MORE THAN A WOMAN

Syrah held her temper, barely, as she paced about the chilly chamber. "You would admire these traits if a man wielded them in defense of his House. I find it curious that they assume the patina of character defects when a woman does so."

"These things do not lie in the province of a woman," Jibril said, matter of factly.

She pointed an accusatory finger at him. "Only because your pride will not allow it to be so."

"I misspoke then. Perhaps I should have said in a woman's nature."

"It must be in *my* nature," she retorted, "else I could not have done it. Am I any less a woman?"

"I have never known a woman I admire more."

Her chin went up. "With all my grievous faults?"

"With all your grievous faults. But ask me the tenth reason I should not lock you up and throw away the key."

"Go ahead," she muttered. "It can't be any more insulting than the other nine."

"If anything happened to you, I wouldn't know how to live."

She Who Laughs Last

Jennie Klassel

LEISURE BOOKS NEW YORK CITY

For Sidonie Gabrielle, Muse
and
Luz Teixeira, Cheshire Cat

A LEISURE BOOK®

August 2003

Published by

Dorchester Publishing Co., Inc.
200 Madison Avenue, Suite 2000
New York, NY 10016

ISBN 0-8439-5231-8

The name "Leisure Books" and the stylized "L" with design are trademarks of Dorchester Publishing Co., Inc.

Printed in the United States of America.

Visit us on the web at www.dorchesterpub.com.

She Who Laughs Last

Prologue

Lady Syrah Dhion had long ago concluded that you couldn't order up people by design. She herself was no fairy-tale princess—all knobby knees and sharp elbows and peculiar eyes, neither blue nor green, but an annoying hazy in-between color; and nondescript pale hair so straight and thick that no amount of crimping could tease it into the ringlets so much in fashion. The likelihood of her turning into a raving beauty was not all that promising.

Oh, there were handsome men about, of course. But in Syrah's admittedly limited experience, a chivalrous gallant with golden hair curling about a noble brow, eyes blue as sapphires, and bewitching little dimples was more likely to be gazing at his own reflection in a looking glass than admiring her.

A fairy-tale Prince Charming presented an even greater problem. To expect charm as well as beauty in one man without a surfeit of insufferable conceit was asking altogether too much of the good Lord.

The prince who rode through the gate of her father's manor house one bright autumn morning in Syrah's thirteenth year certainly didn't look very charming. He looked downright forbidding as he sat ramrod straight upon a

1

sleek Arabian stallion and took in the scene before him in one cool appraising sweep of his golden eyes.

By all accounts, Prince Jibril was not held to be a handsome man. During the days preceding the royal family's visit, Syrah had been too embarrassed to seek details of his appearance from her mother or her governess. She was left with the dubious word of servants that the prince was stern of countenance and—here began the tittering—a man of noteworthy size and possessed of legendary stamina.

Syrah had not been impressed. So the man was tall, strong, and could run or swim long distances. What of it? Any number of men she knew merited that description. Her own ancestors, who had sailed in their great ships from the far north to settle on the island now known as the Dominion, were reputed to be giants.

The prince dismounted with the easy grace that bespoke his years commanding the military forces of the Crown. Lord and Lady Dhion stepped forward to welcome the royal family to the hall of the Ninth House. Syrah hung back, shy, hoping to pass unnoticed in the crowd, but her father beckoned her forward to be introduced to King Ahriman, the lovely Queen Alya, and Crown Prince Jibril.

It was then, as he bowed over her hand, that this forbidding prince suddenly and astoundingly metamorphosed into the most beautiful man Syrah had ever seen. She could not have been more surprised had the mythical sorcerer Merlin dropped straight from the sky into the courtyard, waving a golden wand and muttering arcane incantations.

Banished instantly and forever was the shining knight of Syrah's childish dreams. In his place entered the dark warrior, no maiden's dream this prince, but a man inexplicably thrilling, whose power enveloped her and sent a curious warmth spiraling from the top of her head to the tips of her toes. A flock of fluttering golden butterflies took roost in her heart. Little frogs leaped about in her belly. The tiny feet of mice skittered along every nerve.

As though from a great distance, she heard a deep voice inquire, "Are you quite well, my lady? Perhaps the heat is too much for you?"

2

Syrah froze. She must answer the prince. But what if she opened her mouth and nothing came out? What if she started babbling in some unknown tongue? What did one say to a man who just moments before had been a mere curiosity but now assumed the consequence of the man at the center of her whole world?

"Quite well, Your Highness," she managed to reply, almost snatching her hand from his as she backed away smack into her little brother, Eben, who let out a loud squawk and shoved her forward again—right into the prince's arms. Syrah died a thousand deaths as the prince set her firmly on her feet, ruffled her hair, and strolled on into the hall with the rest of the royal party.

Spitting mad, Syrah whirled on Eben. "You little monster! Look what you did. I will never forgive you, never. I'll get you for this." She burst into tears and tore across the courtyard to the stables, where she huddled in her secret spot in the hayloft and agonized over every moment of her meeting with the prince and her subsequent humiliation at the hands of her detestable little brother. She did not emerge until the pipes sounded the summons to the midday meal, but while everyone else headed toward the great hall for the welcoming feast, Syrah crept up the back stairs to her small chamber, and for reasons she did not fully understand cried herself to sleep beneath the covers of her trundle bed.

During the three days that the royal party stopped at the hall of the Ninth House, Syrah could not decide whether she wanted Prince Jibril to notice her or not. One moment she was praying he would; and the next, with equal fervor, praying he would not. For the most part, she hugged the shadows, lurking behind pillars, peering around corners, ducking behind merlons on the parapet to watch him best all comers in wrestling and swordplay.

He hadn't taken any notice of her, of course. Why should he? At thirteen, she would seem a child in his eyes, invisible amidst an entourage of grand ladies with real bosoms, seductive smiles, and exquisite finery. He was hardly likely to pay attention to an awkward girl garbed in the modest

3

high-necked gown of a maiden, who was not even allowed to pin up her hair but must still wear it loose or woven into a long braid.

That was not the worst of it, for even young maidens could pass among the grown-ups, giggling and blushing, to be remarked upon, complimented, and teased. Syrah, on the other hand, had to be ordered by her mother to attend the festivities in the great hall. Shyness at the thought of Prince Jibril turned to out-and-out panic whenever she found herself in his vicinity. She begged to be excused when her father and mother insisted she present herself before the company, and escaped at the earliest opportunity to the enchanted kingdom she had created among the rolling hills and thick woods of her father's lands.

There, Syrah was not the gawky girl whose bosoms were still but rounded little mounds surmounted by rosy nipples as small as tea roses, whose neck and legs seemed entirely too long, her eyelashes too short, her nose too freckled. Although her governess assured her that she looked every bit as she ought for a young lady who had become a woman only a few months before, Syrah knew, just knew, she would never be the beauty her mother was. But in her own kingdom, she could be child or woman as she chose, princess or Gypsy, a golden carp, a soaring eagle.

So it was, on the afternoon of the last day of Prince Jibril's visit to the hall of the Ninth House, that the Lady Syrah could be found—and she certainly hoped she would not be, thereby incurring her father's serious displeasure—sprawled amidst tall aromatic grasses far from the Great House. She had spent the past hour memorizing the shapes of clouds, so that when they floated around again someday she would have them fixed firmly in her mind. Her father had taught her that clouds were not just one shape or another and were constantly blowing away or falling as rain, but Syrah still wanted to believe the ancient tale of her ancestors that told of a goddess who wove the clouds into beautiful shapes from threads of purest silver.

Tiring of that game, Syrah imagined she captained a full-rigged ketch sailing around the convoluted edge of an island cloud, deciding which bay was likely to have pirates lurking in wait, which would shelter the ships of the great navy of the Dominion. Then she set sail across a placid sea toward even more distant island clouds, and the sapphire waves rocked her into sweet slumber.

An hour later, Syrah's eyes popped open as the first drops fell. Gone were the goddess at her loom, the lurking pirates, the sapphire sea. Instead, she stared up into a leaden sky and rain that fell in quick light drops now, but promised to come down in great slanting sheets any minute. She shot to her feet, hoping to outrun the storm, then realized she must be at least a mile away from the Great House. She would be soaked by the time she reached it, and she wouldn't be able to sneak up the back stairs without being seen.

She started out at a brisk trot toward a distant stand of trees, then broke into an all-out run as roiling clouds let loose a torrent. She loved running like this, free beneath the sky, her hair streaming out behind her, with her heart beating in cadence with the stinging drops against her face. Forgotten were the dire consequences of her disobedience in the sheer exultation of the moment.

She saw the horse just as she reached the bottom of the hill. She skidded to a stop in the wet grass and froze. Nothing on earth was going to propel her across the final hundred feet that would bring her beneath the sheltering canopy of the dark wood. There could be no doubt about that sable stallion; a magnificent beast, a mount fit only for . . . a prince.

Jibril had been wondering what she would do when she reached the woods. He'd been watching the slim graceful girl as she flew across the meadow, first with grim determination, then more slowly as she realized she couldn't outrun the rain. Once she even stopped completely, turned her face to the sky, threw out her arms, and whirled around in a dance of primitive abandon worthy of the most debauched Dionysian reveler.

Of course, now she looked like nothing so much as a half-drowned bunny rabbit nose to nose with a hungry fox, and would likely remain rooted to the spot until spring if he didn't do something to snap her out of it

Syrah knew her duty: Kneel before your prince until he bids you rise. And there could be no doubt that it was her prince lounging against the trunk of an ancient oak with arms folded across his chest, waiting for her to do just that. Down she went onto one knee, head bent, hands clasped one in the other in the ritual gesture of allegiance known only to members of the noble Houses. It mattered not that she must look ridiculous, drenched to the skin with her hair plastered to her skull.

"I think, perhaps, we can dispense with the formalities under the circumstances," Prince Jibril remarked. "Not that it's going to do you much good, but you might as well come in out of the rain."

Syrah mustered what dignity the humiliating situation afforded, and ventured forward. He so reminded her of the black panther on the shield of the First House, with his thick black hair and those mesmerizing golden eyes, that she feared he might well seize her as a cat would its prey. But then again, he might . . . Well, she wasn't quite sure what else he might do, but she felt sure it would be dangerous and thrilling and not at all unpleasant.

"You are far from home and alone, Lady Syrah. Does your father allow you such liberties?"

"No, Your Highness," Syrah mumbled, her eyes fixed firmly on her ruined half boots. A moment later her head snapped up. He knew who she was when he hadn't spared her a single glance in the past two days?

Jibril smiled down at her. "Have I said something to surprise you?"

"No, my lord. It's just that I didn't think . . . that is, I hadn't supposed you . . ."

"Come out with it, child. I don't bite."

"I'm sure you don't," she assured him.

"Bite," she added.

Dear Lord, she must sound like a ninny.

"I didn't think you had noticed me, my lord."

"You hug the shadows, as conspicuous in your unwillingness to be seen as you would be if you forced yourself to my notice."

"I apologize if I offended you, my lord. Your presence in my father's hall is a great honor to the Ninth House."

Jibril couldn't understand why the girl was apologizing. He had noticed her by her very absence from much of the entertainment Lord Dhion had provided for the pleasure of his royal guests. Thinking she might be sickly, he had inquired of his host why she was so little seen in the hall. Lord Dhion had explained that Syrah was only just entering her womanhood and not yet entirely comfortable in company, as much a girl still as a young woman.

Gazing now at the sodden figure before him, Jibril was inclined to believe Lady Syrah was very much a woman, although she might not believe it herself just yet. It was charming, really, how unconscious she was of the enticing picture she presented with her white gown clinging to the gentle curve of her young breasts, her supple waist, and the long slim legs of a colt. Why, if a man should gather her to him, it would be like cradling a delicate flower, like tapping a crystal goblet with a small silver spoon, like . . .

He cleared his throat. "How old are you, Lady Syrah?"

"Thirteen, my lord. Fourteen come the summer solstice."

"That old?" he teased, trying to bring some semblance of order to his rioting senses. "Not old enough, I fear, to have the good sense to know that a young lady has no business wandering about in the wilds alone."

"Yes, my lord," Syrah said, mortified at the reproof.

"Surely you know the dangers? You might meet with wild beasts or brigands; men who might . . . well, who might not treat you with the respect you deserve. I trust you will not be so foolish again."

Syrah's mumbled "No" came out suspiciously like a sob.

Jibril hadn't meant to upset her. But then, he knew nothing of the tender emotions of thirteen-year-old girls.

"There, there," he said gruffly, reaching out to put his arm around her shaking shoulders, then thinking better of it and giving her a brotherly pat on the head. "Don't cry,

Lady Syrah. I was your age once and I cannot say I was any wiser than you are. Shall we head back now that the rain has slowed somewhat?"

He swung up onto the stallion and leaned down to pluck her off the ground. To Syrah's astonishment, she found herself cradled in his lap with his strong arm around her waist, holding her against an impossibly broad chest as he spurred the powerful beast into an exhilarating gallop across the fields. It was all too short a ride as far as Syrah was concerned, not only because she was flying along in the arms of the Crown Prince of the Dominion, but when they trotted into the stable yard her father was just mounting his own horse to go in search of her.

Taking just a moment to greet the prince, Lord Dhion shot his blackest look at his wayward daughter. "This is the last time you will disobey me, Syrah. If need be, I will lock you in your room and feed you naught but worms and water until you learn that young ladies do not go roaming about the countryside unescorted."

"Yes, Papa," came a small voice from the bedraggled bundle in the prince's lap.

"If I might, sir," Jibril said, giving Syrah a little squeeze, "your daughter may have been so foolish in the past as to put herself in danger, but today I must take the blame for her absence. I happened upon her as I was setting out to exercise my horse and asked her to point the way to a pleasant ride. As you can see, we were caught out in the storm."

Lord Dhion had only to glance at his daughter's face to see that the prince's words had astonished her as much they had him. He wasn't about to gainsay the Crown Prince, so he contented himself with replying, "I thank you for clarifying the situation, my lord."

"It would grieve me to see your daughter punished for an offense she did not commit, although I agree a propensity to wander about by herself is most foolish," the prince replied. He tried to look stern as he set Syrah on the ground. "I trust in future you will obey your father in all things when he has only your welfare at heart, my lady."

"Yes, my lord," Syrah just managed to whisper before she turned and fled into the house.

Throughout the evening meal, Syrah kept her eyes firmly on the dishes before her, unaware of the prince's amusement at her discomfiture. Later, when she begged to be excused, her father had to order her to remain in the hall for the evening's entertainment.

Knowing all too well that it was useless to try to force Syrah to dance or play at riddles, Lord Dhion steered her toward a far corner where an impromptu round-robin of chess was in progress. Bolstered by a copious amount of the fine Bordeaux the king had presented upon his arrival, he was in an expansive frame of mind. To Syrah's acute embarrassment, he prodded her forward and proclaimed, "The pick of my best bitch's new litter to anyone who can beat my daughter here at chess."

It was a wager Lord Dhion knew he was unlikely to lose. At the age of thirteen, Syrah could already trounce everyone in the household. Her great uncle Amorgos had recognized her talent early on, and she had mastered the most complicated moves he could teach her by the time she was twelve. She was soon devising her own successful strategies, and her ability to read another player's intention was nothing short of astonishing.

Every player took Lord Dhion up on his wager. Syrah proceeded to handily eliminate one after another until only Prince Jibril's good friend, Kalan Ankuli, remained in contention. He put up a good fight, but she finally feinted with her knight to checkmate him in a move she had invented only a few days earlier. So filled with admiration for her skill was Captain Ankuli that he urged her to play a final game with the prince himself, who was said to be unbeatable. Panicked at the prospect, Syrah pleaded a sudden headache and fled to her room.

Lord Dhion and his household gathered in the courtyard the following morning to bid farewell to their royal guests. He discovered Syrah lurking behind Eben's nurse and scolded her forward. She knelt and pledged the allegiance of her House, but did not follow her parents back into the great hall as the royal party clattered away over the wooden bridge. She wandered off toward the extensive rose garden her mother tended so lovingly, overwhelmed by an inexplicable feeling of loss.

She did not hear the horse and its rider until they were upon her and Prince Jibril was leaning down to whisper, "They say, Lady Syrah, that worms taste like chicken. Don't you believe it. They taste exactly like worms and wriggle terribly upon the tongue. I hope you will not have occasion to discover this for yourself."

Syrah thought she felt his lips graze her cheek, but surely it was just the touch of his long black hair as he straightened up to ride away. Surely it was just her imagination.

A year passed, then another and another. One night in early spring, Syrah went to bed an awkward girl, and at the rising of the sun she emerged from her chamber a willowy desirable young woman. All too soon, clouds were just clouds, the sky merely blue, rain a nuisance. And impossible dreams of whispering princes and the deepest wishes of the heart lay swaddled in silk cocoons, awaiting the silent command that would transform them into the exquisite dance of love and desire.

Chapter One

Syrah tried to remember everything she had learned to expect from a man in the throes of amorous pursuit, and felt quite certain that tongues had not been mentioned. Such a thing had never entered her mind. The only tongue in her mouth was her own. There couldn't possibly be room for two. Evidently, the dairymaid had omitted a vital piece of information, because there most certainly were two tongues in there now, and one of them wasn't hers.

The hands, she had expected. One cradled the back of her head, holding her still while the strange tongue acquainted itself with hers. The other drifted in sensual exploration over the swell of her breasts, revealed all too wantonly by her garish low-cut gown, then trailed down over her stomach and out along one thigh. It slipped beneath the hem of her gown and inched up her inner thigh with the clear intent of exploring her . . . Well, that really was going a bit too far. Her own hand descended, with equal determination but limited success, to wage war with it.

The hard bulge by her right hip might be the clasp of the wide leather belt that encircled the man's slim waist, but most likely it was the "it" the dairymaid had hinted at before she succumbed to yet another fit of giggles. In truth, Syrah hadn't needed a detailed description, because her brother, Eben, had an "it," which she had seen many times when she bathed him as a baby. If what she was feeling tonight was one of those, well, the poor man must have something terribly wrong with him. It was much bigger than Eben's, even given the comparative difference in size between a boy and a man of about thirty—huge, in fact— and it hadn't been there when he first pulled her down onto his lap five minutes ago. She certainly couldn't ignore it now.

Everything appeared to be under control, except, perhaps, for her own tongue, which had developed a mind of its own and was enthusiastically copying every dip and sweep of his. Her left hand couldn't seem to make up its mind whether to pull his away or press it more firmly where it was determined to go. And although she didn't have to worry about a burgeoning bulge of her own, a little pool of liquid heat had bubbled up from heaven-knew- where not far from the busy arena of contention between their hands.

Into this frantic scramble of diminishing thought and waxing sensation came a voice that immediately brought Syrah back to herself and the reason the nineteen-year-old daughter of the Ninth House was engaged in a lewd per- formance worthy of a common harlot with the Crown Prince of the Dominion.

"Your wine, my lord," the serving girl said, her eyes wide with shock at the appalling scene before her. Her chaste young mistress—the Lady Syrah Dhion!—in the arms of a man who in moments would be dragging her off to one of the tavern's private rooms for the purpose of fornication. It mattered not that he was Prince Jibril of the First House; his intent was no different from any other man's bent on taking his pleasure in exchange for a few coins.

"What are you gaping at, girl?" Jibril demanded, extract- ing his hand from the folds of the wench's skirt.

"Your wine . . . yes, my lord, wine . . . for fornica—" A

film of nervous perspiration popped out on the girl's forehead.

Syrah took control of the situation before her maid collapsed into a fit of hysterics.

"She is just jealous of my good fortune this night, my lord," she purred as she ran her hand over the hard sculpted chest beneath his ivory linen shirt, imitating a favored gesture of the women of pleasure she had observed earlier in the evening. She looked up at Mayenne with unmistakable warning in her eyes. "Is that not so, Nini?"

The maid's thoughts chattered in her head like magpies. For the life of her, she could not imagine who this Nini could be. Her name was Mayenne, wasn't it? Then a thread of comprehension snaked its way through the din: She was supposed to be Nini, the serving girl Nini!

"Yes, yes, most fortunate . . . jealous, as she says, my lord," Mayenne croaked as she backed away.

"Stop, girl."

Mayenne froze at the prince's command. Had he so much as tapped her with the feather of a tiny bird, she would have shattered into a million pieces.

"This wine tastes strange. Bring me some other."

Mayenne turned terrified eyes toward Syrah. She had measured out the last of the powdered herb into this flagon. If the prince didn't drink it, he might not succumb to its sleep-inducing effect and then . . .

Then he would take her lady to the back of the tavern, and he would fornicate with her, and her lady would be despoiled, and no man would take her to wife because another had claimed her maidenhead. They would be cast out with only the clothes on their backs and a crust of stale bread to sustain them. They would have to live in a rude hut in some damp dark wood, at the mercy of whatever outlaws might lurk therein. And they would have no one to defend them, because Eben would have to shun her lady, even if he was her brother. And they might have to leave the forest and become wanderers on the roads of the Dominion, prey to Gypsies, and Gypsies were dark devils, Mayenne knew for a fact, because her mother had told her

13

so, and they were a lusty people, and she and her lady would be forced into slavery, helpless in the face of all that lust, and . . .

Syrah could see from the glazed look in Mayenne's eyes that she had careened off into one of her fantastical melodramas; perhaps lost her wits entirely. It would be up to her alone to rescue the plan from certain failure if Prince Jibril did not drink this particular wine.

She wasn't exactly sure where the idea came from, but she snuggled closer and dipped just the tip of her little finger into the wine, then sucked it with an appreciative "Mmmm." When he chuckled, she did so again, but this time she offered the finger to him. He took it into his own mouth, sucking slowly, staring deep into her eyes, evidently well pleased with her sensual teasing.

He waved the quaking servant away, and turned his attention to the luscious mouth of the girl in his arms.

He grinned down at her. "So you like this wine, do you?"

"It is sweet and well spiced, my lord."

"Then I shall drink it to please you, little one. And I do intend to please you this night. Let us drink it together. Take a measure into your mouth but do not swallow."

Syrah had no intention of swallowing, but she did as he asked and was surprised to feel his mouth close over hers. His hand tilted her head slightly and the dark wine trickled between her lips into his mouth. "It is ambrosia when I take it from your sweet mouth, little one."

It had been a night chock-full of astonishing discoveries for Syrah, and this latest addition to her catalog of amatory activity certainly deserved further research. But not tonight, not with this man, and certainly not with the drugged wine that was intended to plunge Prince Jibril into a sleep so deep that he would not awaken until she had him safely under lock and key.

"Patience, my lord," she crooned. "The night is young. Let me please you with this first flagon; then you shall fill me with your sweetness from the next."

She caressed his smooth-shaven cheek. "Perhaps we might go somewhere more private. I have a room at a nearby lodging house with a fine feather bed."

"You read my mind, sweetling."

He glanced around the room to see the men of his guard similarly engaged, although none dallied with a wench as desirable as the girl he held. In fact, he had been surprised to find such a one in this hellhole. Not that she was perfect, by any means. Her skin was sallow, she was missing a tooth, and the style of her dull brown hair did not flatter her. But her eyes were extraordinary—not quite blue and not quite green—and she had a mouth a man would not soon forget and breath as sweet as spring mint. Her body beneath the garish gown was promising: high firm breasts, a slim waist, and long legs. There was a delicacy about her, an endearing air of innocence. So, although he had not been seeking female companionship this evening, she promised sweet pleasure and would prove an interesting diversion.

He eased her from his lap and summoned the serving girl who was hovering anxiously in the doorway. "Fill a carrying flask with this wine, girl, and be quick about it."

With his arm around Syrah's waist, he led her to a table by the far wall, where his old friend and captain of his personal guard, Kalan Ankuli, was fondling the enormous breasts of a plump red-haired wench.

"I find I'll be engaged for the evening after all," the prince said.

Kalan frowned up at him. "I don't like the idea of your going off alone. I'll follow and wait for you."

"Nonsense. I can have nothing to fear from this little darling. Besides, I wouldn't want to spoil your last night of freedom. It is not every day a man marries. You must take your pleasure this evening to fortify you for the morrow."

Syrah was barely able to suppress a gasp of outrage. The man was consorting with loose women on the eve of his wedding day! Of course, she knew men were capable of such degeneracy. Her own cousin, Vicq, had been plucked out of a harlot's bed only minutes before he was due to kneel at the altar with his bride. He had marched back down the aisle of the cathedral in solemn splendor, happily unaware that his fine leather breeches were still not fully laced, providing an intriguing glimpse of what his virgin bride would see in its full glory in just a few hours.

Syrah had only been ten at the time, and thought the whole thing hilarious. But then, she had not fully understood the reason for the disorder of his clothing, and was simply enjoying the horrified gasps of the ladies and the snickers of the men in the throng of dignitaries gathered to witness the nuptials.

"Trust me, sir," Syrah said to the prospective bridegroom with what she hoped was a lascivious smile. "Your friend will be safe in my hands."

"Well, you weren't very enthusiastic about coming to this hellhole in the first place, Jibril," Kalan allowed. "You might as well have some pleasure for your trouble."

"I intend to, believe me."

Jibril beckoned the serving girl to follow, and led Syrah across the smoky room and down a dark hallway, where a cacophony of grunts, squeals, gasps, and groans from behind closed doors provided proof, if any were needed, that fornication was indeed taking place.

Syrah had to wonder why all that noise was necessary for the simple act of procreation, which, so far as she had allowed herself to imagine, would be quickly concluded in respectful silence with, perhaps, a few pleasurable sighs and expressions of gratitude on both sides when the transaction was concluded. The hullabaloo that reverberated through the hallway and followed them out into the night most certainly belied that assumption. She set aside this new piece of information for future contemplation, and turned her attention resolutely to her own objective, which most certainly did not include fornication, although the tall man beside her would probably beg to differ.

By this time, Jibril would have had considerable difficulty begging to differ. For some unaccountable reason, he was quickly losing command of his ability to speak. The words that he did manage to form were slipping and sliding around his tongue in the jumbled confusion of a man who had far exceeded the sensible quota of spirits for the evening. He hadn't, as far as he could recall. He'd only drunk two flagons of wine, perhaps three; not enough to account for the fatuous smile he couldn't seem to erase from his face as he leered down at the woman who was taking him . . .

Where the devil was she taking him? And where was Kalan, who usually dogged him like a second shadow when he was out and about? Speaking of shadows, he must be in some sort of parade, because four shadows marched along the stone wall beside him. There he was, the tall one, and the slim woman leading him by the hand as though he were a child. Another woman trudged along close behind, and only a few steps behind her, a shorter shadow carried a large satchel and what appeared to be a frying pan.

It was all very odd, probably a dream. And although he was far past the point where he could sort out reality from hallucination with any degree of certainty, two clear thoughts did flash across Prince Jibril's mind just before the cobblestones rose up to meet him: He wasn't going to wake up in his own bed tomorrow and that wine had tasted downright peculiar.

Chapter Two

"Deeeaaaddd!"

Mayenne fell to her knees in the narrow alley. "He's dead," she wailed. "Dead, dead, dead."

"Stop that at once," Syrah hissed.

"I told you we shouldn't have brought her along," snorted Eben Dhion, heir apparent of the Ninth House and fourteen-year-old coconspirator. "Silly twit."

"If you don't be quiet, Mayenne," Syrah snapped at the keening maid, "I'm going to stuff a rag into your mouth. He is not dead, he's asleep."

"What the devil is going on down there?" an angry voice shouted from an upper-story window. "Can't a man get a decent night's sleep around here?"

Eben stepped up smartly, seeing that his sister had her hands full restraining the distraught maid from throwing herself across the prostrate form of the future King of the Dominion.

"We're real sorry, mister," he called out. "My pa's in his cups again on account of how my ma just up and ran off with the priest. Not that I'm blaming her, mind you. Pa couldn't do no more pokin' after he met up with that shark. The beast chewed his poker right off, it did. It wasn't a

18

pretty sight, I can tell you. Anyhow, my sister and me, we come out looking for our pa. And we find him here passed out in this alley. And he looks dead, so my sister—well, she isn't all there in her head, if you know what I mean, not since she fell off the roof trying to get the pig down—so she thinks he's dead and—"

"I don't need to know your life story, boy. Just shut her up so I can get some sleep," the man snarled, and slammed the shutters closed.

"Perhaps a little less embellishment in future, Eben," Syrah suggested, releasing a sniffling Mayenne.

"I got rid of him, didn't I?"

She reached out to ruffle his golden curls. "So you did."

He jerked his head away. "Don't do that."

"Why?"

"I'm not a child."

Syrah smiled to herself at this latest display of independence. Eben was growing up so fast; too fast really. It couldn't be helped. While other boys his age applied themselves to their lessons and played at the games of war that simulated the lives they would lead as men, Eben had watched as his birthright slipped from the fingers of a feebleminded father, and the few defenders of the Ninth House went down to defeat at the hands of their hateful cousin, Ranulph Gyp. His boy's life had ended three months ago when Syrah led their little family and a few faithful retainers into a moonless summer night to disappear forever—or so it was believed—beneath the raging waters of the southern ocean. Syrah knew what they did this night might be Eben's last hope to reclaim his patrimony.

"I'm sorry, Eben. I keep forgetting. Good work," she added, clapping a hand on his shoulder in a man-to-man sort of way.

Silence descended on the little group as they gazed down at the sleeping form at their feet. Somewhere a baby cried, cats screeched, small rodents skittered through the shadows.

"We've got to get him out of here," Syrah said.

Eben fixed the maid with an accusing stare. "How much did you put in the wine, anyhow?"

"Don't you go looking at me like that," Mayenne retorted. "I gave him what your great aunt Rosota mixed up. Can I help it if it was too strong?"

Syrah sighed. "She must have thought we were kidnapping a blasted giant. I was certain he'd make it as far as the lodging house. We aren't going to be able to carry him that far. We'll have to stay here for the night." She glanced up and down the alley. "Let's see what's behind these doors."

They tried every door but found all barred from the inside, save one that led into a long narrow hallway filled with unemptied chamber pots. The stench was appalling. Mayenne stumbled back into the alley and gave over to noisy retching.

"Don't even think about it," Eben warned his sister when he saw her assessing the space with the clear intent of declaring it suitable for their purposes.

Syrah glared at her brother "I'm open to suggestions."

He considered the alternatives; there weren't any. However, it was pride rather than practicality that brought him to grudging agreement with her. After all, he was the man of the party, and men didn't let a little thing like the stink of deepest hell get in the way when a man had to do what a man had to do.

"Fine, but if we all die of putrid fever, it will be on your head," he grumbled, and stalked out into the fresh air.

Syrah followed him. "It won't be so bad," she cajoled him. "We'll just move the pots outside. Come on, help me. We don't have much time."

She ventured back into the foul darkness and bent to pick up the first pot, only to realize that the other two hadn't followed. She reappeared in the doorway, hands on hips, her patience hanging by the slimmest thread. "I could use some help, if you don't mind."

One look at Eben's mutinous expression assured her that the seventeenth armiger of the Ninth House had no intention, now or ever, of doing anything with a chamber pot save for its allotted purpose. Mayenne's greenish hue left

Syrah in no doubt that she could not expect help from that quarter either.

Ten minutes later, half a dozen chamber pots rested on a doorstep at the far end of the alley and Syrah was wishing, not for the first time, that she had never embarked on this mad scheme in the first place. What had ever led her to believe she could kidnap Crown Prince Jibril Chios, hold him for ransom, and hire the most famous mercenary in the Dominion and his band of outlaws to storm her hall, oust her cousin, and restore the hearth and honor of her House?

The plan had fiasco written all over it. It was utter insanity. It was doomed to fail. It was the only way.

Of course, carting away chamber pots in the middle of the night with a prince of the royal blood snoring peacefully in a dark cobblestone alley hadn't figured in that moment of inspiration on the cliffs of Pailacca. In her mind's eye, Syrah had envisioned a sack of gold coins, a quick strike in the dark of night to commandeer the hall, and the pennant with the azure, green, and gold shield of her House flying from the east tower once again.

Chamber pots simply had not figured.

Or coffins.

Syrah considered the matter of the coffin, which, she had to admit, was one of the more inspired elements of her scheme. They would spirit their captive out of Suriana in a coffin. The problem was, at the moment it was sitting in the room at the modest lodging house they had rented for the past three nights while they trailed Prince Jibril wherever he went. If they couldn't bring Jibril to the coffin, then they would have to bring it to him, and before first light.

Since Mayenne was proving a distinct liability when confronted with the least complication, Syrah decided the maid should remain behind to guard their captive while she and Eben went to fetch the cart and coffin. It took all three of them to lug Jibril into the hallway. They removed his wide leather belt, scabbard, and falchion; tied his hands and feet with strong silken cords; and gagged him with a soft clean cloth.

21

Syrah stood back, admiring their handiwork. "There, that should do it."

"That just goes to show that women don't know anything," Eben scoffed. He knelt at Jibril's feet and ran his hand over each leather boot. "See?" he exclaimed triumphantly as he drew a short two-edged dagger from a secret compartment in the side of the left boot. "It's a good thing you have a man along."

Syrah shook her head and laughed. "It certainly is."

Mayenne had been mercifully silent throughout the proceedings, but the prospect of being left alone with the prince was already plunging her into an abyss of dreadful imaginings: He would awaken. It would be but a moment or two before he became fully aware that all was not well, but when he did, mighty would be his wrath. He would pierce her with his terrible yellow eyes, compelling her to free him from his bonds. And when the gag was removed, he would speak the words she so richly deserved—"You die!"—and he would slit her throat. But wait! He would know there had been others; she would be spared only long enough to name her accomplices. They would drag her through the streets by her hair—that was going to hurt a lot—but not anything compared to the instruments of torture that awaited her in the foulest dungeon beneath the palace, where hideously deformed jailers would have their way with her again and again. And when they had taken their foul pleasure, she would be dragged naked before the King of the Dominion—how embarrassing!—and he would laugh an evil laugh as she begged for her life, and promise her a death so terrible that she would have no choice but to name her lady as the true villain of the piece. And they would hunt her lady down like a pack of ravenous beasts, strip her naked, and throw her to the men of the garrison, whose lust had deflowered many a poor maid, and . . .

"For pity's sake, Mayenne, are you listening?" Syrah demanded.

"He's going to wake up, my lady. I just know it," Mayenne sniveled, wringing her hands.

"He is not going to wake up. You'll be perfectly safe. I've

barred the door that leads up the stairs, and I want you to bar the door to the alley when we leave. If he gives you any trouble, use the frying pan, but just tap him with it. I don't want to come back and find his brains all over the floor."

That horrifying prospect had Mayenne's complexion turning from the color of chalk to pea-green pottage in a matter of seconds and Syrah snapping, "Don't you dare throw up again! You've got to keep your wits about you or we'll all end up with our heads on pikes on the castle wall."

"We ought to use the frying pan on her, if you ask me," Eben grumbled as he and his sister hastened away.

Filled with dread beyond bearing and certain this was to be her last night on earth, Mayenne slid slowly down the wall, curled into a ball of despair, and promptly fell asleep.

Syrah stared into the darkness with a deep sigh. She was bone weary, but she knew there would be no sleep for her this night. It had taken almost two hours to lash the coffin onto the little cart and drag it up the steep hill to the alley. And here they were with dawn hours away, crammed into a pitch-black hallway that reeked of human waste. Their dray pony was locked up for the night in a public stable, and they couldn't retrieve it until the proprietor opened in the morning, which probably wouldn't be until six at the earliest.

She hadn't anticipated this complication. One couldn't very well expect the man to cooperate in his own abduction, of course, but the least he could have done was keep to his feet until they got him to the lodging house.

The subject of all this careful planning stirred on the floor beside her, nuzzled her thigh, shifted his head into her lap, and threw one arm over her legs with a deeply contented sigh. She reached down immediately to move him away, but found her hand unaccountably smoothing back the thick dark hair that fell in waves to barely graze his shoulders. She snatched the hand back and gave it a good slap to remind it that behavior of that sort would not be tolerated. Caressing this man in the course of her clumsy se-

23

duction in the tavern was necessary, but there could be no valid reason to do so now, none whatsoever.

As for the head cradled in her lap alarmingly close to the spot where a pesky pool of liquid heat was beginning to bubble up again, she really ought to return it to the cradle of his own arms where it rightly belonged. Still, the poor man had an uncomfortable day ahead, so why not let him be for now? She would just keep a close eye on the hand, and the heat was not all that bothersome. In fact, it felt . . . very pleasant.

As the dark hours of the night crawled by, Syrah found herself thinking about the girl she had been before tragedy came into her life. Before a virulent fever of the brain swept through the Great House, carrying off her sweet mama and leaving papa virtually bereft of his wits. Before cousin Ranulph swooped down like a vulture and took possession of the hall.

How eloquently Ranulph had spoken of his concern for the safety and well-being of his beloved cousins. How earnestly had he affirmed his familial obligation to protect Lord Dhion's interests until his uncle regained his health.

Syrah had informed Ranulph, none too diplomatically, that they had no need of his assistance and he could return to his own hall, thank you very much. At nineteen, she was perfectly capable of managing Papa's estates. In any event, she had already petitioned King Ahriman to allow her to sit as regent for Eben.

Ranulph wasn't about to vacate the hall, nor did Syrah have any means of forcing him out. He went right ahead and settled in to await the king's decision.

A few days later, the rumor reached the Great House that Prince Jibril had decided to marry. Ranulph must have known that Syrah would be among eligible daughters of the noble Houses deemed an appropriate consort for the prince. He had other plans for her, as Syrah was to discover.

"You may set your heart at rest," Ranulph had assured her. "The burden of your brother's care is not to fall upon your own frail shoulders but on mine."

"Whatever do you mean?"

Ranulph affected surprise. "As your husband, the well-being of the Ninth House is my sole care."

"Husband? We are not betrothed," Syrah exclaimed. "I cannot imagine why you should think so."

Ranulph sighed and shook his head. "I was afraid of this. I urged your father to tell you when you reached your sixteenth birthday. But no, good man that he is, he wanted to give you the opportunity to realize for yourself the happy outcome of such a match."

"You must be mad," Syrah said. "Papa would never enter into a betrothal contract without my knowledge."

Ranulph smiled indulgently. "Syrah, Syrah, you are so very young yet. So innocent of these worldly matters. No doubt you still entertain your girlish dreams of marriage—love and all that nonsense."

Syrah narrowed her eyes at him. "Indeed?"

"I hope you do not take my meaning amiss," Ranulph continued smoothly. "Our union will be based on the mutual affection that has grown between us since we were children. Who knows? We may very well come to love one another. Whether we do or not, we will be happy together. How else can it be when we have the blessing of our families to sustain us?"

Even now, three months later, Syrah felt as though someone had punched her in the stomach when she recalled Ranulph's look of triumph as he unrolled a parchment adorned with her father's seal and put it in her hands. It appeared to be a contract of betrothal, drawn up at her birth, that bound her to Ranulph as surely as though they were already married.

Syrah read and reread the dreadful document, then rolled it up carefully and set it aside.

She fixed Ranulph with a flat stare. "No."

Ranulph raised a brow. "No?"

"I will not marry you. I do not acknowledge the validity of this contract. Papa's illness may prevent him from proving it a forgery, but I shall submit it to the king's counsel for his determination."

A dispatch from the king a week later informed Syrah

that after serious consideration he must deny her request to sit as regent for Eben. He did not consider it fitting for a young woman to assume such a responsibility. Instead, he had appointed her great uncle Amorgos to take on those duties for the time being. The king made no mention of the betrothal contract.

Great Uncle Amorgos had duly arrived, but collapsed and died two days later, ostensibly from a surfeit of eel pie. Syrah had again petitioned the king. After two weeks of almost unbearable suspense, the king replied that he would take her request under advisement, but that for the moment he would entrust the business of the Ninth House to Lord Ranulph. Again, there was no mention of the betrothal contract. A third letter, in which Syrah informed the king that she believed Ranulph might have murdered her great uncle and that she feared for Eben's safety and her own, had elicited no response at all.

It was then that Syrah realized she must act. She must see her little family safely away from Ranulph and find allies where she could. She would buy them, if necessary.

Yes, Syrah thought wistfully as she settled the prince's head more comfortably in her lap, he was lost to her. Even had evil had not befallen her House, forcing her to these desperate measures, it was not certain that Jibril would have chosen her to be his wife. Other candidates might be more to his taste: curvaceous Josana of the Fifth House, who had only to thrust her huge breasts in the direction of any man who still had his teeth and stood upright on his own two feet to gain his undivided attention; scheming Beline, with all that breathless admiration for a man's least accomplishment and a bottomless well of flattering words; or Chrasine, angelic Chrasine, insipid, boring, beautiful Chrasine.

Syrah finally fell into a fitful doze, awakening with a start to see a faint sliver of light under the door to the alley. It would soon be dawn and the streets would be filled with early risers going about their business: fishermen trooping toward the harbor, bakers firing their ovens, priests hurrying to early mass. They must move quickly.

Still, Syrah hesitated before waking Eben and Mayenne. Six years ago, she had swept through the heart of a storm cradled in Prince Jibril's arms. For a few minutes on a warm autumn day, ancient tales that spoke of heroes and valiant quests, gods and the daughters of men, fair damsels and impassioned princes, and all the secret imaginings of a young girl's heart had sprung to life. Perhaps somewhere in her heart that girl still dreamed, but never again would she touch this mesmerizing man, breathe in his strangely thrilling masculine scent, feel the heat and energy of him.

And to think he might have been her husband. But, no, that could never be now. Somehow she *would* convince the king to let her be Eben's regent until he attained his majority in six years. By then, Syrah would be twenty-five, well past marriageable age, and Prince Jibril would long be wed to another. No, there would be no husband for her, no children, no hall of her own. Some might say it was too high a price to pay. But the bitter lessons of the past year had taught her that honor had no price. Honor was only as strong as the ties of blood. Honor was all.

Syrah pulled herself up short. These bitter memories and regrets could serve no purpose. She had work to do.

"Wake up, wake up," she whispered as she groped about in the darkness. She found a shoulder and shook it hard. Mayenne shrieked.

"Shhhh," Syrah warned, "we mustn't wake the house." She listened tensely for footsteps or signs that someone up above had heard, but all was quiet. She opened the satchel at her side, drew out a large kerchief that would serve as a blindfold in case the prince awoke, and tied it in place. Confident that he could neither loosen his bonds nor see his abductors, she turned her attention back to Eben and Mayenne.

"From now on, we never address each other by name. Is that absolutely clear? One slip of the tongue could lay waste to the whole plan."

Yawning and grumbling, Eben went on his way to the stable to retrieve the pony. Syrah decided she and Mayenne would have to maneuver the coffin into the narrow confines

27

of the hallway in order to load the prince without danger of being seen, an endeavor that proved far easier to conceive than accomplish. After several attempts to lift the dead weight of the royal scion, it became obvious they would have to devise another strategy. If they couldn't lift him, perhaps they could roll him. They set the coffin on its side, eased him in like a rolled-up carpet, and righted it.

Unfortunately, he came to rest nose down, a most undignified position for a prince of the royal blood and one bound to be extremely uncomfortable during a long day's ride on rough and rutted roads. Syrah reconsidered: If they rolled him from a facedown position, he would come to rest faceup like a proper corpse.

Well satisfied with this ingenious solution, Syrah placed a soft rose-scented silk pillow beneath his head and tucked thick woolen blankets on each side to protect the royal torso, taking care that the breathing holes that Eben had gouged out with his knife were not obstructed.

The sky was just beginning to glow with the first delicate pinks and yellows of the new dawn when Syrah and Mayenne dragged the heavy coffin into the alley. While a grumpy Mayenne plopped down on the doorstep to rest, Syrah turned her attention to what she considered the pièce de résistance of this phase of the plan. She rooted around in the satchel for the stubby piece of black chalk and the pouch of yellow powder she had used to disguise her face the previous evening, and set to adorning the lid of the coffin with a drawing of the stark bones of a grinning death's head.

She sat back on her heels to survey her handiwork, wishing that she had been more diligent in her drawing lessons. The skull looked more like her late great uncle Amorgos deep in his cups than the terrifying symbol of the plague it was intended to represent. Still, it would serve to discourage curious travelers from venturing too near the cart and its occupants. To complete the effect, they would tie scarves over their noses and mouths, as though loath themselves to breathe the foul air that wafted from the remains of the deceased.

Eben jogged around the corner leading the little piebald pony. "I thought the dolt would never show up," he grumbled as he set about hitching the horse to the cart. "He stank to high heaven of sour ale and garlic, and wanted to tell me all about the jolly poke he had last night."

"What's a poke?" Syrah inquired.

Eben shot her a look of pure astonishment. Everyone knew what a poke was, even a fourteen-year-old boy. Well, obviously not everyone, and he certainly wasn't about to get into a discussion of the facts of life with his own sister. "It's a card game."

"You'll have to teach me sometime."

Eben rolled his eyes.

Loading the coffin onto the cart proved every bit as frustrating as settling the prince into it had been. They started out well enough, standing it on end against the back of the cart, and with Syrah and Mayenne lifting from the bottom and Eben guiding it from the flatbed above. They had trouble progressing past this point, however, for they would just manage to get a purchase when the skittish little pony would stumble forward. They were finally forced to unhitch the beast and load the coffin first. By the time everything was secured and the horse back in harness, they were out of sorts and very hungry.

"That's the worst of it," Syrah declared as she took up the reins. "Stop your complaining. Some market stalls must be open by now. We'll get some food and be out of the city in no time."

Half an hour later, they were resting comfortably beneath a tree not far from the open-air market, bellies full of dates, new-baked bread, and goat cheese; and feeling a great deal more optimistic about the day ahead. Several contingents of the palace guard had thundered past, but no one had spared them so much as a glance. No doubt the search for Prince Jibril was under way. The sooner they quit the city the better. The only danger left, as far as Syrah could see, lay in crossing the great grass parade ground where the planting and harvest festivals were held each year.

They would most certainly draw notice—a coffin with the

mark of the plague upon it would not be ignored—but that was exactly what she had planned for. All three had tied the black kerchiefs over their noses and mouths. They would present a vision of such horror that no one would dare approach.

Syrah gave herself a mental pat on the back as they set out. Everything was going so well. The face of Great Uncle Armogos grinned up from the lid of the coffin, proffering unmistakable warning of the horrendous cargo within. Passersby gave them a wide berth. The prince slept on, snoring softly.

They were passing the market. They were coming to the far end of the parade ground. They were nearing the great upper gate of the city.

They were in deep trouble.

A company of the king's men bore down on them; the thunderous echo of a hundred steel-shod hooves on the hard-packed ground a harbinger of certain doom. Syrah only just managed to resist the first irrational impulse to whip the little pony into a mad dash for the gate, and quickly drew the cart to a halt. There was not a moment to lose.

"Quickly, Mayenne, throw yourself across the coffin and grieve loudly for your father."

"My father? But he's not—"

"Keen!"

". . . dead."

"God's teeth, Mayenne! Keen!"

"Keen?" Terrified beyond all understanding, Mayenne would have been hard pressed to boil water, much less keen for a father she knew to be alive and well.

Eben had by now recovered from his own moment of horror at seeing the onrushing contingent of heavily armed men, and took matters into his own hands in the time-honored way of a boy of fourteen: He reached over and punched the witless maid so hard that she burst into tears and collapsed into a convincing little heap at the foot of the coffin, a perfect picture of a grief-stricken daughter.

It was, Syrah prayed, a tableau so touching, so pitiful, so

poignant that it would melt the heart of even the most battle-hardened soldier. The fateful moment was almost upon them, and Syrah was surprised to feel not fear but pride. Pride in her quick-witted little brother, in the unswerving loyalty of her maid, in the three of them that they dared risk all in defense of the honor of the Ninth House.

It seemed impossible that the implacable charge of horses and men-at-arms could stop in time to avoid running right over them, but a shouted command rose above the din and the entire company pulled up as one in a huge cloud of dust not twenty yards from the cart. For a full minute, the only sounds on the warm morning breeze were Mayenne's piteous sobs, the heavy breathing and shifting of horses, and the occasional clink of metal. Enough noise, Syrah hoped, to mask a gentle snore.

Three officers rode forward to survey the scene before them. Syrah could almost feel the ground open up beneath her feet when one of them proved to be none other than the captain of Prince Jibril's personal guard from the tavern last night.

Surely, he could not recognize her, dressed as she now was, scrubbed clean of the hideous makeup with half her face covered with the black bandanna. He would not associate this humble peasant girl with the brazen strumpet Prince Jibril had left the tavern with. Yet, when she raised her eyes to look at him, he stared back with a slightly puzzled look.

"Do I know you, girl?"

"Nay, sir, I cannot believe that you do," Syrah replied, quickly dropping her gaze and staring fixedly at the ground. It could only be her eyes that had prompted his curiosity, her damnable blue-green eyes that she now thought her very best feature, unusual eyes in this land of mostly dark-eyed people—eyes that might now mean her very death.

He looked unconvinced. "Perhaps not, but your eyes—"

"Captain Ankuli, sir," a voice screamed, "it's the plague!" Shouts of "plague, plague" and "run for your lives" spread through the company, and the orderly line that surrounded

31

the little cart broke as riders backed their mounts away from the awful face of Great Uncle Amorgos and all it implied.

"Stand," Captain Ankuli roared in a voice of command not to be ignored. "There has been no plague in this land for three generations. Stand, I say, or you will be confined to barracks at my pleasure." Order and an uneasy silence descended again as the captain rode forward to assess the coffin.

"What means this sign, boy?" he said to Eben, who stood ramrod straight and met his suspicious stare with admirable composure, considering the circumstances.

"Aye, sir, it is true our pa did not die of plague. As you say, by the mercy of our Lord Father in heaven, our land has been free of the Black Death for many years. Yet we knew of no other way to warn the good people of this city of the loathsome contamination that took him from us. Pa—may he sing with the angels above—was a trader, you see, newly returned from the great deserts beyond our waters—"

"Exactly what contamination might that be, boy?"

Eben's eyes filled with tears. "Spittle fever, my lord. That was the name Pa gave while he still possessed a tongue to speak with. After it fell out, well, he couldn't very well—"

Captain Ankuli snorted in disbelief. "Spittle fever, you say? I have never heard of such a malady."

"Dromedaries," Eben explained.

"Dromedaries?"

"Great beasts of the desert, sir. Nasty-tempered, they are, inclined to spit a foul green phlegm when seriously annoyed."

"Brother," Syrah chided between clenched teeth, "there is no need—"

"Being unfamiliar with the irritable nature of the beast," Eben continued blithely, "Pa thought to pat one upon the nose—very much as you might stroke your own fine mount, sir—and this dromedary, who was in amorous season and unappeased, if you know what I mean—"

"Enough now," Syrah growled.

32

Eben was well launched on his tale and not to be deterred from the telling. "As I was saying, this dromedary was in amorous season and testy indeed—quite like any of your men, I'll wager, sir, when the need is upon them, or you yourself—"

"Brother," Syrah fairly shouted in an effort to curb Eben's feverish imagination, but to no effect whatsoever.

"Well," Eben continued, glowering at the interruption, "the beast did not take kindly to Pa's innocent touch and let loose great green gobs of fetid spittle full in his face—"

Syrah let out an audible groan and sent up a silent prayer of gratitude to Captain Ankuli when he managed to interrupt Eben's enthusiastic rendition of their pa's fateful encounter with the bad-tempered dromedary.

"Enough, boy. We get the idea. You have my sincere condolences on the death of your father. Still, I am curious about this coffin." He walked his horse slowly around the cart, eyeing it suspiciously, and came to a stop so close to Mayenne that he brushed her sleeve as he reached down to wiggle a finger into one of the breathing holes.

For the first time since Mayenne had become her personal maid a year ago, Syrah welcomed the splendid display of histrionics that resulted from the captain's unexpected touch, as the red-eyed maid let out a spine-chilling shriek that sent Captain Ankuli's horse stumbling back. At the same time, it catapulted the nervous little dray pony into a wild panic that sent it hurtling right through the mounted line and off across the parade ground. The cart swerved, bounced, and tilted precariously as shrieking maid and snoring prince careened toward an uncertain fate. Eben and Syrah could only watch in horror as a burly soldier swung his mount around and went in pursuit, gaining quickly, then leaning down and deftly plucking the caterwauling Mayenne from her dangerous perch up into the safety of his arms. He slowed for only a moment, then continued the chase as the pony made straight for the bustling open-air market.

Syrah held her breath, praying that the rider could stop the cart before it crashed through the tents and shoddily constructed wooden stalls. Just when it looked as though all was lost, the soldier gathered Mayenne hard against him with one hand and bent low from his horse to grab the pony's bridle and bring the terrified beast to a halt. Mercifully, the coffin remained securely lashed to the cart and appeared undamaged, although the well-being of its occupant was another question altogether, not to mention the appalling possibility that the wild ride had yanked him from his deep slumber.

Syrah suddenly realized that she had not drawn a single breath in the past two minutes. When she turned to Eben, he was as blue in the face as she was. They stared at one another, dumbfounded. The men of the mounted militia, however, were howling with laughter, and even Captain Ankuli was grinning as Mayenne's savior led the pony and, unknowingly, the Crown Prince back across the parade ground.

The captain turned his attention back to Eben and Syrah. "I'm still curious about those holes, young ones." Syrah's mind went blank, but with heroic presence of mind, Eben took the field once again.

"The boils, sir."

"Boils."

"Well, we tried, don't you know, but right up to the moment he drew his last breath—God rest Pa's immortal soul—there were these great boils breaking out all over his body—some in places it wouldn't be proper to mention in front of my sisters here. The healer said we had to keep lancing them, even after Pa passed on, or the pressure would build up and Pa would explode. And there's gases, too, sir, although I don't quite understand them, but the coffin maker said we should make holes to let the gases out. We thought that ever so clever of him. Not that it matters to Pa, of course, but this coffin cost a lot of money for poor folks like us and we didn't want to ruin it on account of our ma's been rather poorly herself of late with a vile disease of the bowel—"

Syrah finally managed to break in. "Let's not burden the good man with our sorrows, brother." She looked up at the

34

captain brightly. "Unless you'd care to hear more, sir?"

Captain Ankuli grimaced. "I think we've heard quite enough. Be on your way. I suggest you get your father buried before nightfall. I would send a man to escort you, but we have other business to attend to. You may not have heard, deep in mourning as you are, that the Crown Prince is missing. We are concerned for his safety."

"No," gasped Eben, clapping a hand to his mouth for full dramatic effect. "Say it isn't so, Captain."

Kalan was grim. "It is so."

"But what of his personal guard?" Syrah inquired. "Do they not accompany him wherever he goes?"

Kalan chose not to answer that. He should never have let Jibril go off alone. He had been derelict in his duty, all for the sake of a quick tumble with a tavern whore. The blame for his friend's disappearance sat squarely on his own shoulders. He would find Jibril if he had to turn over every rock, tear apart every outhouse and chicken coop with his bare hands, and interrogate every living soul in the Dominion. Even now, his men were rounding up every whore and serving wench in the city. Not only had he dishonored his commission and his House, but far more grievous, he had failed a friend. Jibril might forgive him, but he would never forgive himself.

"Tell me, young ones, have you seen anything amiss today?"

Eben scratched his head, according the question the serious consideration it deserved. "No, I cannot say we have, sir." He brightened. "There was that cat with two tails, but I wouldn't call that terribly strange. I myself once saw one with three; but then the third tail turned out to be a fifth leg and—"

Syrah hissed a warning. "Be still, or I will lock you in the privy when we get home and feed you naught but worms and water."

She turned to the captain. "Please accept my sincere apologies, sir. My brother's imagination often runs away with him. I'm sorry we have been a bother to you when you are on a mission of such grave importance. We will pray for

35

the prince's safety. I am sure if anyone can find him, it will be you."

"I will find him, fear not."

Kalan gave Syrah another speculative glance. "I feel sure . . . You have lovely eyes, girl. Mayhap we will meet again and you will permit me to discover what other treasures you possess. I would have your name and village."

"Nini of Dunataea, sir," she lied prettily, choosing a village at the farthest corner of the Dominion.

"Well, Nini of Dunataea, until we meet again . . ."

"Not if I have anything to say about it," Syrah muttered under her breath as he rode away with his men falling into orderly ranks behind. She smiled at the sheer conceit of the man, but sobered immediately at the thought that he might remember her eyes long after they had released Prince Jibril. Well, she would confront that problem when the time came. Right now, all she wanted to do was get as far away from Suriana as possible.

"Hurry up, get back on the cart," she snapped at Mayenne, who hadn't moved a muscle since the burly soldier finally managed to pry her arms from around his thick neck and set her down. She stood transfixed, watching the retreating soldiers with the fatuous smile of the truly besotted. Syrah had to turn her around bodily and boost her up onto the cart, where the girl spent the remainder of the day in lustful imaginings and poignant regret.

As Syrah guided the little cart through the gate, she turned to her brother, who rode beside her whistling a cheerful tune.

"Spittle fever?"

Eben grinned. "Not bad, huh?"

Chapter Three

The dromedary smiled a shy smile. "May I offer you some wine, my prince?"

Jibril gazed into the beast's wide-set innocent eyes, eyes the color of a warm summer sea. "Do I know you, dromedary?"

"Nay, sir, I cannot believe that you do. I am newly come from Dunataea."

"Is this your first tournament, then?"

"Aye. I pray you will be gentle with me."

"I will try, but if we are to reach the goal, mayhap I will have to ride you hard."

The dromedary blushed prettily. "I am yours to command, my lord. They say that once firmly seated you will reach the goal, whether the ride be rough or smooth. I am honored that you have chosen me to be your mount this day."

The prince only smiled and turned to survey the course with the practiced eye of the military strategist. As far as he could see, it presented no difficulties more challenging than those of the biannual games hosted by the First House at the planting and harvest festivals. Only rarely had he been bested in competition, and never in battle. If he was awesome in hand-to-hand combat, he was nigh invincible in the saddle. Whether seated upon his fearsome stallion leading a charge, or astride a delicate untried dromedary in a friendly competition on a summer's afternoon, he could guide and control with the slightest nuance of hand, knee, or heel without resorting to the whip or spur.

Novice though she was, this dromedary possessed the fine long legs to clear every hurdle, dry ditch, and water jump without unseating him. Lithesome and responsive, she would undulate prettily beneath him as he guided her through the intricate twists and turns of the obstacle course. She would hold steady as he leveled and released his lance, and provide the speed and stamina to carry them down the long straightaway to the goal.

She was a fine mount, the most promising he had ever encountered, and lovely really, with those azure eyes and silken fur. "You will do very well for me, dromedary. It pleases me to introduce you to the pleasures of the race."

"You are too kind, my lord," the dromedary murmured. "More wine?"

"Perhaps just a drop, but then I must see to my weapons." The prince strode toward the great white tent above which the pennant of the First House—a sleek black panther rampant on a crimson field—fluttered in the warm breeze.

"Ah, there you are, Jibril," his old friend, Kalan, greeted him. He glanced over at the little dromedary. "She's a fine specimen, my friend. Sweet tempered from the look of her. Most unusual in the breed, I understand."

"A novice," the prince said nonchalantly.

Kalan let out a shout of delight. "A novice? You actually found a novice?"

Jibril gave him a smug little smile. "Actually, she found me. I had no intention of riding today and was merely wandering about the paddock to while away the time until you completed your ride. I noticed her right off, of course; you don't see a dromedary like her every day. Once or twice I caught her glancing my way, but then she would duck her head and pretend she wasn't looking at me at all. Tell me if that isn't as much an invitation as if she'd sidled right up to me?"

Kalan clapped a hand on his friend's shoulder and laughed. "A dromedary could spit you full in the face with great green gobs of fetid spittle, and you'd believe it was an invitation."

"I wouldn't go that far," the prince said dryly. "But she is a delectable little mount, is she not? And anxious as all get out to run her first race."

Kalan swung up into the saddle of his own mount, a sturdy roan-colored dromedary that had run many a race. "Well, you didn't want to come to this competition in the first place, so you might as well have some pleasure for your trouble."

"I intend to," the prince replied as his friend trotted off toward the starting line.

Still, he could not help feeling that something was not quite right about this day. He glanced about the field; it was just a field like any other. He watched as Kalan took the first set of hurdles; it was a competition like any other. He glanced over at the dromedaries in the paddock; they were just dromedaries.

He shrugged off the disquieting premonition, and sauntered over to the paddock where his charming little dromedary awaited him. She gave him a dimpled smile. "Some wine, my lord?"

"I think not. I dare not imbibe too much before a race."

"Oh, yes, of course, my lord. I just thought . . ."

"What did you think, little one?" he teased, smiling at her evident disappointment.

"I sent specially for this wine; it is delicately spiced and sweet upon the tongue. To celebrate . . ." She pinkened slightly beneath the silky down on her cheeks. "To celebrate my first race, my lord."

Jibril laughed. She was really quite charming. He would indulge her. He could remember his own first race at the age of fourteen: the apprehension that perhaps he was not ready, the fear of ridicule should he not acquit himself well.

"Since you have gone to the trouble and ask so prettily."

He raised the flask to his lips, and although he found the wine much too sweet for his own taste, he emptied it to please her.

After a long shy silence, the little dromedary said, "Your lance, my lord."

"What of it?"

"I hear it is a very fine lance indeed. Longer than most and well forged."

This was a subject guaranteed to please the prince. He was uncommonly proud of his lance and knew it to be the envy of many knights. Ladies of the court had been known to pay troubadours very well indeed to compose pretty verses about it.

"How did you hear of my lance, little one?"

The dromedary stirred uneasily. "It is the talk of the paddock. Indeed, its fame has spread even to my humble village. Will you carry it this day, sir?"

"But of course. Would you like to see it before I mount you?"

If the dromedary had pinkened earlier, she now turned positively crimson with embarrassment. "No!" she gasped. "I mean . . . I am sure it is as fine a lance as any in the Dominion."

The prince adjusted a stirrup and gave her a comforting pat on the rump. "You are nervous, I see. That is only to be expected. However, know that we are partners in this race. I will see to my lance and wield it well. You need only respond to my commands. You will know what I ask of you from the feel of my hands upon your flanks, the grip of my knees, the shift of my weight as I lean into you—"

"Plague, plague," screamed a voice from the crowd that had gathered near the starting line. "Run for your lives!"

Pandemonium reigned as spectators scattered in all directions. Mothers called out for lost children, husbands for their wives. Priests fell to their knees begging heaven's mercy and were trampled beneath the feet of the surging mob. Shrieking dromedaries broke from the paddock and galloped to and fro in mindless panic.

"Stand, I say," cried a voice from the heart of the tumult.

"There is no plague upon this land. 'Tis only spittle fever. You have naught to fear."

"Spittle, spittle," chanted the crowd. "Naught but spittle, naught to fear."

Throughout this bizarre episode, Jibril had the strangest feeling that he was there, yet in some real sense he was not there at all. He could see the scene in his mind, but realized with a sudden surge of panic that he could not see it with his eyes. He could hear—yes, that was Kalan's voice, and the spine-chilling shrieks certainly had not been his imagination—but he didn't seem to be able to move a muscle.

". . . prince did not return to the palace last night . . . fear for his safety."

Jibril frowned. He was missing? Nonsense, he was right here.

". . . three tails . . . fifth leg." Well, it was possible, the prince supposed. He himself had once seen a heifer with two heads.

". . . worms and water."

It was said worms tasted like chicken, but Jibril had always had his doubts about that. In any event, he hoped he would never have occasion to discover that for himself.

"I will find him, fear not." That was Kalan again.

"I'm right here, you fool," Jibril shouted, but he couldn't hear the sound of his own voice.

And suddenly he knew that he *was* there, but for some reason Kalan could neither see nor hear him. It had all been a dream—the dromedary, the tournament, the maddened mob. But not . . . *the tavern, the wine, the wench!* That wine, which had tasted so peculiar, must have been drugged, and now he lay bound hand and foot, gagged and blindfolded, in some sort of crate, bumping along in the back of a cart.

Now that he was fully awake and aware of his circumstances, Jibril began to examine his present predicament in much the same way he would gather information about a dangerous adversary before deciding on a course of action.

It might all be a practical joke. Some woman who fancied him had arranged for him to be kidnapped; the soft scented pillow beneath his head might attest to the hand of a woman in his abduction. He could soon find himself in a feather bed in a boudoir redolent of roses.

He discarded the idea almost immediately. No woman of his acquaintance was clever enough to plan and implement such an elaborate scheme.

Perhaps it was a cuckolded husband, someone dismissed from his employ, a disgruntled officer under his command. Abduction might serve to avenge some wrong by making the prince look ridiculous, but beheading was a steep price to pay for petty vengeance.

He might be a pawn in some dispute between the noble Houses. There had been that tragic business a few months back when that lout, Ranulph Gyp, had commandeered the hall of the Ninth House. The family of his father's old friend, Lord Dhion, had fled, only to be lost at sea. No craft, however well caulked, rigged, or manned, could have survived that terrible storm; certainly not the rickety little boat that set out in the darkest hour of the night in the midst of the tempest. Jibril himself had commanded the search for survivors, but nothing was ever found, save for a few planks, the pennant of the Ninth House, a rag doll, and a salt-stained gown of delicate blue silk that must have graced the supple form of Lady Syrah.

A now familiar pang of loss pierced through Jibril. He had known many women, but throughout the years it was Syrah who had haunted his dreams, a lovely laughing girl dancing in the rain. He had known that day he would make her his queen.

Ranulph Gyp's nefarious schemes had ended all that. The desperate act that sent the Dhion family to the bottom of the sea had ended forever the noble line of the Ninth House. Not for two generations had one House risen against another, but Ranulph Gyp had determined to take that which had been denied him, namely, the Lady Syrah and the strategic lands that would come with her dowry. King Ahriman himself had deemed the contract of betrothal suspicious, having hinted many times over the years to his old friend that he would look with favor on a marriage between the Crown Prince and the Lady Syrah. Although deeply honored by the king's marked favor, Lord Dhion had told the king he would not mention the prince's intentions to his wife or daughter, believing that the choice should be Syrah's alone when she came of age.

Had the bastard threatened Lady Syrah, even violated her? Jibril's stomach clenched at the thought. Gyp would pay for his greed. Jibril would see to it personally.

The cart jerked to a bone-wrenching stop. A hissing dispute about spilt porridge erupted between a boy and a whining woman.

"Don't look at me." The boy.

"I did it last time." The whiner.

"I helped with the chamber pots."

"Did not."

"Did too."

"Don't make me laugh. You never help with anything."

"I do too. You were just too busy throwing up to notice."

Another woman intervened with calm authority. The boy was assigned the distasteful task of cleaning up the mess, which he did with much ill grace.

Once they were under way again, Jibril resumed his analysis of his present predicament. Mercenaries had been known to take hostages to exchange for imprisoned comrades, but none had ever dared seize a member of the royal family.

There remained but one sensible explanation for his abduction: ransom for gold, pure and simple.

It did not even cross Jibril's mind that his kidnappers would be a match for him now that his mind was clear. Still, he had to admire their clever strategy so far. They had known he was at that stinking tavern. Although it had been an impromptu visit, they were prepared for the eventuality.

He allowed himself a moment of chagrin, reflecting that lust had landed him in this humiliating position. It was all the more ironic that he had given in to temptation when he was about to begin one of his periodic bouts of abstinence to test his self-control—no easy feat for a man of his strong sexual appetite.

But there had been something about that girl in the tavern, an innocent sensuality that was infinitely more seductive than the wiles an experienced harlot might use to lure a man to her bed. The thought had even crossed his mind that she might be a virgin, but that was ridiculous. She had served as a tool of the conspirators to entice him to drink drugged wine; they would only employ a woman well versed in the art of seduction. He wondered what her price had been. A few coins, a new dress? Had she even known who he was?

Drugging him had certainly been their only option. It would be impossible to take him by force, given his strength and physical prowess, not to mention the fact that his personal guard accompanied him everywhere. Still more impressive was their sheer audacity in slipping him out of the city right under Kalan's nose, a fact that would no doubt infuriate Kalan once he learned of it. It remained to be seen just how they intended to keep him prisoner, and more interesting still, how they intended to collect the ransom from the king.

Jibril was intrigued. Here lay a challenge worthy of his abilities: anticipating their moves, setting the trap, and bringing them down. And he had not the slightest doubt that in the end the game would be his.

Chapter Four

"You are awake, Your Highness?" a man's voice inquired.

Prince Jibril grunted that he was.

"We are going to remove your gag and try to make you comfortable for the night. We will not harm you, but it is in your best interest to cooperate. Do you understand?"

Jibril offered another grunt.

Someone loosened the gag, and Jibril flexed his jaw and ran his tongue over his dry lips.

"Water, please," he croaked.

As the long day wore on, Jibril had considered a number of strategies to gain his release, the first of which was to listen carefully to all that went on around him. It was what he did not hear, however, that surprised him: Many times as the hours dragged by he heard other carts upon the road, yet passersby spoke not a word to his abductors. Something about them kept others away, but for the life of him he could not come up with an explanation.

"We will bring ale and water in a moment, sir. No doubt you wish to relieve yourself first. I will untie your ankles and assist you in standing up."

Jibril tried to take the measure of the man: well spoken and properly deferential, but not overly so. A man who knew his place and was accustomed to dealing with the nobility. He might be a high-level servant, chamberlain, or a private secretary. Of middle age, possibly older.

The man untied the cords around his ankles, assisted him to his feet, and guided him off the back of the cart. "I will loosen your breeches, my lord. I believe you can manage the rest by yourself."

"I can."

A few minutes later, Jibril found himself seated in reasonable comfort against the wall of what must be a stable, judging by the smell of hay and manure. A stout rope wound several times about his waist secured him to the wall. His ankles were bound again but loosely enough to allow him to extract his knife from the secret compartment in his boot merely by bending his knees and bringing them to his chest. Hearing the man leave the stable and believing himself alone, he immediately fumbled for the knife. It would take but a moment to cut the ropes and free himself.

"You will not find it there, Your Highness." A woman's voice: soft, confident, possibly educated.

Jibril affected nonchalance. "You are thorough," he allowed.

She made no reply. He tried again.

"We have not reached our destination?"

"We have not."

Her reticence irritated him. He had long observed that women volunteered more in the way of explanation than was required by a simple statement or question. Perhaps it was because they were rarely welcome in the conversation of men and their opinions and advice so little requested or heeded. Or they sought to please by appearing more interested in the subject under discussion than they in fact were; it was a common enough ploy to snare a man's attention and flatter his ego. Or perhaps they simply had not the intellect to see that brevity was often more effective than verbosity, and infinitely less annoying. He sought a reason why this woman would be different and concluded that she had been forbidden to speak to him.

Still, she would likely prove a weak link. Subtle intimidation might loosen her tongue.

"You do not understand what it is you do, girl."

Silence.

"You are involved in treason against the Royal House."

"Yes, my lord."

"It is an act of folly and sure to fail."

"I see." She didn't sound particularly worried.

"Your masters cannot kidnap a prince of the realm and expect they will succeed."

"You are here, my lord, are you not?"

Jibril was suddenly wary. Was that a hint of amusement in her voice?

"It is one thing to drug a man and bind him, and quite another to hold him captive and collect ransom or exchange him for another, no matter how clever your masters may be."

Syrah almost laughed; he thought her but a servant doing the bidding of others. She would not disabuse him of that notion. It might be possible to carry out the entire scheme without his ever guessing her role in it. Such a misapprehension might prove useful when he set out to find his abductors.

It was going to be enjoyable matching wits with him. Her father had admired Prince Jibril as the best military tactician he had ever seen. What wiles would he bring to bear to strike fear into a lowly serving wench?

"Aye, my lord, it is quite another thing," Syrah conceded in a tremulous voice. "But my masters assure me they will succeed and I will be rewarded for my assistance."

"That may be what they tell you now, girl, but when the time comes to divide the spoils—"

He stopped at the sound of approaching footsteps. He would explore this avenue of intimidation the next time he found himself alone with her. He only hoped she would continue on with them in the morning. She might be persuaded to help him, and if he could not frighten or cajole her into releasing him, he could always seduce her.

Syrah hastened into the stable yard to waylay Aleden. "I

47

will take the tray in to him. We can remove the blindfold as long as we wear the hoods. We'll need to free his hands so he can eat. We need several lengths of chain; the rope was good enough for the coffin, but he's clever and I doubt it would hold him for the night."

Ten minutes later, a chain secured by a small lock had replaced the stout rope around the prince's waist and a shorter chain bound his ankles. Satisfied that he posed no danger, Syrah signaled that Aleden could return to the house.

"My lord, I am going to set out your meal, remove the blindfold, and free your hands so you can eat in comfort. Please do not move until I say you may. If you do not cooperate you will not eat. Is that clear?"

"Clear enough."

He heard the rustle of skirts as the girl set about laying out the food near his knees. Then she moved behind him and reached through the slats of the stall wall to remove the blindfold. Light from an oil lantern exploded into his eyes, as stunning as the sun at midday. It took a full minute for his eyes to adjust. He raised his arms above his head at her command to allow her to loosen the rope that bound his wrists.

He was confined, as he had thought, in a stable, but the cart, horse, and crate—probably a coffin, since he had been stretched out full length in it—had been left outside. There might have been something distinctive about them that would help him track these people down.

The girl still stood behind him. He caught a whiff of fresh herbs as she moved about, rosemary and a hint of the wild thyme that graced the open pastures of the Dominion. He only hoped she would not remain hidden while he ate; her appearance would be a vital clue to the manner of people he was dealing with, and he had to admit he'd been wondering what she looked like. Comely, plain, or downright ugly, he would seduce her if it would gain his release.

Jibril focused his attention on the food before him and saw at once that he was dealing with people of quality or servants of such, who valued cleanliness and the good manners of the table. Wealthy merchants, nobility even. An immaculate white linen cloth had been spread out on the hay-strewn dirt floor. A small bowl of water for washing his hands stood to one side and beside it a soft cloth to serve as a napkin. A wooden trencher etched with a pattern of vines and flowers held chunks of succulent roasted mutton and a flagon was filled to the brim with ale. A large bowl, decorated in a similar motif, held a generous serving of bean and pea pottage with thick chunks of bacon—well seasoned from the savory aroma of it. The bread was wheat, as befitted a noble table, not the coarse rye or barley of the peasant. Figs and cheese were set out for desert. There was even a small container of fine salt. The only implement was a wooden spoon for the pottage. Naturally, they would not allow him the use of a knife, but they had seen fit to cut the meat, bread, and cheese into bite-size pieces.

"I trust the food meets with your approval, Your Highness. The ale is newly brewed and the bread but half a day old."

Jibril looked up to see the woman standing before him. She had taken great care to conceal her features. Her head was covered with a hood of the same rough homespun as her belted tunic. Even her eyes were concealed behind a panel of close-knit mesh. Only her hands were visible, the fingers long and delicate, the nails well trimmed. Something about her bearing as she settled down on a rude bench against the far wall and folded her hands in her lap made him think she might be highborn, or more likely a lady's personal maid.

The woman's question amused him. He flashed a smile meant to tease and charm. "And if I don't approve, will you then bring me rare beef, sugared wafers, and new Beaujolais?"

Syrah laughed, softly beguiled as he had intended her to be. "Nay, my lord. Here you are as much a prisoner as a prince. You must be content with humble fare until they release you."

Jibril gave her a lazy smile. "When I am free to enjoy such a fine meal, I hope you also will be free to join me."

Syrah caught the double entendre and couldn't resist replying, "I shall most certainly be free, but I fear it will not be in my best interest to accept your kind invitation."

"A pity," Jibril replied, delighted with her quick comeback, proof of some intelligence. He wondered briefly if she had some part in planning this mad abduction, but dismissed the idea almost at once. She had said "when they release you," implying that others made the decisions. He pressed on with the flirtation. "Then I must content myself with your presence at this unpretentious supper. Will you join me?"

"Nay," was all Syrah trusted herself to reply, wanting nothing more than to launch herself across the short distance that separated them and snuggle up against him as she had in the tavern. She might not have understood the strange excitement she had felt in his strong arms six years ago when she was but thirteen, but there was no doubt that last night he had kindled a fire that could only be the desire the milkmaid had warned her about. And although Syrah might not understand all the details of lovemaking or suspect the depth of her own carnal nature, the longing to touch this man again and be touched by him was almost irresistible.

She wondered if he would feel the same desire for her as the chaste Lady Syrah as he had for the tavern wench. No, it had been a harlot he sought, a woman skilled in the art of pleasing a man's every desire. What did Lady Syrah know of a man's desires? Why, she had barely known how to kiss. The few chaste kisses her father's squires had stolen scarcely counted when compared to the expertise Prince Jibril wielded with his warm sensuous lips and teasing tongue.

Jibril made quick work of the food. When he was finished, Syrah slid the cloth and dishes away, keeping well clear of him. Once again, she moved behind him and reached over the stall wall to retie his wrists, this time behind his back. She had just fetched the blankets and pillows from the coffin when Aleden, chamberlain of the Ninth House, and Eben, each wearing a hood, appeared at the stable door.

"You must be tired, my lady," Aleden said. "The boy and I will keep watch tonight. Cook is keeping your dinner warm."

"Yes, I am tired, Aleden. Double-check his bindings. I've left him some slack so he can get comfortable, but stay well away from him and don't let him draw you into conversation. He's under the impression that I'm just a servant and I want him to think the same of you two. He's going to be looking for someone he can cajole or intimidate. If he's confused as to who's who, all the better."

Eben squared his shoulders. "He can't put anything over on me. I found that knife in his boot."

"You did indeed," Syrah said, "and he went right for it when he thought no one was looking."

"He did?" Eben crowed. "What did he say when it wasn't there?"

"That we were thorough, and there was considerable admiration in his tone."

"I'll wager it annoyed the devil out of him," Eben said with satisfaction.

Syrah laughed. "I imagine it did. But don't get cocky. He's devious and dangerous. I'll feel better when we get him to the island."

Long after cook had fed and fussed over her and retired to her own bed, Syrah sat on a low stool staring into the dying embers of the kitchen fire. The silence of the old manor house settled around her, familiar and comforting now after three months.

It was here, to the home of her newly widowed great aunt Rosota, that she had brought her family and five faithful servants when Ranulph occupied her hall and tried to force her to marry him. And close by, on a remote stretch of cliffs on the edge of the southern ocean, she had grieved for the loss of Eben's patrimony and life as she had known it in the hall of the Ninth House. Here she invented the story of their deaths at sea and swore a solemn oath that she would reclaim all they had lost.

She really ought to take herself off to bed, tired as she was, but she needed this quiet time to review the events of the past four days, check for mistakes, and go over for the thousandth time each step ahead. Tomorrow they would complete the journey along the coast to the cave at the foot of the Pailacca cliffs. At nightfall, when the tide was at its lowest ebb, they could cross the rocky causeway to the barren outcrop of rock known as the Isle of Lost Souls, believed to be haunted by the tortured souls of monks gone mad from mortification of flesh and spirit. There, in the ruins of the ancient hermitage, they would hold their hostage until the king paid his ransom.

Syrah could not ask for a better place of concealment. Few had dared set foot there since an earthquake three hundred years ago sent the great abbey crashing into the sea and left the pitiable anchorites to die unmourned and unshriven. The prelate of Pailacca had declared the cataclysm the devil's work and had forbidden his flock to venture across the causeway, lest Satan seize their souls.

Great Uncle Amorgos, scholar and rationalist, dismissed the legend as so much foolish superstition, and proved it so when he took Syrah and Eben on an afternoon expedition to the island. All three had returned with their souls intact.

So it was that the island came immediately to mind when Syrah was casting about for a safe place to hold the prince. It wasn't foolproof by any means: Great Uncle Amorgos was not the only skeptic in the Dominion, but so isolated was the island from the usual routes of commerce that visitors were few.

Syrah finally collapsed into bed but lay for a long while staring at the timbered ceiling. She was worried about that captain who had commented on her eyes. Would his description of the maid from Dunataea prompt Jibril's memory of the tavern wench, or even Syrah herself? Surely he would not remember her at all, much less the unusual color of her eyes.

As for that Captain Ankuli, she would see to it that they never crossed paths again.

Chapter Five

By the time Prince Jibril was again laid out in his coffin the next morning, he had gathered a number of important facts about his captors.

First, as to their number: He had seen but three the night before—the woman, the man, and the boy—but the comings and goings of the morning proved there were five, all of whom he had assessed and named according to their character and probable vulnerability.

The woman in charge, who smelled so sweetly of rosemary and possessed some wit, he called the Lady's Maid. A second woman, who had brought his morning meal, he called simply the Wench. He marked her as the most vulnerable of the group, if her nervous demeanor was anything to go by; she had skittered and stammered as though he would burst free of his metal chains any moment and visit the fury of hell upon her. The Man was unflappable and confident, although Jibril did not think he wielded any authority. There were two boys. Boy One was obviously a servant, possibly a groom, who spoke not a word. Boy Two, however, would bear careful study. He carried himself with an air of confidence and innate pride, and although he deferred to the Lady's Maid, Jibril suspected the lad was more accustomed to being obeyed than obeying others.

As to the makeup of the group, Jibril had surmised that at least three of them were related. He had heard, but not seen, an Old Man as well. The Old Man was the father of the Lady's Maid. While the cart was being loaded out in the stable yard, she had cried out, "No, Papa, you cannot go into the stable. Let me help you back to the house. You must rest and gather your strength." Apparently, the Old Man was quite ill and not involved in the present circumstance. Boy Two was almost certainly related to the Lady's Maid, probably her brother if their banter and bickering were anything to go by.

In sum, they were as unlikely a band of miscreants as Jibril could imagine. He could understand that the people who had masterminded his abduction might not choose to show themselves at present; they were shrewd to use others to do their dirty work for them. However, their absence irked him. Surely, they should have felt it necessary to employ a strong force of ruffians to seize and guard a prisoner of his own renowned strength and intelligence. Had Prince Jibril been a man who allowed emotion to cloud his reasoning, he might almost feel insulted that they should think him so easy to take and contain.

The second important fact he had gleaned was that he had been conveyed to the south coast. A fog had rolled in during the night, bringing with it the telling tang of the sea; fresh sprats, possibly netted that very morning, constituted the main portion of his morning meal. That he had been conveyed to the south coast was easily deduced from the angle and movement of the sun, seen through a narrow slit in the stable wall.

He only hoped they hadn't slipped more sleeping herbs into his morning ale. That question was answered as the Lady's Maid led him out of the stable, blindfolded once again, and assisted him onto the cart.

"I am sure that you would prefer not to be drugged again," she said. "But we must prevent you from appealing for help should the opportunity arise. I regret I must replace the gag."

"May I speak before you do so?"

Syrah considered the request, wary lest he sway the others with honeyed words. In the end her curiosity won out.

"You may speak, but be brief. We have far to go today."

Jibril drew himself up into an attitude of command that had served him well in both the heat of battle and formal affairs of state. He chose his words with care.

"I am your prince, first son of the House of Chios. I am sworn to uphold the word and law of my father, your king, to whom you owe all allegiance and obedience. You are involved in an act of treason. The penalty, you surely know, is ignominious death by beheading; your bodies hung by the feet from the gibbet until the flesh rots and dribbles from your bones; your heads atop a spike on the battlements."

A squeal of terror was cut short by a howl of pain and outrage as someone's boot—probably Boy Two—made contact with what he assumed was the Wench's shin.

Having scared them witless, or so he hoped, Jibril continued in a more soothing and earnest tone of voice. "But your king knows mercy also and will not punish the innocent. Judging by the kindness and concern you have shown me, I believe that all of you are innocent of planning my abduction. You but follow the orders of others. I tell you this: Release me now and I will ask the king to show compassion in his consideration of your part in this treason. Release me now and it will go well with you. I swear this upon my honor of my House."

He towered above them. In a voice both soft and terrible he made known his royal will: "You will release me—*now*."

Gag firmly in place once again, Jibril considered his next move. The dramatic speech that would have left his most battle-hardened troops quaking in their boots hadn't deterred the motley little band from their course one whit, although a woman—most likely the high-strung Wench— had been led away sobbing and moaning. The self-possessed Lady's Maid had thanked him politely for his offer to intercede on their behalf, and without further ado assisted him into his coffin, solicitous as ever of his comfort. He could have sworn that she was smiling all the while.

Jibril did not take kindly to the idea that this woman was mocking him. He would put her in her place. He grunted several times to indicate that he wished to speak. She left off adjusting the cushions beneath his head and loosened the gag.

"You find my plight amusing, girl?"

She smoothed his long dark hair with gentle fingers. "Nay, my lord. We hold you by necessity, not by choice. We do not wish to humiliate or dishonor you."

"Honor! What do you know of honor?"

The hand stilled. He heard a sharp intake of breath.

Good, he thought, he had hit a nerve. "The traitor sheds his honor when he betrays the covenant between the king and his people. When you dishonor me, you dishonor your king."

She made no reply, but Jibril felt her tense beside him. He pursued his attack.

"Where lies the virtue in drugging a man, binding him, taking him against his will from family and friends? Is gold worth the life of a man? Metal for flesh?"

The woman's breathing quickened.

Jibril pressed on. "What of the thief—for that is what you are—who takes what he has not himself earned? The harlot who lures the drunken man to her bed, then empties his purse while he sleeps?"

Stung by his tirade, Syrah finally snapped, "Well, that's something you would know about, isn't it? What did you say? 'Metal for flesh'?" she taunted.

"It is the weakness of most men. I am a man."

"And a woman? What is her weakness?" Syrah said through clenched teeth.

"Love. Her weakness is love."

Syrah certainly did not want to speak of love with the man who had haunted her dreams for so many years; a man now lost to her forever. Stilling her anger by sheer force of will, she retied the gag.

Her skirts rustled as she stood. Before she pushed the lid of the coffin into place, Jibril heard her say, "Believe me, I know of honor. And all too well the price we pay for it."

Chapter Six

The second day of the journey passed much as the first with only two breaks from the jarring tedium: once to allow the prince to relieve himself, the second for a simple meal of bread and cheese. A storm broke in the late afternoon and an argument flared between the Lady's Maid and Boy Two as to whether they should stop and seek shelter. Once again, the Lady's Maid prevailed in a voice of calm authority, and they continued on, the Wench and Boy Two grumbling at the indignity of getting wet while their captive lay snug and dry.

By the time they reached their destination, the prince had concluded that the Lady's Maid might very well be more than a minion. She might even be a true lady, the daughter of a noble House. Her speech, grace, the delicacy of her hands as they smoothed the hair from his brow, even the scent of oil of rosemary, marked the refinement of her taste. If such were the case, he would have to reconsider the role of a noble House in this mad scheme. For the time being, however, he looked forward to a most delightful seduction, whether it would win his release or not.

Syrah had had about all she could take. Her bones ached from the jolting of the cart; her ears rang with the constant bickering between Eben and Mayenne; her clothes were damp. And the man in the coffin had utterly unnerved her.

She sat now in the cave at the landward side of the causeway that would lead to the Isle of Lost Souls when the tide went out, and tried to keep her spirits up. Despite a cheery fire over which Mayenne was heating up an iron kettle of stew and the prospect of having the prince securely under lock and key in just a few hours, Syrah longed for this part of the scheme to be over. The sooner she had Prince Jibril off her hands, the better.

How dare he preach to her of honor? She wanted to shout that it was easy for him, easy to defend his honor with the shield of his royal power and the strength of his arm. Ranulph Gyp had seized her hall by dint of force and guile. By his silence, King Ahriman had withheld his strength and succor. Who then possessed virtue—the usurper, the king, or a small band of three risking their very lives to counter a chilling twist of fate and right a dreadful wrong?

"The tide's starting to go out," Eben announced, bringing with him into the warm cavern the bite of sea air and the dark chill of the night. I'm starving. Isn't the stew ready yet?"

"It will be ready when it's ready," Mayenne snapped.

Syrah thought her head would explode if she had to listen to one more squabble today. "Enough! Not another word from either of you. I will feed you worms and water, I swear I will."

"I'd like to see you try," Eben retorted.

"Now where have I heard that before?" drawled a voice from the dark ledge beyond the fire. "Worms and water. It doesn't sound very appetizing."

Prince Jibril lounged against the cavern wall with his legs stretched out in front of him. Now that they had finally unpacked him, he was reasonably comfortable, even with his hands tied behind his back.

Eben squatted near the fire, warming his hands. "You'd be surprised, my lord. I like them pickled myself, but fried is good too. It depends on the worm. The fat red ones have the most meat but they're tough to chew. The little green ones aren't bad raw, but I rather think that's an acquired taste. Myself, my favorites are those gooey gray grubs with all the legs that you find under rotten logs. Unfortunately, it's not the season," he added with a sigh.

Jibril laughed. "You sound like an adventurous lad."

Flattered, Eben assured him that he was. "I'm pretty smart too." He could not help adding, "I was the one who found the knife in your boot."

"Now that was very clever of you. We have need of men like you in the service of the Crown. I suspect you might be officer material. Do you ride?"

"Of course, I do," Eben enthused, already envisioning himself leading the charge into the enemy camp. "We breed—"

"Enough!" Syrah interjected sharply before Eben could complete the sentence. "Brother, I would like a word with you."

She led a mutinous Eben out of the cave and sat him down on a boulder several yards down the shingled beach.

"Are you out of your mind?" she fumed. "That man is going to move heaven and earth to find us when this is over. He's going to file away every single bit of information he can glean from us."

Eben hung his head. "I know, I know. I'm sorry."

Syrah paced back and forth in front of him. "It's a bit late for that, don't you think? You might just as well have told him our names, our House." She took a deep calming breath. "Eben, this is not a game. It is a matter of life and death. There are times when I think I must have been out of my mind to believe we could do this. But we've gone too far to go back now. Even if we were to release him now, there would still be the devil to pay. We don't have any choice but to go forward."

"I'm sorry," Eben repeated. "He said I was clever—"

Syrah threw up her hands. "Can't you see what he's doing? He's flattering you, trying to win you over to his side."

Eben's chin went up a notch. "But it was clever of me to find the knife. You even said so yourself."

Syrah softened; she had not meant to hurt his pride. "Yes,

it was very clever. If you hadn't found it, he would have been able to cut himself loose and it would have been over right then and there. But, Eben, you have got to control your tongue."

Eben hopped down off the rock. "I already said I was sorry. You've made your point. I just wish . . ." He picked up a heavy shell and hurled it into the surf.

"What? What do you wish?"

"That it was different. That when I was armiger of our House, he and I would be comrades, maybe even friends someday."

"You will be," Syrah said earnestly.

"I'm sure he's just going to forget all about this," Eben snapped as he headed back toward the cave.

Syrah gazed out at the brooding silhouette that was the Isle of Lost Souls. Somehow she would make it right for Eben. Prince Jibril might very well guess the truth when mercenaries drove Ranulph from her hall and the family of the Ninth House miraculously reappeared. Syrah would make sure the blame rested squarely upon her own shoulders. If the price had to be paid with her own death or imprisonment, then so be it.

She, too, just wished . . .

The boy's blunder had confirmed what Jibril already suspected: Two of the conspirators were highborn. He had already surmised Boy Two and the Lady's Maid were brother and sister. Now he knew they came from a family wealthy enough to breed horses. Only the nobility and a few rich merchants could afford such an expensive hobby. That they were not of Arabic descent was evident from the pale skin of their hands. They were the children or relatives of one of the twenty-eight Houses.

Twenty-seven now, he reminded himself: The Ninth House no longer existed.

Jibril set aside this important information for the moment to take careful stock of his new surroundings. The trek from the cave over slippery rock and shifting sand to the base of a cliff and up a narrow twisting path had been harrowing.

The Man had guided his every step, solicitous for his safety. The Wench had set up such a hullabaloo—something about losing her soul to the devil—that Jibril was profoundly grateful when she was ordered back to the cave.

He heard the clang of an iron door and the grating turn of a key. The Lady—for so he had determined her to be and renamed her accordingly—ordered him to stand with his back to the iron bars while she removed first his blindfold and then the rope that bound his hands before quickly stepping back out of his reach. Jibril took a few moments to massage his wrists and stretch his aching muscles, then turned for his first sight of the chamber.

It was unlike any he had ever seen: a single room of good size divided in two by iron bars. At floor level was a square opening, not large enough for a man to crawl through but sufficiently so that smaller objects could be pushed into the section that served as his cell.

Considerable effort had gone into making his cell comfortable. It was furnished with a thick pallet covered with two woolen blankets and the scented pillows from his coffin; a chamber pot; a pitcher of clean water for drinking and washing; even a Bible and a chess set. A clean tunic and breeches were folded neatly on a stone bench built into the wall.

"Just like home," he remarked to the hooded figure watching him from the other side of the bars. "But where exactly am I? This is a most unusual chamber. I have never seen its like."

Thinking no harm could come of it since the prince would surely know the place was the Isle of Lost Souls when his soldiers came to release him, Syrah explained that in ancient times mad monks were confined to the cell where they could do no harm to themselves or others. Priests used the outer chamber to pray for their souls and perform exorcisms.

Not wishing to be drawn into further conversation with him, Syrah turned to go.

"My lady," the prince said softly, testing whether she would respond to the title.

She hesitated a moment before hurrying out, but that slight response was enough to confirm Jibril's conclusion.

He did the same when the boys wrestled the coffin through the narrow door and plunked it down. Boy One backed out the door, while Boy Two leaned the coffin lid against the wall.

Jibril burst out laughing when he saw the grinning skull. "Oh, wonderful. You are clever indeed, my young lord."

The boy started to speak, then thought better of it and left the chamber. Touché, Jibril thought.

He turned his attention to the large metal padlock on the door of his cell. He might have been able to force it open given the right tools, but since they had left not one scrap of metal upon his person other than his ring, he would somehow have to get hold of the key.

The Lady returned an hour later with a sheet of parchment and a piece of sharpened chalk, which she handed through the bars, keeping well out of his reach.

"Your family will be concerned for your safety. You may write a brief letter confirming that you have not been harmed and asking that the ransom be paid. Please append your signature and the mark of your House."

"You are very thoughtful," Jibril said. He scribbled a note and passed it back to her, grinning as he did so. "What next? You must prove to the king that I am truly your prisoner. Will you take a piece of my ear, a finger?"

Syrah snorted. "Your person is safe, my lord. I would, however, have your ring."

"I will not part with the insignia of my station. If you want it you will have to come and get it."

"I would be a fool to do so."

He grinned. "Indeed you would, for your person is certainly not safe with me."

Syrah caught her breath. For a moment she was thirteen again, standing in a sunny courtyard with butterflies in her heart, frogs in her belly, and tiny mice dancing along every nerve. She was grateful that he couldn't see her face, for she could feel the warmth of her blush as it overspread her cheeks.

She rolled up the parchment with exacting care and said crisply, "I will see that this reaches the king. While I am gone, you will be well looked after. If we have neglected to provide you with any necessity, you have only to ask."

Jibril affected a plaintive puppy dog sort of look. "You are leaving me all by myself, then?"

Syrah had to laugh. "No, my lord, not alone. You will have the company of the poor demented souls who once dwelt in this chamber. And my cousin, of course. I understand you excel at chess; he may prove a creditable opponent."

Jibril heaved a sigh. "Small consolation without you."

"I promise you a game of chess when I return."

"I will win, you know. In the end I always do."

"Not this time, Your Highness."

The next three days dragged by. The Lady and her brother had gone off to deliver the ransom note to the king. Jibril could not imagine how they would go about it without being apprehended. Simple but ample meals arrived twice daily, delivered by the ever-silent Boy One, likely cooked by the Wench in the cave at the other end of the causeway. Jibril's steady companion turned out to be the Man, whose chess game offered little in the way of a challenge. He was, however, willing to converse with the prince on a number of safe topics such as the weather, hunting, and the exotic land of Egypt from which the prince had returned only a few days before his abduction.

At night, Jibril lay on his pallet imagining what the Lady looked like beneath her shapeless gown, and planning seduction.

Chapter Seven

"You stink," Eben groused again as they trudged along the road toward the king's hunting camp.

"I'm supposed to stink, you ninny. It's part of the disguise. If you don't like it, stay here and I'll do this on my own." Syrah had taken to breathing through her mouth to minimize the foul stench that hung about her. She sounded like a whiny invalid with a bad cold.

"Well, you do."

Syrah was in no mood to put up with her brother's gibes. "Eben, please, I beg you. This is no time to get into another quarrel. So I stink. So we have to wear these filthy scratchy clothes. Should we just stroll into the king's camp, hand him the ransom note, and wait around for him to send for the gold?"

Eben was feeling uncharacteristically pessimistic after the long exhausting ride from the coast. "What I think is, we're going to get caught. This isn't much fun anymore."

Syrah stopped so suddenly that Eben careened into her. "We need to talk," she muttered and veered off toward a copse of firs where they could not be seen or heard from the road. Eben chose a spot upwind of his sister and plopped down on a bed of fragrant needles.

Syrah leaned against a tree, determined to keep her temper under control. "I understand," she began carefully, "that you're nervous. I told you the other night at the cave that this is not a game. Sometimes I think you're right, that the whole scheme is madness. I just couldn't figure out what else to do. Great Uncle Amorgos died. The king didn't seem to care what happened to us. I wouldn't trust Ranulph to save my life, despite all that rigmarole he kept spouting about having our best interests at heart. It all seemed so simple when I first got the idea: If we couldn't fight our cousin ourselves, we could pay someone else to do it for us."

Eben picked up a pinecone and aimed it at a rock some paces distant. "I know all that. I just don't see why we had to kidnap the prince. Why not just some rich man? Then we wouldn't have the whole army after us."

"Because Prince Jibril is important and we—"

"I don't see why we just don't go back to the island and explain everything. He's nice. I'm sure he would help us. He wouldn't even be mad."

The same thought had occurred to Syrah more than once, but she wasn't about to admit it. She paced back and forth as she explained her reasoning. "First of all, we're going to need a lot of gold to get that mercenary to work for us, and the king has more gold than anyone. Second, the prince goes out drinking almost every night, so it wasn't all that hard to follow him and put the drug in his wine and—"

"Ha!" Eben snorted. "You liked that part of it, admit it. Mayenne said you looked like you were really enjoying yourself, cuddling and kissing him."

Syrah glared at him, choosing to ignore the interruption. "He isn't going to be so nice once he's free. He's going to be furious, especially if he ever finds out it was just two women and a boy who bested him."

Eben couldn't let that pass. "I am not a boy. I'm a man."

Sinking to the ground, Syrah buried her face in her arms. "Yes, yes, you're a man," she said wearily.

A hopeful note crept into Eben's voice. "I could talk to him. Man to man. He'd listen to me."

"I don't know, Eben, I just don't know." After a short silence she raised her head with a deep sigh. "No, I think we should go ahead as we planned. We can't take that chance. But after we deliver the note tonight I want you to go back to the island by yourself. Collect Aleden and Mayenne and Clim, and go back to Great Aunt Rosota's manor. You'll be safe there. I can do the rest of this alone. If I get caught, no one could prove you were involved. Then someday when you're older, you'll come up with your own plan."

Anger propelled Eben to his feet. Syrah looked up to see, perhaps for the first time, the young man who was destined to be the seventeenth armiger of the Ninth House.

"This is my fight too," he said fiercely. "I'm fourteen, almost fifteen. You can't just send me away as though I were a child. You're my sister. Do you think I'm going to slither off like some slimy snake and leave you? Do you think you're the only one who knows about honor?"

Suddenly it was all too much. Syrah began to cry.

Eben stalked around the clearing. "Do you think I don't understand what you're going to have to give up if you become my regent? Do you think I don't know about you and the prince, that you wanted to be the one he married?" He snorted in disgust. "You could have kidnapped someone else, but the truth is you didn't want to. You kidnapped him because you wanted to be with him before he married someone else."

The truth of Eben's words sent bitter tears streaming down Syrah's cheeks. For long minutes only her sobs and the cawing of a raven high in the branches of an ancient fir sounded in the stillness of the darkening wood. Having voiced its opinion of human folly, the irritated bird flew away.

Her tears spent, Syrah spoke into the silence. "You're right, Eben. You're not a child anymore. I just didn't see it. It is your fight too. More yours than mine even. I can't do this without you."

Eben cleared his throat and put out his hand to help her

up. "So what are we doing sitting here like bumps on a log? Let's go."

How chamber pots came to play a part in the restoration of the Ninth House might someday become the stuff of legend, but at the moment all Syrah wanted was to hurl the stinking vessels as far away from her as possible. She wanted to slink off into the concealing night before that damnable Captain Ankuli recognized her. She should have realized he would show up at the king's hunting camp, which now served as headquarters for the search for Prince Jibril.

Syrah jammed the tattered straw hat well down over her forehead to hide her face. So far no one had shown the least interest as she limped pathetically from tent to tent on her necessary but foul errand. On the contrary, the soldiers, squires, and assorted functionaries who swarmed around the camp gave her the widest possible berth. She waited until the skinny sentry trotted off to the bushes to relieve himself before approaching the king's tent. She sent up a silent prayer to the patron saint of slop girls, whoever she might be, and slipped inside.

Her entrance precipitated an instant exodus of King Ahriman's inner council, who were gathered around a table poring over a map of the northeastern quadrant of the Dominion. Syrah flattened herself against the tent wall and lowered her eyes as they filed past her. Only the king seemed unconcerned with her appearance and went on with his study of the map while Syrah took careful note of the furnishings of the tent and possible hiding places for future reference.

Two chamber pots—one clean, one clearly in need of emptying—were concealed behind a privacy screen embroidered with a hunt scene of leaping stags and baying hounds. Syrah dithered about for several minutes until the king finally made a great show of sniffing the air and suggested, not unkindly, that she finish her work and be on her way. She sketched an awkward curtsy and babbled her thanks as the king pressed a copper coin into her filthy palm.

The sentry shooed her away as she emerged into the sweet night air. She slipped around to the back of the tent, and keeping well away from the many campfires set out to see how Eben was getting on with his part in the night's mission.

Eben pulled another wad of sweet taffy from his pocket. He dusted off the lint and waved it enticingly at the squire who stood guard over the king's silver-embossed hunting saddle. "Aw, come on, I got more than I can chew in a week."

The pimply squire had already eaten more of the sticky stuff than even the ironclad stomach of a twelve-year-old boy could handle. He reached for the grimy blob, thought better of it, and bolted around the corner of the hounds' pen to throw up in a bramble bush.

While the squire was well occupied with relieving his stomach of its cloying content, Eben reached under his shirt and pulled out the ransom note and the letter that Prince Jibril had written the previous day. He was just about to slide them under the edge of the leather saddlebow when a furtive rustle in the trees had him dropping to the ground and rolling under a heavily laden baggage cart.

"Eben," came a whisper out of the darkness, "where are you?"

"Under here."

Syrah doubled over to peer between the wheels of the cart. "What in the world are you doing under there?" she whispered.

Eben scrambled out still clutching the letters. "Trying not to get a whiff of you."

"Hurry. We need to get out of here."

"I can't believe how much taffy it took to get that squire to throw up," Eben grumbled as he slid the two documents under the pommel. At dawn, perhaps sooner, someone would notice and take them to the king.

They melted into the shadows just before the squire returned. He turned around several times looking for the friendly lad who had shared his sweets with him, but the boy was gone. A bit of tan parchment poking out from beneath the saddlebow caught his eye. He unrolled one of the scrolls, held it up to the light of a lantern, and managed to puzzle out the words "god" and what might be "prince." The pieces of parchment looked pretty important, all fancy writing and rolled up nice.

The squire tore through the camp, rehearsing what he would say when he came face-to-face with the king: He had been on duty since the evening meal. He had taken but a minute to relieve himself. When he returned, someone had slipped the letters under the saddle. He had no idea who could have put them there. He had made a diligent search of the surrounding area and found no one. He had brought them straightway to His Majesty.

The sentry on duty outside the king's tent looked down his nose at the sweating squire and informed him archly that His Majesty was busy with important matters and had given strict orders not to be disturbed.

"Aren't you gonna give him these?" the squire demanded. "He's gonna want to see them."

"I got my orders not to interrupt the meeting. Get along now, boy. I'll give them to him when they're finished."

"But it's about Prince Jibril!"

"Says who? Are you telling me you can read?"

"Well, no, only a little," the squire admitted. "But I know most of my letters."

"I said, it can wait."

Determined to acquaint the king with the happy news that God had the prince in His safekeeping—for so he had decided as he sprinted through the camp—the squire snatched the letters from the sentry and dashed through the tent flap. He slid to an abrupt stop and threw himself down onto the carpet.

"It wasn't my fault, Your Majesty," he cried. "I had to throw up—taffy don't sit too good with me—and then there they were, just lying there on the saddle, and I thought

71

you'd be wanting to see them as it's all about God and Prince Jibril."

"Calm down, lad," King Ahriman interrupted, bringing the squire to his feet. "You have news of the prince?"

"And God, sire."

"And God," echoed the king with remarkable patience.

The boy thrust the letters into the king's hand. "I found these on your hunting saddle, sire."

The king unrolled one of the letters and scanned it quickly. "Thank you, son. You were quite right to bring these to me immediately. You may go now. If you should find any sign of the person who left them, I know you will report it at once."

"I will, sire, of course, sire, yes," the squire jabbered. He scampered through the tent flap and threw a sneering look over his shoulder at the stupefied sentry as he fled back to his post, resolved never to eat taffy again as long as he lived.

Chapter Eight

Your Most Serene and Gracious Majesty:
His Highness, Prince Jibril, is being held for a ransom
of one thousand gold discs. Have the ransom conveyed
to your camp within twenty-four hours. At midnight
two days hence, you will dispatch one lone horseman
with a satchel containing five hundred gold discs to the
north end of the bridge that spans the river Korian near
the village of Spiros. He must come alone. You will
receive another note at that time with instructions for
the delivery of the other half of the gold. Be assured
that we will know if a trap is being set for us. Do not
score or mark the discs in any way for future identifi-
cation. When the full ransom has been paid, return to
Suriana and the whereabouts of the prince will be
made known to you. Failure to follow these instructions will have dire consequences.

Your most loyal servants, the Kidnappers

"Curious," mused King Ahriman, "most curious."

He rolled up the ransom note and canvassed the faces of
his most trusted counselors and military commanders.
"What shall we make of this odd demand?"

Jasan Arcos, First Admiral of the King's Navy, frowned. "Odd, Your Majesty? It seems perfectly straightforward to me."

"You think so?" said the king. He fixed his eye on Ranulph Gyp, armiger of the Twenty-seventh House and now pretender to the high seat of the Ninth. Ranulph had been one of the first to rush to his side after news of Prince Jibril's abduction had resounded across the width and breadth of the Dominion. "Lord Ranulph, what say you?"

Flattered that the king should single him out for his opinion, Ranulph leaned back in his chair and pursed his lips in judicious consideration of the problem. "It would appear, sire, that we are dealing here with blackguards who are no strangers to this sort of villainy. Foreigners, I should say, for there is not one among your subjects who would dishonor His Highness so."

He paused for effect. "They will most certainly kill Prince Jibril. It is the way of the Infidel."

"So, you think the kidnappers plan to smuggle the gold out of the Dominion?"

"Most assuredly, sire."

"And what of our pirate friends who plague our coasts?" the king wanted to know. "Might they not be behind this?"

Ranulph shifted in his chair, uncomfortable with the appraising look in the king's eye. "As you are aware, sire, I know little of pirates. My estates lie well inland from the coast and I am unfamiliar with their nefarious ways. But I cannot believe even they would have the audacity to plot so heinous a crime and threaten one so dear to your heart."

The king nodded. "You may be right. You will no doubt learn a great deal more about what a pirate will and will not dare when you assume the high seat of the Ninth House."

A sly smile flashed across Ranulph's face. "Aye, sire. I have much to learn of piracy."

The king waved his hand, dismissing the subject. "Quite. Let us hear from some of the others."

Ranulph relaxed back in his chair, sure now the Ninth House would be his. The king had as much as said so. He did not care one whit about Prince Jibril, the man who might have ruined his chances of marrying Syrah. The kidnappers could slice and dice him for all he cared. In the end, everything had worked out wonderfully well, with the last of the Dhion family at the bottom of the sea and the king's present assurances. Of course, he had lost Syrah, as sweet a morsel as any man could want in his bed, but a lord of the Dominion who held two high seats would never lack for female companionship. Besides, King Ahriman had two unmarried daughters. Though neither could hold a candle to Syrah, Ranulph would be more than happy to make do with a royal princess.

A spirited debate ensued over the advisability of paying or withholding the ransom; the likelihood of Prince Jibril coming to harm; and the best way to apprehend the kidnappers when they showed up to collect the gold. The king remained silent. Finally, he turned to the captain of Jibril's personal guard, who had not spoken a word. "Captain Ankuli, we have not yet heard your thoughts on this matter."

"With all due respect to my colleagues, Your Majesty, I too find the ransom demand strange indeed."

The king gave Ankuli his full attention. "How so?"

"The first thing that strikes me is the amount of the ransom. If you will excuse me for saying so, sire, one thousand gold discs is an outrageous ransom to demand."

"Quite right," the king said dryly. "Not even the combined effort of my wife and six daughters could make a dent in such an amount in a decade of outfitting themselves."

"Then there is the manner of the ransom. Why are we not to deliver the full sum at one time? Why split it?"

"My question exactly," agreed the king.

Captain Ankuli addressed Ranulph Gyp, barely able to hide his dislike of the man. "My Lord, I beg to differ with you. I do not believe that the gold will leave the Dominion. If that is the intention, why the warning not to mark the discs lest they be identified as part of the ransom? It would make no difference if the gold is to be spent abroad whether the discs are marked or not. But it would make all the difference if the gold is to be used here in the Dominion, where marked discs would leave a trail straight to the kidnappers."

Captain Ankuli turned back to the king. "Shall I continue, sire?"

At the king's nod, the captain went on to remark that the kidnappers would be foolish to believe the bridge that spanned the river Korian would be a safe place to collect the ransom. The banks of the river at that point were thickly wooded, an obvious place for concealing soldiers. "I can reach only one conclusion," he said.

The king smiled. "They do not intend to collect the ransom at the bridge."

Ankuli nodded. "They know we will have the gold conveyed from Suriana. No doubt they will be watching the roads. They also know we will take no chances and send half to the drop-off point at the bridge as instructed. But with the other half here in the camp, they will attempt to steal it right out from beneath our noses when they think we are all out lying in wait for them at the bridge."

"Exactly, Captain. They demand one thousand gold discs when even half that sum is a small fortune. Well, we shall accede to their demands. Half the sum will be conveyed to the bridge and a convincing number of men deployed to make it appear that we are setting a trap. In the meantime, we will secure the camp. When they show up here we will nab them."

Stung by the king's casual dismissal of his own opinions, Ranulph leaned forward. "But what of Prince Jibril, sire? They will certainly kill him. The Infidel is without mercy."

"I have always thought the Infidels badly maligned, Lord Ranulph," the king said, raising his tankard of ale to his lips. "They showed no less mercy in the Holy Land than did our own Crusaders. In any event, I doubt they have any part in this."

The king rose, a signal that the meeting was over. "Captain Majan will take command of one division to see the gold delivered to the camp no later than the day after tomorrow. We will convene again in the morning to finalize our plans."

The men filed out of the tent, all except Captain Ankuli, who remained behind and came to rigid attention before the king. "Permission, to speak, sire."

"Yes, Captain?"

Ankuli took a deep breath. "Your Majesty, I wish to be relieved of my command."

"Indeed?"

"I have disgraced my command, sire. It is my fault Prince Jibril was taken. I failed in my duty to protect him."

The king snorted. "Nonsense. My son was taken because he can't keep his breeches laced up."

"Nonetheless, sire, I failed him. As my prince and as my friend. His very life is in danger because of me."

The king threw his arm over the captain's shoulders as he escorted his son's oldest and staunchest friend to the tent door. "The only danger my son faces, Kalan, is a serious blow to his pride. As for his life, I wouldn't worry. His note to me is in code. He assures me his captors are amateurs, at best, and that he is in no danger. In any event, the 'dire consequences' hinted at in the ransom note are a far cry from 'we will cut him up and send him back to you piece by piece.'"

Vastly amused by the thought, the king went on, "And they are, after all, 'my most loyal servants.' Oh, by the way," he added with a wave of his hand, "they are holding him on the south coast. The Isle of Lost Souls, to be precise."

Ankuli was astonished. "You know all that from a brief note?"

"Jibril is nothing if not clever, in both word and deed. He is, after all, my son," the king added with a mischievous smile.

"I will organize the rescue party immediately, sire."

The king leaned back and steepled his fingers. "I think not, Captain. I am no longer concerned for Jibril's safety, and those left behind to guard him are likely minions, hardly worth the taking. It is the mastermind we must snag. He must be here, close by."

Captain Ankuli was first and foremost a soldier, a man of action, not much given to the study of the subtleties of human nature. "Surely, sire, the leader of these blackguards would not put himself in the way of discovery. He may be close by, but he will not seek to enter the camp himself. He will send underlings to do the job."

King Ahriman shook his head. "There you are wrong, my friend. The ingenious mind behind this business would not leave the retrieval of the ransom to any other but himself. His pride demands it.

"In the meantime, I want you to keep an eye on Gyp. Somehow he fits into this but I cannot figure out how. He certainly doesn't have enough brain matter between his ears to devise such a clever scheme or the ballocks to carry it out. But he's involved, even if indirectly, and I want to know how."

"Yes, sire."

The king chuckled. "I must confess that I look forward to meeting the author of this clever business. He is most assuredly a man after my own heart."

"You just threw it away? Why?" Eben demanded. "I always wanted to see royal poop. I have a theory about it."

Syrah closed her eyes and shook her head in disbelief.

"Did you get a good look at it?"

Syrah set down the pear she was about to eat. It suddenly looked far less appetizing than it had a moment ago.

"No, Eben, I did not get a good look at it. I did not look at it at all."

Eben munched thoughtfully. "That's where you made the mistake. Important people like the king and God probably poop purple. He frowned. "Maybe God doesn't poop at all."

Syrah groaned. Once launched, her brother could rarely be brought to earth until he had revolted everyone within hearing distance.

"Now that I think about it, I imagine poop could be very profitable," Eben enthused. His mind whirled with possibilities for interesting new trades. "We could import dromedaries—"

"Eben, if I ever hear another word about dromedaries, I'm going to cut out your tongue and sell that in the bazaar."

"I was just trying to make conversation. You're so touchy tonight. It's not that woman thing, is it?"

Syrah rolled her eyes in the darkness. "No! Now let's get some sleep."

Not that Syrah expected to sleep a wink. She needed to go over every detail of her plan. Nothing must be left to chance. King Ahriman was reputed to be as clever as his son was; he might very well figure out that the kidnappers would not be at the bridge. He might set a trap at the hunting camp.

They had set up their own well-concealed little camp on a wooded knoll high above the main road where they would be sure to see the soldiers returning with the gold. Syrah did not expect the shipment to arrive before the following afternoon. Most of the king's men should be in position long before midnight on that day. The king himself would certainly lead them. It wouldn't take but a few minutes for her to enter his tent, ostensibly to empty the chamber pots, and make off with the five hundred gold discs they had left behind.

"You'll make sure the horses are all ready to go? Fed and watered?"

"That's the tenth time you've asked me that," Eben complained.

"I'm sorry, Eben. I'm nervous. It's just that we need to get back to the island as quickly as possible and make sure the prince knows someone is coming to get him. I wouldn't want him to worry. We have to be well away before the soldiers arrive. We must all be back at Great Aunt Rosota's manor by then."

Eben giggled. "I wouldn't want him to worry," he parroted.

Syrah gritted her teeth. "Well, I wouldn't. He deserves our consideration and respect."

Jennie Klassel

"He's a military commander, for heaven's sake, Syrah.
He's going be too busy planning how to catch us and roast
us alive to worry about when his papa is coming to get
him."

"That's very comforting, Eben. Thank you for reminding
me."

"Do you think he'll ever find us?" Eben asked in a worried voice a few minutes later.

"I hope not. Remember, he thinks we're dead."

"We are, aren't we? When we get the hall back we can
say we were hiding from Ranulph. He won't be able to
prove it was us."

Syrah heard Eben settle down. The little noises of the
night piped up around them: crickets, nightjars, amorous
frogs.

Eben giggled again. "If the mercenary thing doesn't work
out, we can always go into the poop business."

Syrah laughed despite her worries. "An excellent idea.
How much poop do you think five hundred gold discs
would buy?"

Far down in the valley one of the king's soldiers, too drunk
even to stand, took another deep draught of sweet ale and
could have sworn he heard the laughter of children on the
wind.

Chapter Nine

Midnight in the king's hunting camp. A nearly full moon cast long shadows across darkened tents and cold fire pits. A few horses stirred restlessly in the paddock. Hunting hounds slept sprawled over one another. A screech owl swooped low to seize a large gray mouse; a little squeak of terror was lost in the whoosh of great wings.

Sentries patrolled the perimeter, eyes probing the deep shadows for even the slightest movement. Agile young squires monitored the two paths leading to the camp from perches high in the trees. Ten of the king's fiercest personal guards ringed the royal tent. The silence was eerie, expectant.

King Ahriman drained the last of the splendid Bordeaux from his jeweled goblet and rose to his feet. "I think we're well secured here. Let's ride out to the bridge to see if anything has transpired there. They won't make a move until they think I've left the compound."

Squires stood to attention as the king exited the tent with Captain Ankuli and several high-ranking officers following close behind. When all had mounted, his personal guard did the same, and the party headed out of the compound. At the main gate the king halted.

"You understand," the king said to the captain of the camp guard, "that no one who is not known to you personally shall enter the camp?"

"Yes, sir!" the soldier replied smartly.

"No one shall enter and no one shall be allowed to leave until I return. We will circle around and come up the back path on the other side of the hill. It should take about two hours."

"Yes, sir!"

The king turned to Captain Ankuli. "We will have our conspirators in chains by morning. They cannot escape us."

Syrah and Eben retreated deep into the copse as the royal party galloped by on its way toward the river Korian. Led by the king himself on a huge white destrier, the grim-faced riders rode as one, a juggernaut that promised death without mercy, doom without redemption.

"I'll wager he left a lot of guards at the camp just in case we show up. And no one is going be allowed in or out," Eben whispered.

Syrah drew a deep breath, trying to calm her frazzled nerves, then wished she hadn't. She might not have control over any number of a thousand things that could go wrong, but at least her disguise was sure to pass muster. If anything, she looked and smelled even worse tonight than she had on the first occasion she played the role of slop girl. Her lank hair fell across a face thick with grime; her shapeless gray shift hung in tatters nearly to the ground; and her booties were more holes than leather. With Eben an ebullient mentor, she had perfected an inane jabbering that declared her a nitwit of the lowest order and a bumbling, lurching gait that would not have shamed an unrepentant drunkard on a three-day binge. She passed Eben's sniff test and emitted a stench that could fell an ox.

"Someone has to empty the slops. I'm counting on the fact that no one would forbid me to service the king's privy."

"Yes, but what if they ask you why you're there in the

middle of the night? They're going to ask you how you know the king's not in bed as usual."

The question gave Syrah pause. "I'll say I saw him ride by the village and thought it would be a good time, so I wouldn't be disturbing him."

Eben looked doubtful. He frowned, deep in thought. "I know: Use a poop story. They'll think you're crazy as a bedbug."

Syrah could not hide her admiration. "You are the smartest boy . . . sorry, the smartest man in the whole Dominion."

Eben gave her a playful punch in the shoulder that sent her stumbling two steps back. "It's about time you noticed."

The fateful moment had arrived. Syrah took Eben by the shoulders and looked into his blue eyes, silvered now by the pale moonlight. "If they catch me, you must get as far away from here as possible. It's not going to do us any good for both of us to get caught. I want you to promise that you won't try to play the hero and free me."

Eben grunted an unconvincing agreement.

"Promise me, Eben, on our mother's grave. Say it."

"I promise, on our mother's grave."

Syrah gathered him against her, held him tight for a moment, and murmured, "I love you." She released him before he could pull away in embarrassment.

"You'll have the horses all ready where we agreed?" she said as matter-of-factly as she could. "Wait two hours, not a minute more. If I'm not there . . ."

There was no need to finish the sentence: They understood one another. Without a backward glance, she set off resolutely toward the king's camp bearing two chamber pots suspended from a yoke across her shoulders and affecting a pathetic limp. She did not hear her brother's soft words as she disappeared along the shadowed path into the trees.

"I love you, too, Syrah."

The first shrill whistle shattered the eerie silence, repeated as the warning signal passed from tree to tree. Syrah stumbled to a halt, fighting the overpowering urge to turn and run. On shaking legs, she forced herself to limp forward just as though the warning could have nothing to do with her. She had not gone fifty feet before the lookouts were dropping from the trees and soldiers with swords drawn were emerging from the darkness all around her.

Authoritative commands to "halt!" and "surrender or die!" metamorphosed into bellows of "ugh!" and squawks of "phew!" as the camp's defenders rushed forward, then reeled back. Syrah whirled in a circle staring wildly about her, a piteous figure sketched in the moonlight. She let out a heart-stopping howl of terror, dropped to the ground, and curled into a quaking ball.

The captain of the camp guard directed his troops to scour the woods for possible accomplices, although he doubted anyone with a nose in the middle of his face would have accompanied the stinking girl up the hill.

"Get up, girl," the captain wheezed. "Gather your pots and follow me."

Syrah could not honestly have said how much of her fear was put on for maximum effect and how much was real. As she trudged up the hill surrounded on all sides by grunting soldiers, she took comfort that at least no one had skewered her on the spot. But she knew they would question her closely. If God were on her side she would be allowed to get on with her work.

The interrogation was mercifully short, although there was one sticky moment when the inevitable issue arose of what she was doing emptying chamber pots in the middle of the night. One guard, more skeptical and presumably with a stronger stomach than the rest, fired off the crucial question.

Syrah wasn't sure she could carry it off, but suddenly Eben's voice seemed to be right there inside her head, and she let loose. "I got to do the poop! My pa says there's a big demand for poop. We sell it, don't you know, to the farmers for their fields. They pay good money for poop from important people, 'cause they say it's better quality 'cause of what important people eat."

"No one cares about your pa's trade," the guard snapped. "Answer the question: Why are you here at this hour?"

"Everyone knows the king went to catch the bad men that stole the prince, your guardship," Syrah whined. "I got to get the poop now 'cause it's a full moon tonight and my pa says it's always best to collect during the full moon, and the moon didn't come up until just a bit ago. Sort of the same, like when you plant parsnips, don't you know? I got a powerful liking for parsnips myself, especially when they're grown with—"

"Enough!" the guard said. "It all sounds like nonsense to me, but His Majesty isn't going to want stinking chamber pots fouling the air when he gets back, so you'd better get on with it. Do it quickly and be gone."

Eben would have been proud, Syrah thought, as she practically sprinted across the camp toward the king's tent. The skinny sentry she had encountered the day before was leaning against a tree flirting with a woman whose tentlike homespun tunic barely concealed the largest bosom Syrah had ever seen. A coquettish giggle floated across the clearing.

Syrah stuck her head cautiously through the flap and slipped inside. A single lantern burned low beside a handsomely carved teak chest. Knowing she had not a moment to lose, she set the yoke down on the thick oriental carpet. She extracted the little dagger Eben had found in Prince Jibril's boot from her pocket, regretting she would have to destroy the beautifully wrought silver clasp that secured the lid. To her surprise the chest was not locked. She lifted the lid and gasped at the sight of hundreds of discs burnished golden and rosy in the soft glow of the lantern's light.

The coins, newly minted in honor of the Crown Prince's thirtieth birthday, bore his likeness in profile: the haughty high-bridged aristocratic nose, the determined chin, and the firm but sensuous line of his lips. Inscribed on the reverse in bold Latin script, the motto of the First House proclaimed "The Honor of Our House, The Honor of the Dominion."

Syrah allowed herself a moment of profound regret as she traced the face of her lost prince with the tip of a finger.

Spurred on by fear and the urgency of the moment, she shrugged the sentiment aside and set to examining a random selection of discs for identifying marks. Finding none, she scooped handfuls of the golden discs into each pot until the chest was empty. Five hundred gold discs weighed a good deal more than Syrah had expected, but she felt sure that with the weight distributed equally across her shoulders by the yoke, she would have no trouble carrying it away.

On a sudden whim, she returned one disc to the chest, setting it precisely in the middle before she closed the lid.

She had just secured the silver clasp when the sound of furtive whispers approaching the tent set her heart slamming in her chest. Panic informed her every move as she shoved the yoke beneath the king's bed and hauled the pots behind the privacy screen. Just as a hairy hand pulled back the tent flap, Syrah dove behind the screen and crouched low, gathering her skirts close around her ankles and hunching over to peer through a narrow slit dividing the two halves of the screen.

The flirting lovers slipped in.

Syrah sank her teeth into her lower lip to keep from laughing aloud at the incongruous pair. No doubt they had seized a few stolen moments to cuddle and coo. The sentry appeared horrified when his amour towed him along behind her toward the king's bed.

"No, Honey-pot! That there's His Majesty's bed," the guard exclaimed in a panicked whisper.

"A camp bed's a bed for all that. You think all he does is sleep in it?"

Using every ounce of strength he possessed, the sentry spun her away from the bed. He struck a righteous pose. "His Majesty is a married man."

"My sweet innocent man, my busy little bee," she crooned enfolding him in beefy arms, "I have so much to teach you."

Her lover's head surfaced from the chasm between her huge breasts. "I ain't so innocent."

Honey-pot subsided slowly onto the thick carpet like a

poked pudding, bringing the miffed guard sprawling atop her with a resounding splat. "Show me then, my king!"

"Uh . . ."

"You are my master, I your willing slave."

"Er . . ."

"Use me without mercy, my magnificent savage."

"Ooofff!"

"Mount me, my strapping stallion. Ride me, my lusty steed."

"Aaaargh!"

"Take your mighty sword in hand."

"Yikes!"

"Storm my quivering bastion."

"Yow!"

"Thrust, thrust, thrust!"

"Unh, unh, unh."

"Faster! Harder! Faster! Haarrrder!"

"Unh, unnhh, unh, unnnhhhh."

"Oooh, oooh, oooh!"

"Aggh, aggh, aggh."

"Oooh, aaah, oooh, aaah!"

"Agghh, ugghh, agghh, ugghh."

"Aaaaiiiiieeeeee!"

"Yooowwwwzzaaaahh!"

If love was blind, Syrah thought wryly as the lovers' cries faded away, God should just have gone all the way and made it deaf and dumb as well.

She blinked away the ludicrous episode she had just witnessed, took a deep grounding breath, and managed to close her gaping mouth. The magnificent barbarian and his willing slave now lay panting and puffing just out of sight on the floor at the far side of the king's bed.

Syrah told herself she simply could not have seen what she had seen: the skinny rump clutched between enormous jiggling thighs like the white belly of a dead flounder rising and falling on the swells of a storm. She could not have heard what she had heard: groans, moans, grunts, and yes, snorts, whinnies, and whickers.

In point of fact, Lady Syrah Dhion, first daughter of the Ninth House, could not possibly be crouching in the privy of the royal bedchamber, clutching two chamber pots full of gold, and watching what her governess had once described ever so delicately as the Sacred Act. What was holy about the preposterous tableau she had just witnessed she could not imagine. Surely the good Lord could have come up with something more . . . decorous to entice a man and woman into the married state and obey His commandment to be fruitful and multiply.

An astounding thought struck her. Could Great Uncle Amorgos and Great Aunt Rosota have . . . ? King Ahriman and Queen Alya? *Her own parents?* Unthinkable, impossible. Not squealing and screeching like Honey-pot and her busy little bee. It simply did not bear thinking about.

She consigned the night's revelations to the growing list of amatory sport begun in the sleazy tavern, and pressed her eye to the narrow opening in the screen to see the guard poking his head through the tent flap to check that the coast was clear. Honey-pot clambered to her feet, crammed her huge breasts beneath her tunic, and with a step surprisingly light and stealthy for a woman of her impressive proportions, stole after her little bee into the night.

Knowing she had not a moment to lose, Syrah held her breath, poured the contents of the king's chamber pots over the shining golden discs, and settled the yoke across her shoulders. With a whispered prayer, she gathered her courage, slipped out of the tent, and made her way through the camp. No one paid her the least attention, except to move away as she passed. She followed the path down the hill past the lookouts and sentries, and limped down the road. After a quarter mile, she veered off along a faint track. Not far ahead, she could see the small lake, glazed with moonlight, where Eben was to have the horses ready.

Syrah had considered and discarded any number of means to move the gold to a safe hiding place until she secured the services of Obike Zebengo, the mercenary she would hire to eject Ranulph Gyp from the hall of the Ninth House. To attempt to transport the gold along the main roads of the Dominion would be madness. Every cart and carriage, satchel and saddlebag, purse and pocket would be subject to search as the king's soldiers fanned out across the island in pursuit of the kidnappers. In the end, she concluded that it should not be moved at all but hidden close by the king's own hunting camp. She would return for it when it was wanted.

She followed the shoreline to a tree that had fallen over, its heavy branches half submerged in the water. A quilt of water lilies had flourished in the shallows there, thick enough to conceal the gleam of gold from even the most assiduous scrutiny. She waded out into waist-deep water and carefully lowered the heavy yoke and the pots into the thick mud, making sure the lily pads closed over the spot.

Buoyed by the night's success, she laughed up at the moon. "I'm rather clever, if I must say so myself."

A soft whistle sounded from the thick woods. Syrah clambered up onto the bank and hurried several yards along the shore until she came to a spot where little ripples lapped against a pebbled beach. Wading out again, she pulled a small piece of rose-scented soap from her pocket and ducked beneath the cold water to wash away the foul smell that clung to her.

Another whistle sounded from the trees. She hurried into the woods toward the soft whicker of her little white palfrey. Eben and the horses were but vague shadows within the deeper darkness. Without a word, Syrah dried herself, donned a clean tunic, and buried her tattered shift beneath a pile of leaves and brush weighted down with heavy branches. They moved off along the shore, keeping well within the concealing shadow of the trees. Ten minutes later, they came to a narrow path that eventually met up with the main road five miles beyond the bridge that spanned the river Korian.

Only the creatures of the night watched from the shadows as two hooded riders swept out of sight down the moonlit road toward the southern coast.

* * *

One hundred and sixteen men snapped to attention in the ominous silence that filled the night. One hundred and sixteen pairs of eyes stared straight ahead. One hundred and sixteen jaws clamped tight. Two hundred and thirty-two feet shook in their boots.

The voice was remarkably calm, the words very nearly dispassionate. "I find myself somewhat perplexed. Let us review the situation together."

King Ahriman Chios, hands clasped behind his back with head bent in pensive mien, strolled slowly back and forth before his elite guard, six of his most astute counselors, eighty-five crack troops, eight squires, one royal chaplain, three cooks, and two laundresses.

"Not two hours ago, I was in possession of one thousand gold discs from my personal treasury. Two hours ago, this camp was sealed so tight that the Holy Father himself would not have been able to gain entrance without a personal invitation by my own hand. Two hours ago, a flea would not have been able to crawl into my private quarters without being stripped and searched."

The king paused, surveyed the assemblage before him, and frowned a bemused little frown.

"How then, I ask myself, can it be that I am now in possession of only five hundred gold discs? That a slop girl waltzed into this camp without so much as a by-your-leave? That a mortal creature hundreds of thousands times larger than a flea entered my tent, purloined my gold discs, and slipped off into the night as invisible as the Holy Ghost?"

The king's eyes swept through the ranks and fixed on the captain of his camp guard. "Captain Ziem, perhaps you can enlighten me."

Captain Ziem promptly keeled over backward in a dead faint.

"I see not," the king said dryly.

The sentry froze as the king discovered him cowering in the furthermost rank. Before the king had even opened his mouth, the sentry sank to his knees.

"She dangled them right there before my eyes, sire," he jabbered, "and they were so big and juicy, and we didn't

90

use the bed, my word upon my immortal soul, sire." Fortunately for him, terror choked off his rambling confession.

The king's eyebrows shot up. "Big? Juicy?"

"Jugs, sire," the sentry forced out through chattering teeth.

The king struggled to make sense of the sentry's words. "Jugs?"

"I'm a b-busy little bee, sire, and—"

"The chamber pots, you mean? Big juicy chamber pots?"

"Titties, big juicy titties!" the sentry wailed in despair. His eyes rolled back in his head as he toppled forward into blessed insensibility.

"Good heavens," King Ahriman muttered. "I'm surrounded by imbeciles." He stalked off toward his tent. Behind him, Captain Ankuli barked out an order to stand down and strode after the king. He found him contemplating the chest, where a single gold disc seemed to wink up at them.

Steeling himself to receive the full force of the king's fury, he said, "Your Majesty, I take full responsibility—"

His jaw dropped in amazement as low chuckles followed by loud guffaws escalated into booming laughter. "Oh, clever, clever girl," the king hooted. "A slip of a girl with more brains than every man in this camp combined, myself included."

Holding his sides, King Ahriman sank into a chair. "Oh, my, oh, my," he gasped. "What must Jibril make of her? She must be leading him a merry chase. What I wouldn't give to be a fly on the wall."

Chapter Ten

Jibril awoke in a state of aching arousal, trying to catch hold of the threads of the dream: a beautiful young girl whirling beneath a rain of falling stars; a maiden with waving hair of spun honey borne on the breast of a raging sea; a lover trembling beneath him as he sank into her welcoming virgin heat.

The threads twisted away and dissolved, leaving behind only the sound of light joyous laughter in the soft light of dawn. Jibril was suddenly aware that the laughter was real, echoing in the stone corridor beyond the barred door of his prison. The Lady and her brother had finally returned. Excitement surged through him, but he feigned sleep as the door swung open.

"Let's tell him now," urged the boy.

"No," the Lady whispered, "let him sleep."

"Come on. I want to see his face when we tell him we got the ransom and didn't get caught."

It was all the prince could do not leap to his feet in surprise. The ransom had been paid. Somehow these two unlikely felons had outwitted the king and his troops. Jibril would have given anything to see his father's face at the exact moment he realized he'd been duped.

"Tell me, young ones," he said conversationally without opening his eyes, "how much am I worth?"

"A thousand gold discs," the boy crowed.

The prince sat up, adjusting the blanket to conceal the evidence of his waning arousal. He smiled at the two hooded figures. The boy positively vibrated with excitement and the Lady appeared relaxed, and something else— perhaps just a little shy? "I find that rather flattering."

Before the woman could silence him the boy enthused, "We only took five hundred, but I bet we could have gotten a lot more. We should have asked for two thousand; then he'd have left one thousand in the tent."

Syrah steered Eben toward the door. "We have more than we need. I doubt His Highness wishes to hear himself discussed as though he were nothing more than a commodity to be bought and sold. His food should be ready by now. Bring it and start loading up the cart. You need to leave soon."

The sound of the boy's delighted whoops could be heard as he leaped down the stairs and dashed across the causeway.

"I must commend you, my lady. During your absence, it has become clear to me that you do not serve others but are the architect of my abduction. Your brother is an able second-in-command. Am I not correct?"

At first he didn't think she would answer him as she moved to the window and lifted down the wooden shutters to allow the sun to stream into the chamber. "Perhaps you have it aright, my lord, perhaps not. Soon we'll go on our separate ways and you will never know."

The prince laughed. "You think not? You have provided me with every comfort and accorded me the dignity of my station. Ah, but my pride, my lady, my pride has received a mortal blow. I will find you."

"From what I have observed, I suspect it will take a far more deadly weapon than any I possess to lay waste your pride," Syrah retorted.

"But that is where you are so very wrong," the prince said. He pressed his hand to his heart. "You are a weapon unto yourself. A beautiful woman can pierce a man's heart with far more ease than the sharpest arrow."

Syrah settled herself on the stone bench and folded her hands primly in her lap. "Beneath my habit I may be as beautiful as Helen of Troy or as scrawny as a plucked chicken; I may have spots upon my face and a wart on the end of my nose. In any event it does not signify. It is entirely possible that someday we will meet again and you will be none the wiser."

"I shouldn't count on it if I were you," he said as he rose and let the blanket drop to the stone floor. With apparent lack of concern that a lady was present, he arched his back and stretched his arms high above his head, then strolled to the corner of his cell where he poured water into the ewer and set about his morning ablutions.

He glanced over his shoulder at the sound of a horrified gasp to see the Lady leap to her feet and cover her mouth with both hands. He leaned nonchalantly against the bars.

"Is something amiss, my lady?"

Something was most definitely amiss.

A naked man was smiling at her. Naked. Smiling. At her.

A strangled giggle caught in her throat as Syrah froze, riveted by the astounding display of manhood jutting forth from a nest of curly black hair. Any questions she might have had about the "it" were forever banished, replaced by a sinful urge to touch it, stroke down its impressive length.

"My lady?"

Syrah willed her eyes upward to focus on his face. "No, nothing amiss," she said as she backed away toward the door to the corridor. Every bone and sinew in her body seemed to have melted into a pulsing puddle somewhere in the region of her groin.

Without warning, Eben came barreling around the corner and was only just agile enough to keep the tray from crashing to the floor as he collided with her. He took in the scene before him—the grinning prince, his retreating sister—and erupted into gales of laughter.

Syrah fled. Their rowdy amusement at her expense snapped her out of her mortified retreat. Dashing back up the stairs, she shot the prince a look that would have slain him on the spot had he been able to see it, gave her brother a swift kick in the behind, and stalked back down the stairs into the new day.

Syrah floated through the first searching beams of the rising moon, her skin luminescent, and her long hair a pale swirl on the gentle ripples near the shore. The busy hum of the sea filled her ears as she tried to imagine what it would have been like had she truly drowned. It was said the body did not decay in the cold waters of the deep. Would she then drift along with the current on a silent journey through the oceans of the world until she was swept over the edge into a vortex of stars? Or would the fishes find her a dainty morsel and nibble away until her white bones settled softly into reefs of pink coral?

A plaintive whicker sounded from the shore where her snow-white mare, Angel, was tethered to a stunted bush. Roused from her reverie, Syrah waded to shore. She rubbed her body with a rough cloth until her skin sang, slipped a clean shift over her head, and donned a clean tunic, belting it low on her hips with a delicate cord woven of fragrant marsh grass. There was something pleasing, she reflected as she led Angel into the cave, about the simplicity of her garments. She had left all but three of her gowns behind when she fled her father's hall. Two she had cast into the sea to wash up on the shore: Jetsam from the supposed wreck of their little ketch. Her favorite, azure silk embroidered with delicate vines and tiny suns for the flowers, nestled in a chest of fragrant cypress at her great aunt's manor house. She would wear it—azure, green, and gold, the colors of her House—in triumph as she swept through the great doors to reclaim her hall.

It had been a hectic morning, what with loading the cart and hatching last-minute plans to cover every eventuality. Eben and Aleden were to return Mayenne and Clim to Great Aunt Rosota, and then travel on to Suriana in the guise of a man and his son conveying a harvest of flax to market. The road led past the king's hunting camp and across the river Korian; they would ascertain that the king had indeed broken camp and returned to the capital. A few coins in the palm of a very young child would see a note delivered to the palace gate, informing the king of the prince's whereabouts.

Syrah calculated it would take two days for the king's troops to reach the Isle of Lost Souls, even if they rode hard through the night. By then, Eben and Aleden would be safely back home and Syrah would be well away from the island.

"You must be very careful," Syrah cautioned for the umpteenth time. "When you're in Suriana, don't go near that tavern or the lodging house. Keep well out of sight until you are absolutely sure the child has delivered the message to the palace. Then leave the city immediately."

She paced back and forth in front of them, afraid she might have forgotten something crucial. "If you suspect the plan is going wrong, don't wait around to find out. Get away as fast as possible. I will still release the prince as planned."

Eben finally threw up his hands in disgust. "You'd think we want to get caught, Syrah."

"We understand, my lady," Aleden ventured, as wearied as Eben by Syrah's oft-repeated instructions but too much the deferential retainer to let her see it. "But allow me to say again how unhappy I am leaving you here alone."

Syrah wasn't so sure she wanted to be left alone with the prince either, but not for the same reason. "I've explained all that. I can't be seen on the roads or in the city; that captain might recognize me if we should meet. We can't get Mayenne to set foot on the island, and even if we could drag her over there, we'd be mad to leave her alone with him. He'd have her unlocking his cell in no time. Clim, God bless him, is just too slow-witted. Someone has to look after the prince. Don't worry about me. I'll be well away before they come for him."

"But, my lady—"

Syrah stood firm. "No, old friend. Trust me, this is the best way. Besides, I can't hold a candle to Eben when it comes to talking us out of sticky situations, although I didn't do so badly that night at the camp if I say so myself."

Eben finished harnessing the sturdy little dray pony to the cart. "The full moon story was pretty good, but I'd have slipped in something about worms."

"Well, excuse me," Syrah glared, hands on hips. "I thought I did a pretty good job for my first time. You don't see my head on the block, do you?"

"Block?" Mayenne squeaked from her perch on the back of the cart. "I thought you said they were going to hang us. Now you say they're going to chop off our heads?" Dangling by the neck before a bloodthirsty mob was one thing; having one's head removed was another. Mayenne wondered what the proper attire would be for a beheading.

Syrah hurried on before hysteria set in. "No one's going to hang and no one's head is going to plop into a basket."

Too late. Mayenne's fevered imagination was off and running. At least there would be a basket; she wouldn't get mud all over her face. But wait. When they led her to the block, she would have to kneel before her executioner. He would plant his feet wide; the muscles of his thick sinewy thighs straining against his tight leather breeches, the thick bulge of his manhood nearly at eye level. He would lick his lips in anticipation just before raising his terrible weapon to pierce her tender flesh. . . .

"Oh, Lord," Syrah groaned, seeing the glazed look in her maid's eyes. She took a brisk tone. "Mayenne, you will pull yourself together at once. No one will ever know who we are. Clim will be safe; Eben and Aleden will be home in no time."

"But what about you, my lady?" Mayenne wailed.

"I only have to stay here two days and—"

The maid's head swiveled toward the island. "But you'll be alone here with *him*."

"You know very well he can't harm me." Syrah waved her hand toward the others. "All of us have been alone with him at one time or another. Do we look harmed?"

"N-no." A terrifying new thought struck Mayenne, leading her on toward yet another doomsday scenario. "But what about your souls? Do you still have your souls?"

Eben flapped toward her, his face a credible devil's mask. "Noooo, I have taken their souls. My minions will visit terrible torture upon them. They will drink naught but brimstone and eat worms of fire—"

Mayenne leaped off the cart and fled screaming down the beach.

"That was quite unnecessary, Eben," Syrah snapped and went after her. She found the girl huddled behind a large boulder and drew her into her arms.

"It's all right, Mayenne," she soothed. "Eben was just teasing you. God protects the souls of the righteous."

"But we've sinned, my lady," she sobbed. "We stole the prince."

"We did, but it was in a good cause. God will understand. Has He not smiled on our venture so far?"

Mayenne admitted that He had. "But I'm so scared for you, my lady. Don't send me away. I don't know what I'd do if anything bad happened to you."

Syrah felt tears welling in her own eyes. This simple girl was willing to stay, in the face of all her fears, for her mistress's sake. "You have important work to do, Mayenne," she said. "I'm giving Papa and Morgana into your care. I can't think of anyone I trust more than you to look after them."

Mayenne searched Syrah's face. "Really?"

"Really."

When they returned to the others waiting beside the cart, Mayenne lifted her chin and announced, "I think we should get going. I have important work to do."

Syrah puttered around the cave. She checked for anything incriminating that might have been left behind, stirred the fire, brushed her hair.

She had enjoyed her first day of privacy in weeks. Angel had needed exercise, so Syrah took her out for a long satisfying ride along the cliffs, keeping a sharp eye out for soldiers who might be searching for the prince along the coast. She swam in the sea and munched on fruit and nuts.

The tide was out now and she couldn't come up with any good reason to procrastinate any longer. The prince must be hungry. Aleden had taken him a hearty breakfast before the cooking utensils were packed away, but he'd had nothing to eat since.

She picked up the basket and set out across the causeway. This wouldn't be too difficult. She could handle it. But she would be damned if she was going to serve dinner to a naked prince.

Chapter Eleven

Jibril heard a quick light step on the stairs and the sound of the bolt sliding open.

"Are you fully clothed, my lord?" came a hesitant voice.

Jibril had to laugh. "Do you want me to be?"

"What a question."

"Hold on," he called. "It won't take but a moment to get these breeches off."

"Don't you dare. If you aren't wearing every stitch of clothing you own, you're not going to get your dinner."

"But you'll have to open the door to find out, won't you?"

A muffled *hmph*. "Do you want to eat or not?"

"I do."

"Then put your breeches on."

"I have a suggestion, my lady."

"Yes, what is it?"

"If it offends you to see me naked, you could remove your own clothing. Then perhaps you'd feel more comfortable."

A groan. Definitely a groan. "You're playing with me."

"Not yet."

"That's it." The bolt slid home.

Jibril was not about to forgo his dinner. "Please don't run

off in a huff. I'm a hungry man. I assure you I am covered from head to foot and modest enough to enter the confessional."

Syrah stuck her head around the edge of the door and instantly wanted to wipe the mischievous smile from his face. Without a word she stomped across the room. She set out the food on a tray and slid it through the hatch. She crossed her arms and tapped an impatient toe.

The prince settled onto the stone bench with the tray across his lap. He looked up at her. "Won't you be seated? It's unnerving to dine with a sulking child looming over me."

"I do not sulk. And I am not a child."

Jibril took a slow appreciative survey of her supple form. "Hmmm, you may be right."

Syrah retreated and perched at the edge of her bench, determined to keep her visit as short as possible.

Jibril addressed the simple meal with gusto and made short work of bread, cheese, and dried fish. "No ale?"

"You will soon be back to carousing with your friends and may visit every low tavern in the city for all I care, but tonight you must make do with water."

Gone, Jibril noted, was the usual polite deference to her royal prisoner, replaced by an endearing female irritation in the presence of a man bent on mischief.

He cocked an eyebrow at her. "And what do you know of carousing?"

Her chin went up a notch. "Enough."

"You have caroused yourself then?"

"That's for me to know."

"And for me to find out?"

"Impossible," she muttered, "absolutely impossible." With a swish of skirts she headed toward the door.

"I have not yet finished my meal," he called after her. "Will you not stay until I've eaten these succulent dates?" He took a tiny bite.

Syrah's hands settled on her hips like a harried governess eyeing an unruly child. "I've no doubt the ladies of your acquaintance swoon when you address them with such

101

clever innuendo, but let us remember our positions here."

His eyebrow twitched and a devilish smile tugged at the corner of his mouth a mere second before she snapped, "Don't you dare say it."

"Say what?"

"You know," she said through clenched teeth.

"I can't imagine what you mean. Perhaps you don't want me to eat this date."

"You know very well what I mean."

"I do?"

"Oh, you're . . . you're . . ."

"Charming. No? Irresistible then."

Exasperated, Syrah threw up her hands. "Why can't you act like a normal prisoner? You ought to be furious, vindictive, terrified. You ought to be scheming to escape. Your very life might be in danger and here you sit like a prince at a party."

Jibril started laughing, nearly choking on another teensy bite of date. "But I am a prince."

"It isn't funny," Syrah seethed.

"With all due respect, your naughty little band does not exactly strike fear and trembling in my heart."

"Naughty! You see this as some childish escapade?"

"Well, you must admit—"

"How dare you!" All the pain of the past year, the loss of her mother, the lonely burden of seeing her family's fortunes restored, facing a future without love and children—without him had he but known it—exploded in that moment. "We have risked our honor and our very lives to right a terrible wrong," she shouted at him. "And you think it merely a joke?"

Syrah was unaware of the tears coursing down her cheeks. "You can have no idea what I . . . what we have suffered, what desperation drives us to such madness."

"My lady, please—"

"I'm not a fool. I tell the others that we cannot fail. This morning I sent them to safety. They think we will all go on together but I intend to finish this alone. You will hunt me down. I don't care. I will see it done and then you may make an example of me to all the world."

Jibril damned the iron bars that prevented him from taking her in his arms, this clever bold woman weeping like a child. Words would have to do.

"You have nothing to fear from me," he said gently. "Tell me what troubles you and I will help in any way I can."

Syrah shook her head, remembering the long fruitless days she had waited for word from the king; how she had feared for Eben's life and locked herself in her room when Ranulph tried to force himself on her. "No, you cannot help me. It is far more complicated than you can imagine."

"The power of the Crown can do anything, my lady."

Syrah dashed the tears from her cheeks and smiled ruefully. "Yes, the power of the Crown can do anything. If it so chooses."

She straightened up, in control again, and picked up the basket. "I apologize for my outburst, Your Highness. I must go now. The tide will soon be in. I leave you to enjoy your dates. If you continue to nibble at them at this rate, you may possibly finish by Twelfth Night."

She was at the door when he inquired, "You will return tomorrow?"

"At night, yes. But it will be very late because of the tide. I have left sufficient food for the day."

"I believe you owe me a game of chess."

"I will honor that promise before we part. But I must warn you that you cannot win."

"You have proved yourself a wily opponent, but you cannot win every game in life. Or do you mean to drug me again to befuddle my mind?"

Syrah laughed. "That would hardly be fair. In any event, it will not be necessary."

"I am rather good at games myself," Jibril said. "I do not care to lose. My pride, you know."

Syrah glanced at the chessboard in the corner of Jibril's cell. He was in the middle of a game he was playing against himself to pass the time. She cocked her head. "Black to checkmate in five," she said, curtsied, and departed.

Jibril stared down at the chessboard and let out a low appreciative whistle. "So it is: black to checkmate in five."

Just after dusk, the wind shifted to the southeast, presaging the storm to come. The sea swept to shore in great rolling waves, driving the waters of high tide almost to the entrance of the cave where Syrah stirred the little fire to dispel the chill damp. In the ruins high on the cliffs of the Isle of Lost Souls, the wind scraped and shrieked against the ancient stones as seabirds abandoned their nests in the cliff face and let the wind carry them inland to calmer waters.

Lying on his pallet with arms crossed behind his head, Jibril stared up at the rounded vault of the stone ceiling thinking about the poor souls who had lived out their mad lives in the confines of this very cell. Had they heard in the shrieking wind the voices of their demons? Had they flung themselves at the unforgiving bars, begging to be released? Had some compassionate monk come to soothe them with prayer and perhaps a small flagon of wine?

Come to think of it, he would rather like some wine himself right now, perhaps a rough red to match the mood of the coming storm. And a certain young woman smelling of rosemary to drink it with.

Jibril had never met a woman like his mysterious Lady; a woman as bold and clever and determined as any man he knew. But for a few minutes she had allowed anger and pain to rule her. Bars of metal only had shielded her from defeat as she cried her heart out—and from the comfort and aid he could offer.

That she would decline his offer of help puzzled Jibril. He could understand if she still feared his retribution and the king's justice, no matter his assurances. But what had she meant when she said the power of the Crown could do anything—if it chose to? Had his father denied a petition or failed to award fair judgment in some dispute? Could someone in the royal family have broken his word of honor?

Jibril rose gracefully from the pallet and stretched out the muscles of his back, arms, and legs, using the bars for leverage. He was accustomed to using his body hard in training at arms, riding, and of course, in the sweeter pleasures of a woman's arms. Inactivity did not sit well with him.

The Lady had said his troops would come to release him no later than tomorrow night. The storm would probably delay them, but she could not risk remaining in the area beyond the next morning. He might not be able to convince her to accept his help, but there would be time enough to discover some vital piece of information that would help him track her down and keep her from further folly.

And to make love to her.

Syrah ventured out into the rising wind. The tide was low now, but an occasional wind-whipped wave swept over the causeway, eating away at the sand and leaving the rocks strewn with slimy seaweed, making it all the more treacherous in the dark of night. She could feel the rain on the wind and knew she had to decide whether she would risk the walk out to the island. The prince wouldn't starve if he had to wait another ten or twelve hours for food. But what if his soldiers were delayed or the message had never reached the king? She couldn't very well abandon him without any way to free himself.

No, she would have to go to him; he was her responsibility. She drew her cloak closer around her and picked her way gingerly across the treacherous causeway to the island. She had just reached the halfway point on the steep path to the top when the rain started to fall. Slipping and sliding, she scrambled up the last thirty feet and ducked into the dank stairwell. How she was going to get back to the cave she could not imagine.

First things first. Food for the prince and a quick formal farewell. She would leave his knife on the stone bench and toss the keys across the room through the bars of his cell. It would take but a second to slam the outer door and slide home the bolt. He would have food enough for several days, and since he was so very clever, she had no doubt he would find a way around the bolt eventually. He would then be free to await his troops or make his way back to the capital on his own.

This time, she promised herself as she shook the rain from her cloak, she would keep her emotions under control, no matter what he said. She trudged up the steps and set the basket down outside the bolted door.

Taking no chances, she called above the wailing wind, "Are you decent, my lord?"

"It hardly matters," came the shouted reply. "It's dark as Hades in here. There is nothing to see to put a blush upon your cheek."

A few minutes later, Syrah finally won the struggle with the tinder and lit the little lantern. Without looking at the prince she bustled about the room, making sure the shutters were well secured against the wind and setting out items from the basket just so onto the tray.

"I have a surprise for you," she said as she worked. "You've been an admirable prisoner; I thought you should get a little reward." She slid the tray toward the bars and held up a small leather flask.

"Wine!" the prince exclaimed. "I was just thinking about wine. Ah, but perhaps not, knowing our history."

Syrah pleaded ignorance. "Our history? I don't understand."

"Come now. You are the wench from the tavern, are you not?"

"There are many wenches, my lord."

"I disagree. Some wenches are more memorable than others."

Syrah carefully cut the wedge of yellow cheese into small pieces. "And her face, my lord? This wench you speak of. Would you remember her face?"

Jibril dipped his hands into the water bowl and dried them with the cloth. "I remember a face, but I doubt it was her true one. Or should I say, your true one?"

"As I say, there are many wenches, Your Highness. I suggest you eat quickly. I must get back to shore as soon as possible."

Jibril paused as he was about to pop a piece of brown

bread into his mouth. "Surely you can't be thinking of returning in this weather. I won't allow it."

"I beg your pardon? Did you say 'allow'?"

"That is precisely what I said. I order you to remain here until the storm is over. You will obey me. I am your prince."

"You are my prisoner."

"Prisoner, prince, whatever. I'm not about to let some featherbrained woman get herself swept out to sea."

Syrah was on her feet. "Featherbrained?"

"Only a simpleton would risk the causeway in such weather."

"Simpleton! I'll have you know the only reason I came to the island was so you wouldn't starve to death over here." It wasn't true, but it was certainly all she would admit to.

Jibril was still trying to get his temper under control. He rarely lost it, but somehow the idea of this girl taking such a risk struck a raw nerve. There had been another girl who had been claimed by the sea, lost forever. And the dreams.

"You will stay here until I say you may leave," he said tightly.

Syrah bit off another retort. It was ridiculous to get worked up. He could shout orders at her and snarl until he was hoarse, but in the present circumstances the panther had no teeth. She could and would leave when she chose to.

Letting him think he had won the argument, she settled down on her bench and nibbled at her own bread and cheese.

"You mentioned wine," the prince grumbled some time later.

Syrah held the flask out to him, dangling at the end of her outstretched arm, then stepped back quickly in case he tried to grab her. He drank deeply and handed it back.

"I trust I'll not awake tomorrow to find myself bouncing around the countryside in a coffin," he said with a grin, trying to lighten the atmosphere. "A novel experience, I must say, but not one I'd care to repeat until I die. At which time, the journey will seem neither long nor uncomfortable."

"The wine is not drugged, my lord." Syrah took a small sip. "See? I drink it myself."

The prince was about to suggest they share it mouth to mouth as they had at the tavern, but there would be time enough to seduce. He didn't want to scare her off.

He moved the chessboard toward the bars and started setting up the pieces. "You were quite right about my game yesterday. Black in five. You are no novice."

Syrah shivered as she spread her damp cloak on the cold stone in front of the hatch.

"You're cold."

"A little," she conceded. "My boots and stockings are soaked through."

The prince pulled the blankets off his pallet and handed them to her through the bars. "You'd better take them off and wrap yourself up well."

A few minutes later they were settled, Syrah snug in the wool blankets, the board between them, the two little armies of onyx and ivory facing off in the soft glow of the lantern, the tempest howling without.

The prince plucked one black and one white pawn from the board and held them behind his back. "Choose."

If Syrah chose white she would have the first move.

"Left hand," Syrah said.

The prince held up the black pawn. "I cede the first move to you. You will have the advantage of me."

"I decline. I require no advantage. It occurs to me that it is not the first move that gives the true advantage but the last."

The prince smiled at her. "Well said."

At first Syrah was careful to slide the board back and forth between them so he wouldn't be able to catch hold of her hand, but as the play deepened she forgot all about it.

The prince played an aggressive game, as men were wont to do in sport, firm in his strategy, decisive in his moves. Syrah lured him this way and that, appeared weak, then strong, was patient.

Jibril broke the long silence almost an hour later as he pondered her latest move. "We are well matched, but I'm sorry to have to tell you that you play like a woman."

Syrah snorted. "I have heard that before and I have always taken it to mean that a woman is not sufficiently aggressive and is unwilling to give up even the most useless pawn."

"You have it aright," Jibril answered as he maneuvered his queen to hold off her bishop.

"I would also add that my opponent is most likely to make that observation when he is losing. A clever ploy."

"But not," she added as her hand went to her knight "always a successful one."

She took his queen and sat back on her heels. "Checkmate, Your Highness."

Jibril stared at the board. "I'll be damned."

"Surely not, unless you're playing with the devil," Syrah said with a laugh. "Losing a game of chess does not qualify as a mortal sin."

Jibril tipped his king, acknowledging defeat, then replayed the last four moves. "If nothing else, I should do penance for sheer stupidity. Where did you learn that move? It's brilliant."

Syrah blushed. "I must confess it is my own, but you are welcome to use it."

"I see now where you come by your skill in strategy. In the past few days you have checkmated not one but two kings. That is no mean feat." He pulled the board into the cell and set up the pieces for another game. "Tell me, my lady, how you outwitted my father."

Syrah was tempted to reveal her charade with the chamber pots, but that would be boasting, a sin of pride. Besides, she might have to use that stratagem again someday, although she fervently hoped it would never come to that.

"I'm sure His Majesty will fill you in on the particulars. In the meantime, I leave it to your imagination."

Jibril shot her a mischievous grin. "My imagination has been busy with other things of late."

Syrah could easily guess what those "other things" were if her own imagination was anything to go by.

Jibril glanced up to see her lifting aside the wooden shutter to look out at the storm. "You will not leave until I say so."

Irritated by the prince's peremptory tone, Syrah was tempted to remind him just who was in control here, but getting into another argument with him would serve no purpose.

"If you are concerned that I might be swept away and you would be left here to an uncertain fate, be at ease, my lord. I will make provision for you to free yourself before I leave." Seeing his surprise, she added, "But not even with your renowned skills could you do so in time to apprehend me."

"What would you say," Jibril said quietly, "if I were to tell you that your safety is my primary concern?"

Syrah's heart skipped a little beat. "I would have to question your motive; you might be trying to sweet-talk me into releasing you and surrendering."

The prince leaned against the bars, his voice serious for once. "No ulterior motive, I assure you. I lost one young woman to the sea. I would not lose another."

Syrah's heartbeat escalated to a resounding *rapa-tapa-bop*. "I am sorry to hear that," she said, thrilled her voice could sound so normal. "Was she . . . were you close?"

"We might have become so had she not been so misguided."

"Misguided?" she said carefully.

"Yes. Very much like yourself. She set out on a crusade of sorts with little thought to the consequences. But we all know women make poor crusaders."

"Do we indeed?"

"You women are too emotional. You are unable to see the larger picture. She drowned, along with all her family. Perhaps you heard of it. Lady Syrah Dhion?"

"Yes, I know of it. And what was she to you, if I might inquire?"

"I had thought to wed her."

The simple statement struck Syrah dumb while warring emotions almost deprived her of breath: outrage, anger, exhilaration, and passionate regret. She would not cry, she would not.

Steadying herself, she said, "I'm sorry for your loss. I don't know the circumstances that led Lady Syrah to such a terrible fate, but I am sure she acted with honor and in good conscience."

"Perhaps."

She was not going to ask. She asked. "Did you care for her?"

"I met her but once several years ago. She was lovely. Impetuous, bright, as beautiful as a young colt. I wanted to wait until she was of age to approach her. I think we would have suited. Well, that is all past. I only bring it up because you, too, appear to be set on a course of utter folly. I can only guess why you need such an enormous sum of money, but no good can come of it. It cannot be worth dying for."

It suddenly became imperative for Syrah to get away from the dim confines of the stone cell. Away from him. Without a word she closed the outer door, slid home the bolt, and ran down the steps to the partially destroyed entryway where she wept into the storm.

Jibril paced back and forth in his cell, cursing himself for his harsh words. Offending her had been stupid when his aim was to convince her to give up her crazy scheme. Surely she knew by now that he wasn't going to exact retribution for this farce of a kidnapping.

The sound of the door opening brought Jibril to the bars. He couldn't tell if she'd been crying but she set about tidying up the supplies that had been stored in his coffin in that very precise way women have when an emotional storm has passed.

"I didn't mean to upset you."

She took some spare clothes from a cloth satchel and refolded them carefully. "I'm not upset. You're not acquainted with the facts, but you are entitled to your opinion."

The howl of the wind had tapered off to a steady moan. She was preparing to leave. Jibril scrambled to find a way to lure her to him. He needed to keep her from her folly, true, but he needed something more: to hold her against him, breathe in that faint scent of fresh herbs, explore her warm, sweet mouth. She might not admit to being the tavern wench, but he had no doubt she was the same. He wondered about the true color of her hair, whether the missing teeth and sallow complexion had been but artifice. He could not be mistaken about her soft curves and long firm legs. He recalled his fleeting impression that she might be an innocent. If indeed the woman who was so studiously ignoring him now was that delectable girl, he could no longer doubt that first impression.

"I believe we have unfinished business, my lady."

Syrah pulled dry stockings from the satchel and turned away to put them on. "I think not. We've had our chess game. Your men should be on the way to release you. I've explained that you will be able to free yourself after I leave." She glanced around the cell, taking care to avoid looking at him. "Have I forgotten anything?"

The prince's eyes danced with amusement. "I believe we had an agreement to enjoy one another's company."

Syrah sniffed. "I remember no such agreement."

"Were you not to offer me wine from your sweet mouth? Were we not to share your feather bed?"

"Oh, for heaven's sake. You know very well—"

"So you don't mean to honor your word?"

Syrah folded her arms and glared at him. "You are working on a false assumption."

"Not so. Shall I quote your very words?"

"I have no interest in the promises of some common harlot. You are mistaken."

Jibril grinned. "Trust me, my lady, I am unlikely to forget so sweet an invitation. I will compromise with you. We will forget the feather bed—for now—but it can do no harm to share the last of the wine."

Syrah paused at the door, her satchel at her feet. She needed to leave. She wanted to stay. He was lost to her, destined for another. He was here with her now.

Jibril stood perfectly still, willing her to come to him. He could not see her eyes behind the mesh panel of her hood, but he was sure her gaze was locked on him like a doe frozen in the hunter's sights. "Come to me," he said softly.

Syrah shook her head, as much to clear her jumbled thoughts as to deny him. "You know I cannot."

"I will not harm you. On the honor of my House."

A man might swear fealty to his lord on bent knee and still break his word. But for Prince Jibril to swear upon the honor of his House was like putting his hand upon the Bible to swear an oath before God. Syrah could not but believe him.

Leaning casually against the bars, the prince radiated that lazy masculine energy that would become power and grace in motion. He drew her to him, moth to flame, a half smile on his lips, his eyes watchful, golden in the flickering light of the lamp. Doubly dangerous, seductive, and utterly confident in an infuriating male way that did not demand submission but somehow expected it as his prerogative.

"Very well," Syrah agreed briskly, as much to puncture the bubble of his conceit as to prove to herself she was in complete control of her own feelings. "We'll drink a toast."

"Let me think," the prince mused. "I won't drink to the success of your enterprise; I would as soon you abandoned it. I can't very well drink to your cleverness since it reflects rather poorly upon my own and that of my father. I might drink to your beauty, but you choose not to reveal it to me."

"Such a toast would be wasted," Syrah agreed. "I am not at all in the fashion of the ladies of your court. And you know very well why I do not show my face."

Jibril stared at her so intently that Syrah felt as though he could see right through the material of her hood. "You are beautiful, my lady; you cannot hide it. I see it in the delicacy of your hands and the grace of your manner. If your face is not a model of perfection, it matters not. Beauty is not always of the body; it is revealed equally through goodness of heart, arises from laughter, carries in the music of the voice."

Syrah could hardly draw a breath. She tried for a light tone despite the hammering of her heart. "You are quite the poet, my lord. Your words would bring comfort to many a maiden who lacks beauty of face and form but is possessed of other, less-valued qualities. You must admit, however, it is a woman's appearance that first brings her to a man's notice. It does not seem to signify that he himself may be far from handsome; she must be fair."

Jibril shrugged. "It is the way of men and women. Yet look at us. I meet you in a tavern; your hair is dull, your complexion sallow, made more so by the harsh yellow of a harlot's gown; you appear to be short a tooth or two. We meet again and I cannot see you at all. Yet I know you are fair. Therefore, I will drink to your beauty whether you admit to it or not."

He reached out for the flask. Syrah took a few cautious steps forward and held it out to him at arm's length. Before she could even cry out, his hand shot out and seized her wrist. Slowly, inexorably he drew her toward the bars. Desperate to resist, she tried to anchor the heels of her half boots on the edge of a flagstone and use the weight of her whole body against the strength of his arm.

"Give over," the prince commanded.

"Never!" She jerked back so suddenly that he let go and she landed smack on her backside. In a flash he grabbed an ankle. She planted her other foot against a bar and used her weight to push back. His left hand closed around that ankle too and he dragged her forward again until her legs were spread-eagled on one side of the bars and her upper body on the other.

"Swine, skunk!" she yelled.

"No kicking, you hellion," he grunted. "My God, I've hooked marlin that were easier to land."

"Slimy, slithery snake! I should have known better than to trust you!"

"Lady—"

"Dog! Swine!"

"If you'll just stop squirming and be quiet—"

"Purple-pooping—"

"I'm warning you—"

"Spittle-spewing dromedary!"

"Dromedary?"

"Worm!"

"Enough!" the prince roared.

Syrah was out of breath and, for the moment, out of epithets. "Let go of me," she snarled.

"I will when you calm down."

"You can't possibly expect me to be calm under the circumstances. So much for your word of honor," she snapped.

"I've not broken it. I said I would not harm you. I did not say I would not seduce you."

Syrah looked down in horror at her tunic and shift, which had bunched well above her knees. "This is your idea of seduction?"

"It does lack a certain polish, does it not?" Jibril laughed. He reached for her hand through the bars, but she quickly extended her arms high above her head.

Jibril clasped both ankles in one hand while the fingers of the other traced a soft meandering path up her leg. "I require a certain degree of cooperation if I am to improve my technique."

"You cannot possibly expect me to cooperate."

One finger trailed another inch up the inside of her thigh. "Don't you dare."

Another inch. "Soft, like silk."

The lantern flame suddenly flickered wildly and went out.

Jibril could feel her wriggling about and wrestling with some piece of clothing. A light ping of metal against stone alerted him to the possibility that she might have a weapon in her hand.

Releasing her ankle, he sighed like a bad actor upon the stage. "Alas, my beauty, I fear we must postpone our tryst until a more propitious moment."

Dredging up every shocking epithet she had ever heard from the mouths of her father's stable boys, Syrah searched blindly until her fingers closed upon the key she had thrown across the room lest he yank it from the ribbon around her neck. She moved along the wall until she came to the coffin and groped about inside for more lantern oil. Then she remembered that the last of it had gone on with the cart.

"There's no lamp oil. You'll have to do without."

"We don't need it."

"We?" she snapped. "There will be no 'we.' I'm leaving."

Jibril was on his feet as she lifted aside the shutters. "No, wait. Truly, I meant only to kiss you; it was you who turned it into a brawl. Whatever else you may think of me, I am a man who honors my word. I would not harm you. I will not hold or try to bind you until my men arrive. I want only a kiss. A kiss of farewell."

Syrah stood in the outer doorway, one hand upon the iron cross bolt. The merest hint of dawn was creeping through the window to breach the inky darkness, outlining Jibril against the vertical bars of the cell. She had only to toss the keys to him, pull the door shut, and it would be over. Forever.

"See here, I will cover my eyes with the kerchief." She heard him moving about the cell. "There. I have tied it tight. There is not the slightest possibility I will see your face."

The wind had risen again, masking all sound in the room. Jibril did not hear the soft rustle of her skirts and the little sigh of longing that escaped her as she moved toward him. It was her scent that alerted him that she had drawn close, a sweet distillation of wind and wild herbs and exciting femininity. He extended a hand into the darkness and felt her arm beneath the rough fabric of her cloak.

"Take it off," he murmured. She did not resist as he carefully lifted the hood over her head and let the cloak drop to the floor. "I will know you by touch only, my lady, but it will suffice."

His fingers moved gently over her hair and found the pins that secured the bun at the back of her neck. Her hair fell in a wave to her waist and she arched her neck, feeling the sensual weight of it.

"A kiss," Syrah managed to say, "you said a kiss."

"Ah, yes." His mouth settled over hers for a few seconds. He pulled away. "Your kiss, my lady," he said gallantly.

"Oh."

"I fear I have disappointed you."

Syrah cleared her throat delicately. "Well, I thought perhaps . . . it would be more . . . seeing as this is a farewell kiss and all."

"A farewell kiss when lovers are to be separated forever must needs be brief, aching with poignancy and regret."

"We're not lovers," she said faintly.

"Allow me to remedy that," he murmured as he took her mouth again, this time in unmistakable hunger.

All caution fled. Rational thought, common sense, and sound judgment dissolved as Syrah slipped into a stream of erotic discovery that bore no resemblance to her carefully compiled list of amatory activity. The sniggering dairymaid's catalogue of a man's pleasures, the indifferent fumbling of the whores, the rutting cacophony from the tavern's back rooms, the ludicrous mating she had witnessed in the king's tent—all were forgotten. A purely male energy surrounded her, aroused her every sense, fired every nerve. Her own passion exploded, granting her power over him even as he sought to possess her, commanded her to submit.

Suddenly, she was seized with mindless panic. The first gray light of dawn had banished the safety of darkness; the prince would see her face and all would be lost.

The blindfold. Had Jibril kept his word?

In the feeble light she trailed her fingers across the sharp angle of his cheeks until she felt the soft cloth. It was firmly in place. She gently pulled his head forward as far as the bars would allow and kissed each eyelid. "Thank you, my lord."

Reluctantly, she tried to disengage herself from his embrace. "I must go now."

Jibril stroked down the gentle curve of her back, cupped the enticing globes of her buttocks, and drew her toward him. "The kiss is not finished, my lady."

"It's not?"

"I think it will not take long," he said with a hint of laughter in his voice.

117

"Well, if it can be done quickly."

Their lips and tongues met in another fiery kiss, more ravenous, if possible, than the first. His fingers trailed a fiery path from one exquisitely sensitive spot to another, down the graceful arch of her neck to the pulsing hollow at the base of her throat. Syrah moaned at the sweep of his fingers across her breasts and the nip of his teeth and the suckling of his lips through the coarse fabric. She gasped when he knelt before her, lifted the hem of her shift, and pulled her firmly against the bars. The tip of his tongue found a spot amid the pale silky curls of her sex that she had never known existed, and had she not clung to the bars with every ounce of strength she possessed she would have crashed to the floor as his mouth worked upon her until a wave of unimaginable pleasure swept over her.

Jibril was on his feet raining soft kisses over her face and murmuring words of approval as Syrah drifted back from a world where seconds might be hours and minutes centuries. "What happened?"

Jibril pried her fingers from the bars. "We kissed."

His dry mischievous tone snapped Syrah out of her erotic thrall. "You mock me, sir." She hastily set about righting her clothing and settling the concealing hood on her head.

"On the contrary, you have my utmost admiration," said the prince as he listened to her set herself to rights. "I cannot remember a time when a lady was able to complete her part of a kiss so quickly."

"That is quite enough," she said waspishly. "I'm sure I do not take your meaning, nor do I care to discuss it. You may remove your blindfold now."

She bustled about the cell making haste to depart, looking everywhere but at him. She carefully surveyed the room to make sure she had left nothing incriminating lying about. She set his jeweled dagger on the stone bench beneath the window. Finally, she screwed up the courage to look at him.

He lounged against the wall, arms crossed across his chest, an unreadable look in his amber eyes. He did not speak.

Increasingly uncomfortable as the silence stretched between them, Syrah paid close attention to smoothing the folds of her cloak.

A distant memory teased at her. She was thirteen, standing alone in a garden ablaze with thousands of roses, feeling an inexplicable sense of loss. A prince had leaned down from a towering stallion and whispered soft words in her ear. She squeezed her eyes tight and stifled a sob. She was a woman grown now. The six years that had passed between that moment in her mother's garden and this stone prison had become a lifetime. And everything that might have been would never be.

"I ask you again, my lady, to confide in me and allow me to assist you," the prince said.

Syrah shook her head, afraid to speak lest she come apart.

"You are brave and clever, but wisdom lies in knowing your limitations and having the courage to seek help when you cannot possibly carry the full load."

"You say that because I am a woman," Syrah stated flatly. "You would not make such an offer if I were a man."

"True. Men can command other men. Women cannot. I suspect your mission will become even more treacherous, and your little band, loyal as they may be, cannot offer protection that requires strength and, yes, courage."

Syrah stiffened. "You think only men are strong? You believe women lack courage to do what must be done? Let me acquaint you with the true nature of things: Men break in the storm; women ride it."

"I am not about to debate philosophy with you, madam," Jibril said, his temper rising. "I have offered my assistance. You decline it not because you can do without it but because your pride will not allow you to do so. You are one of those crusaders who is blinded by the rightness of his cause, whose way is the right way, the only way."

Syrah marched to the door. "You are wrong. I most certainly require assistance in this matter. In fact, I do require a man to help me see it through. But that man is not you."

"If you hope to insult me, my lady, you have succeeded," Jibril said quietly.

Syrah suddenly wanted to weep. "No," she cried. "You don't understand and I'm sorry that I cannot tell you why. You are bound by your duty as my prince to redress the wrong I have committed against you. You cannot make an exception of me because I claim a just cause and, especially, because I am a woman."

"You forget who I am and the power I wield. I can make exceptions as I choose," Jibril declared.

Syrah glanced at the brooding dawn. She could tarry no longer, but it pained her to leave with discord between them. In an effort to soften their parting, she observed quietly, "I do not forget, Your Highness. More than you know, I respect your station and your power. However, it seems we are well matched in our faults. I suspect your way is the only way, even as my way is the only way. Your honor compels you to offer your assistance. My honor compels me to refuse it."

Jibril smiled. "And I am a man and you are a woman."

Syrah glanced at him one last time. "Our kiss . . . I expect there's more to it. Surely, you . . ."

Too embarrassed to go on, she knelt formally and rose. She tossed the key into his cell, pulled the door closed before she could change her mind, and shot home the bolt.

Jibril had his cell door unlocked before she had even reached the bottom of the stairs. Now he watched from the open window as the woman picked her way across the treacherous causeway. She gained the safety of the shore and disappeared into the mouth of a cave a short way up the beach.

"Damned fool," Jibril said. As he waited for her to reappear he examined the bolted door. The ancient wood was cracked and crumbling; it would be but a few minutes' work to carve into the doorjamb and jimmy the bolt. Not quickly enough, however, to allow him to give chase.

The Lady emerged from the cave leading a small white palfrey. She tied her satchel to the saddle, climbed up, and urged the horse into a gentle trot up the beach without a backward glance. She suddenly brought the little mare about and sat staring back at the windswept island. The hood still concealed her face, but Jibril knew she was focused on the window of his cell.

The wind lashed at her cloak as they stared at one another. A sudden blast lifted the hood away from her face. She grabbed for it and pulled it close again, but not before a few tangled tresses of flaxen hair escaped its confines and whipped about her face. She wheeled about so quickly that her horse nearly lost its footing, and raced out of sight around a steep headland.

Jibril remained at the window long after she had disappeared. The wind was pushing the spent clouds out to sea; streaks of pale blue appeared and soon the rising sun transformed the drab cliffs into a towering precipice of rust and gold.

It took only ten minutes for Jibril to chisel away the rotting wood and push back the bolt. He picked up the basket, draped the leather flagon of wine over his shoulder, and went out into the fresh morning air. He set up a comfortable little space in the lee of a large boulder and stretched lustily. Then he settled down to watch the azure water of the southern ocean surge over the causeway and deposit a delicate silver froth on the sand. He stripped off his tunic, closed his eyes, and let the warm rays of the sun wash over him.

"The kiss, my lady," he murmured into the sweet-scented air, "is not finished."

Chapter Twelve

Master Sprum trotted along the long marble corridor that led from his own little domain in the south wing toward the great hall of the palace. Save for his semiannual reports to the king, he was rarely summoned to the royal presence.

"Phew, phew, phew," he wheezed as he juggled an armful of the dusty scrolls and leather-bound journals he had been poring over since the morning meal. This was the second summons today. How the Crown Prince expected him to carry out his research into the genealogies of twenty-seven noble Houses with these constant interruptions, he really could not say.

So cloistered was Master Sprum in the musty chamber that housed the King's Rolls that the happy tidings of Prince Jibril's rescue and return to the palace had not reached him until the following morning. In the event, it was the prince himself who brought the news when he suddenly appeared at Master Sprum's door. So taken aback was he that the plump little Keeper of the Rolls tumbled from his chair and had to be assisted to his feet and dusted off by the royal personage himself no less. In a few clipped words, the prince had ordered Sprum to discover the names of a brother and sister of any noble House who met one simple criterion: The girl would be between the ages of seventeen and twenty-five, the boy between ten and fifteen.

"Oh, dear, oh, dear," Master Sprum chanted as he pattered down the last flight of stairs that led to the gallery overlooking the great hall. He would have to explain yet again why the search was proving so very difficult. His Highness did not seem to comprehend the complexity of the task. The brother and sister might be the children of sitting armigers; grandchildren or great-grandchildren; nieces and nephews, great nieces and great nephews; first or second or even third cousins. Any one of these might be entitled to the honor of being addressed as Lady This or Lord That. Taken all together, the keeper was looking at twenty-seven Houses whose extended families must number close to twenty thousand.

The little man paused briefly in the gallery to collect himself before he presented his findings to the prince. He did not think the prince would be happy with his progress to date.

Oh, dear, oh, dear.

Jibril looked up from the chessboard just as the Keeper of the Rolls reached the bottom step of the staircase. "Finally. Stop dithering, Master Sprum. Come here and tell me what you have discovered."

The keeper approached the little party gathered about the huge hearth: Prince Jibril and his friend Kalan, who faced one another across an inlaid marble chessboard; King Ahriman, lovely Queen Alya, and the two youngest princesses.

"Well?" Jibril demanded.

Master Sprum took a deep breath and prepared to deliver his report. Before he could launch into his usual apology, the king said to his wife, "My dear, these are weighty matters that would no doubt bore you. Perhaps you and the girls would be more comfortable in your own quarters."

"Anything that concerns my son," said the queen, fixing her husband with a wifely stare that brooked no nonsense, "is of the greatest interest to me." She waved the princesses away and settled herself more comfortably upon the velvet-padded chaise longue. "Proceed, Keeper."

Master Sprum cleared his throat. "I have now completed my research into the extended genealogies of the first Twelve Houses." A wistful expression spread over his wrinkled features. "With the exception, of course, of Your Majesties, of the Ninth House."

A heavy silence fell on the group.

"Just so," the king said gruffly. "Pray, continue."

"I have found two sets of siblings who meet the criteria."

"Yes, yes," Jibril said impatiently.

"Lady Fruza of the Eighth House is eighteen years of age. Her brother is ten, but perhaps his character would lead one to believe him to be several years older. Then—"

"I believe we can discount these two," the queen interrupted. "Fruza's mother is a particular friend of mine, and I know for a fact that she and the children have been abroad these past three months visiting her mother."

Master Sprum looked crestfallen. "I had such hopes for that one. Well, the other possibility lies in the Fifth House. The Lady Josana is seventeen and her brother is fifteen."

Prince Jibril paced back and forth before the hearth. "No, no, impossible."

"Why so?" inquired the king.

"She is too, er," Jibril said, glancing sideways at his mother, "robust."

"Robust? What do you mean by that, son?" said the queen.

Amused at his son's discomfiture, the king pitched in, "What Jibril is saying, my dear, is that the lady is rather well endowed, if you catch my meaning."

The queen's brows came together in a puzzled frown. "But you said your kidnapper wore a shapeless garment. How then could you perceive her . . . qualities?"

The king and Kalan looked at the prince expectantly.

Jibril rolled his eyes toward his mother, willing the two men to help him out of this quandary.

"Ah," said the king.

"Ha!" said Kalan.

"Really!" the queen said repressively, catching the drift of the conversation. She rose and sent her son a dark look. "We will speak of this later, Jibril." She swept from the chamber in a swish of her velvet skirts, her little dog pattering along behind her.

"So," the king remarked with a glint in his eye, "tell us exactly how you 'perceived her qualities,' son. Seduction, I'll warrant. Not a bad strategy to obtain your release. Seeing that you were still on the island when Kalan arrived, I can only presume you were not entirely successful."

Prince Jibril dropped down onto the chair he had vacated earlier and stared down Kalan, wishing nothing more than to plant his fist in the middle of that smirking face.

"It occurs to me that you can have nothing to boast about in this farce," he snarled. "I seem to recall your own singular lack of success with this woman."

Kalan had nothing to say to that. He still had not recovered from the humiliation of discovering the coffin in the prince's cell chamber and realizing how he had been deceived. A sharp twinge shot up his leg from his right foot, reminding him of the fury that had seized him in that moment. He had gone quite berserk, aiming kick after kick at the wood panels, breaking three toes despite his thick leather boots. Unable to shatter the coffin, he had then taken an axe to it and reduced it to splinters. To make matters worse, Jibril had insisted on bringing the lid with its grinning skull back to the palace, where it was prominently displayed in his study.

"Uh, Your Highness," Master Sprum interjected timidly into the tense silence between the two men. "If I might complete my report?"

"Obviously you have nothing useful to report," the prince snapped as he turned his attention once more to the chess game. He was losing. He never lost. Well, almost never. "Go away, Master Sprum."

"Leave off, Jibril," the king admonished him. "The keeper is doing his best. Girl," he said to a hovering serving maid, "give Master Sprum a flagon."

A few minutes later, the keeper was settled on a low stool

in the far corner of the chamber wiping the perspiration from his brow, determined to work through the night. One more encounter with Prince Jibril such as this did not bear thinking about.

Kalan leaned back and propped his chin on his hand as he awaited Jibril's next move. "You seem to be having some difficulty this evening," he said smugly.

Jibril glared down at the board. Kalan's unusual strategy had indeed forced him into a number of foolish moves. "I'm distracted, is all."

"Excuses, excuses," Kalan said airily.

Stung, Jibril moved quickly to cover Kalan's black bishop with his white queen.

Kalan immediately struck back with his knight. "Checkmate!" he crowed.

Jibril stared down in astonishment. "How in hell did you . . . ?"

"Heh, heh, heh."

"By the saints!" Jibril's eyes narrowed as he regarded his smirking friend. "Where did you learn that move?"

Enjoying his triumph, Kalan took a deep draught of ale. "Wouldn't you like to know?"

Jibril studied the board. "Indeed I would," he said softly. "Indeed I would."

"As a matter of fact, I picked up that little maneuver some years ago. I've never had a chance to use it before. It was on that visit to the hall of the—"

Jibril leaped to his feet, propelling chess pieces in all directions. He stormed this way and that before the hearth, running his fingers repeatedly through his hair. "I don't believe it! Sweet Lord, it can't be. How could it? I saw the wreckage with my own eyes! Why that little . . . Sprum," he roared. "Where the devil is Sprum?"

The Keeper of the Rolls shrank back against the wall, trying to make himself as inconspicuous as possible.

"I see you," the prince bellowed. "Get yourself over here this minute!"

"Calm down," the king said. "Get control of yourself, Jibril."

On legs that could barely support him, Master Sprum edged toward the prince as though happening upon a wild boar in rutting season. "Y-yes, my lord?"

Jibril glowered down at him. "You have completed your study of twelve Houses, save one?"

Master Sprum could but nod, coherent speech being beyond him under the prince's intense regard.

"Listen carefully, Sprum: We have an older man, a father, possibly quite ill. A daughter, seventeen to twenty-five. A son, ten to fifteen, probably closer to fifteen. A younger child, perhaps a baby. An older female relative, possibly a grandmother or aunt, living somewhere along the south coast. A noble family, wealthy enough to breed fine horses.

"Now, search your mind, Keeper. Of the first twelve Houses does any particular House come to mind?"

Sprum scrunched his brow. "Hmmm. The Eighteenth? No, no sons. Horses, you say? I suppose . . . Um, well . . ."

"Yes?" the prince demanded.

Sprum's mouth fell open. "Upon my word, I vow . . . Oh dear, oh dear. Let me think. Wait!" he exclaimed as he bustled back to his parchments and books. "Ah, yes, here it is. Well, well, I never. If I didn't know better, I would say that the family you describe could be none other than—"

"The Ninth House," Jibril said. "Of course."

Chapter Thirteen

Courtiers, soldiers, squires, and servants scattered before him like startled chipmunks as Jibril stormed from the great hall. The passageways resounded with the sound of slamming doors, metal-toed boots upon stone floors, and a stream of remarkably creative invective. Two statues and a set of rare crystal bowls were reduced to shards in the wake of his passing.

The Ninth House!

When he had reached his own chambers Jibril threw himself into his favorite chair and kicked off his boots, and tore the key of his cell on the Isle of Lost Souls, which he now wore on a thin leather cord, from his neck. He threw it across the room, then immediately leaped up to retrieve it. He stalked from hearth to window to door and back again across the thick carpets.

I lost one woman to the sea and I would not lose another. Misguided . . . very much like yourself She set out on a crusade of sorts with little thought to the consequences, but we all know women make poor crusaders . . .

Jibril seized a bowl and hurled it against the far wall.

She was lovely. Impetuous, bright, as beautiful as a young colt. I thought to wait until she was of age to approach her.

He finally came to a standstill before the window. He threw it open to let the night breeze wash over him and cool his anger. How could he have been so stupid?

We have risked our very lives to right a terrible wrong . . . you can have no idea . . . what I . . . what we have suffered, what desperation drives us to such madness.

Jibril threw himself onto the bed and stared up at the scarlet canopy.

You think only men are strong? You believe women lack courage to do what must be done? Let me acquaint you with the true nature of things: Men break in the storm; women ride it.

Ranulph Gyp. Sweet Lord, Lady Syrah was going after Gyp!

The realization sent Jibril storming back down the stairs in his stocking feet. He charged into the great hall where the king and Kalan were sitting much as he had left them.

"She's going after that bastard Gyp," he raged. He turned on the king and pointed an accusing finger at him. "It's your fault. She begged your assistance. But no, you wanted to play a cat-and-mouse game with Gyp. You thought to put her off until you had a better understanding of Gyp's true intentions. That poor old man—Lord Amorgos—was most certainly poisoned. Lady Syrah feared for her brother's life. Perhaps for her own. Certainly for her virtue. She took the only course open to her. She faked their deaths so Gyp would not hunt them down. She wasn't going to buy him off with her gold and he wasn't going to vacate her hall now that he held it. No, she intends to hire mercenaries to get rid of him."

God Almighty, how she could think to deal with such men?

"Do you know what she said to me when I offered her my assistance and she declined it?" Jibril shouted at his father. "I boasted that the power of the Crown could do anything. Do you know what she said, do you? She said, 'Yes, the power of the Crown can do anything. *If* it so chooses.'"

Jibril dropped into his carved teak chair, his fury suddenly spent.

King Ahriman finally spoke into the long silence. "There is some truth in what you say. As you well know, I never intended to put the Ninth House into Gyp's hands, but it was imperative to keep an eye on his dealings with that blackguard Najja Kek. He wants that estate because it spans almost a hundred miles of the coast to the west; there are hidden bays enough to anchor a dozen pirate ships and caves to hide all manner of goods."

The king leaned forward. "I do not need to defend my actions to you or anyone else, Jibril. I have reigned thirty-two years and my sole care has ever been for my people. These damnable pirates loot and kill at will and must be stopped. But I will defend myself on one point: I received two letters from Lady Syrah. I appointed Amorgos as Eben's regent, certain that that kind man would do everything in his power to safeguard the interests of Lord Dhion during his illness."

The king summoned a serving girl to bring him more wine.

"Lady Syrah's second letter read much as the first. She petitioned me to allow her to sit as regent herself. I apprehended no particular alarm in her words, nor any intimation that she feared for the family's lives. Had Gyp tried to coerce her into marriage by compromising her virginity, she would most certainly have made mention of it."

The king frowned. "I wonder. Squire," he called to a lad stationed across the hall, "find Master Quarlos and tell him I require his presence in my study immediately."

Ten minutes later the king faced a curious but composed Quarlos across his desk. Jibril and Kalan sat to either side.

"Knowing how gossip tears through the palace," the king said with a smile, "you are no doubt aware that earlier this evening we learned that Lady Syrah of the Ninth House is alive, as are Lord Eben, Lady Morgana, and my poor friend Lord Dhion."

"Glad tidings indeed, sire," Quarlos said. "But is it not true that her ladyship is responsible for the Crown Prince's abduction? I have heard such."

"That would appear to be the case. It seems she took

some foolish notion that Lord Ranulph intended to remain in her hall indefinitely and that the family was in some danger from him. It is nonsense, of course, but you may recall that she sent me two letters regarding the regency for Lord Eben."

"I do indeed, sire."

The king folded his hands and leaned forward. "During the course of his captivity, my son had the impression that Lady Syrah's concerns were of a very serious nature. We are uncertain of the particulars, but I wonder if perhaps she sent a third letter that did not reach me. As my private secretary, you handle all my correspondence, which is why I have summoned you this evening."

Quarlos frowned, deep in concentration. Finally, he shook his head. "Nay, sire, as I recall you received but two letters from Lady Syrah. If there was a third, it did not reach the palace, else I would have known of it. It is not unusual for letters to be lost along the road."

"You are quite certain?"

Quarlos nodded emphatically. "Quite certain, sire."

"Well, then," the king said, leaning back, "that is that. We must look elsewhere for answers."

Jibril was on his feet almost before the door closed behind Master Quarlos. "He's lying."

"Yes," said the king. "I believe he is."

Jibril settled back in the brass tub that had been specially built for his six-foot three-inch frame. Wisps of spice-scented steam curled lazily through the heated bathing room as Jibril allowed the hot water to work out the stress of the evening's revelations.

Unable to sleep, he had roused two of his guards for an impromptu practice session with the falchion, sending them back to their pallets bruised and befuddled. Startled maids were summoned to prepare a bath for him in the middle of the night. Lady Peliana had appeared at his chamber door to offer her own unusual talents to console the prince in his hour of distress, but had been summarily sent on her way.

Jibril closed his eyes, remembering that sweet sodden girl

kneeling before him in the rain; the whore who had felt so right in his arms; the lone rider flying down the beach, her blue cloak and pale hair streaming behind her. These three women were but one: Syrah.

Jibril's arousal was almost painful. Where was she now? He wanted her, needed to feel her trembling beneath his lips, taste again the salty-sweet dew of her release. He wanted her here, now. His enchantress.

His queen.

Chapter Fourteen

Harlot. Slop girl. Now an itinerant vendor of honeyed almonds and dried fruits. What would her next role be? Syrah mused. Acrobat? Shepherdess? Nun?

At least she wasn't painted up like a tart or lurking in some foul privy. Hanging about this inn for the last two days, clad in a new blue tunic with clean hair and fingernails, was definitely a step up in the world.

Eben, perched upon a fence rail, presented a perfect picture of a shiftless young man with nothing better to do with his time than leer at buxom serving girls. Syrah wasn't sure all that leering was part of the act. Eben was, after all, fourteen, a time of life when eyeing the attributes of every passing female admitted a young man into the sacred precinct of male obsessions.

Syrah crossed the inn yard to lean against the fence next to her brother. "I just wish he'd get here," she complained. "If I hear one more lewd suggestion, someone is going to get hurt."

"One of the stable boys said he was coming today for sure."

Syrah popped an almond into her mouth. "We're not likely to miss him. If he's anything like his description, we'd have to be blind. A black giant. Not someone we're likely to miss."

"I heard he's got cuts all over his face. Not the kind you get in a fight. They're decorations. They say he was a prince in his own country and one day he got angry and killed his brother and ate him."

"Good heavens, that's utter foolishness."

"Sometimes people eat other people," Eben asserted. "I don't expect they taste very good. Not like worms."

"Don't start, Eben," Syrah warned.

A shout rang out from the upper story of the inn. "It's Zebengo. He's coming."

Suddenly, the yard was filled with people jockeying for the best position to see the legendary mercenary ride through the gate. Syrah climbed up beside Eben, her heart beating faster as the sound of approaching hooves thundered along the lane. Three horsemen galloped into the yard, stirring up a cloud of dust so thick Syrah could barely see them as they dismounted and threw their reins to the stable boys.

An enormous apparition appeared out of the swirl of dust, dwarfing his companions and everyone present by a good foot. His ebony skin gleamed in the sun, gold glittered amid impossibly white teeth, and black eyes surveyed the yard with a chilling intensity. For a moment they settled on Syrah, and she wished herself anywhere but here; a privy would do quite nicely at this point.

The giant winked at her and disappeared into the cool darkness of the inn.

"Did you see that?" Eben breathed.

Syrah nodded. She'd seen. She just didn't believe it.

"No doubt about it," she said. "The man ate his brother."

Syrah shifted onto her back and stared up at the sky, blacker than black, sprinkled with tiny stars. When she was very young she had believed the stars were fairy dust. Then a sour old priest had decreed that stars were holy lights shining through tiny windows in heaven. Stars were whirling spheres of fire impossibly far away, Great Uncle Amorgos had explained.

Whatever they were, Syrah wondered if you could somehow fly to them. And if you could, would you find people just like you? Were there fair damsels and charming princes? Did they live happily ever after?

She flopped over onto her belly. Eben slept soundly a few feet away on the other side of the fire. They had set up camp in a picturesque little glen where the moss was soft and thick upon the ground, but Syrah had gotten precious little sleep the past two nights.

A tear slid down her cheek. She brushed it away, willing herself not to cry again. Prince Jibril haunted her every moment, day and night. Oh, she put on a brave front for Eben, but it had taken willpower she never knew she possessed to get on with the plan after she left the Isle of Lost Souls.

Perhaps the prelate of Pailacca had been right: You did lose your soul if you ventured onto that haunted crag. But it wasn't the devil that had claimed Syrah's soul. It was a dark-haired, amber-eyed, hard-bodied man who had teased her and infuriated her and made her laugh. Who had awakened her to desire and kissed her and touched her and sent her soaring toward the celestial light of heaven and the spinning spheres of fire and the clouds of sparkling fairy dust.

"Bosomsmmms," Eben murmured in his sleep, jolting Syrah from her own erotic imaginings.

She heaved a sigh and resolutely steered her thoughts toward her plans for the morrow. She would find a way to speak with Zebengo alone; explain precisely what she required of him; and secure his interest with one or two gold discs, promising half an agreed-upon sum at the start of the enterprise and half when Ranulph had been ousted from her hall.

Zebengo couldn't possibly guess she was in a position to offer a fortune of five hundred gold discs, if necessary, for his services. Most likely he would demand fifty, possibly as much as a hundred. Syrah felt secure that should he demand more, she held the advantage.

By this time tomorrow night everything would be settled. They would have their mercenary.

How hard could it be?

He's just a man like any other man, Syrah reminded herself sternly as she poked her head around the door to the main room of the tavern in search of her quarry. Except there was a lot more of him. Two benches pushed together could barely contain his muscled bulk. One enormous paw encircled an entire pitcher of ale. Why, his neck must be as thick as her own thigh! His thigh must be as big around as a tree and his . . . Syrah blinked several times, trying to blot out the unladylike image that popped into her mind's eye but without much success. Ever since Prince Jibril had unveiled his own impressive endowment to her maidenly gaze, she sometimes found herself speculating about the . . . proportions of other men. A thousand Hail Marys weren't likely to afford absolution for such a grievous sin; she was almost certainly going to burn in hell.

"What are you waiting for?" Eben urged. "Go talk to him."

"I'm going, I'm going." She squared her shoulders, stepped across the threshold, and froze to the spot. Every eye turned toward her, or so it seemed. Conversation stopped. Male eyes assessed, female eyes narrowed.

Syrah lifted her chin a notch and made her way through the rough-hewn tables toward the far corner where Zebengo sat with his two cohorts. The patrons turned back to their companions, the hum of conversation resumed.

One thing was clear: Zebengo commanded the room simply by being in it. Men and women went about their business—eating, drinking, gaming, lusting—seemingly oblivious of the famous mercenary in their midst, but truth be told, this was not a man to be ignored. And well he knew it, Syrah reflected, as he lounged indolently against the wall. Treat this just as you would a chess game, she told herself.

She bobbed a little curtsy. "Good evening, sir. I wonder if I might have a few minutes of your time."

A lazy, rather charming grin spread across his broad face. "Only a few minutes? Two, three?"

"Yes, I'm sure that would do for this evening," Syrah replied, encouraged by his willingness to speak with her. Perhaps this wasn't going to be so difficult after all. "If that's all you can manage."

"All I can manage?" Zebengo turned to his companions. "This sweet little thing wants to know if I can manage two or three minutes." All three men burst out laughing.

Syrah frowned, unable to see the humor in her simple request. "Of course, I'll need at least ten minutes to finish. We can resume tomorrow if that's convenient. I'd rather get it over with this evening, but I understand if you have another commitment."

Syrah's eyes narrowed. The men were holding their sides, gasping for air.

"Really, gentlemen," she scolded, "I fail to see what's so funny. I am here on business. You are in the business of hiring yourselves out for pay, are you not?"

One man pounded on the table, so convulsed with laughter he could barely draw a breath; the other slid to the floor.

Syrah was fast losing patience. If the matter were not so urgent, she would have emptied the pitcher of ale over their heads and marched out the door.

Thoroughly fed up, she pulled five gold discs from her pocket and slapped them down on the table.

There, that ought to get their attention.

"So you see," Syrah concluded, having neatly managed to skip over the entire kidnapping episode, "my cousin need employ only a few dozen men to hold the Great House. He believes my family perished at sea and only awaits the king's official proclamation to assume the high seat. He holds the hall legitimately and there is no one to challenge his claim."

Zebengo tilted back his chair and studied the two expectant faces across the table. "You seem certain the king has given Gyp his assurances. I make it my business to know everything that goes on in the palace and I have heard nothing of it."

"I can't really know for sure," Syrah conceded. "All I know is the king didn't lift a finger to help us after our great uncle died. I sent him an urgent letter; I told him I suspected poison and I feared Eben might be in danger. I asked him to appoint me regent. Then Ranulph would have had to leave."

"And the other thing," Eben reminded her.

"I don't want to talk about that, Eben. It's not important."

"Well, I think it is. Ranulph tried to force her to . . . He was furious when my sister wouldn't marry him. I guess he thought if he bedded her, she'd have to agree."

Zebengo tilted his chair back against the wall and folded his arms across his chest. "What did he do, Lady Syrah?" he said softly.

Syrah looked down at her hands in her lap.

"He lured her out to the stable when he thought everyone was at chapel, and when she tried to fight him off he hit her, is what the bastard did," Eben said with a growl.

"Eben, please—"

"I'm going to kill him. I'm going to hack off his—"

"Eben!"

"I take it, my lady, that you came to no serious harm," Zebengo interjected.

Syrah straightened up. "No, no harm at all," she said briskly. "Fortunately, two squires rode into the stable yard and Ranulph stormed out. I did not think it sufficiently important to tell the king. In any event, it was obvious by then that His Majesty had little interest in our affairs. I had not even the courtesy of a reply. You know the rest."

They had moved into a small alcove for privacy. Zebengo pulled back the curtain and summoned a serving girl to bring more ale.

"My services do not come cheap," he informed them when the girl had departed.

Syrah watched him carefully. "We are well aware of that. I'm sure we can come to some arrangement."

"Make me an offer, my lady."

"Perhaps you should state your terms first, sir," she said. "Then we shall see how well we understand one another."

The mercenary laughed. "I believe we already understand one another very well."

Syrah smiled prettily at him. "All this is so new to me, sir. Matters of business lie outside the province of a woman's skills. I cannot imagine how to go about it."

Zebengo wagged a long finger at her. "I suspect you know very well how to go about it. I cannot think of ten men who could have planned such a scheme as you propose."

"You flatter me, sir."

Zebengo poured more ale. "Let me say—just to lay a foundation for our negotiations—that my assistance to the Crown in tracking down a band of brigands recently brought me and my associates one hundred and fifty gold discs."

Syrah affected surprise. "So much?"

"It was a very dangerous assignment."

She pounced. "As I explained, retaking our hall poses little or no risk to you or your men. I expect we should take that into account."

The mercenary threw back his head and laughed. "Well played, Lady Syrah."

Syrah blushed. "Thank you."

Zebengo stretched and stood up. "It grows late. I leave for the capital in the morning on other business. When I return I'm sure we can come to terms."

"Then you'll help us?" Eben said.

"Yes, I will help you. On one condition: You and your sister will remain here until I send word that it is safe for you to return to your estate."

"What?" Syrah and Eben exclaimed in unison.

"Impossible," Syrah cried. "We had to leave many servants and their children behind. I will have to warn them. They are my responsibility and I won't have them put in danger."

Zebengo pinned her with a cold eye. "You worry about their safety. What of your own? What do you think Gyp will do to you when he learns you're still alive?"

"That's right," Eben said to her. "He'll go after you like he did before. But there's no reason I can't go with you, Zebengo. I can fight. I'm not afraid. I stand for my father, armiger of the Ninth House. It is my duty."

"Your duty to your people is to stay alive," Zebengo replied harshly. "Otherwise there will be no Ninth House."

Eben tossed another pinecone into the fire; it sizzled and sparked as the flames fed on it. He frowned. Something about Zebengo bothered him, but he couldn't quite put a finger on it.

"I've been thinking."

Syrah ran a silver comb through her long hair, still damp from a dip in the cold stream at the bottom of the glen. She had been daydreaming about hot baths and oil of citrus and ginger and rosemary; Mayenne brushing and brushing her hair until it shone; scented linens and cook's wonderful persimmon pudding.

"Mmmm?"

"I've been thinking about Zebengo."

"What about him?"

"There's something wrong about him."

Syrah leaned closer to the fire. The evening had turned cool and she didn't want to curl up in her warm blankets with wet hair. "He comes from another country; that's probably why you think so. After all, everything we heard about him led us to believe he would be a barbarian and he isn't at all. He's polite, intelligent, and well spoken."

Eben gazed into the flames. "That's just it. He's a mercenary, but he's obviously educated and he speaks our language so well you would think he'd been born here."

"I noticed that, too. Perhaps he's been here a long time."

"Didn't you think it was strange that he went off to the capital without finishing his business with us? And he didn't even ask us if we could afford a hundred and fifty gold discs."

Syrah paused, trying to reason it out. "He knows we're children of the Ninth House. Papa's rich."

"Yes, but wouldn't he be wondering how we would get at our treasury when Ranulph holds the hall?"

Syrah pulled a blanket around her shoulders and stared into the fire. "Perhaps if he thought if we could give him five gold discs just to get him to talk to us, we'd have a lot more."

Eben scooted beneath his blankets and curled up facing the fire. "I really liked him, but I still think there's something wrong about him."

Long after Eben had fallen asleep, Syrah was still staring into the dying embers. She, too, had liked Zebengo, but Eben had raised some good questions. The mercenary was due back at the inn tomorrow evening, but before they dealt further with him Syrah intended to get some answers.

Fifty miles away the king, also, was staring into the embers of a dying fire.

"I don't like it," Jibril said for the third time.

"It's a good plan, son."

Jibril leaped out of his chair. "Didn't you hear what Obike just told us? Gyp tried to force himself on her. And we're going to send her back into his clutches? I won't have it."

"Sit down. You're letting your feelings for this girl get in the way of your common sense. It's a perfect strategy to get Gyp once and for all and you know it. We'll take every precaution to ensure that she's not harmed."

Jibril glared at his father. "I don't have feelings for her; I'm just sorry for her, that's all. She's gone through enough. In the space of a single year she loses her mother, takes on the care of a father who can barely remember his name, and the management of a huge estate. Gyp forces his way in, kills Amorgos, threatens her brother, and tries to rape her. She's not going to know it's just a ploy for us to get at Gyp. She's going to see herself as a sacrificial lamb. And believe me, she's not going to thank us when she figures it out."

Obike Zebengo laughed. "From what I've seen of Lady Syrah, she's not exactly a little flower."

"I'll drink to that," Kalan said.

"And I," said the king.

Nine men sat around the enormous stone hearth of the king's fishing lodge a few miles outside the capital. The servants had been sent away, leaving behind an ample supply of ale and wine. The king had asked five of his elite guard to join them. They had come together less than six hours after the message from Zebengo reached the palace that the Dhions were alive and that Lady Syrah and her brother had tried to hire him to drive Ranulph Gyp from their hall.

"How much did she offer you, Obike?" the king inquired.

"Nothing yet. She's finessing and damned good at it."

"Would it surprise you," the king said, "to know that the lady holds five hundred gold discs from my personal treasury?"

"Not at all." Zebengo grinned. "It didn't take much imagination to realize she was the mysterious lady kidnapper."

He turned to Jibril, who was scowling at his boots. "It couldn't have been too unpleasant an interlude. She's lovely."

"I never saw her," Jibril muttered.

"Maybe not her face." Kalan smirked.

Jibril was halfway out of his chair before the king ordered him to sit down again.

"Enough of this, Jibril. Kalan, be silent. I have no patience with either one of you. It is my decision to go ahead with our plan. Let us review it."

He paced slowly back and forth before the hearth.

"Kalan, you and five guards will accompany Obike back to the inn. You will take Lady Syrah and her brother into custody in full sight of the patrons and servants. Treat them as you would any other enemy of the Crown. You will, of course, be careful not to injure them in so doing. Bring them to Suriana. I will have them brought before me in my public receiving room. It will be interesting to observe Lord Ranulph's reaction to their capture. I will then announce my intention to take under advisement the appropriate punishment for their treason. Out of deference to their noble station, I will be magnanimous and spare them the dungeons; they will be held in heavily guarded private chambers."

The king paused. "Any questions so far?" Meeting with no response save a low growl from his son, he continued.

"I will meet privately with Lord Ranulph to seek his counsel as to what is to be done with Lady Syrah and her brother. He will be flattered. I will encourage his input; after all, they have sullied his reputation with baseless accusations. I expect he will do one of two things. Either he will insist they be banished from the Dominion because of their treachery, or he may think better of it and forgive their foul accusations on condition that I order Lady Syrah to marry him. He will, of course, welcome Lord Dhion, Eben, and little Morgana to return to his protection in their hall."

"I don't like it at all," Jibril muttered.

"You have made that abundantly clear," the king said dryly. "If he's smart, Gyp will counsel me to choose the latter option. While members of the Dhion family still live, he will never take the high seat. Precedent decrees that in such an event the Ninth House be stricken from the Rolls and its land confiscated by the Crown.

"I will order Lady Syrah and Eben to return to their estate under escort. Lest Lord Dhion meet the same fate as his uncle, I will keep him here at the palace on the pretense that he is too ill to travel. And then we shall see."

"May I speak, Your Majesty?" one of his guard said.

"Of course, Majan."

"We of the guard often hear stories that may not reach your ears. Gyp is a well-known lecher and has debauched many serving wenches in his own hall, some as young as twelve. He is said to be brutal in his pleasures. I must agree with Prince Jibril that Lady Syrah will be in much danger."

"Finally," Jibril snorted, "someone with common sense. Gyp tried to force her to his bed once. He won't hesitate to do so again."

The king frowned. "I think not. I can safeguard her by implying my consent to a marriage between them, but withhold my official sanction for the time being. With such a prize within his reach, Lord Ranulph will not dare cross me."

King Ahriman returned to his chair and took up a jeweled goblet. "What we need here is time, gentlemen. We need eyes and ears in that hall to discover the nature of Lord Ranulph's dealings with his pirate friends and their plans for the time when he will supposedly hold a considerable stretch of the western coastline."

He sipped at his wine. "To accomplish both objectives—protect Lady Syrah and Lord Eben and obtain information—we will send several of our trusted servants to attend her, including several of my guard in disguise. And you, Obike, will appear at Lord Ranulph's door to discuss some nefarious business of your own with him. Offer him your services. After all, you are the Dominion's most notorious mercenary, are you not?"

Zebengo smiled broadly. "Yes, Your Majesty. You have made me so."

Jibril cast a suspicious glance in Zebengo's direction. "You seem very eager to stand as Lady Syrah's champion."

"Indeed I am, Jibril. After all, I have seen her face."

Jibril scowled into his ale.

"Come, old friend, do not be cast down," Obike said, throwing his arm around the prince's shoulders as they staggered up the broad staircase that led to the private east wing of the palace. They had, between them, consumed nearly an entire keg in the hours since the king had adjourned the meeting and retired to the side of his beautiful queen.

"Now that you have found your fair damsel in distress, do you think I would foil your plans to save her from a fate crueler than death and then to make her your queen?"

Convinced he couldn't take another step without falling flat on his face, Jibril sank down at the top of the staircase and belched. "You don't know what you're talking about. Damsel in distress? That little hellion will have her cousin trussed up like a goose ready for the spit before I can even saddle my horse to ride to her rescue. And Eben will probably talk him to death before the fire is lit."

Obike held on to the newel post as he carefully lowered himself onto the step beside Jibril. "Come now, you are in love with the girl, that is obvious. She is everything a man like you could want—intelligent, brave, resourceful. And from what you and I are able to put together—I her face, you the rest of her—she must be a very desirable woman."

"She's irresponsible, reckless, and a danger to herself and others, is what she is," the prince said with a growl. "There's no stopping her when she gets an idea into her head."

"You exaggerate," Obike said. "She seemed reasonable enough to me, or at least as reasonable as one can expect a woman to be. Why, when I told her she couldn't go home until I had secured the hall, she hardly objected at all."

Jibril's head snapped around. "Are you insane? You told her she wasn't to ride with you when you set out to take the hall?"

"Shouldn't I have?" Zebengo said cautiously.

"No, you damn well shouldn't," Jibril shouted, startling a guard stationed outside the royal bedchamber at the far end of the corridor. "She thinks she's on a holy crusade. She probably intends to ride over the drawbridge like King Richard storming the gates of Jerusalem. She isn't going to be content to trot up on a little palfrey after the enemy has quit the field!"

Jibril looked glum. "This is not a reasonable woman we're talking about. You probably won't have to worry about coming to terms with her tomorrow. We'll be lucky if she isn't a hundred miles away, offering five hundred gold discs to some blackguard who couldn't find his own shaft in full sunlight."

Chapter Fifteen

The blacking boy gave a high leather boot a final swipe with his polishing cloth and set it down on the bench beside him. He took another and set to work scraping mud from the sole.

"All I know is he got the biggest feet in the world," he told Eben. "I got to charge him extra 'cause it takes twice as long to do his boots and I got to use twice as much blacking. He's real particular, too."

Eben leaned forward and whispered, "I heard he ate his own brother."

The boot boy shook his head. "Naw, it was his father he ate. Everyone knows that."

"Maybe that's why he's here in the Dominion," Eben suggested. "He ate his father and then he had to run away because they were going to tie him naked to a stake in the hot sun and smear honey all over him and let the army ants eat him alive."

"It'd take a lot of ants to eat Zebengo," the boot boy sniggered. " 'Sides he's too smart to get caught. He never gets caught, even when the king sends a whole troop of soldiers after him. Prince Jibril came looking for him here once. I seen him myself."

"And?" Eben prompted.

"Well, it was strange 'cause the prince didn't try to capture him or nothing."

"Eben! Eben, where are you?"

Syrah came dashing around to the back of the stable and skidded to a halt, gasping for breath. "I thought I'd never find you. He's here. He just rode in. I didn't expect him until much later, and I haven't even had time to question that maid who promised to meet me behind the bake house."

Eben scrambled to his feet. "Syrah, this boy just told me that—"

Syrah grabbed his arm and dragged him toward the inn. "We don't have time. Tell me later. I want you to find Zebengo. Tell him I've decided seventy-five gold discs is a fair price and I'll join you in his room shortly. Keep him talking until I get there. Stay near the window. If I learn anything suspicious, I'll whistle and you make some excuse to get out of there."

"What am I supposed to talk about until you come?"

"You'll think of something. You always do."

"So you fancy him, do you?" The blowsy maid snickered.

If this was going to get her the information she needed, Syrah decided she was going to fancy the black giant. "I think he's powerful good-looking. And so savage with those scars on his face. I've heard stories of what savages like to do to women, and the women keep coming back for more."

The serving girl looked Syrah up and down. "You're not his type. He likes a big woman with a lot of cushion on her. Ain't many can accommodate him, if you get my meaning."

"You mean he's . . . ?"

"Biggest I ever seen."

Syrah's eyes went wide. "You mean you've been with him? What was he like?" she asked breathlessly.

The girl took another handful of honeyed almonds from Syrah's basket and crammed them into her mouth. "Couldn't hardly walk the next day."

Syrah couldn't believe she actually asked the next question, but somehow it just slipped out. "Someone told me he likes to make a woman use her mouth."

"Nothing unnatural about that," the girl scoffed, reaching for the dried fruits. "Never met a man didn't want that."

This was more information about carnal sport than Syrah wanted to hear at the moment. She steered her inquiries into less thought-provoking waters.

"I heard he's a prince and he ran away on a pirate ship after he carved up his brother and ate him."

"It was his uncle, not his brother. Everyone knows that."

"Anyhow, that's how he came to the Dominion."

"Don't know about him being a prince. Maybe it's true—he grew up in the palace."

"*What?*"

The girl wiped her hands on her grubby apron and stood up to leave. "I heard tell him and Prince Jibril are friends, even if Zebengo is a mercenary." She looked dreamy. "Prince Jibril, now there's a man I wouldn't mind a tumble with."

Syrah sat paralyzed, watching her sashay off toward the kitchens, trying to wrap her mind around the girl's words.

Suddenly she was on her feet. "Oh, God, I have to get Eben out of there!"

Tucked into the embrasure of the window, Eben had a good view of the stable yard. If Syrah needed to find him he'd be in full view. He was becoming increasingly uneasy. He'd found not only Zebengo in the upper chamber but two other men he didn't recognize; he hadn't seen them around the inn and they weren't the same ones that rode in with Zebengo two days ago. All three sat around the table picking at a cold supper of fowl and salted hare, cheese, bread, and figs. He'd caught the two men eyeing him more than once. Something wasn't right here.

"Sure you won't join us?" the mercenary asked.

"Thank you, but I'll wait till my sister gets here.

"Where did you say she'd gone?" Zebengo asked around a mouthful of pheasant.

Eben eyed the distance to the door. The mercenary was asking too many questions. "I didn't."

Zebengo raised an eyebrow. "It's a secret then?"

Eben needed to stall. "I guess it wouldn't hurt to tell you, now that we're partners and all."

"Certainly not," Zebengo assured him.

"She went down to the lake to get some frogs."

"Frogs."

"Frogs," Eben confirmed.

"And what does she do with her frogs?" Zebengo inquired, unable to visualize the lovely Lady Syrah slopping about in the mud in search of frogs.

"She blows them up."

A piece of pheasant fell out of Zebengo's open mouth and plopped into his ale. "You're telling me Lady Syrah blows up frogs? You mean she piles them up and lights black powder?" he said when he could again find his voice.

Eben frowned. "Why would she want to do that?"

"You just said she blew them up, did you not?"

"I don't understand the question. Oh, I see what you mean." Eben nodded. "No, she does it the other way."

"There's another way?"

"Of course. You blow into their mouths and they just sort of explode. Not everyone can do it," Eben continued, warming to his story. "It takes a lot of practice. We're all very proud of her." He beamed.

He pulled some dried almonds from his pocket and munched thoughtfully. "It sounds easy, but you'd be surprised. First you get your frog. Not just any frog will do. It can't be too big or else you can't get your mouth around it."

Eben ignored the gagging sounds coming from the vicinity of the commode.

He cupped his hands just so. "You can't squeeze too hard or it gets all squishy, which defeats the purpose, don't you agree? You want it full of air."

One of the men scraped back his chair with a groan and dropped his head between his knees.

"You have to be careful not to look in its eyes because it

149

knows what's coming. Frogs sense these things and they don't take it very well. You start slowly, just a few puffs, to get into the rhythm of it, and—"

A low whistle sounded below. Eben shifted position slightly; from the corner of his eye he could see Syrah gesticulating frantically below. He surveyed the room, noting one man still crouched over the commode. The other had regained his composure but looked somewhat ashen.

Eben hopped off the windowsill and strolled over to the table, hoping no one else had heard the whistle. He selected a gingered fig and slurped it into his mouth. "So," he continued, glancing at Zebengo to see if he believed the outrageous story, "that's how you begin."

The big man was watching him carefully; he didn't look at all repulsed, as he should. Eben drifted toward the door.

Suddenly, Zebengo was out of his chair with an agility surprising in a man of his size. He positioned himself between Eben and the door, an insurmountable mountain of solid muscle.

"Hell," Eben muttered, then hurtled across the room, and catapulted himself straight out the window.

Syrah's heart stopped dead in her chest. She could not even summon up a scream. Just when it appeared Eben was going to slam headfirst into the hard-packed dirt of the stable yard, he flipped over and landed neatly on his feet.

Shouts could be heard from the inn. Curious faces crowded the windows. People milled about in confusion. Eben grabbed Syrah's hand and dragged her behind him as he ran toward the stable where a piebald mare, still saddled, nibbled at a pile of hay. Footsteps pounded behind them. Eben threw Syrah across the saddle like a sack of grain, leaped up behind her, and seized the reins.

Hands grabbed at his legs but he kicked them away. Syrah started to slide off the saddle as more hands clutched at her skirts.

"Hang on, hang on," Eben shouted. Syrah made a desperate grab for the saddle horn but in vain. A strong arm came around her waist and pulled her hard against an implacable chest.

"Go, go," she shouted at Eben.

He hesitated for a second, kicked the mare's flanks, and streaked out into the night.

Syrah struggled against the impossibly strong grip that held her fast. She kicked back, trying to find a shin but connecting only with a thick leather boot.

"Give over, traitor," a voice threatened. "You are well and truly caught."

"Never," Syrah shouted, sinking her teeth into a hairy forearm.

He let go of her in surprise. "You bit me!"

Syrah sprinted across the stable yard and plunged into the cheering mob that had gathered for the entertainment. She made it as far as the hog pens before the breath was knocked out of her when she was tackled from behind. As she lay shaking with anger and terror, her hands were bound and she was flipped over.

She squinted up into the hard eyes of her captor, none other than the captain of Prince Jibril's personal guard.

"Nini of Dunataea. We meet again."

Chapter Sixteen

"This is your place," the Voice said as a gentle hand set her down. "I have made it so. Guard it well, child."

Syrah Eliaza Oriana Dhion stood amidst sweetly scented grasses and wildflowers of saffron, ivory, and blush-rose. Far above in a cobalt sky, a golden-haired goddess sat at her loom weaving clouds from delicate strands of silver silk.

"I love this place. I will never leave it."

"Someday you must choose," said the Voice. "Farewell."

The moon rose and the child danced in its silver light. The rains came and the child danced beneath the sweeping clouds. She danced for joy. This was her place and she would never leave it.

One rosy dawn, when Syrah was no longer a child, she espied a garden. In the midst of sparkling glass flowers stood a beautiful man, gentle of countenance, with flowing golden hair. She ventured forth from the world of waving grasses, but when she reached the garden he shook his head and pointed to a distant dark wood.

"The garden is beautiful but it is not your place," he said as he faded away.

Syrah gazed into the shadows of the wood where a terrifying beast with yellow eyes awaited her, its head that of a panther, the rest the body of a man. "Come to me, Syrah," it said. In its embrace she had no memory of the waving grasses and the garden of glass flowers. Here was her place.

"No, Syrah, this is not your place," the beast said as it led her back to the edge of the wood. It pointed to a distant hill upon which stood an edifice of unyielding gray stone. "You must journey there, for that is the way to your place."

Syrah set out. On the way to the grim castle she passed by her place of waving grasses. But they stirred in the breeze no more. They lay crushed and broken and foul things crept among the stunted stalks. She wept until she could weep no longer. One day, she vowed, she would return. The foul things would be driven from their dens and the grasses and flowers would flourish once more. She had vowed to guard her place well, and so she would again.

The cold gray keep closed about her, a world of chill stone and still, stale air. So thick were its walls that at first she heard only her own breathing. Then came the sound of a bell tolling, a door opening, footfalls.

"No!" she cried aloud, "this cannot be my place. Voice, where are you? Help me."

Syrah's eyes opened to see the anxious face of an old woman peering down at her.

"Are you all right, my lady?"

"Yes, yes," Syrah replied, struggling to sit up. "I must have been dreaming."

"I've brought you a bit of bread and sweet wine," the woman said. "You've had a hard time of it. You'll need your strength. They'll be coming for you soon."

Syrah gazed about the small dismal room. She had fallen asleep as soon as her head touched the cold stone of the bench. It had been a long hard ride to the capital; they traveled overnight, stopping only once to rest the horses. She had had nothing to eat since yesterday noon and only water to drink, but she could not take a single bite of the bread the old woman held out to her. Wine, please," she murmured.

"My name is Depta," the old woman said, passing a glass

of mulled wine to her. "You are the talk of the palace. The hall is packed."

"Yes," said Syrah, "I shall make a fine show, shall I not?" She looked down at her blue tunic, so bright and clean just twelve hours ago, now wrinkled and filthy from her tussle with Captain Ankuli in the stable yard. She reached up to smooth her hair, which had come loose from the blue ribbon that tied it back from her face, and picked out bits of hay and leaves.

The old woman chuckled. "They say you are a she-devil and a traitor."

Syrah wet her lips with the sweet wine. "Perhaps I am."

"Nonsense," Depta snorted. "I often attended your mother and father when they came to the palace. They held their honor high and their child would do no less."

Heavy steps approached the thick wood door. Two tall grim-faced guards appeared. "It's time," one of them told her.

Syrah smiled at the old woman. "Thank you, Depta. Your kind words give me courage."

The guards took their places, one on each side of her. Out in the hallway two others fell into step behind her.

"Don't you worry, my lady," the old woman called after her. "All will be well."

Syrah studied the patterns inlaid on the marble floor of the oval-shaped room where great personages waited to be summoned to the presence of the king. Laughing-eyed dolphins sailed over white-frothed, sea-green waves, a fitting symbol of an island nation that stood neutral in times of war and unrest and welcomed all peoples to its shores.

She was no great personage, she thought ruefully, and wondered why she had not been left to wait in some dank cell. Beyond the open door, she could hear the excited buzz of the crowd in the receiving room. Once or twice a curious face would appear at the door, trying to catch a glimpse of her, only to be waved away by an imperious guard.

A horn sounded. An expectant silence settled upon the crowd. Syrah heard the rustle of silks as the ladies of the court curtsied low. King Ahriman would be entering the chamber; Jibril would surely be at his side.

Once, when she was fifteen, Syrah had ridden to the hunt with her father. For weeks she had pestered him until he reluctantly agreed to let her ride with him. Thrilled at the prospect and wishing to acquit herself well, she had risen early every morning to practice with her small bow. The stable boys set up a target against a bale of hay. Syrah practiced first from a standing position, then from atop a small gray gelding trained specially for the hunt.

The great day arrived. She rode out beside her father beneath a brilliant sky. Soon a magnificent stag was sighted high on a hillside and the chase was on. They cornered the sleek powerful beast in a glen speckled with sun and shadow. Winded and spent, it gazed calmly at its pursuers.

Syrah could not even lift her bow. Tears flowed down her cheeks as the proud stag went down in a hail of arrows. It raised its head one last time before it died, and Syrah felt it was looking straight at her, imparting some truth she was too young to understand. Her father had gathered her in front of him on his stallion, and she had wept into his chest all the way back to the Great House. She had never ridden to the hunt again.

As the guard led her into the long sumptuous hall, Syrah understood at last what the stag had wanted her to know: You cannot lose the race if you have run it well.

A stout self-important man arrayed in the official robes of his station, stepped forward. "Ahem. As Minister of Justice for his Most Merciful Majesty, King Ahriman, Lord of this Domain, I am charged to open this inquiry.

"Lady Syrah Eliaza Oriana Dhion, you stand before your king, his ministers, and the peers of this realm charged with the crime of high treason against the Crown," a somber voice intoned. "Do you understand the nature and the gravity of the charge laid against you?"

Syrah studied a pair of russet suede boots and the scarlet hem of the sweeping robes of state that must belong to the king. To her right, a pair of lavender silk slippers poked from beneath a pale silver gown embroidered with purple

155

and white flowers. Queen Alya. To her left, she could see a pair of gleaming, knee-high black boots, no doubt Jibril's.

"Yes, my lord," she said firmly without raising her eyes.

"I am commanded to read the charges against you. First—"

"A moment, Minister," a deep voice commanded. "Have the others brought before us before you begin."

Syrah froze. Others? She heard a door to the side of the room open; footsteps echoed through the vast hall as several people were brought before the dais.

The king spoke. "You have been brought before me so that you may bear witness to the charge of high treason against a member of your House."

Syrah turned to see Lord Dhion, Great Aunt Rosota, Aleden, and Clim standing uncertainly beneath the blazing chandeliers. Little Morgana held her grandfather's hand; the thumb of her other hand was stuck firmly in her mouth. Eben was not there, nor Mayenne.

Oblivious of her surroundings, Syrah glared at the guards who had herded the little group in. "How dare you leave a sick man standing like this?" she demanded. "Bring a chair for my father immediately—and one for my aunt as well."

A soldier looked to the dais uncertainly. The king signaled his assent with a little wave of his hand. Chairs were brought. Morgana climbed up onto her grandfather's lap and gazed solemnly around her. When she saw her sister she smiled. "Srah! I missed you. Will you pway with me?"

With a low cry Syrah started toward her, only to be restrained by a firm hand on her shoulder. Frightened, Morgana began to cry. It was all Syrah could do not to scream out her anger and frustration.

With a swish of silver skirts the queen rose and descended from the dais. She leaned down to Morgana and brushed her tears away. "Don't be frightened, little one," she crooned. "Your sister cannot play right now, but perhaps you will see her later." She plucked a minted pastille from a silk pouch at her waist and popped it into Morgana's mouth, patted her on the head, and resumed her seat on the dais.

The king cleared his throat. "Read the charges, Minister."

"Syrah Eliaza Oriana Dhion, these are the charges laid against you.

"First, that you did abduct the first son of the First House, Crown Prince Jibril Mekon Jirod Dhion, seizing him unawares and against his will by cunning, deceit, and artifice. Do you understand the charge?"

"I do understand, sir."

"Second, that you did procure dangerous herbs and potions and administer said herbs and potions to the Crown Prince by deceit in a glass of wine in order to render him malleable and senseless."

"Third, that you did confine the prince in a crate—"

"Coffin," Syrah muttered.

"Lady Syrah," the minister said severely, "do you find these proceedings amusing?"

She looked up at him, all innocence. "Oh, no, sir. I'm quite sure you don't intend them to be."

A few chortles ricocheted through the crowd.

"Very well," the minister said with a frown, "I shall proceed."

"Fourthly, that you conveyed His Highness to a place of confinement unsuitable to his rank and station."

Syrah bit back a sarcastic retort. After all her hard work. What a spoiled, ungrateful—

"Fifthly, that you did demand a ransom of one thousand gold discs from His Majesty for the release and safe return of his son and threatened 'dire consequence' if he did not accede to your demand.

"Sixthly, that you did, in the guise of a slop girl, trespass on His Majesty's private property, namely the hunting camp located near the river Korian, to retrieve said ransom."

A murmur of distaste washed through the crowd.

"Lastly, that during the course of his confinement you did threaten the Crown Prince with a—"

"Chessboard," Syrah said aloud, then clapped her hands over her mouth.

The minister glared down at her. ". . . a sharp instrument, namely a knife, when he tried to . . ."

On and on he droned. To the relief of everyone in the hall, he finally rolled up his parchment with a flourish and retired to his chair.

The king rose. His voice was soft, yet it carried the full length of the room.

"Lady Syrah, do you understand the gravity of the charges here stated against you?"

"Yes, Your Majesty."

"Do you understand that the penalty for high treason against the Crown is death?"

Syrah fought to control the fear in her voice. "Yes, Your Majesty."

"Do you wish to speak in your own behalf?"

For a moment Syrah was back in a sun-spangled glen, sobbing as a beleaguered stag stood his ground with dignity and grace. He had run his race well. She could do no less. She looked up into the king's eyes, so much like Jibril's.

"No, Your Majesty."

"Very well, We shall take this matter under advisement."

"Your Majesty, might I speak?" Syrah said.

"Of course, child. Your silence troubles me."

"The others you have brought before you should not suffer because of my actions. I alone am to blame. Our loyal steward, Aleden, tried to dissuade me at every turn but in the end had no choice but to obey my orders. Young Clim there is utterly without guile, being deaf and dumb. My great aunt Rosota sheltered us but she had no part in the abduction. Morgana, of course, you must hold blameless. As for Papa—Lord Dhion—he is ill, as you surely know. I beseech you to release them."

A quiet smile reached the king's eyes. "You speak eloquently, Lady Syrah." He descended from the dais and placed a hand on Lord Dhion's shoulder.

"How fare you, Akritos?"

Lord Dhion gazed up at him, confusion evident in his

eyes. "Well, sire. But I do not understand why we are here."

"Don't worry yourself about it. I invite you to remain here at the palace until your health is restored. My own physician will attend you. Lady Amorgos may remain by your side if she so wishes." He ruffled Morgana's hair. "And this little moppet will want to stay near her grandpapa. We shall have the nursery prepared."

Signaling the guard, the king ascended the dais as the little group was herded out the side door. He leaned back in his great chair.

Syrah bowed her head. "Thank you, sire."

Murmurs of approval swept through the crowd. Despite the size of the hall, its atmosphere was close and hot, but no one seemed inclined to seek cooler air outside. They gazed expectantly at the king as he prepared to speak.

"I am grieved, Lady Syrah," he began. "Grieved and surprised to see the first daughter of the Ninth House standing before me accused of treason, and her brother, the future armiger, not yet apprehended, under the same indictment. I did not think to see such a thing in my lifetime. We do not speak here only of treason," he continued solemnly, "but of honor. You bring dishonor upon your House when you dishonor us. Do you not understand that, child?"

Syrah's head snapped up. "If you would speak of honor, Your Majesty, you would do well to look to your own."

An awful silence settled over the room. No eye blinked. No muscle twitched. Not a hair stirred.

For long moments the king stared straight into her eyes. "Indeed?" he said softly.

Syrah met his gaze, her voice shaky at first but gaining strength with each word. "A king owes loyalty to his subjects, even as they owe loyalty to him. We lay our allegiance at your feet, if necessary our very lives. In return, you undertake to protect us and see to our welfare. It is a covenant, sire, one that you broke with my House when you allowed that *jackal* to enter my father's hall and feed upon us even as we lived."

Blind fury drove her on. "Where were you when my beloved uncle, Lord Amorgos, lay dying? Where were you

159

when Ranulph Gyp killed three men of our guard—one who had served us for twenty years, another thirty, yet another with a newborn son? Where were you when my cousin tried to force me into marriage, claiming a writ of betrothal my father would never have countenanced? And where, sire," she shouted up at him, "were you when I beseeched you to come to our aid as the jackal turned his eyes on my brother?"

King Ahriman rose slowly from his chair and in a quiet voice that sounded like thunder in the awful silence he informed the stunned crowd, "Lady Syrah is overwrought. Guards, clear the hall."

Syrah was past knowing what was going on around her. She sank to the floor and covered her face with shaking hands.

A few moments later a soft hand smelling of jasmine caressed Syrah's cheek. "Come, child, get up now." The hand guided her to her feet and smoothed her tangled hair back from her face. The queen smiled at her. "Take heart, child. All will be well."

Syrah looked around, surprised to see that the only people remaining in the huge hall were King Ahriman, Queen Alya, the prince, whose eyes she could not meet, and two other men, one she did not know, and the other the hateful Ranulph.

A guard brought a chair. Syrah sank down gratefully and folded her hands in her lap.

"We will leave aside for another time the accusations you lay at my feet," the king began. "Instead, let us examine your allegations against Lord Ranulph. I received two letters from you after the death of your mother. In one you described your father's illness and requested leave to serve as regent for Lord Eben until such time as your father could resume the high seat. After careful consideration, I chose to appoint Lord Amorgos for that post. His death was sudden, certainly, but there is nothing to indicate it was unnatural. Your second letter mentioned your suspicions but you brought no proof to my attention. Lord Ranulph offered to sit as regent, seeing it as his familial duty, and I saw no reason why he should not."

"But I sent a third, urgent message, Your Majesty," Syrah cried. "I told you my cousin tried to coerce me into marriage and that I feared for all our lives if I did not marry him."

"I received no such letter. Step forward, Master Quarlos."

The secretary almost stumbled on his official robes as he approached the dais.

"Master Quarlos, Lady Syrah insists she wrote a third letter beseeching my aid. What say you?"

Quarlos cast a surreptitious glance at Ranulph. "As I told you, sire, no such letter reached my desk. I would most certainly have brought it to your attention immediately had there been one."

Syrah leaped from her chair. "You're lying!"

"Sit down, Lady Syrah," the king ordered.

"Can't you see he's lying?" Syrah pleaded.

"Master Quarlos has served as my personal secretary with great merit for many years. I have no reason to doubt his word," the king told her sternly.

"Far more serious are the charges you have leveled against your cousin," he went on. "Not the least of them murder."

"My great uncle was in the best of health when he arrived at our hall. In less than a day he lay dying," Syrah said through clenched teeth.

"If I might speak, Your Majesty?" Ranulph interjected.

The king turned curious eyes upon him. "Certainly, Lord Ranulph. You are most closely concerned in these matters. I would hear what you have to say."

"When I first went to Lady Syrah to offer my assistance in her time of need, I saw at once that the strain of the last months had taken a serious toll on both her health and her reason."

Syrah was halfway out of her chair when the king barked, "You will stay seated, Lady Syrah, or we end this audience here and now."

"Given the recent death of her beloved mother and her

fears for her father's life," Ranulph continued smoothly, "the unfortunate death of poor Lord Amorgos was the last straw. I believe my dear cousin could not credit that fate could be so cruel. She must have a reason and so blamed me. I assure you, I felt the death of Lord Amorgos as keenly as she."

The king leaned back in his chair and steepled his fingers in concentration. "What of her allegation that you tried to coerce her into marriage?"

"You have seen the contract of betrothal yourself, sire. If she says I laid hands upon her, she mistook my intention, as young women are wont to do. I sought only to comfort her."

Syrah had to clench her teeth to keep from screaming.

"We seem to be at an impasse here," the king remarked. "Lady Syrah says one thing, Master Quarlos another, and Lord Ranulph still another. Let us adjourn. We will take the matter under advisement. In the meantime, Lady Syrah, you will be escorted to a more comfortable chamber. My wife will send women to attend you. You may even walk about the gardens, if you choose. Under escort, of course."

Syrah curtsied as the king led his wife from the hall through tall doors behind the dais. The four guards who had escorted her to the hall took up positions by the door, ready to march her away. For the first time since she had entered the hall Syrah allowed herself to look at Prince Jibril. He had not spoken a word during the entirety of the proceedings, yet there was not a moment when she had not been aware of him.

With an unreadable expression in his eyes, he bowed and strode away across the marble floor, the echo of his boots fading until he was out of sight.

Whatever the course of her life might prove to be, Syrah reflected sadly, he would not be part of it. And if she should find her true place he would not be there to share it with her.

* * *

"Jackal. What an apt description of the man," the queen fumed as she tossed her crimson robe onto the silk coverlet and climbed into the high bed beside her husband. "All that sanctimonious drivel about 'poor Lord Amorgos' and the welfare of his 'dear cousin.'"

The king settled himself more comfortably with his hands behind his head. "I'm going to send her home with Gyp. I hate to deceive the girl, but I can see no other way to find out what the scoundrel is up to. It provides the perfect opportunity to put spies in place inside the hall. I wish I could tell her, but the more she knows the more danger she'll be in."

The queen snuggled down beside her husband. "I think it's cruel. I know she was misguided when she kidnapped Jibril but he was never in danger. You can't deny her cause was just."

"Quarlos," the king said grimly. "He's been with me for twelve years. I never thought him a greedy man, but Gyp must be paying him an enormous sum to betray me like this."

"Perhaps Gyp holds some power over him. You might want to find out what it is. He might be able to provide useful information."

The king smiled down at the lovely woman who was his queen, the mother of his eight children, still beautiful in his eyes after thirty-one years of marriage. "A good idea, my dear. You're rather wise—for a woman."

Alya reached beneath his white sleeping robe and began tickling him mercilessly.

"Stop, stop," he gasped.

"Take it back."

"Yes, yes, I take it back," he said, laughing. He flopped onto his back and stared up at the star-spangled purple canopy of their bed. "I thought Jibril was going to go for Gyp's jugular."

"I thought he was going to go for yours," the queen remarked. "I thought he was going to toss Syrah over his shoulder and flee into the night with her."

"Yes." The king chortled. "It was all he could do to keep his seat. Our boy's in love, Alya. She will make him a splendid queen."

"As I have you?" she teased, batting her eyelashes at him. The king laughed and reached for her.

Chapter Seventeen

Reports of Prince Jibril's release and the subsequent arrest of none other than Lady Syrah Dhion brought every man, woman, and child in the Dominion to the market squares and village fountains, avid to hear every last detail. They were insatiable. Every recitation of the events altered in the telling; every delicious scrap of rumor, gossip, and innuendo titillated and teased; surmise upon surmise piled up until it scarcely signified what the truth of the matter might be.

A number of facts were universally acknowledged.

The prince had been discovered barely clinging to life, horribly mutilated, a raving lunatic. The Holy Father himself had dispatched an exorcist to rid the prince of the fiends that now possessed his soul. The outlook was not good.

The king had had to be confined by his own guard in an iron cage, manacled hand and foot, where he howled ceaselessly day and night for vengeance. The queen had fallen insensate to the floor when she beheld the wretched relic that had been her beloved firstborn son carried upon a litter into the palace. The prince's childhood friend and captain of his personal guard had fallen upon his sword. Two of the prince's former mistresses had taken the veil.

Little was actually known of Lady Syrah Dhion, save that she had risen from the dead. Her brother, Lord Eben, had disappeared. Cannibalism was suspected.

The roads of the Dominion were nearly impassable as thousands of the curious set out for the capital with high hopes of witnessing, if not an actual exorcism or inquisition by torture of Lady Syrah, at the very least her execution. The fact that an Inquisitor had never been allowed to set foot in the Dominion, torture had been banned generations ago, and a public execution hadn't taken place for over a century did nothing to dampen the enthusiasm of the excited pilgrims upon the road.

Others flocked to the Isle of Lost Souls. For a few coins, enterprising young men led breathless sightseers across the causeway to view the fearsome ruins and stand in the very cell where Prince Jibril had courageously met his awful fate. Vendors did a brisk business in ale and meat pies, as well as trinkets to commemorate a visit to the historic site. Vials of sand from the beach, certified genuine, were especially popular, and cost only a few bruxa.

One soul amidst the excited throng took no part in the endless exchange of gossip and speculation. She trudged along heavy of heart, knowing she must go to the capital but having no idea what she was going to do when she got there. All Mayenne knew was that her lady needed her. She had already frightened herself half witless with visions of the tortures her lady must be suffering. She must do something to save her.

And Lord Eben, what of him? Mayenne wondered for the thousandth time. Some said he had escaped, but others whispered that her lady had carved him up like a leg of mutton and devoured him piece by piece. Mayenne knew this could not be true: Her lady disliked mutton.

Whatever the sacrifice, she, Mayenne, must save her mistress. She choked back a sob of remorse. If only she hadn't gone off to visit her father that terrible night, she could have fought off the troop of soldiers that had swept down upon the manor house. She had been but a quarter hour away on her return when twenty grim-faced guardsmen appeared over the rise escorting a little cart. Upon it huddled Lord Dhion, Master Aleden, Lady Amorgos, little Morgana, and poor Clim. Mayenne had just enough time before they came abreast of her to scamper into the deep shadow of a little copse. She could see the hard-set lines of each soldier's face in the cold moonlight and the bewilderment in the eyes of Lord Dhion. Aleden slumped against the side of the cart, while Lady Amorgos cuddled Morgana in her lap. To her dying day, Mayenne would never forget the pitiable sobs of her little charge as the wagon passed by. Lady Syrah had given the care of her papa and little sister into Mayenne's hands, and she had failed her. A tear ran down her cheek.

"Quit yer shovin'," a man behind Mayenne snarled, then quickly apologized. "Sorry, Brother, didn't see yer staff in this crowd."

"Not at all, my son, the fault is mine. I came by this mangled leg only recently when I was attacked by a crazed dromedary in the desert where I had gone as an act of penance for sins best left unmentioned. I have not yet learned to wield my staff well," a voice said, cracking a little on the last few words. "As it were," he added with a barely suppressed snicker, fortunately lost in the hubbub of the crowd.

Mayenne nearly screamed with relief. A voice that spoke of dromedaries could mean only one thing: Lord Eben was somewhere nearby. She craned her neck this way and that until her gaze came to rest on a slim figure clad in a brown friar's robe thumping along with the help of a stout staff. He angled toward her through the flowing stream of humanity and signaled with a jerk of his head that she should follow him. Neither spoke as they slipped down a grassy bank and crouched behind a landslide of enormous boulders.

"Oh, Master Eben," Mayenne sobbed as she sank to her knees, "I'm so glad to see you. I've been so afraid and I didn't know what to do, and I can't think who's going to braid my lady's hair and make sure her gown is clean when they cut off her head, and my father broke out in this terrible rash, and she said I was brave but I'm not or I would have stole them off the cart, and they say my lady ate you but she never eats mutton, and I know those demon jailers are mounting her right now—"

"Good Lord," Eben muttered, but he squatted next to her and put his arm around her shoulder and said kindly, "Mayenne, calm down, everything's going to be all right."

She turned teary eyes toward him. "It is?"

"Yes."

"How?" she asked tremulously.

Eben plopped down beside her. "I haven't quite got that figured out yet."

Chapter Eighteen

Syrah smoothed the folds of her pale yellow gown as she settled onto a wooden bench beneath a trellis draped with honeysuckle. She closed her eyes, the better to let the sweet scent wash over her. Bees buzzed, birds chattered, and beetles clicked as they went about their business in the palace gardens. Beyond the high walls in the city below, wagons clanked, children shouted, horses whinnied. The four guards who escorted her everywhere took up positions at a discreet distance talking among themselves.

A cool breeze had sprung up and Depta had insisted on running back to her chamber to fetch Syrah a wrap. Syrah could see her now, bustling along the long gravel path with a deep green velvet cloak draped carefully over her arm.

For someone who had committed treason against the Crown, Syrah reflected, she was being accorded every attention a favored guest might expect. Except for the guards, of course, and the fact that she was not allowed conversation with anyone other than the three women who had been assigned to see to her needs. Though guarded in their speech they were friendly and cheerful. This morning the queen had seen fit to send one of her own ladies-in-waiting to inquire after Syrah's welfare, an event that had the maids beaming and chattering amongst themselves.

Something was not right here, Syrah thought. Two days had passed since she had flung her accusations at the king; surely time enough for him to decide her fate. Ranulph had tried to approach her as she came out into the gardens a short while ago but was stopped by the guards, which had been fortunate for him because Syrah would have scratched his eyes out. If the king had been set on making an example of her and the price of her treachery, the proclamation would have gone out by now. More likely she would spend the rest of her life in prison. One bright spot in such a scenario was that she would never again find herself in her cousin's hateful presence.

"It's lovely here," she said to Depta, who had wrapped the cloak about her, all the while clucking and fussing.

"That it is, my lady. My father was under-gardener here for fifty years. I can still point out trees he planted with his own hands."

Syrah smiled up at the old woman. "It's a fine legacy, Depta. We should all leave the world a better place than we found it. I tried, you know, to do the right thing," she said wistfully, "but I will be remembered, if I am at all, only as a traitor."

"You did the right thing in the wrong way, is all," Depta said. "There is no dishonor in that, my lady, only a lesson to be learned." She patted Syrah on the shoulder and headed back toward the palace at a pace remarkably spry for a woman of her years.

Despite the threat of rain, Syrah could not bring herself to return to her chamber. She had spent too many hours pacing back and forth in the dark hours of the night when sleep would not come. When next the king summoned her, perhaps it would be to condemn her to a life inside thick walls where she would never again feel the glory of a storm on the wind.

She gathered her cloak about her and settled the hood over her unbound hair. Tendrils whipped in the wind as she walked to a parapet and gazed out over Suriana toward the home she would never see again. Eben was out there somewhere. She feared for him but firmly believed he would someday take the high seat of the Ninth House. The king could not be so cruel as to deprive him of his hall. Surely, even he must see the evil in Ranulph.

"Lady Syrah," a deep voice said, bringing her back to the moment, "will you speak with me?"

Jibril was standing beside her.

"Of course, my lord," she replied, amazed that she could speak at all, so disconcerted was she by his nearness. Too shy to look up at him, she continued staring out at the roiling clouds of the coming storm.

"I wish," he began after a few moments' hesitation, "that we had met under other circumstances."

Syrah's heart contracted. Did he not remember another day, another storm? Had only she carried that memory in her heart all these years? Of course he would not remember, she chided herself. She had been so young, endowing that insignificant little scene with all the romantic yearnings of a young girl's heart. He would have forgotten it long ago.

"I want you to know that I bear you no ill will," he continued. "I must admit my pride took a beating when you feinted with that knight. I never saw it coming."

Syrah stared up at him in amazement. She had drugged him, kidnapped him, carted him halfway across the Dominion in a coffin, imprisoned him, and sold him back to his father as though he were a bull in the market square, and the man was upset that she had bested him in a game of chess?

He smiled down at her, and for the first time since an ill wind had blown through her hall and changed her life forever, laughter bubbled up from her heart and the happy, mischievous young woman she had once been gazed out on the world again.

"Walk with me, Syrah," he said softly.

They walked, and talked, careful to avoid any mention of the subjects uppermost in both their minds—the intimacy they had shared and the momentous decisions being made about her future at this very moment. He told her a little about his life and his travels. She spoke of the delightful eccentricities of her great uncle Amorgos. She discovered he disliked eel. He learned of her love of poetry. When the storm broke he led her to a portico that ran the length of the west wing. They had just seated themselves on a stone bench out of the wind when a page appeared to summon the prince to his father's study room. A heavy silence settled between them as the boy trotted away.

Syrah fixed her eyes on her folded hands, pale against the dark green of the cloak, willing him to leave quickly so he wouldn't see her cry. "Thank you, Your Highness," she said to his boots. "It has been an honor to know you, if only for a short time."

"And thank you, my lady," he said as he took her hand and pressed a gentle kiss upon it, "for the honor of being your prisoner."

Not even her mother's death had left Syrah as sad and bereft as this moment when she heard her prince stride away down the long covered arcade, and out of her life.

The guard stationed at the end of the short hallway that led to Syrah's chamber came to attention when Prince Jibril suddenly appeared around the corner. If he thought it strange that the prince should be wandering around the west wing of the palace in the middle of the night he gave no sign of it.

"Stand down, Orini," the prince said. "All's well here, I take it."

"Yes, my lord. It's been quiet enough. Lord Ranulph came by earlier, wanted to speak with the lady, but I told him I had strict instructions no one was to disturb her. He said as he was her cousin he had a right to see her, but I wasn't having any of that. He went off in a snit, said he'd report me to His Majesty in the morning."

"I wouldn't worry about it," Jibril said, making a mental note to report Gyp to His Majesty in the morning.

"I came by to speak with Lady Syrah myself," he continued casually. "Perhaps you'd like to take a break."

"That I would, my lord. I'll be off now, and come back, say, in an hour?"

"Make it two."

Jibril paced back and forth before the door for some minutes. All evening he had paced. From one end of the great hall to the other until his father had finally ordered him to go pace somewhere else. Along the corridors of the north, south, and east wings of the palace. Up and down the ballroom. In the end, his pacing had brought him here, to Syrah's door, which was where he wanted to go in the first place.

He rapped lightly on the door. "Lady Syrah?" Receiving no reply, he knocked again, louder this time.

"Go away," came an angry voice. "I told you, I don't want to talk to you."

She must think he was Gyp. "It's Prince Jibril, Syrah."

"Oh."

"May I come in?"

"It's late. I'm . . . Yes, of course, my lord."

Jibril walked in, closing the door softly behind him. Syrah was standing in the middle of the room, clad in her sleeping gown, clutching a long poker in one hand and drawing a fringed blue silk shawl close around her shoulders with the other.

"I hope you were expecting someone else," the prince said dryly. He gently pried the poker from her fingers and carried it back to the hearth.

"I'm sorry, Your Highness, I thought you were Ranulph coming back. I heard him out there in the hall earlier. The guard told him to go away."

Jibril leaned against the mantel and regarded her gravely. When the guards had marched her into the king's receiving room, she'd looked like a street urchin, adorable, with her smudged face and her hair all which way. In the garden she'd been a shy, charming young lady. Tonight, the most desirable woman he'd ever seen stood before him.

She wasn't exactly beautiful, feature for feature—not at all in the fashion of the court, as she'd once told him—save for wide-spaced eyes the color of the Dominion's seas and full rosy lips. The nose was too haughty, the little chin a tad too determined, the cheekbones too sculpted. No lady

173

of fashion would boast of hair so straight and pale.

Syrah shifted uneasily beneath his scrutiny. "Your visit is unexpected. I was just about to go to . . . I'm not in any state to receive you, sir."

Jibril smiled. "I admit I've never before been received by a woman wielding a poker, clad only in her sleeping gown, but then, Lady Syrah, you are not just any woman."

Syrah edged past him toward the door that led to her little dressing room. "I'll just go put on something more . . . well, something," she finished desperately.

He grinned, enjoying her discomfiture. "That won't be necessary."

"It won't?"

"I'll only have to take it off again."

"Oh."

He arched one black eyebrow.

Her eyes narrowed. "You're teasing me again."

Jibril relented. "Yes. No." He ran a hand through his hair and wandered over to the window. "I don't know. This situation is so bizarre."

He could see her reflection in the glass, and behind her in the sleeping chamber, a bed piled high with goose-down pillows and a white coverlet neatly turned down. Even as the sight fired his blood, his common sense fought to keep the upper hand. Someday in the not-too-distant future he would take her to his bed as wife. It would shame her if he took her now before they had spoken their vows. Tomorrow the king would inform her of his decision to send her back to her hall; he would imply his consent to a marriage between her and Gyp. If Jibril claimed her now, she would surely look upon him as an opportunist who had sought only to satisfy his lust. Even when Gyp had been brought low, she might view his seduction with horror and disgust. She might never forgive him. He must leave. Now.

"It is well past the midnight hour, my lord," she said, "so I gather you have come to bring me tidings of my future. You know of the king's decision? Is it so terrible, then?"

Jibril lifted her chin so he could look directly into her eyes. "Syrah, I want you to know that your future is not so bleak as you now imagine." He brushed a tear from her cheek. "The matter before the king is difficult to explain. Despite what he said when you were first brought before him, he does not view you as a traitor. On my word of honor, any decision he makes regarding your future will not be a punishment, though you may view it as such."

Syrah looked up at him, worried. "Do you view me as a traitor?"

"No, my lady," he replied as he lowered his head and brushed his lips across hers. "At this moment I see you only as the most desirable woman I have ever known."

He started to straighten up, fighting an arousal he might not be able to control, but she threw her arms around his neck and kissed him back with a passion that had his self-control hanging by a thread in seconds.

"Syrah, Syrah," he murmured. "I would not dishonor you—"

"You said our kiss was not finished. Let us finish it now, before—" she pleaded.

"Your husband . . ." he protested against her sweet lips, hoping she would pull back, because he certainly could not.

"I will not marry against my will."

"If you were to marry the man of your own choosing, Syrah, what vow would you make to your husband?"

"I don't understand."

"Tell me," he insisted.

"I . . . I would say that I will love him, and him alone, forever. I would place my heart, my soul, and my body into his safekeeping."

"And would you have him say the same? That he loves you, and will love you and you alone, forever. That he will hold you safe and give his heart and soul into your safekeeping?"

She looked up into his eyes uncertainly. "Yes. That is what I would have him say."

She struggled to free herself from his arms, but he held her fast against him. "Let us not speak of this," she cried. "There will be no husband for me, can't you see? Tomorrow the king will pass sentence on me. He may spare me the block, but I'll most certainly be imprisoned for the rest of my life, or at the very least forced to take the veil."

"We are here now, my Syrah," Jibril said softly. "Let us finish our kiss."

She was softness, cool silk and warm skin beneath, as he lowered her onto the bed. He was raw power above, waiting, allowing her to learn the feel of him.

"So sweet, my Lady . . . your lips, your breasts—"

"I've dreamt of you—"

"I've dreamt of you—"

"Here beneath me . . ." He groaned as she tangled her hands in his hair and brought his lips back to hers, seeking, demanding. "Your hair spread out—"

Her tongue traced the line of his lips, his jaw, down to the hollow of his neck. Her hands explored the hard planes and strength of him, shoulders, arms; spanned the broad chest, slid around to the tensed muscles of his back, down to the tight curve of his buttocks.

"Let me see you, Jibril."

She ran her hands up the softer skin of the inside of his thighs, caressing him with her fingers, running her lips over him, finally exploring him with her tongue.

"No, stop," he gasped.

Syrah looked up at him, surprised. "Stop? I don't understand. I thought—"

"I won't be able to wait, Syrah."

"Oh, I didn't know—"

He laughed, wrapped her in his arms, and settled her beneath him again. "I know you didn't."

"You're laughing at me," she accused.

"Never, my lady." He knelt between her thighs. "You may be sure that I take you—and this—very seriously," he murmured as his lips grazed the pale curls there, and his tongue sought entrance to her warmth.

"Again, Jibril . . . yes, kiss me as you did on the island . . . yes, there. . . ." She arched up against him. "Oh, oh . . . ohhhh . . ."

And then she was lost, and when she opened her eyes

again, for a moment she was bewildered to see him there above her.

"Now, sweet Syrah, I claim you."

He slid into her, and paused but a moment before he thrust hard. He held her trembling in his arms as she buried her face against his neck and braced against the pain, then softened.

As he moved against her, he fed their hunger for one another, fired their blood, and when he could no longer hold back his need, she cried out with him, cradled in his arms.

She had no regrets. She could endure whatever the king decreed for her today. She would have only to close her eyes to find herself again in the shelter of Jibril's arms. Her life might be harsh, monotonous, cold—it no longer mattered.

Shortly before dawn he'd left her bed. She had reached for him, trying to draw him back down beside her, but he had bent over her and said gravely, "Forgive me, Syrah."

She had reached up to caress his cheek. "There is nothing to forgive."

Chapter Nineteen

Depta took in the disheveled young woman clutching the tangled sheet to cover her nakedness, and waylaid the maids before they could enter the sleeping chamber.

"So he came to you, did he?" she said after she'd sent them off to fetch water for Syrah's bath. "Can't say as I'm surprised. You'd have to be blind not to see the way he's been looking at you these past days."

Unable to meet the old woman's eyes, Syrah slipped from the bed and quickly donned her sleeping gown. She stared down in dismay at the stained sheets and blushed to the roots of her hair.

"Don't you worry, my lady," Depta said kindly, "I'll just take those sheets away now so no one sees them. We'll keep this just between you and me."

"Thank you, Depta. He . . . We . . ."

"You don't have to explain, my lady. I'm not one to judge."

"Thank you," Syrah said, profoundly grateful for the woman's kindness. She stood staring out the window at the dull day, listening to the sounds of Depta bustling about and the maids preparing her bath. After the morning meal, she would be escorted to the king to learn her fate.

"Please fetch the blue tunic I wore when I first came to the castle," she told one of the maids.

"But, my lady," the girl protested, horrified, "it's not right a lady like you should wear such a—"

"Nonetheless, it is what I will wear today," Syrah said firmly. "And please return the lovely gowns to the princesses and thank them on my behalf for lending them to me during my stay. I shall not be needing them in future."

Syrah straightened her shoulders as Depta tucked an errant lock of hair behind her ear. The ominous tread of approaching footsteps signaled the arrival of her guards. She hugged the old woman. "Thank you, Depta, for all your kindness . . . for everything."

Syrah was shown into the king's private study; apparently she was not to be made a public spectacle again. The room was surprisingly intimate, dominated by a highly polished rosewood desk and matching high-backed chair. The white marble hearth was adorned with panthers, emblem of the First House, exquisitely carved in bas-relief, and a thick carpet in subtle shades of crimson, rose, and blue covered the inlaid wooden floor. Tall doors that led out into mist-shrouded gardens had been thrown open, and the mingled scents of sea and roses and damp earth wafted through the chamber.

The king sat back in his chair regarding her gravely. To his right loomed Obike Zebengo, who winked at Syrah just as he had that day in the yard of the inn. To the king's left stood Jibril, his stance wide, hands clasped behind his back. Syrah curtsied, then stood, head bowed, with her hands folded neatly before her. For long moments no one spoke.

"Lady Syrah," the king began, "there are two questions I would put to you before we proceed further."

Syrah met the king's gaze without flinching. "Yes, sire."

"Zebengo here informs me that you tried to procure his services to kill your cousin, Lord Ranulph. Is it true?"

"I wished to hire the man to oust my cousin from my hall, sire. I do not recall saying anything about killing him."

"Nonetheless, Zebengo understood that was your intent."

Syrah lifted her chin a notch. "You would take the word of a man who ate his own brother?"

The king turned to Zebengo with raised brows. "Did you indeed, sir?"

The mercenary shrugged. "The hunting had been poor that day. What else could I do?"

"Quite understandable," the king said with a perfectly straight face.

Syrah's composure almost slipped. They were mocking her, but it had been a stupid thing to say, born of false bravado.

"Now, Lady Syrah, for my second question. Your brother seems to have disappeared. Do you know where he is?"

"No, Your Majesty."

"Would you tell me if you did?"

"No, Your Majesty."

"You will, of course, inform me should you hear from him."

"No, Your Majesty."

For long moments the king just stared at her. He started to speak, thought better of it, and turned to Zebengo. "Thank you, sir, for your service to the Crown in this matter. You will, as always, be well compensated."

Zebengo bowed to the king, flashed Syrah a mischievous smile, and ducked beneath the lintel of a curtained archway behind the king's chair.

"Ask Lord Ranulph to step in," the king ordered a guard who stood to attention nearby.

Syrah stiffened. An uneasy feeling settled in as her cousin strode confidently into the chamber. He bowed low, first to the king and then only slightly less elaborately to Prince Jibril.

"I have requested your presence, Lord Ranulph," the king began, "because the fate of Lady Syrah most nearly concerns your own."

Syrah's unease escalated to alarm as the king continued. "It distresses me to have discord between the noble Houses. It is my responsibility—as Lady Syrah so eloquently reminded me the other day—to keep the welfare of my people uppermost in my thoughts. It is my responsibility to foster peace where there is misunderstanding."

Syrah's eyes widened. "Misunderstanding? You call—"

He held up his hand to stop her. "You will have your say in a moment, Lady Syrah."

"I have thought deeply upon this matter," the king resumed, "and I have concluded that Lady Syrah's actions in kidnapping the Crown Prince do not constitute treason but rather resulted from a simple misunderstanding of your motives for coming into her hall. I do not, of course, condone her actions, but as no real harm came to my son, I shall set aside the charge of treason."

"You are truly magnanimous, Your Majesty," Ranulph oozed.

The king smiled. "It is good of you to say so, but I cannot hold you blameless in this. I understand three men of Lady Syrah's hall died shortly after your arrival."

"Another misunderstanding, sire," Ranulph assured the king.

"Lady Syrah?" the king said, turning to her.

"They were murdered in cold blood." She turned on Ranulph. "Would you also say my great uncle died as the result of a misunderstanding? And my last letter to His Majesty gone astray, was that yet another misunderstanding? And that fictitious contract of betrothal—"

"Enough," the king commanded. "I will repeat once, and once only, Lady Syrah, that no credible evidence exists to support your allegation that Lord Amorgos was murdered. As to the letter, my private secretary assures me no such letter arrived on his desk."

"That does not mean it was not sent," Syrah retorted.

The king dismissed the subject with a wave of his hand. "In any event, I had no knowledge of your concerns. Now we come to the matter of a betrothal between the two of you. I have shown the document to your father, Lady Syrah. Unfortunately, his illness clouds his memory."

The king paced over to the window and stared out into the garden. "It falls to me, therefore, to make the determination. I hold it to be valid."

"No," Syrah practically shouted. "You must be mad to think it so."

"You forget yourself, Lady Syrah," the king said. "I will overlook this unseemly outburst because you are under a great deal of stress."

"She is, sire," Gyp interjected smoothly. "I hope you will forgive my cousin. I'm sure when she calms down she will see that it is all for the best."

Syrah faced him. "I will never marry you. I will die before I allow you to lay one finger on me again."

She turned her eyes to Jibril, suddenly dead calm, her heart cold in her breast.

Forgive me, Syrah.

There is nothing to forgive.

"You knew."

He made no reply, moved not a muscle.

"Lady Syrah," the king said kindly, "I am not giving my official sanction to a marriage between you and Lord Ranulph just yet. I would rather not have to order you to marry against your will, but I do want you to return to your hall and see if you two can iron out your differences. I have every expectation that you will come to an understanding."

"I'm sure we will, Your Majesty," Ranulph said, the triumph in his voice unmistakable. "We are both most grateful for your perspicacity and generosity, are we not, cousin?"

Syrah might have been carved from marble.

"Lord Ranulph, I imagine you will want to go on ahead to prepare for Lady Syrah's return. In the meantime, she can consult with my physician regarding Lord Dhion's health and choose a suitable nursemaid for Lady Morgana. My own guard will escort her to you in, say, a week's time. I understand her personal maid is no longer serving in the hall, so I will send several of our own servants along to attend her."

After Ranulph had bowed himself out with many expressions of gratitude for the king's benevolence, Zebengo stepped from behind the curtain. Jibril stood rock solid, as he had from the beginning.

"Do you wish to say anything, Lady Syrah?" the king inquired.

Syrah was all steely politeness. "No, Your Majesty."

"You may go. Oh, one more thing. I believe you are in possession of five hundred of my gold discs."

"No, sire, I am not."

"No?"

"I possess but four hundred and ninety-four, sire. One I left in the chest in your tent. Zebengo holds the other five. I am sure he will be more than happy to return them to you," she said sweetly.

With that, Syrah sank to one knee, bowed her head and folded her hands in the ritual gesture of allegiance of her noble House, then rose gracefully and swept from the room.

"I don't believe I have ever met a woman quite like her," the king observed after the door had closed behind her. "She'll bear watching. I want you in place, Zebengo, as soon as possible. Get to Gyp before she arrives; tell him you think you might know where the rest of the gold is. That should catch his attention."

"If she arrives," the mercenary replied with a grin. "I suspect she is already hatching plans of her own." He extracted five gold discs from a pouch at his waist and set them on the desk. "Let it not be said I take money that I have not earned. I doubt coming by the rest from the lady will prove so easy."

With a courtly bow he stepped through the open doors to the garden and slipped away into the fog.

The king looked over at Jibril. "I suppose that went as well as could be expected."

"Yes," the prince replied dully.

"She said 'you knew.' I don't suppose you'd care to tell me what that was about."

"No, I wouldn't," the prince said tightly and strode from the room.

For the next three days Syrah went through the motions of living. She rose, bathed, dressed, played in the nursery with Morgana, and sat with her father, reading to him or just holding his hand as he slept. She consulted with the king's physician, who assured her that he had seen like cases and that a prognosis for a partial recovery, while not certain, was good.

Otherwise, she did not leave her chamber, although the weather had turned fine and the gardens shimmered with color. She politely declined to see a priest and did not attend chapel. She ate what Depta set before her. She embroidered a soaring golden eagle, symbol of her House, on the sleeve of her blue peasant's tunic. At night, she sat in a chair by the window, following the path of the waning moon until it dissolved into the pink light of dawn.

Surprisingly, it took no great effort to set aside the pain of Jibril's betrayal. Someday she would have to face up to it, but for now she simply closed the door of her heart to him. He had set out to seduce her knowing the king had promised her to Ranulph. Once she had wondered whether he would feel the same desire for her as the Lady Syrah as he had for the harlot in the tavern. Now she knew, although the harlot surely had the better of it; she, at least, would be paid for her services. He had said it himself: Lust was the weakness of men and he was a man. And love, he had said, was the weakness of women, and now Syrah knew it was true. Love him she might, but forgive him? Never.

Thinking back over her audience with the king, Syrah could not shake off the feeling that there was more to his decision to send her home than he had let on. "Papa," she said one evening as she sat with him by the fire, "His Majesty showed you a contract of betrothal between my cousin, Ranulph, and myself. Do you remember?"

"He might have," replied Lord Dhion. "My memory has been rather poor of late, you know."

Syrah sat forward and pressed his hand. "I want you to try to remember, Papa, if you ever agreed to such a betrothal. It's very important."

"I remember discussing a betrothal with someone," Lord Dhion said with a little frown, "but I don't recall who. It must have been a very long time ago. Perhaps your mother would know.... Ah, I forget sometimes that she's gone on before me," he said sadly.

Syrah's voice was low and urgent. "Papa, please listen to me. I know it's hard to remember—you've been very ill—but the king believes you pledged me to my cousin Ranulph. What did he say when he showed you the document?"

Lord Dhion gazed into the fire as if he could find an answer to his daughter's question in the flames. "He said ... he asked me ... Is that what he meant, that I offered you to Gyp?"

"Yes," Syrah said, tears welling up in her eyes.

"Why, no, daughter," Lord Dhion said, his voice suddenly strong, his eyes clearer than she had seen them since the fever struck him down, "I would never pledge you to that dreadful boy."

"Did you tell the king that, use those very words?" Syrah asked, hardly daring to breathe.

"Why, I believe I did."

"And he understood?"

"Oh yes, my dear. I distinctly recall him saying he wouldn't marry a scullery maid to that snake."

Syrah burst into tears. "Oh, Papa, Papa," she said between sobs, "I love you so much."

Lord Dhion pulled her into his embrace, wrapping his arms around her. "Don't cry, little Syrah. We have seen too much sorrow."

She looked up at him. "You don't understand, Papa. I am weeping for joy."

Later that night, Syrah asked the guard who stood before her door if she might take a walk in the gardens. Orini, for that was his name, had hemmed and hawed and finally agreed to a short stroll. The sea fog had lifted and a skinny sliver of moon cast just enough light to negotiate the pathways that crisscrossed the gardens.

Syrah gazed out over the city toward the west, toward home. Had it been only three months since she last stood in her beloved hall? It might have been a year or a lifetime. Three days ago she had been so convinced she would never see it again that she had not offered up a single prayer beseeching God to grant her a reprieve from unthinkable, unbearable exile. Yet to her astonishment, the king had that morning granted what she dared not ask of the greater power.

What could he mean by it? Why had he declared the betrothal contract to be valid when he knew for a fact that Papa had never contemplated such a match? Why would he allow Ranulph to carry off such a deceit? Or *think* he was getting away with it?

Something very strange was going on here, something that had nothing to do with her own crimes or the purported betrothal or discord between two noble Houses. Ranulph might not know it, but he was a player in some game of the king's devising. And she, Syrah, was a pawn. She might not know the whys and wherefores of the matter, but she knew a game of chess when she saw it.

So the king would dangle her before Ranulph for his own purposes, would he? She need have no fear of her cousin now, for she would be under the king's protection. While they were occupied with their little game, she would be free to play her own and have, as it were, the home advantage. The king had unknowingly granted her the first move.

She really must thank him.

King Ahriman could hardly believe it. "You wish to leave at once?"

"Yes, Your Majesty. I have thought on it and see the wisdom of your decision."

The king frowned. "You have?"

Syrah clasped her hands behind her back like the polite little girl she'd been taught to be. "I know my father would do the same were his health good enough to understand the matter."

"Indeed. And you would not question his decision?"

Syrah's eyes widened. "Of course not, sire. He is my papa."

The king drummed his fingers on the arm of his chair. Without taking his eyes from her he said, "Jibril, what do you make of this? Lady Syrah has resigned herself to make it up with her cousin and wishes to waste no time in doing so."

Jibril moved away from the mantel and perched on the edge of the king's desk, one long leg swinging back and forth.

"What are you up to, Syrah?" he said quietly.

Syrah gave him an inquiring look.

"You know very well what I mean. You would not make it up with Gyp if the four horsemen of the Apocalypse were at your door."

"Perhaps I thought so once," she said humbly, "but now ... I must take a husband, sir, as you advised me only recently." She looked him straight in the eye. "I believe you even suggested the words of a vow that would be suitable on the occasion of my marriage."

"Syrah," he said with a growl.

She stepped away from him so she could see the king. "Have I displeased you somehow, Your Majesty? You commanded me to return to my hall, and that is what I want, as well. My father and sister are in good hands. I see no reason why I should presume on your good graces any longer. You have been very kind, very thoughtful. We are all most grateful."

The king looked at Syrah long and hard. Finally, he sighed and said, "You have my permission to depart in the morning. But let me just give you a word of advice, Lady Syrah. You are a clever woman, but wisdom lies in knowing your limitations."

Syrah nodded. "I know. I received just such advice from your son, Your Majesty."

"Evidently you did not heed it," the king replied.

"But I did, sire," Syrah said emphatically. "I am more aware than ever of my limitations."

The king leaned forward and folded his hands on the desk. "If you harbor any thoughts of ridding yourself of Lord Ranulph, I will be seriously displeased. Is that understood?"

"It is, sire."

The king waved his hand. "Go."

Jibril picked up a small copper Buddha from the king's desk, a gift from some traveler upon the Silk Road, and hurled it against the fireplace as the door closed behind Syrah. It hit the marble with a resounding metallic ping and bounced back onto the carpet, where it lay at his feet, its face a study in undisturbed tranquility.

"She . . . is . . . absolutely . . . infuriating! She's driving me to distraction."

"Obviously," the king observed dryly as the Buddha sailed across the room and landed in a potted plant.

"I should let Gyp have her," the prince declared, marching across the carpet and plucking the unlucky little idol from among the roots of a twisted miniature yew. "Let her drive him crazy. That's what I should do."

Jibril stalked about the room tossing the Buddha from hand to hand. "She's got another insane scheme in her head, you realize that, don't you? She won't have to hire some cutthroat to take the hall now because she'll be right where she wants to be—under your protection. All I can say is, God help Gyp."

The king managed to snag Jibril as he marched by again, but not before the Buddha found more or less permanent sanctuary on a windowsill high up on the wall above the hearth.

"Sit down, Jibril," the king ordered.

The prince dropped into a chair and glowered at his father.

"No doubt she means to take full advantage of her new circumstances. We will just have to see that she doesn't do anything to put herself in danger. Obike will be there with two or three of his most trustworthy men. I have already assigned Depta to accompany her; that woman has the eyes of a hawk and the hearing of an owl."

"And what am I supposed to do?" Jibril growled. "I'm a man of action, for God's sake. I'm a soldier."

"You, son," the king said, "have the most difficult part in all this. You will find Eben Dhion. She won't make a move without him. After all, she has put herself in the way of danger for his sake, not her own. She set out to reclaim his patrimony and to hold him safe until either Lord Dhion can resume his duties or her brother is old enough to do so."

The king had Jibril's attention. "And?"

"You will find him before she does and recruit him to our side. If he is as clever as you have painted him, he will keep her in check until we have achieved our objective."

"And then?"

The king's eyes lit up with mischief. "Then, son, you will ask her to repeat that vow you taught her—on the occasion of her marriage."

Jibril leaned against the acacia as the light in Syrah's chamber went out. A fire must have been laid in the hearth; he could see a faint glow through the slats of the shutters.

He imagined her snuggled down against plump pillows, her lips slightly parted, rosy in the firelight; her hair tousled, a tendril caressing a smooth cheek; her firm breasts rising and falling with each soft breath. He imagined her sleeping gown tangled about her long slim legs, her heat. She would be dreaming now, an angelic smile on her sweet lips.

Dreaming up diabolical new ways to drive him out of his mind.

Chapter Twenty

"That's about the most amazing thing I ever heard," Guardsman Orini said. "You hear stories, of course, but you're the first I ever met who actually saw it with his own eyes. It's no wonder you and your sister want to devote yourselves to a life of prayer, not after what you've been through."

The young monk handed the guard another chunk of bread and nibbled at his own thoughtfully. "I try to see it as part of God's great plan. He made Adam and Eve and put that snake in the garden so's we'd see their sin and not make the same mistake they did. He probably made cannibals for a good reason, too. He seems to know what He's doing, wouldn't you agree?"

Orini agreed and thought as how he might light a candle at the little roadside shrine where Lady Syrah was kneeling—just in case God had any cannibals in mind for him.

"Anyhow," the monk continued, "he's probably explained it all to Pa and Ma now that they're in heaven with Him, but you can't expect people to take the long view when they're sitting in a cauldron of boiling water with naked men poking at them with sharp sticks."

"It's a miracle you and your sister managed to escape."

"It certainly is," Brother Pundomom agreed, standing up and brushing crumbs from his rough habit. "If that herd of dromedaries hadn't stampeded through the camp we'd have been stew ourselves by morning. The Lord moves in mysterious ways."

Orini shuddered. He had faced death several times since becoming a member of Prince Jibril's elite personal guard— once even taking an arrow in the leg in pursuit of three notorious highwaymen. But ending up in a cannibal's stomach held little appeal, even if it was part of God's great plan.

Lady Syrah had finished her prayers and was making her way down the hill in the company of the young woman Brother Pundomom was conducting to the priory at Dunataea where she was to enter the novitiate. Orini had learned her name was Nini and thought it a pity such a pretty little thing would be shut away behind high stone walls for the rest of her life.

"Brother Pundomom," Syrah said, "I count myself fortunate to have met you and your sister on the road today. She has just been telling me of your recent adventures. Your story is most inspiring."

"No more than your own, my lady," the monk replied. "It is known across the width and breadth of our fair isle, although much exaggerated, I fear. They say your brother has been eaten by cannibals. Alas, I now count myself somewhat of an expert on the subject and it would compound my own grief to know that you have suffered the same loss."

Orini tore his eyes from Nini just long enough to interject, "It's all nonsense, if you ask me. There's no cannibals in the Dominion; they're all off in that heathenish place you just come from, Brother."

"I'm sure there's nothing to it," Syrah assured the little group. "Still, I fear some great evil has befallen him. I light a candle to our Lady every day for his safe return." She sighed deeply. "I wonder if I shall ever see him again."

Brother Pundomom placed a comforting hand on her shoulder. "Be of good heart, my lady. It has often been my experience that we must make our way through a long dark tunnel in order to find the light at the end. It is all part of God's great plan."

Syrah beamed at him. "How well you put it, monk—a long dark tunnel! You are truly wise for one so young."

Brother Pundomom beamed back. "And you, my lady, are a woman of great understanding, if I may say so."

"Lady Syrah, we must be on our way if we are to reach the inn by nightfall," Orini said. He turned to the monk's blushing sister. "I, too, feel fortunate to have met you upon the road, Nini of Dunataea. The world outside your convent walls will have lost a fair flower indeed the day you take your vows."

While Eben Dhion dragged a quivering, moon-eyed Mayenne behind him toward their little cart, Guardsman Orini handed Lady Syrah Dhion up onto her palfrey. He bounded up into his own saddle, and with one last glance back at the lovely Nini, signaled the escort to continue on its way.

A smile spread across Syrah's face as they rounded a bend in the road. A long dark tunnel. Why, there just happened to be one beneath the great hall of the Ninth House.

From the top of the steps that led into the great hall, Ranulph had greeted Syrah with utmost civility, quite as though not a week previous she had called him jackal and murderer. Her chambers had been prepared for her, he informed her, and a light repast awaited her after a journey that must have been terribly tiring. In the evening he would host a banquet to celebrate her safe return.

Every man, woman, and child who served the Dhions had been assembled in the courtyard, decked out in their finest tunics. The sun shone bright and a gentle breeze carried the scent of fresh herbs and medicinal flowers from the garden, which mingled with the agreeable aroma of horses and leather and hay fresh strewn over the hard-packed earth.

A strained silence settled over the crowd when Ranulph had concluded his little speech. Where shouts of joy should have greeted the return of the beloved Lady Syrah, only polite murmurs of welcome could be heard. Children held fast to their mothers' skirts. Men stood uncertain, caps in hand. Women gazed at her with tears welling in their eyes.

Captain Ankuli, who had ridden ahead to secure the road and prepare for the arrival of Syrah and his men, extended his hand to assist her from her horse. As Ranulph moved forward to embrace her, Ankuli took her arm in an unmistakable gesture of guardianship and guided her through the crowd.

Syrah grinned up at him. "Are you expecting me to try to escape, Captain? My cousin must have two dozen guards on the walls and your own troops surround the Great House."

"I wouldn't put it past you, my lady," he muttered darkly.

Syrah paused on the top step to look down at her people with a warm smile. "How pleased I am to be home and see all my old friends here to greet me. We have come through great trials together, and I promise you that all will be well again in the Ninth House."

A great cheer echoed through the courtyard. Shielding her eyes against the bright sun, Syrah looked up to see not one but two pennants snapping in the breeze above the east tower: the eagle of the Ninth House, and above it in pride of place, the three harts of the Gyp family and the Twenty-seventh House.

"You dare!" she hissed, whirling around to face Ranulph.

"We are to be joined, my lady, not only in holy matrimony, but our Houses as well," he said with aplomb.

"You will remove your colors from my hall."

"But, Syrah," he replied with charming smile, "I thought you would be pleased. His Majesty has charged me to defend and protect the Ninth House. It is a fitting symbol, our colors together, is it not?"

She started toward him, but Captain Ankuli's hand tightened on her arm. "This is not the time or place, Lady Syrah," he murmured. "Leave off."

Syrah cast her cousin a look of pure loathing and allowed Captain Ankuli to lead her into the great hall. Ranulph am-bled along behind, slapping his leather gloves against his thigh, a sly smile of triumph on his handsome face.

The servants of the Ninth House might choose to watch their tongues in the presence of Lord Ranulph, but their love for their lady and their joy at her return resonated in their every action. The Great House sparkled, vases of flowers adorned every table, the gardens sported nary a single weed. In her chambers, the linens smelled of rosemary and tiny purple violets lay scattered over the ivory silk coverlet. The brass tub gleamed, enough hot water to fill ten such tubs was at the ready, and her favorite bath oils and lotions were close at hand.

Cooks and bakers, dairymaids and scullions bustled about; serving men bore so many platters and bowls, tureens and trenchers, goblets and cups from the kitchens that there was scarce room for the cellars of fine salt on the banquet tables. Every dish Syrah had favored from the age of two, when she splattered her first spoonful of honeyed mush over her doting mama's hair, had been lovingly prepared. Great roasts of beef, fish, pheasant, fowl; sauces, green and red and yellow; savory pies of leeks and cheeses; new-baked bread; puddings and sweet tarts and honeyed fruits.

Syrah sat at the high table beside Ranulph, composed and gracious, making sure everyone, even the lowliest scullion, had an opportunity to come to the lower tables to partake of the great feast. If her heart was heavy because the three dearest to her in all the world—Papa, Eben, and Morgana— were not there to share the joy of coming home, it did not show in her smiling countenance. She made small talk with Ranulph, inquiring after his family, estate matters, and the new foals. He, in turn, acted the perfect host, solicitous as to her every need as the long meal progressed course upon course. Occasionally, his hand came to rest on hers or he would stretch his arm along the back of her chair and lean close, as though he had some intimate thought to share with her and her alone. Syrah's pleasant demeanor did not falter, though she discreetly removed his hand or leaned away toward Captain Ankuli, who sat to her left, to utter some casual pleasantry.

Everyone knew by now, of course, that Lord Dhion and Lady Morgana had stayed behind in the capital at the king's request and under his protection; they were safe. No one knew the whereabouts of Lord Eben, or for that matter, their lady's personal maid, Mayenne. A few gullible souls still held out for the cannibal theory, but most scoffed at such nonsense. As Lady Syrah exhibited neither perturbation nor fear as to Lord Eben's well-being, she must believe him to be alive and well.

The ale and wine flowed, the musicians fiddled and piped, children careened throughout the hall intoxicated by too many sweets and the thrill of being allowed to stay up far past their bedtimes. Yet beneath the cheerful chatter and bawdy repartee, the belching and flirting and laughter, lay another, darker mood. And when Ranulph rose to his feet to propose a toast to Lady Syrah, the crowd turned a watchful eye upon her, as though they would take their cue from her.

"It is with great joy that we welcome Lady Syrah home at last," Ranulph began. "The Ninth House has known more than its fair share of pain and loss during the past year. Here, tonight, we may put those dark times behind us at last. Lord Dhion, Lord Eben, Lady Morgana, and this precious jewel of the Ninth House beside me were not lost to us after all.

"I do not deceive myself that my arrival in this hall was not the cause of a grievous misunderstanding," he continued. "I have assured Lady Syrah, and now I would assure all of you, that I came with only the best interests of the Ninth House in mind. Lord Dhion's illness left his lands undefended, his children unguarded. As their cousin, I could do no less."

He slanted a fond look at Syrah before he continued. "Lady Syrah would now be the first to agree that she mistook my intentions. She embarked on a course of action, which, as you know, involved the royal house. His Majesty is a wise and compassionate man, and taking all into account, has allowed your mistress to return to her home free of the taint of treason."

A murmur of approval flowed through the crowd. "To His Majesty," Ranulph cried, raising his goblet. "To His Majesty!" they echoed back.

Solemn again, he continued. "His Majesty has informed me that Lord Dhion has shown improvement under the care of his own physician and is much cheered by having little Morgana nearby. As to Lord Eben, we have every expectation that he will be with us any day now."

Throughout this performance, Syrah had been watching the crowd for any hint of affection, respect, or loyalty for her cousin; she found none. The eyes of many of the men were filled with distrust; those of the women, hard anger and fear.

Ranulph's arm snaked about Syrah's waist, drawing her closer to his side as he continued to address the crowd. "Finally, on this happy occasion I wish to share with you my own joy. His Majesty has granted me leave to press my suit with this fair lady and has given me every reason to believe that he will look with favor on my success."

Syrah only just managed to keep her countenance, as stunned by Ranulph's announcement as the crowd. A few cries of "no" and "not possible" punctuated the confused babble. She stepped forward, anxious to avert an ugly scene.

"My friends," she said, giving Ranulph a patronizing little pat upon the arm, "in his zeal my cousin perhaps gets ahead of himself. The king has not yet sanctioned such a marriage. He has said only that my return here will enable Lord Ranulph and me to discover if we will suit. I cannot say whether we will or not, but even if we so decide and His Majesty sanctions our union, I would not be so undutiful a daughter as to marry without my papa's blessing. His health improves daily, true, but he is not yet well enough to attend to such matters."

"Very clever, Syrah," Ranulph said softly, "but make no mistake: You will call me husband, and soon."

*   *   *

"Pssst, my lady."

Syrah peered up the dark winding staircase that led from the kitchens to the house servants' quarters on the second floor of the north tower. "Who's there?"

Pleading exhaustion after her long journey, Syrah had left the banquet early and gone down to the kitchens to thank the staff for the superb feast. Anxious for some time alone, she had chosen a roundabout way to reach her own quarters rather than return through the great hall.

"Please, my lady, it's me, Clea, Mayenne's sister."

Syrah gathered up the skirts of her green silk gown and hurried upward toward the voice. She emerged into a dark hallway illumined only by the single flame of a tallow candle clutched in the hand of a girl who bore a striking likeness to Mayenne, save that she was considerably plumper.

"This way," Clea whispered and led Syrah into a large closet filled with linens and towels. She pulled the door shut and turned to Syrah with tears in her eyes.

"I'm so glad to see you, my lady. I've been ever so worried. When I heard you was taken, I swooned, I swear I did. First everyone said you was drowned, and then you wasn't dead at all, but they was going to chop off your head, and then they wasn't. It got so I didn't know what to think. And then they said Mayenne wasn't taken. I got down on my knees to thank the virgin, but now I don't know where she is and my pa's ever so worried."

"Hush, Clea," Syrah said. "Mayenne's fine."

The girl's eyes were huge in the candlelight. "You seen her, my lady? The Gypsies didn't get her?"

Syrah smiled. Vivid imaginations must run in the family. "No, the Gypsies didn't get her, and yes, I've seen her."

"Is she coming here, too?" the girl asked eagerly.

"Not just yet, Clea."

"But who's going to look out for her? Who's going to keep the Gypsies from ravishing her?"

"You must trust me," Syrah said firmly. "She's in good hands and you'll see her soon."

"Oh, thank you, thank you, my lady. You can't imagine

how awful it's been since you went away. All us girls is scared out of our wits."

"Why are the girls afraid?"

The maid clamped her mouth shut, her eyes darting this way and that.

"You will tell me, Clea, why the girls are afraid," Syrah commanded.

Clea wrung her hands. "I know he's your cousin and all, my lady . . ."

"What about my cousin?" Syrah said, a cold hard knot forming in her stomach.

"He took Lyrlon to his bed and then when she wouldn't go with him no more, he beat her and she ran away."

"But Lyrlon's just a child. She can't be more than twelve!"

Clea nodded. "Twelve, my lady. He wants the younger ones. And I hear he does bad things, things that hurt. Nobody wants to go with him, but if he wants you . . ."

For a moment Syrah thought she was going to be sick. No evil that had befallen the Ninth House—not sickness, not betrayal, not even murder—could approach the horror of a man who would use a child to satisfy his lust.

"Thank you, Clea, for telling me," Syrah said gently. "I promise you I will do everything in my power to stop him."

Too shaken to return to her chamber, Syrah made her way back down the stairs to a small door that led out into the kitchen gardens. She sank down on a cracked stone bench in an alcove that was all but hidden by falls of ivy. As a child she used to hide here when her father was particularly displeased with her over some mischief or another. Over the years it had become her thinking place.

How in heaven's name was she going to rid her hall of this devil? Short of plunging a knife through Ranulph's black heart she could see no way of bringing him down without help. Seeking out another mercenary was out of the question, if her experience with Obike Zebengo was anything to go by. It hadn't been a complete disaster, of course. Eben had escaped and he'd take care of Mayenne; Papa and Morgana would be well looked after at the palace.

She was back in her own hall under the king's protection—
and most assuredly under surveillance as well. Ranulph's
hands were tied, for the moment anyhow.

Syrah drummed her fingers on the cold stone, wondering
yet again about the king's motives for sending her back. He
might still be intending to marry her off to Ranulph despite
the fact that Papa had told him the betrothal contract was
a forgery. But why not just sanction the marriage and have
done? No, for some reason the king had his eye on Ranulph,
and what better way to put spies in place than send her
home with a retinue of palace servants and a contingent of
the king's own guard?

Whatever her cousin had done to merit the king's scrutiny, Syrah had every intention of finding it out and using
it to her own advantage. In the end, she might have all the
help she needed to rid her hall of Ranulph—from the king
himself.

In the meantime, there were other matters that needed
her urgent attention, not the least of which was to keep the
younger female servants out of Ranulph's clutches. The
older, more experienced women would be able to handle
him. Some might even welcome the opportunity to share
his bed in exchange for some bit of finery. But girls of
twelve, or even sixteen, were all too vulnerable, and the
best protection Syrah could offer them would be to send
them home to their families.

Ranulph was bound to wonder why ten or fifteen servants had disappeared from the hall, especially if he had
his eye on one or more of them. Syrah was going to have
to come up with a good reason for dismissing them and
find a way to get them away from the Great House. In this
she would have allies aplenty among her own staff, and
after all, a contingent of the king's men, brawny fellows all,
might be persuaded to escort the girls away. Depta would
act as guardian, and heaven help the man who cast even
one lascivious glance at the bevy of little maids.

Syrah leaned back against the cold wall and gazed up at
the stars. Perhaps Great Uncle Amorgos was up there some-

where looking down at her right now, for she could swear she heard him saying, as he had a thousand times, "Your opponent is your best ally, child. Observe him well, for it is he who will point the way to your victory."

Chapter Twenty-one

"Please, please," she moaned as she sought his mouth and arched up beneath him. The raw strength of him above her, the fierce demand of his arousal, drove all thought from her mind. She wrapped her legs around him, clinging to him, drowning.

"Look at me, I want to see your eyes as I claim you."

He slipped one arm beneath her shoulders and the other beneath her hips, using his full strength to raise her to receive him.

And then he was gone, his potent dark presence fading into a blackness so empty and desolate that her cry of ecstasy metamorphosed into a whimper of loss and despair.

Syrah came awake in a tangle of damp bed linens, throbbing with unsated desire. Every night the dream was the same; he came to her, filled her with his power, dissolved in her arms, and left her alone in the indifferent night.

She swiped at the tears on her cheeks, pushed aside the mosquito netting, and padded to the east-facing window. Beyond the low-lying hills she could just see the half-moon settling into the waves of the southern ocean. Bats swooshed through the soft air, scooping up the flying insects of the night; two cats faced off somewhere in the courtyard below, hissing and screeching; the howl of a hungry baby was suddenly stilled as its mother took it to her breast.

Syrah rested her head against the cool stone of the window frame and thought about babies, Jibril's babies, whom she would not bear, would never take to her breast. The night after he had come to her chamber her courses had begun, and she now knew he would never come to her again, except in dreams, and perhaps there would even come a night when she would not dream the dream, and then, truly, he would be gone.

She had not seen Jibril since that day in the king's study. He had ridden out the next morning without a word of farewell, not even, she thought with some asperity, another "apology." Depta had informed her that news of pirate incursions to the north had reached the palace, and the prince had set out at once to investigate. More than fifty heavily armed men rode with him.

Syrah was determined not to ask Captain Ankuli for news of the prince, even though rumors were rife of skirmishes with casualties on both sides. Had Jibril been injured, the captain would surely let it be known. As to that, Syrah was curious why the guard that escorted her from the capital remained at her hall and under the command of so important a personage as the captain of Jibril's personal guard. Ranulph, too, must have been curious: One of the maids reported to Syrah that she had overheard the captain telling Lord Ranulph that he had been charged to keep an eye on Lady Syrah, lest she take it into her head to get into mischief again. The king might not trust her; but it looked as though he trusted her cousin even less.

The first sweet call of a morning lark drifted up from the meadow, announcing the coming dawn. Syrah settled down on the window seat and rested her chin on her knees to watch the sun come up. She did not want to return to her bed; she did not want to dream the dream.

Far to the north, Prince Jibril cast only a cursory glance at the reddening sky as he pounded through the trees and made a running dive into the frigid waters of Lake Zando. He exploded up through the surface with a dismayed yelp and wondered if he'd ever be able to take a breath again. Every part of his body screamed the order to get it to shore before it froze solid. Jibril wondered vaguely if the royal shaft and family jewels of the First House would just shrink away, never to be seen again, leaving the task of carrying on the royal line to one of his younger brothers.

By sheer dint of will, he managed to tread water for a full two minutes before he floundered out and stomped back to camp. His men probably thought him insane to be bathing so early in the morning. Any sensible man would have waited until evening when the sun had warmed the surface waters of the bottomless lake that now filled the crater of the ancient volcano.

Good sense had nothing to do with it, Jibril thought wryly, as he dried himself and dressed in the privacy of his tent. Truth be told, his morning dips were just about the only way to subdue the fierce arousal that had plagued him every morning since he'd left Syrah's bed. Not to mention at night, or the hours in between astride his stallion, which made for a truly uncomfortable ride. It was fitting penance for losing his vaunted self-control and seducing his future wife.

If he was having trouble now when half the Dominion lay between them, it was going to be hell in three days' time when he came face-to-face with her in her father's hall.

From the moment he set eyes on the grown-up Syrah Eliaza Oriana Dhion, the self-discipline of a lifetime had evaporated into thin air where she was concerned—and then she'd been got up in the costume of a whore, with missing teeth and a sickly complexion. She hadn't been able to hide those eyes, of course, or the lovely breasts and long, sleek legs, but he had resisted more alluring bodies than hers during his bouts of celibacy. No, it was the energy of Syrah herself that had swept him away, by turns innocent and wanton, mischievous and serious, impulsive and determined. In short, arousing in every way.

With a sigh, he buckled on his sword belt and went to

break his fast at the cook's cart. Sleepy villages sprang into furious activity when the royal troops were camped nearby, offering services of every sort: cooking, laundering, mending, bedding. Jibril had no objection to his men seeking their pleasure when they were off duty, but women were never allowed in the camp for that purpose.

The stout woman who ladled out porridge for Jibril grinned at him with mischief in her eyes. "A fine morning, my lord. You do seem to enjoy your morning dips. Cold enough for you?"

Jibril narrowed his eyes at her, then gave up and burst into self-deprecating laughter and sauntered away.

The activity on the north coast was winding down. Fifteen smugglers were in custody, their longboats impounded, and a small fortune in pirated spices confiscated. But the main ship was long gone by the time Admiral Arcos rounded the point with two ships of the Dominion's navy.

Jibril spent the morning questioning the prisoners and learned that none other than Najja Kek had captained the ship. The man was a legend in the southern ocean. For years he had plundered the merchant ships that plied the waters between the great desert kingdoms to the south and the bustling ports of call to the north and west. What particularly interested Jibril was that Kek had sailed so close to the coast of Dominion. Generally, he gave the island a wide berth, preferring to send the smaller ships under his command into coastal waters. He had no compunction whatsoever about putting his men in the way of the Dominion's formidable navy to avoid being taken himself. Yet he'd been within a mile or so of the coast not ten days past and had set a course to the west when his lookout spotted the prince's troops on shore. Something unusual was afoot. Jibril dispatched a messenger to the king and another to Kalan, warning him that Kek might be paying a visit to Ranulph Gyp in the near future.

By late afternoon, most of the troops had departed for the capital with the prisoners and their plunder. Twelve remained behind to patrol the north coast and three others were to ride southwest with Jibril at first light.

Jibril couldn't decide which was more daunting: another swim in the waters of Lake Zando or the coming confrontation with Lady Syrah Dhion.

Chapter Twenty-two

Guardsman Orini couldn't believe his eyes. What the devil was Nini of Dunataea doing here? Only four days previous she'd been on her way to enter the novitiate, and now here she was bustling across the great hall of the Ninth House. He watched the girl's progress as she disappeared up the stairs that led to the family's private quarters. Odd, he hadn't remembered her being quite so plump, but he couldn't mistake the curly black hair and that enticing derriere.

Tossing back the last of his morning ale, he followed the derriere up two flights and down a long hall, where it turned into Lady Syrah's chambers. He had just enough time before the door closed to glimpse four women gathered about Lady Syrah. He heard the murmur of voices pitched low through the heavy door but couldn't make out the words. Determined to discover what mischief was afoot, he stationed himself in an alcove halfway down the hall to wait for the deceitful little Nini to reappear.

A quarter of an hour later, the door opened and the women dispersed; two toward the back staircase that led down to the kitchens and one down a hall that led to the nursery. Nini trotted straight toward the alcove where Orini lurked. It took but a second for him to jerk her against him and cover her scream of surprise with a big calloused hand.

"Not a sound, wench," he growled. The girl nodded her head and stared up at him with huge frightened eyes. "What the devil are you doing here?"

"I w-work here, sir," the girl stammered in a whisper.

Orini frowned down at her. Now that he saw her up close, he wasn't so sure it was Nini after all; she didn't have the little dimples that had so taken his eye. "What's your name, girl?"

"I'm Clea, if you please, sir."

"Not Nini?"

"I don't know any Nini, sir. I'm Clea."

Orini still held the girl tight against him. His body couldn't help responding to the feel of her nicely cushioned bosom against his chest, but this was no time for dalliance. Clearing his throat he said, "I saw a girl upon the road four days ago who was traveling with her brother. She said her name was Nini. She looked exactly like you."

Clea wasn't finding being pressed against the full length of the big guard all that unpleasant, either, but since he wasn't doing anything about it, she decided he had other things on his mind. "Some mistake me for my sister, sir. My pa used to get us mixed up all the time. She's Mayenne, I'm Clea."

Suddenly, the full import of what he'd said hit Clea square in the face. "You saw her? Is she all right? Did the Gypsies get her? Our ma always said Gypsies were lustful devils, but my lady said she's just fine and they didn't get her."

Orini shook his head; the girl wasn't making sense. "Are you telling me Lady Syrah saw your sister on the road?"

Clea quivered with excitement. "It must have been Mayenne! She's Lady Syrah's maid."

Orini's mind was spinning with possibilities. Lady Syrah had known this Mayenne wasn't on her way to the priory at Dunataea. A terrible suspicion took shape.

"Tell me, do you know Lord Eben? What does he look like?"

"All the girls know Lord Eben, sir; he's right handsome with eyes just like my lady's and yellow hair, except hers is straight and his is all curly like. Maybe that's Lord Eben you saw. My lady said Mayenne's in good hands, so I bet it's him. He won't let the Gypsies get her."

"Get along with you, then, Clea," Orini said grimly, but he couldn't resist patting her upon her delicious little derriere as he sent her on her way.

For long minutes Orini remained in the alcove, swearing himself all sorts of fool for letting Eben Dhion and this Mayenne play their little game with him. As for Lady Syrah . . .

Orini knew he'd have to confess to Captain Ankuli how he'd been tricked; the captain wasn't going to take it well. Not that the captain himself hadn't fallen victim to Lord Eben's tricks. Orini had been one of the mounted guard that day on the parade ground when the boy had spun his tale of vicious dromedaries; and he'd never forget the sight of the captain taking an axe to that coffin on the Isle of Lost Souls. Not that Orini had any intention of reminding him of it.

He stalked down the hall to Lady Syrah's door, intending to confront her with his suspicions, only to be brought up short when the door opened and he found her looking out at him.

"Captain Orini," she said brightly. "How fortunate; I was just coming to look for you. Won't you come in?"

Orini took a step back. "Wouldn't be proper, my lady."

"That's no problem; Depta's here with me."

Some of the wind had gone out the guardsman's sails, but he lowered his head and stalked into her sitting room. "My lady," he began sternly, "I need to speak with you on an important matter—"

"I, too, have an important matter to discuss with you, sir," Syrah said. "I wish to ask a favor of you. Since time is of the essence, perhaps you would allow me to speak first."

"But of course, my lady."

"We have a problem here at the hall, sir, of the utmost delicacy. I am told that Lord Ranulph has pestered some of our girls with his unwanted attentions. You will understand my concern when you hear that one of our girls, who is but twelve years of age, ran away in order to avoid returning to his bed."

"The devil you say! Twelve?" Orini roared, completely forgetting himself.

"Yes," Syrah said, seating herself on a low stool. "So, you see, I must get the younger girls away as quickly as possible. My cousin leaves for his own hall later this morning for a few days, and I want them gone when he returns. I have spoken with his steward and convinced him we are overstaffed. I wish you to see them safely back to their families. My women have informed me there are fourteen girls who are most at risk."

So the stories about Ranulph Gyp were true, Orini thought grimly. He only hoped Lady Syrah had been spared the knowledge of just how her cousin took his pleasure. A lady should not know of such things.

"I will help you in any way I can. Captain Ankuli left me in charge in his absence. I will see the girls to their homes at once. We can spare four men to provide an escort."

Syrah gave him a brilliant smile. "I knew I should find an ally in you, sir."

Guardsman Orini was halfway across the courtyard before he realized he hadn't gotten around to asking Lady Syrah about the incident on the road, but he was grinning as he made his way toward the stables. The priory at Dunataea would not be taking a little novice with dimples, curly black hair, and a bottom that would make any man tremble. But with any luck, he would.

"What the hell?" Prince Jibril muttered, pulling up beside Kalan. "Is that Orini down there? What in the name of all that's holy is he doing with all those women?"

The two men stared down at the odd little caravan as it made its way through the valley below. Guardsman Orini led the way astride a brown gelding, followed by two wagons full of young women and Depta on an old gray mule, the whole flanked by four guards.

"Not women; girls, I'd say," Kalan said as they picked

their way down the steep slope and the gay chatter of young girls' voices drifted up to them. "Orini has some explaining to do."

By the time the prince and Kalan reached the bottom of the hill, Orini had spotted them and signaled the convoy to halt. Depta nudged her irascible mount up beside him and they waited in silence as the two frowning men trotted up.

Jibril's gaze swept over the wide-eyed girls, then settled on Orini, who stared straight ahead, evidently expecting the worst. "Explain," he said tersely.

"It's like this, Your Highness," Orini began, only to be drowned out by an explosion of giggles and squeals as the girls realized they were in the presence of none other than the Crown Prince. They began jostling and pushing as they tried to execute awkward little curtsies. Panicked, the dray ponies struggled in their traces and disaster was only just averted when two of the guards grabbed hold of their bridles and forced their heads down to steady them.

Jibril signaled Kalan, Orini, and Depta to follow him as he turned his mount toward a weedy field some distance away.

Orini cleared his throat. "It was Lady Syrah, sir. She—"

Jibril groaned. "I should have known. What's she up to now?"

Depta narrowed her eyes at him. "Now don't you go casting blame on her till you know what all this is about, my lord. I reckon you'll be praising her to the skies once you've heard the truth of it."

"If you say so, Depta," Jibril replied with a grin. "Go on, Orini."

"Seems Gyp's been after the young ones. Lady Syrah said the only way to protect them is to send them home to their families. That's where we're taking them. Gyp's off at his own hall. He's going to be powerfully annoyed with her when he gets back. I set two men to see to Lady Syrah's safety night and day."

"Sweet Lord," Jibril swore. "That man's lower than a snake."

"That's not all, sir. That mercenary what captured Lady

Syrah, he arrived yesterday just after Gyp left and he's hanging around. Says he'll stay till Gyp gets back. Says he has business with him. Lady Syrah wasn't real pleased to see him in the great hall. I have to say I didn't like leaving her alone with him about, but she said it was more important to get the girls away."

Jibril threw back his head and laughed. "I'm sure she wasn't pleased at all. I wouldn't worry: Obike Zebengo will behave himself."

"You did the right thing, Orini," Captain Ankuli said.

"Don't see as I could do anything else, Your Highness," Orini said. "One of those girls he used was just twelve. I've got two sisters, twins that age. I'd see him a eunuch if he dared touch them like that."

"Be on your way, then," Jibril told him.

Kalan and Orini went to have a word with the guards. Jibril remained behind with Depta.

He cleared his throat. "How fares Lady Syrah?"

Depta grinned. "Well enough, my lord."

"She's settled in, has she?"

"She's settled in just fine."

"Her spirits are well?"

"Well enough." She chortled, enjoying his discomfiture. "Of course, I only see her during the day. As to her spirits at night in her bed, I couldn't say."

"Ah."

The prince looked so uneasy that Depta relented a little. "Don't think she sleeps all that well. She's got big circles under her eyes. Might be crying at night, can't say for sure."

Jibril nodded and fiddled with his reins. "You know," he said matter-of-factly.

"I do, indeed," she said fiercely. "She's not with child, but you had better do right by her."

"She'll be my queen, Depta."

The old woman sniffed. "She'd better be, or you'll have me to answer to."

An hour later the caravan had departed and Jibril and Kalan sprawled on the grass soaking up the warm rays of the sun after a meal of bread and cheese. Jibril had given his friend a full account of the operation on the north coast. They agreed Najja Kek would probably turn up soon to meet Ranulph Gyp, especially now that it appeared Gyp would soon be in possession of Lord Dhion's estate. The present whereabouts of Eben Dhion were still a mystery, but Orini's shamefaced account of his meeting with the monk on the road left no doubt Eben would be lurking about. They discussed the various ways the boy might contact his sister. Kalan's spies had informed him that on two consecutive evenings she had disappeared from the great hall and they had been unable to determine her whereabouts. She might already be meeting Eben at some prearranged rendezvous.

Prince Jibril's unexpected arrival with Captain Ankuli the following night sent the Great House into a frenzy. Servants scurried about upstairs and down, casting surreptitious glances at the royal personage in their midst. Jibril and Kalan strode into the great hall where they found Zebengo ensconced in a huge cushioned chair by the fire. Syrah sat opposite, working a flowered embroidery onto the hem of a gown. He was grinning at her over the rim of a huge mug of ale. She was glaring back.

Zebengo lumbered to his feet as the prince made his way toward the hearth and bowed. "What an unexpected surprise, Your Highness," he boomed.

Syrah's head snapped up. Her face remained carefully neutral as she stood to greet the prince. She sank into a deep curtsy and allowed him to assist her up. "Welcome, Your Highness," she said in her most formal manner. "You do us great honor."

Jibril bowed. "It is good to see you again, Lady Syrah."

She managed to summon a smile. "And you, my lord. Now, if you will excuse me, I will see that my staff provides you with every comfort." With that, she marched across the great hall and disappeared through a curtained doorway.

Jibril dropped into the chair she had vacated and signaled a hovering servant to bring ale. Kalan pulled up a bench, and Zebengo settled back in his chair.

"You seem to have made yourself at home, Obike," the

prince observed wryly. "I take it Gyp doesn't know you're here."

"I missed him by an hour or two. Thought I'd settle in until he gets back." Zebengo surveyed the huge hall with its high arched windows and brilliant tapestries. "Why stay at an inn when such accommodation is available?"

"And how does Lady Syrah take your presence?"

"If she could spit fire, I'd have gone up in flames hours ago."

Jibril drank deeply. "We think Najja Kek's on his way."

He gave Obike a brief account of the smugglers they'd arrested. "Word is out that Gyp sits as regent for the Ninth House by my father's decree. That opens up almost a hundred miles of coastline for Kek's activities without much fear of interference. I wish to God that I knew what he's up to; you're going to have to find out for me. I need to find Eben Dhion before Gyp does, or before Syrah draws him into more mischief. He might already be around here somewhere. Orini met up with him and Syrah's maid on the road, although he didn't realize it at the time."

Obike laughed. "Did Lord Eben put one over on him with one of his tall stories? The boy's a genius. He had his sister blowing up frogs the night we nabbed her at the inn."

Jibril shook his head in disbelief. "No frogs this time—cannibals. He got me with worms."

"Dromedaries," Kalan contributed.

A burst of laughter from the vicinity of the hearth startled the servants who were setting the high table with every luxury the cooks could scare up for the prince at such short notice. They smiled among themselves. It was good to hear laughter in the Ninth House again.

Syrah wasn't smiling. She only just managed to reach her bench behind the ivy before she burst into tears. It really was too much. No sooner had she sent the girls off to safety with Depta and Orini than that double-dealing mercenary rode into her courtyard just as nonchalant as could be. He'd winked at her and sauntered up the stairs into the Great House as though he hadn't just betrayed her and sold her to the Crown. She didn't dare toss him out on his gold-studded ear, but it was certain he was up to no good since he said he had business with her cousin. Syrah suggested, none too diplomatically, that he stay at the inn in the village. He thought he'd prefer the accommodations here, he informed her, and summoned one of the pages to show him to the best guest chamber without so much as a by-your-leave. Syrah had no recourse but to entertain him until Ranulph returned.

And now Prince Jibril had popped up out of nowhere, and instead of summoning up her undying hatred, the mere sight of him strolling toward her across the hall in those tight leather breeches with that lord-of-all-I-survey look on his face had launched a veritable phalanx of frogs leaping about in her belly, and truth be told, lower still. Of course, he *was* lord of all he surveyed, being the Crown Prince, but that didn't signify anything in her present frame of mind. He had no right to make her feel like this, all weepy and shivery and squishy.

Wasn't it enough that he'd kissed her "like that" on the Isle of Lost Souls? Wasn't it enough he'd made love to her and sent her clear out of her senses when he knew the king was going to toss her in the way of Ranulph? Wasn't it enough she dreamed of him every night and woke up moaning for him and had ugly black circles under her eyes?

He wouldn't care a fig, she decided, wiping her eyes on the sleeve of her gown. His kind didn't. Well, she'd see about that. She'd just march back into the hall and make him give a fig.

She sank back down on the bench with a sigh and began tearing shiny dark leaves of ivy into tiny pieces. His kind: What did she know of his or any other kind? Three weeks ago she hadn't even known how to kiss.

This was ridiculous; she couldn't remember the last time she'd let her feelings run away with her like this. She was a rational being, not some sniveling child. Moping about because some amber-eyed womanizer had had his way with her wasn't going to get rid of Ranulph and avenge Great Uncle Amorgos.

Of course, she'd had her way with him, too, and very agreeable it had been, not to mention an unforgettable learning experience. There, that was the right way to look at it—all part of a young woman's education, just like geography or drawing or darning.

If Great Uncle Amorgos were here, he would waggle those bushy eyebrows at her and tell her this was no way to win a game of chess.

Resolved not to allow the prince to overwhelm her, she made her way up the back stairs to her chambers, where she changed into a peach-colored gown trimmed with satin ribbon. She splashed cold water on her face and summoned one of the maids to plait her hair, then changed her mind and had her pin it up and secure it with a gold-colored comb in the shape of a butterfly. Feeling very adult, very lady-of-the-manor, she went to greet her royal guest with an apparent ease and elegance that would have made her mother proud.

The three men had moved to the high table where a veritable feast had been spread before them. Syrah glided across the marble floor and executed a graceful curtsy.

"I apologize, Your Highness, that you received so poor a reception in my father's hall. Your visit is unexpected. Had I but known, I would have instructed my staff to prepare a welcome worthy of you."

Jibril lounged back in his chair gazing down at the graceful self-assured woman before him, and wondered if there was a role she could not play to perfection. "Lady Syrah, please don't trouble yourself. It is I who should be apologizing for barging in like this. I have been traveling on business and thought to stop by to see how you are getting on."

"You are too kind, Your Highness. I get on very well. How long exactly do you expect to be in the area, sir?"

"I must return to the capital tomorrow morning."

"So short a time?" Syrah said, her tone that of the hostess who is not at all disappointed at a guest taking his leave.

She turned to Zebengo with a smug little smile. "Alas, sir, I must ask you to vacate the chamber you now occupy so that my maids can prepare it for His Highness, though he graces us with his presence but for one night. I am sure you will find one of the smaller rooms nearly as comfortable, although I fear you will have to do without your own privy. There is, however, a commodious chamber pot beneath the bed. I'm sure you will be most obliging; I understand you are a great friend of His Highness."

Zebengo grinned. "But of course, my lady. I have no objection so long as the pot is, as you say, commodious."

Jibril almost laughed. She did not appreciate Zebengo's condescension. For a moment he thought her temper would get the better of her, but the lapse was momentary and the set smile of the accommodating hostess was again in place.

"His Majesty is in good health, I trust, Your Highness?"

"He is, Lady Syrah. I had hoped to speak with Lord Ranulph. I understand he is away."

"He is. He will be grieved to hear that he missed your visit."

She turned to Ankuli with a charming little smile. "And, Captain, no doubt you will want to move into the Great House now that His Highness has granted us the honor of his presence. The barracks are so very unpleasant, don't you think?"

Kalan nodded, wondering if he would merit even a chamber pot. "You are very kind, my lady."

"Well, now that we have everyone settled, I will leave you to your meal." She curtsied and glided from the hall.

"I believe we have just been put in our places, gentlemen," Jibril remarked.

"Yes," Zebengo grumbled, "and you got the privy."

Chapter Twenty-three

Long before dawn, Syrah had saddled Angel and ridden out into the sweet silence of the open meadows and low hills that surrounded the Great House. The sun was rising now and streams of mist trailed upward from the cooler waters of brook and pond into the warming air. The whitewashed stone of the Great House became for a few minutes a faceted diamond as the last of the fine mist drifted upward from the towers into a clear blue sky.

Far below, the morning rituals had begun. A heavily laden cart bearing pails of fresh milk lumbered up the road from the dairy. Housemaids aired bedding from the upper windows of the south tower, and stable boys led fat mares and frisky foals toward the thick carpet of green in the upper pasture. Creon, the beekeeper, scraped honeycomb from a wooden hive tray, while a small boy waved a smoky rag about to ward off the indignant swarm. A scullion toted a pail of scraps toward the piggery.

A year ago Syrah would have reveled in the rightness of it all. Lord and Lady Dhion would emerge from the chapel and make their way hand-in-hand toward the great hall to break their fast. Morgana would toddle about the herb garden trailed by her anxious nurse; Eben would leap down

the front steps and dash off to the training ground, where
Sir Zibon waited with a boy-sized falchion and shield. And
Syrah would have urged Angel into a mad race down the
hill to the lower pasture, tossed the reins to Clim, brushed
the dust from her gown, and strolled up the steps into the
great hall with all the aplomb of a dutiful daughter who
had not just disobeyed her father by riding out without
groom or guard.

A sob caught in her throat, for nothing would ever be
quite right again. Mama slept within the cold marble walls
of the family vault, and Papa, Eben, and Morgana were in
exile for the time being. Ranulph sat in the high seat as
regent, waiting for his main chance, while far away the king
sat upon his throne, spinning a web about them all.

And now Jibril, Zebengo, and Ankuli had convened in
the Great House, most assuredly not by chance. As she
watched the busy scene below, the three men appeared and
began strolling about the grounds, deep in conversation.
Occasionally, they would stop and ask a question of some
servant, then move on. They seemed to have no particular
destination in mind, but Syrah had the impression they
were looking for something, or someone.

Was it possible they knew of the tunnel? She thought it
unlikely. Papa had insisted that she and Eben swear secrecy
upon the Bible before he showed them the secret entrance
to the tunnel, which lay behind a false wall in the shed
where bunches of herbs and flowers were hung from hooks
in the ceiling to dry. When closed, the stone-faced door sat
flush with the outer wall; one removed a small stone to
move the lever that opened it.

Most manor houses had such tunnels beneath their halls,
but that of the Ninth House was different in that it emerged
not into another building, where enemies might expect it
and so lie in wait, but in a small cave that let on to a high
thorny bank just a quarter mile beyond the boathouse. A
small rowboat rested in the cave proper in the event that
enemies burned the boathouse, thinking to prevent an escape by boat down the river.

The tunnel was ancient, Papa had told them. Even he was

not sure when it had been built nor when it had last been used; certainly not during the reign of the current Chios dynasty, which had suppressed bloody warfare between noble Houses more than two centuries ago. Syrah and Eben could believe that, for they had explored it from end to end on several occasions and found it filled halfway to the ceiling in places with heaps of the undisturbed droppings and white bones of a million unpleasant little creatures and the webs of ten thousands of generations of spiders and other creepy-crawlies. Once they had startled a colony of bats and tried to seal up the river-end entrance with heavy stones in the event some curious passerby saw the bats flying in and out and came to investigate.

Syrah never minded their secret excursions through the tunnel when Eben was with her, but she had trudged all the way to the river three times now with trepidation and disgust, hoping to find him waiting for her. He must be somewhere about, biding his time until the coast was clear. She had thought he would come when Ranulph left the hall, but then that blasted Zebengo showed up and Captain Ankuli returned with Prince Jibril. Last night she had left a note in a jar, warning Eben to stay away for the time being.

"She's been watching us for over an hour," Zebengo informed Jibril and Kalan as they emerged from the sheep barn.

Jibril glanced up at the small figure in blue that had now dismounted and settled down amid the waving grass of a far hill. Her white horse had moved down the slope to graze in a patch of wildflowers. "I know. And she knows we're nosing around. She's waiting to see what we're going to do."

"Never knew a woman could be so patient, just sitting up there like that," Zebengo remarked.

"You haven't played chess with her," Jibril said dryly.

"If Depta hadn't told me Lady Syrah left her sleeping chamber for over an hour shortly after midnight, I'd say there's nothing for us to find here," Kalan observed. "But there has to be. Depta followed her as far as the kitchens, but then the lady just disappeared. All these old manor houses have secret escape routes. There's got to be one here somewhere, but I'm damned if I could find it. Orini's back and I have him and two of the men going over the kitchen area again."

A faint whistle carried on the wind, Syrah summoning her horse to her. They watched as she swung up into the saddle and started down the hill toward the Great House, then swerved off toward the fast-moving river at the far side of the meadow. There she paused beside a small boathouse to let the horse drink before turning back toward the Great House.

"Have a look at the boathouse," Jibril said to Kalan.

"You think there might be a tunnel entrance there?"

Jibril looked thoughtful. "No, but I think the lady may want us to search there and find nothing. What better way to turn our attention away from the area?"

"God preserve me from clever women," Kalan muttered.

Over the morning meal of sweet porridge and currants, bread, and fruit, Jibril sketched out a plan for the next few days. Kalan would keep track of Ranulph Gyp, and Zebengo was to offer his services upon his return. "See if you can get him to bring you in on whatever scheme he and Kek are hatching. Perhaps you can convince him you know where Syrah hid the ransom money; you'll forfeit your usual fee to bring it to him if they'll make you a partner. Meanwhile, I'll take Orini and stake out the area around the boathouse over the next few nights."

Jibril broke off suddenly as Syrah entered the hall and made her way to the high table. He stood to offer her his chair but she politely declined. "Thank you, Your Highness, but I broke my fast hours ago. I just came to see if you spent a comfortable night."

"Indeed I did," he lied. His night hadn't been remotely comfortable, despite the elegance of his suite and the softness of his feather bed. He had only to awake to aching arousal from one explicitly erotic dream to fall back asleep and find her driving him wild in another.

"And the meal is to your liking? More ale, perhaps?" She signaled a maid to bring another pitcher. "I've taken the liberty of ordering Cook to pack provisions for you for the journey back to the capital," she said briskly. "I expect the escort the king so kindly provided for me will be returning with you; I have taken their numbers into account."

It could not have been any clearer that Lady Syrah wanted him and his men off the premises than if she had prodded them before her with a pitchfork.

"Thank you, my lady."

"Well," she said brightly as though contemplating a job well done, "it has been a pleasure to see you again, my lord. Please be so good as to convey my deepest respect to His Majesty. I shall not soon forget his compassion and his great wisdom in returning me to my hall."

"I am pleased to see that you are getting on so well," Jibril said.

"I am indeed. I do believe my cousin and I shall soon reach an understanding."

The prince almost choked on his ale. "You intend to marry Lord Ranulph?"

Syrah smiled sweetly. "Is that not what His Majesty and you yourself counseled?"

Jibril could barely restrain himself from vaulting over the table and strangling the maddening woman where she stood with that mischievous gleam in her eye. Most likely he'd end up kissing that elfish smile right off her rosy lips and bearing her off to the nearest bedchamber. Best to keep his seat.

"I'll convey that happy news to my father."

Syrah curtsied low and started for the stairs that led to her quarters. She paused and turned back to Zebengo. "You found the pot commodious, I trust, Zebengo?"

"Most commodious, my lady," he replied.

"Excellent. Then I shall inform the maids that you are pleased with that chamber and will remain there for the duration of your stay," she said graciously and disappeared up the stairs.

An hour later, Syrah watched from her chamber window

as Prince Jibril and his troops made their way across the drawbridge and down the hill toward the main road. There, Captain Ankuli split off with three guardsmen, heading toward the mountain pass that would take him into the northwest quadrant of the Dominion. It was, Syrah noted, also the road to the Gyp holding. Prince Jibril's party set off along the river toward the capital, a hundred miles to the east.

Syrah had insisted Depta return with them, but the old woman stood firm in the face of every objection Syrah could muster. She would stay until the maid Mayenne returned to the hall, as would the three maids who had attended her in the palace. A hulking groom had remained behind as well, asserting, not all that convincingly, that he had his eye on one of the under-cooks for a wife. Three soldiers, big fellows all, had been assigned to look to her safety on the pretext that there had been reports of smugglers along the western coast.

That these eight men and women spied for the king was obvious; that they had been assigned to nab Eben and keep watch on herself as well as Ranulph was equally so. Perhaps the king thought she would bolt if marriage to her cousin became a real possibility; or she might slip away to hire some other mercenary to replace the perfidious Zebengo.

Syrah rather liked the mercenary, despite his treachery. He might undertake any number of commissions if the price was right, but Syrah suspected he followed his own moral compass and would not prey on the innocent. The thought suddenly occurred to her that he, too, came to the hall at the king's behest to discover what Ranulph might be about.

Syrah watched as the last of the prince's party disappeared around a bend in the river, relieved to be rid of his disturbing presence. At least she hadn't dreamed the dream last night. She hadn't dreamed it because she hadn't slept at all.

It had been well past midnight before she felt certain she could slip down the back stairs and through the kitchen to the herb shed without being seen. She had waited a full hour in the cave by the river, the atmosphere so stale and musty that she finally worked a stone loose to let in some fresh air. More cautious than usual, she had doused the light of the lantern before she emerged into the shed. Putting everything back in its proper place had been slow going in the dark. Creeping past the little alcove where Depta snored loudly, she eased the door of her dressing room closed behind her and exchanged the breeches and rough shirt she had worn in the tunnel for the fine muslin sleeping gown she had worn to bid Depta good night. Back in her warm bed she had lain for hours staring up at the canopy, too wound up to sleep.

"You're looking right tuckered out this morning, my lady," Depta said from the doorway. "You'd think you hadn't slept a wink last night."

"I didn't sleep all that well," Syrah admitted. "Perhaps I'll lie down for a bit."

"That's my girl," the old woman said. "I'll see you aren't disturbed."

Syrah slipped out of her gown, and clad only in her chemise, crawled into bed. However, sleep eluded her and once again she found herself staring up at the canopy, one thought chasing on the heels of another.

Try as she might, she couldn't figure out what her cousin was up to, apart from coveting the high seat of the Ninth House. A marriage would certainly give him purchase, but her father still lived, and now that the king's attention was turned upon him, Ranulph wouldn't dare harm Eben. Not yet, anyway. But Eben was only fourteen, and six years was a long time.

If the court physician couldn't effect a cure, Papa would almost surely die. Syrah could never have imagined that such a big strong man as Papa, descendant of the blond giants from the far north, could have become so feeble and frail in only three months. She suspected his illness stemmed as much from Mama's passing as it did from the fever that struck them down, and no physician could devise a cure for grief. Even if he survived, he would never be the man he'd been. He would not sit on the high seat of the Ninth House again. That left Eben. What better way for Ranulph to position himself than to marry her?

She frowned up at a dimpled cherub. No, something else, equally sinister, was in the wind. She couldn't be sure, but she suspected the king had had his eye on her cousin long before she kidnapped Jibril.

She focused in on Ranulph. The man was reasonably well off in his own right, though not nearly so rich as Papa. His lands were not so fertile as theirs, either, the terrain steep and the soil rocky. He derived most of his income from raising sheep for meat and wool. The Ninth House drew its wealth from both land and sea—fertile fields and the bounty of the sea.

Syrah nearly shot off the bed. The sea! That was it. Ranulph wanted access to the sea. And it wasn't fishing he had in mind. It was smuggling.

Chapter Twenty-four

Mayenne had a plan. She would take off her half boots and tippytoe down the long dock, lower herself into the rowboat, untie it from the piling, and silently slip away down the river into the night.

But wait. What if It happened to notice her tippytoeing down the dock? What if a plank creaked or the boat bumped against the piling and It heard?

What if It was waiting for her in the rowboat?

She pressed back deeper into the shadow of the boathouse and stifled a sob. Eben had told her she'd be safe here while he went to the secret place to meet her lady, because the soldiers had already searched the boathouse and they wouldn't bother coming back. He knew this because he'd spent the morning in a tree on the other side of the river watching them.

So if a soldier wasn't snuffling around on the other side of the boathouse, that meant it was a Something, and a Something could probably do things she couldn't, like fly and sneak up on a person without a sound. A Something might even be smarter than she was and figure out what she was going to do before she knew that she was going to do it and be there when she did it.

225

She stiffened; the snuffling had stopped. Now the Something was grunting and mumbling to Itself. It sounded hungry. It was closer, too, just around the corner of the boathouse instead of way over on the other side. She inched sideways along the wall, keeping her eyes glued to the corner.

A scream froze in her throat as a hulking blob loomed out of the shadows.

It knew she was here! But did It know she knew It knew she was here? She didn't know.

But wait. Maybe It didn't. She might still save herself. The blob was behind her so It wouldn't be lurking in the rowboat, would It? She'd just slip around the corner and creep down the dock. She wouldn't bother with the boat; she didn't know how to paddle anyway. No, she would just slide into the river without a sound and leave the blob scratching Its head wondering where she'd gone. Of course, once she was in the river she would have to figure out how to swim, but how hard could that be?

With a fervent "Hail Mary" she slithered around the corner and slunk toward the rushing river.

"Halt in the name of the king!"

Mayenne whirled around and froze to the spot. Detaching itself from the shadows, the blob turned into a man, an enormous man, a soldier who shouldn't be there because Eben said he wouldn't be, but he was, and at least he wasn't a blob, which really wasn't all that comforting, because he didn't look at all friendly and was probably going to crush her in those massive muscled arms or run her through with his long sword or . . .

"What do you here, girl?" the blob man growled.

"Me?" she squeaked.

"You."

She took a step backward. "I was just, er, um, looking for my, um . . ."

The blob man took a menacing step forward. "Your what?"

She grasped for inspiration. "My . . . my dromedary!"

"Dromedary?" He narrowed his eyes at her. "Wait a minute, I know you—"

"No, you don't," Mayenne assured him shrilly.

Foot by foot he backed her down the dock. "Oh, yes, I do. You're that girl Clea. The one who told me her sister . . . No, wait a minute, you're the other one, the one on the road who—"

Shaking with terror, Mayenne scooted back. And then she looked down and there wasn't a dock where a dock should be. For a few moments she flailed her arms around like the sails of a windmill in a strong gale, and with a fearful shriek she toppled backward into the dark water.

"Oh, hell," Guardsman Orini said as he threw aside his sword and dove in after her.

At about the same time Mayenne was going down for the third time, Eben was a quarter mile downstream wielding a long forked stick to push aside the tangled brambles that concealed the entrance to the cave. A faint breeze touched his cheek, followed by a whoosh of unseen wings, then another and another. He ducked his head as bats swooped past him in and out of the cave.

He stood stock-still, trying to sense where danger might lie. Someone had moved one of the large stones that blocked the entrance. He peered into the cave. A faint glow indicated a light, probably a lantern, far along the twisting passage.

He breathed a sigh of relief. It had to be Syrah. She'd moved the stone and was waiting for him. Just in case, he whistled three times, one of the secret signals they had used as children. When the whistle was returned, he pulled himself up and over the stone barrier and clambered into the cave. He stuffed the tallow candle he'd brought along into his pocket; he wouldn't be needing it because Syrah was already here.

He brushed off his breeches and picked off a few brambles before he bent low and made his way toward the light. He hoped she'd thought to bring some decent food; he was heartily sick of bread and cheese and dried fruit. Cold goose sounded good, or salted hare. Maybe even a blackberry tart, his favorite, or . . .

"Expecting someone?" a deep voice inquired pleasantly.

Eben gave a yelp of surprise and jerked upright, banging his head so hard on the low ceiling that led into the larger cavern that he saw stars. Shaking his head to clear his vision, he beheld Prince Jibril seated against the far wall, one knee bent, the other leg stretched out in front of him, with arms crossed over his chest.

Apparently perfectly at ease, the prince reached down beside him and held out a leather flagon as though this were just a casual get-together between friends. "Wine?"

"How—"

"How did I find your rendezvous? The bats. We've been watching the river. When I spotted the bats, I knew there must be a cave somewhere nearby. I must say it's quite cleverly concealed. I expect the tunnel goes all the way back and comes out near the kitchens. We couldn't find that entrance."

Eben considered making a run for it back along the passage, but only for a moment. He was sick of running and hiding out. He plopped down beside the prince and rubbed his sore head. "The herb shed," he said.

"Kalan's going to kick himself for missing it. We'll have to keep him from taking an axe to it this time." The prince laughed.

Eben reached for the wine. "Where's my sister?"

"Zebengo's keeping her busy with a game of chess. Did you know he was here?"

"Yes. I've been watching the house ever since Syrah came back. He's not really a mercenary, is he? I told Syrah I thought there was something strange about him."

Jibril had given a lot of thought as to what he should tell Eben. In the end he decided not to hold anything back. Eben was clever; possibly the smartest young man Jibril had ever met. He was also in serious jeopardy. Gyp wouldn't dare kill him outright, but there were other, more subtle ways Eben could meet an untimely end. The boy needed to know where the danger lay and where he could look for help.

"No, he's not a mercenary. He's the head of internal security for the Crown."

"I knew it!" Eben crowed. "I tried to tell Syrah but she wouldn't listen. That's how she got caught. She found out he grew up in the palace and he was your friend at the last minute, but it was too late. She never listens. I tried to tell her about you, too."

"What do you mean?"

"The way you acted when you were our prisoner—I could tell you weren't really mad. I wanted her to tell you why we were kidnapping you because I thought you'd help us."

"And?"

Eben aimed a rock at an enormous furry spider in a far corner of the cave. "She said we couldn't trust you because the king wouldn't help us. She was really upset about that."

"I'll explain about that later. But why did you kidnap me?" the prince said. "It would have been much easier to grab some rich silk merchant or a money changer, and then you wouldn't have had half my soldiers chasing after you."

"Syrah wanted . . ." Eben began, then thought better of it.

"Yes?" the prince prompted.

"You'd better ask her," Eben muttered.

Prince Jibril decided he certainly would ask her.

They sat for a while in that utter stillness found only in caves deep in the earth. Occasionally, a bat would shoot by or a current of cool air would eddy along the passage, bringing with it the distant sound of the rushing river.

"So what's going to happen now?" Eben said. "Are you going to arrest me?"

Jibril got to his feet, stretched, and buckled on his sword belt. "No. We're going to ride out to my camp and I'm going to enlist you to help me bring down Ranulph Gyp."

Eben leaped to his feet. "Am I going to get to be a mercenary like Zebengo?"

"Better." Jibril laughed, slapping him on the back. "You're going to be a spy."

They made their way back to the outer cave. Eben held the lantern while Jibril fitted the big stone back in place, and they made their way down the riverbank.

The sound of swirling water drowned out all the usual noises of the night until suddenly an unholy wail soared above it from far upstream. The ululation was soon joined by a stream of invective that would have shamed a sailor as a thrashing blur floated into sight around the bend.

"Good God," Jibril exclaimed as the blur resolved into the shape of two humans locked in what appeared to be a lewd embrace. "Is that Orini again? What the devil is he up to now?"

"They should have drowned you at birth," Orini was yelling as he and Mayenne swept past the two astounded spectators on the bank and disappeared downstream into the night.

Three hours later, a damp, disheveled, grim-faced Guardsman Orini trudged into camp leading a bedraggled little figure at the end of a stout rope, her hands bound before her. He looped the rope several times around a tree limb and tied a knot that would have held a charging bull in check, and marched across the campsite to present himself at his commander's tent.

Jibril had only just doused the lantern and settled onto his cot when he heard Orini's voice requesting an audience. The guard stationed outside the tent started to refuse, but Jibril called out an order to show the guardsman in. He relit the lantern and settled down on a traveling chest to hear how Orini was going to explain away the extraordinary spectacle he had witnessed earlier in the evening.

"Guardsman Orini reporting, sir."

"At ease, Orini. You look out of sorts," the prince said, trying to keep from laughing aloud.

Orini stood ramrod straight, his eyes fixed on a point high on the tent wall above the prince's head. "Yes, sir. I mean, no, sir. I've brought in a prisoner. Found her at the boathouse."

"A woman, then?"

"Yes, sir. Lady Syrah's maid."

"That's an important capture," the prince said gravely.

"Now we have them both. I nabbed Lord Eben at that cave we discovered. I seem to have had an easier time of it, judging by the state of your uniform."

"Yes, sir," the guard replied through clenched teeth.

Obviously, Orini was unaware that his prince had witnessed the absurd sight of his usually stolid guardsman in the arms of a screeching banshee as they swept down the river and was too mortified to report it. Prince Jibril decided to take pity on him. He stood up and walked Orini to the tent flap, slapping him on the back. "Excellent work, excellent."

Orini was halfway across the clearing when he heard Prince Jibril calling him back. He turned to see just the prince's head poking through the tent flap. "Oh, Orini," he said with a broad grin on his face, "I should have mentioned that a member of the royal guard does not swear in front of a lady. You will remember that in future, I trust."

Mayenne nodded repeatedly as Prince Jibril outlined what he expected of her. Under no circumstances was she to reveal to Lady Syrah the present scheme. Her duty was to the Crown first and foremost. If she loved her mistress and would keep her safe, she must not betray in any way what she now knew.

She didn't know much, of course. Jibril and Eben had discussed at length what to tell the maid and what to withhold. They concluded it would be safe to tell her that there might be bad men in the area. She would find a big man with knife cuts on his face in the hall. His name was Zebengo and he was there to protect her lady against Ranulph Gyp and the bad men, but he wouldn't be able to do a good job if Mayenne betrayed his true identity to her mistress. Jibril explained that Lord Dhion and Lady Morgana were safe in the palace. Eben would be in no danger when he and Mayenne returned to the hall because the king had placed them all under his protection, and Ranulph Gyp wouldn't dare do anything to anger the king. No doubt Lady Syrah would question her closely as to how she and Eben had been captured. She could tell the truth, omitting this discussion he was having with her now.

"I know how much you love your mistress," Jibril said kindly. "The best way to help her is to say as little as possible. Do you understand?"

"Yes, Your Highness," she said earnestly. "I swear on my ma's grave."

He patted her arm and sent her off to Cook's cart for the morning meal, a small determined figure wearing a man's shirt that had been shortened with a pair of scissors and a squire's breeches held up with a belt of twisted rope. Her dress hung from a branch drying in the warm rays of the morning sun.

Orini scowled at her departing back. "The girl's a hellion. I've got scratches all over my neck and back, and my ears are still ringing from her screeching."

"Nice dimples, though," the prince remarked. He gave Orini a sly look. "And a fine bottom, if you hadn't noticed."

"I've noticed," Orini muttered, a blush creeping up his neck.

"So," Jibril said, turning his attention back to Eben. He shifted on the low stool and leaned forward. "Let's review. We expect Najja Kek to show up any day. Lord Ranulph may or may not know what he's got in mind. Smuggling, yes, but from what we've learned from those prisoners, something much more important is in the wind. I can't even speculate on what it could be, but I'll wager it's something that Najja Kek thinks is going to make him a very rich man."

He shook his head. "What I can't figure out is what he wants from Gyp, other than unrestricted access to the coast. Gyp's not wealthy enough to sponsor Kek's smuggling activities or build better ships for him—"

"He could be," Eben interjected. "We're a wealthy family. If he marries Syrah and sits as my regent, wouldn't he be able to make use of our treasury?"

"Only with the king's permission, but he'd have to come up with a good enough reason."

Eben nibbled at a chunk of brown bread and frowned. "Hmmm. Well, there is the gold."

"That's it!" the prince shouted, leaping up from the stool. Every head in the camp swiveled to behold their commander laughing and pounding the boy on the back. "Eben Dhion, you are brilliant. Someday I'm going to make you my prime minister. You've hit it exactly. Najja Kek is looking for gold, a lot of gold, and you and your sister just happen to have a fortune hidden away somewhere. He may just want it because he's a greedy bastard, but that blackguard lives for conspiracies and intrigues. I doubt he'd stop his wicked ways if he held the king's treasury. But he needs a lot of gold, for some scheme or other, and that's why he's suddenly become Gyp's best friend."

Eben didn't look all that happy. "Why hasn't he just kidnapped us and forced us to show him where it is?"

Jibril, too, had sobered. Kidnapping was a real possibility here. He'd better send Majan back to the capital immediately to bring more troops to protect Eben and Syrah.

"He didn't have the opportunity. You and Syrah disappeared from sight until you showed up at the inn to hire Zebengo. Since then she's been in custody and you've been on the run."

Eben stood up and tossed the bread aside. "Could I have a word in private with you, sir?"

They crossed the camp and made their way up a steep hill behind the temporary paddock where the horses were kept at night. Eben didn't speak until they stood at the top looking out over a broad sweep of rolling farmland. In the distance, they could just see the towers of the Great House.

"There's something you need to know," Eben said, squatting down on a rocky outcrop. He plucked a long leaf of grass and chewed at it in silence for a few minutes. Jibril held his tongue; whatever the boy had to say was obviously important.

"It's like this," Eben finally said. "We hid the ransom in a lake near the hunting camp. No one would ever think of looking there. It was Syrah's idea; she's really clever. But she disappeared for a few days after she left you on the island. I went to Suriana with Aleden to let the king know where you were. But when we got to my great aunt's manor house Syrah wasn't there. We thought at first maybe she'd been caught, but then everyone was talking about you being free and there was no mention of her, so we didn't know what had happened. The next day she showed up but she wouldn't tell me where she'd been."

"She must have moved the gold," Jibril said.

"Yes, I think she did. It made me mad at first because I thought maybe she didn't trust me, but then I realized she was scared for me. As long as I knew where it was I'd be vulnerable. We never got far enough with Zebengo to talk about the gold, because he went off to the palace that night. I think Syrah would have made it clear to him and anyone else who might learn what we were doing that she's the only one who knows where it is. Nobody could hurt me because I wouldn't be able to tell them anything."

Jibril tossed a stone down the hill and watched as it bounced from rock to and rock and out of sight. "You're forgetting one thing. Someone could kidnap you and threaten to harm you if she didn't come forward and tell them where the gold is hidden."

"I thought about that too, but that would be true only while we had the gold. I think she intended to strike a bargain with Zebengo and pay in advance. Then she'd return the rest to the king and see to it that everyone knew. No gold, no problem."

Jibril shook his head. What an amazing woman. He'd always thought he was the master tactician, or at least the equal of his father, but Syrah Dhion might very well be just as good. Her father had been a brilliant man in his own right, of course—before the fever scrambled his wits—but Jibril suspected it was that crafty Great Uncle Amorgos who had seen the real brilliance in the girl and nurtured it in the only way a woman might be allowed to compete with men: the game of chess.

Jibril had never given much thought to the intelligence a woman might hide behind a pretty face, or a plain one for that matter. He loved their warm soft bodies and their sweet scent; the way they could gentle him with a touch or a soft word, fire him with a seductive smile. He reveled in his power to bring them their own satisfaction, and when they surrendered themselves to him utterly in the moment of his own release.

Not that he didn't value wit and good conversation. His mother the queen was a most perceptive woman, and his father placed high value on her counsel, even if he didn't always act on it. And a woman was the equal of any man in the arts, if her talent was nurtured. Women were known to be great healers, though the superstitious often laid their skills to witchery, whereas an equally able man would be lauded for his great learning.

But when it came down to it, Jibril believed women were ruled by emotion, not reason and logic, and for that reason alone were vulnerable and required the protection and guidance of men. Oh, a woman might be sensible enough to see the wisdom of marrying for advantage, especially if she was highborn and understood that the marriage would cement an alliance or improve the fortunes of her family. But deep in her heart she would always harbor that idealized romantic love the poets sang of.

Syrah Dhion might be a fine tactician, very much in the way of a clever man who finds solutions through the application of logic and critical thinking, and she might claim to understand her own limitations and learn from her mistakes. But life was not a game of chess, and ultimately she would be the loser in a contest of wills with a man who was truly bent on her destruction. She held her honor too high. And she would never understand with her woman's tender heart that shadowy place in every man where the beast still lurked and the true passion of the hunt lay in the joy of the kill.

"Do you have any idea where your sister might have hidden the gold? Would she tell you if you asked?"

Eben shook his head. "I don't think so."

"As long as the gold is out there somewhere, you and Syrah are in serious danger. You do realize that, don't you?"

"Yes."

Jibril tried to find a way to express his next thought without Eben jumping to the wrong conclusion. The pride of a fourteen-year-old boy was a fragile thing.

"If she won't tell you where the gold is, you might find a better use for your talents outside the hall rather than in."

Eben scrambled to his feet and glared down at the prince. "I know what you're trying to do and it won't work. I'm not a coward. I'm not afraid of Ranulph and I'm not afraid of this Najja Kek. Syrah is my sister and if she's in danger, then I'm going to be right there with her. If it hadn't been for her I might be dead now. Zebengo may be able to protect her body better than I can, but I'm the only one who has any chance of talking her out of some crazy scheme that might get her killed."

Eben was now shouting at the Crown Prince of the Dominion as though he were a recalcitrant servant. "I may only be fourteen, but for the moment I'm armiger of the Ninth House and I will protect what's mine."

Jibril climbed to his feet and walked over to Eben, who was kicking furiously at a large clump of gamma grass.

"Eben, you're no coward," he said quietly. "You are the son of Akritos Dhion, one of the bravest commanders who ever served the Crown. You are descended through your father's line from the greatest warriors who ever lived, the Northmen. You have shown nothing but courage and loyalty and resourcefulness since tragedy came to your House."

"You said I was afraid," Eben muttered.

"No, that is what you thought you heard. I was only saying that there might be other ways to protect your sister and the future of the Ninth House. But you are armiger. The choice is yours to make."

Eben looked out at the towers of his home. "By God, if I have to make a stand, I'll do it in my own hall."

Chapter Twenty-five

Syrah took a dainty spoonful of persimmon pudding. "I understand from my cousin that you are a wool merchant, Master Sangor. Do you come often to the Dominion?"

"Alas no, my lady," the dark-eyed man replied, "not nearly so often as I would wish. The quality of Lord Ranulph's wool is exceptional, of course, but my chief source lies in the far north. The mercer breed of the Western Isles produces a fleece particularly valued in the Levant, so I am often away for two or three years at a time."

"It must be a very dangerous undertaking," she said with a little shiver. "Those waters are said to teem with pirates."

"That they do, Lady Syrah. Fortunately, there are cargoes far more tempting than mine and I have only been boarded once."

Syrah set down her spoon with a look of consternation. "I am surprised you speak so calmly of the event. It must have been terrifying. I've heard stories . . ."

The merchant sipped at his ale. "There again I am most fortunate. The captain of their ship was that Najja Kek who boarded the *Abamassa* a few years back and took a fortune in furs. He wasn't all that happy that I carried only ordinary fleece," the merchant said, laughing, "but he took it anyway."

Ranulph had arrived at the Great House early in the afternoon with a man he said was a business partner, a buyer and seller of wool. Despite her curiosity to meet this Master Sangor, whom Syrah suspected was a smuggler—most likely the infamous Najja Kek himself—she remained in her chambers until shortly before the evening meal. From the gossip and chatter of servants, she learned the stranger below was tall and quite handsome, in a foreign sort of way. The girls were particularly excited about a scar that slashed from brow to chin, which made him a man of even greater mystery. He spoke with a heavy accent. His clothes were strange but elegant. He wore a long black robe girt at the waist with a heavy gold belt studded with discs of malachite, onyx, and ivory, and he carried a stout walking stick of polished black wood with an ivory handle in the shape of a lion's head.

Syrah had not been surprised, therefore, when she joined the men at dinner to find not a ruffian but a polite and affable man who might have been any wealthy merchant from the capital. Only his deeply tanned skin hinted at a life at sea.

"Najja Kek boarded your ship!" she exclaimed. "But he is said to be merciless to his victims."

"I did not find him so, Lady Syrah. I think his reputation is much exaggerated."

Syrah gave a little shudder. "Well, I'm sure I should swoon if I were to find myself in his presence."

"Come, come, now, Lady Syrah," the merchant said with a charming smile, "you have become somewhat of a legend in your own right. Not even Najja Kek himself would dare to kidnap the Crown Prince of the Dominion and ransom him for a fortune from the king, all without being apprehended."

"You forget, sir," Syrah replied, rising from the table and leading the way to the hearth, "that I did not escape in the end." Taking up her embroidery hoop, she sent a hostile glance toward Zebengo. "Obike Zebengo saw to that."

The merchant settled into a leather-padded chair. Ranulph sat to his right, while Zebengo pulled up a sturdy bench a little farther from the fire.

"I find it strange, if I might be so bold," Sangor said, "that you allow the man who betrayed you to dine in your hall."

"He is not my guest, sir," Syrah replied. "I suffer his presence because my cousin claims to have business with him."

Zebengo shrugged. "You must not take it personally, Lady Syrah. I am a mercenary. It is what I do."

"But I do take it personally," she snapped. "I realize now how foolish I was to trust you. But you see," she said, her voice positively dripping with venom, "I had some silly notion that there is honor among thieves."

"A common enough misconception," Master Sangor remarked.

Syrah's scowl turned to a flirtatious little smile as she met his eyes. "Indeed, sir? Why say you so? Surely a trader such as yourself has no cause to traffic with thieves?"

"On the contrary." He chuckled. "I traffic with thieves every day, for a wily trader will cheat you if he can."

"And do you consider yourself a thief then, too?"

Sangor smiled. "I suppose I do if taken in that light."

"It grows late," Syrah said as she began to gather up her hoop and threads. "I shall leave you gentlemen to your business. Or should I say, to your thievery?"

"My cousin has not yet recovered her equanimity after her little adventure, I fear," Ranulph explained after Syrah left the hall. "I'm sure she did not intend to be impertinent."

"Not at all, not at all," the man assured him. "I find her quite charming."

Ranulph looked at Zebengo. "Perhaps you too would excuse us. My friend here can only spare a few days. He and I have much to discuss."

"Of course."

"No," the merchant said peremptorily, "stay awhile, Zebengo. I confess to some curiosity about your own trade. Your reputation as a mercenary precedes you. I hope you won't think me overly inquisitive if I ask about your dealings with the king in the matter of Lady Syrah. I presume the reward for her capture exceeded her offer to you to remove Lord Ranulph from this hall."

Zebengo took the cushioned chair Syrah had vacated and picked up his ale. "I can't say. I knew the king would meet my price, given the nature of her treason and the insult to the Crown Prince, so I didn't bother to negotiate with her. Had I known she was in possession of five hundred gold discs . . ." He left off with a shrug.

"Five hundred gold discs, a small fortune," mused the visitor. "You wouldn't happen to know if the ransom has been returned to the king?"

"I wouldn't know," Zebengo said. "I met the king's agent, received my reward, and that was the end of it."

"But you think not," the merchant said softly. "Else you would not be here."

Ranulph had been looking from one man to the other throughout, trying to get a word in edgewise and being ignored as each man took the measure of the other. "Yes, yes," he said into the silence. "Zebengo sent me a message offering his services for the recovery of the gold, and I thought—"

The merchant flicked a crumb from his sleeve. "Why not just ask her, Gyp?" he said with a touch of contempt. "She is your betrothed, after all."

"Syrah is difficult," Ranulph said.

"Bah, she's a woman, isn't she? They are easily enticed with a few words of love or some jeweled bauble."

Gyp shook his head. "You don't know her. Syrah is far too clever to fall into such a trap."

He dismissed Ranulph's excuse with a wave of his hand. "Then beat her."

Zebengo shifted in his chair and stretched his legs toward the fire. The simple movement bespoke authority and enormous physical strength. "I take it your interest in the gold has something to do with the nature of your business with Lord Ranulph? Do you seek investment to expand your trade in wool?"

"I am already a wealthy man, Zebengo."

"Perhaps you have some other project in mind then."

Sangor looked at Zebengo with a little smile. "Perhaps."

Zebengo nodded and stood up and stretched. "I am a businessman of sorts myself, but I have little interest in trade. We can discuss my services in the morning. I have one or two ideas about the location of the gold based on something Lady Syrah let fall when I met her at the inn."

He let out a loud belch. "I don't believe it will do any good to badger the lady. If the king himself could not prevail upon her . . ." He shrugged. "Still, a sum of five hundred gold discs, though paltry in view of his own wealth, is still five hundred gold discs. He might take grave exception to our interference."

Sangor acknowledged the thinly veiled warning with a slight nod. "But of course."

Zebengo swallowed the last of his ale and winked. "I've a pretty little thing waiting for me in the garden, so I'm sure you understand that I need to get on with my own business."

The merchant watched the big man saunter across the hall toward the tall doors that led out to the courtyard. "A most interesting man," he murmured.

Nothing could have prepared her. Nothing. Not the dairymaid, the tavern whores, Jibril's mouth upon her as she pressed her belly and thighs against the cold iron bars of the cell, the sniggering serving wench at the inn. Not even the tempestuous hours in Jibril's arms when he brought her again and again to heights of mindless rapture and caught her in his strong arms as she drifted back to earth.

Throwing herself down on the braided silk carpet of her sleeping chamber, she howled with laughter. Depta hurried into the room followed by three terrified maids to behold Lady Syrah Dhion rolling about the floor like a lunatic in the throes of some violent seizure.

"Oh, my goodness, oh, my," Syrah moaned over and over. "Hee, hee, hee," she burbled. "Har, har, har," she hooted.

"Oh, my lady," Depta wailed, "what's come over you? Are you ill? Shall I fetch—"

Jennie Klassel

"No, no," Syrah gasped, trying to ward off their ministrations with a wave of her hand. "It's just that..." she managed to stammer before she collapsed again.

"Fetch the priest!" Depta shouted to one of the maids. The girl cast Syrah one terrified glance and bolted from the room.

Footsteps pounded down the hall and Zebengo burst into the room. Servants crowded the doorway, pushing and shoving to get a better view of the exciting goings-on.

"Let me pass!" a voice cried. The crowd parted reluctantly to allow little Father Ziggi to stumble through. He fell to his knees and began to shout out prayers with the fervor of a man face-to-face with the Antichrist.

"Everyone out!" a voice roared, silencing even Syrah, who lay on the floor utterly spent but still vibrating with the last paroxysms of laughter.

Zebengo glowered at the gaping crowd. Depta stood her ground spluttering that she would die before leaving her lady alone with the menacing giant. He picked her up, set her down in the corridor, and slammed the door in her face. The lock clicked into place.

Hands on hips, he glared down at the disheveled young woman who would one day be the Queen of the Dominion.

He reached down to help her up. "Well?" he demanded. Syrah poured a glass of water and collapsed into a chair. She smirked up at him. "I heard."

His eyes narrowed.

"I heard," she repeated with a decidedly devilish gleam in her eye.

"What exactly did you hear?"

She giggled. "You know. I heard you talking with Sangor. About the you-know-what."

Zebengo knew very well what she was talking about. He cocked a brow. "So you find it amusing, do you?"

"Well, you have to admit..."

She'd been out of sorts and not a little worried after another fruitless trip through the nasty tunnel. The note she'd left in the jar for Eben was gone and the stones had been replaced at the entrance. He'd probably already been and

242

gone, but it might also mean someone else had been there. She had just finished putting the herb shed to rights when she heard voices outside. Easing open the door that led to the herb garden, she slipped out and crept to her bench behind the ivy.

". . . a pinch in a glass of wine will do it."

The heavy accent told her the voice was that of Sangor.

"How long will it last?" That was Zebengo.

"It will see a man through a night, sometimes two."

"Hmph. No different than any other concoction of the kind. Dried sea horse is readily available in any marketplace. Ram's testicle, seal scrotum, stag's horn. All nonsense if you ask me," Zebengo scoffed. "I need no such remedy."

"Nor I," Kek hastened to assure him. "But lesser men than we would."

"What makes it different from the others?"

Syrah strained to hear as Sangor's voice sank lower. "The difference, my friend, is that once used . . ." His voice dropped to a whisper.

Syrah frowned. What in the world were they talking about?

Zebengo let out a long soft whistle. "Let me understand you. You sell a man a love potion—"

"For a few bruxa," Sangor interjected with a laugh.

". . . with the guarantee that his shaft will increase in length and girth a full inch or more and his ballocks . . ."

Syrah certainly knew what a shaft was by now, so they must be talking about—

". . . and give him stamina of a bull . . ."

Her eyes widened and she had to clap both hands over her mouth to keep from laughing.

A rustling sound to her right alerted her that someone else lurked in the shadows eavesdropping. A slim figure rose from behind a bush and darted around the corner. Ranulph.

"And he will have to purchase more if he is ever to acquit himself so well again?" Zebengo said.

"No, no." Sangor chortled. "Therein lies the genius of it— if he is ever going to perform again *at all!*"

Syrah could have sworn she heard Zebengo's eyebrows shoot clear up to his hairline. "You jest."

"Not at all. I came by the substance when my ship was blown off course by a storm. We managed to make land at an uncharted island. The men there had the largest shafts I've ever seen and the ballocks of bulls. I soon learned they consumed a fungus that grows only on the larvae of moths native to the place."

"I presume you sampled the fungus and discovered—"

"Indeed, sir, I did not," Sangor replied, clearly outraged. "I have no need of such a thing."

"Nor I," Zebengo agreed immediately.

Syrah bent over double as a fit of giggles threatened to overwhelm her.

Sangor continued. "So you see, we make the fungus available to all and sundry for a few bruxa. They try it. It works. The next time they take a woman to bed, they are impotent. We are the only source. A man will do anything to obtain it; pay anything."

The two men had moved off then, their voices fading away. "We will be rich beyond our wildest dreams . . . more powerful than all the kings of the world together."

Syrah grinned over at Zebengo, who now leaned against the carved mantel above the hearth with a scowl on his face. "Ranulph was there too, you know, hiding behind a bush," she said, "but I don't think he heard the whole thing. Tell me why Kek—yes, yes, I know Master Sangor is really Najja Kek—told you but not my cousin. I take it he doesn't trust him?"

"Do you trust me?" Zebengo said.

Syrah hesitated, then nodded. "You're not a mercenary, are you? I think you work for the king. You're here to spy on Ranulph. And me. There are others too: Depta, the maids, the groom."

"You're a very observant woman, Lady Syrah."

"Eben tried to tell me there was something about you that didn't fit. If I'd listened I wouldn't have gotten caught."

"Open up," a voice shouted, followed by violent pounding on the door. "By God, if you've touched her, Zebengo, I'll kill you," Ranulph bellowed.

"Please, my lady," came Depta's anxious voice. "It isn't proper for you to be alone in your sleeping chamber with a man."

Syrah rolled her eyes. As if Depta hadn't already found her under far more compromising circumstances.

"The guardians of your virtue are at the gates, my lady. I'll take my leave. I'll ride out with you in the morning and we can continue this discussion."

"That's my betrothed you're compromising in there, you bastard." Ranulph was shouting now. "The king will hear about this. I'll have you dragged out of this hall by your ballocks."

Syrah was murmuring something to herself as Zebengo headed to the door. He stopped. "Did you say something?"

"No," came a muffled giggle.

"Lady Syrah," Zebengo warned.

"I was just wondering if you need some of Kek's fungus so my cousin can get a good grip on your—"

"That would not be necessary, you naughty child," he snapped.

"Of course not," she soothed. "For lesser men, perhaps . . ."

Zebengo wrenched open the door, brushed Ranulph aside, and stalked away down the hall.

Ranulph's explosive temper had cooled by the time he returned to his chambers, only to be replaced by stone-cold rage. Not twelve hours past he could look to the future with every expectation that his carefully hatched plans would succeed beyond his wildest dreams. Wealth and power were to be his. The long years of living in the shadow of the Dhions would be over. No longer would the Twenty-seventh House be the poor relation of the Ninth, the lesser in wealth, social standing, and influence with the Crown. The combined estates would make him one of the largest landowners in the Dominion. The possession of over a hundred miles of coastline would cement his partnership with

Najja Kek. Should the pirate meet an untimely end—a common occurrence among his kind—others would take his place and be glad to ally themselves with him.

And Syrah Dhion would be his at last.

The contract of betrothal was a forgery, of course, but had his father lived a few years longer he would certainly have promoted the match between Ranulph and his cousin, his ambition no less than his son's. To that end, Ranulph had spent a great deal of time with Syrah as they grew up. At nine he was already urging her to play with him in the hayloft, teasing her into wrestling matches that inevitably ended with her pinned beneath him. At the age of thirteen, titillation turned to full-blown lust, which even his couplings with serving girls in his father's house could not assuage. He had only just averted disaster by taking control of the Great House when rumors arose that Syrah appeared to be Prince Jibril's choice for consort. She had foiled him, but only temporarily, by sneaking away and cooking up that ridiculous kidnapping episode.

Ranulph tossed back a cup of wine and poured another, brooding over the day's events. The first sign of trouble had come when his steward reported that Syrah had sent away over a dozen servants, claiming the hall was overstaffed. That they were all female and young did not escape Ranulph's notice. His cousin had most certainly heard the rumors about Lyrlon. That the girl had thrown herself in his way and crept into his bed would have signified little; his penchant for young girls had been the stuff of gossip for years. However, the fact that Syrah had dared to interfere did not sit well with him.

The business with Najja Kek and Zebengo was far more serious. Ranulph had been curious when Kek sent him a message ten days ago, hinting that a prize infinitely more valuable than the spoils of smuggling lay within their grasp. Tonight, Kek had taken himself off to bed shortly after Zebengo went off to his dalliance. They must have thought him a fool if they imagined he had not noticed the subtle interaction between them. That proved to be the case; Ranulph had overheard just enough of their conversation in the garden to realize Kek was throwing in his lot with Zebengo.

By God, he'd show them that Ranulph Gyp was not a man to be trifled with.

Chapter Twenty-six

Syrah had to promise on her father's heart that she would behave herself before Zebengo agreed to relate the rest of his conversation with Najja Kek.

Zebengo had been skeptical of Kek's claim at first. He still harbored some doubts, but other substances were known to ensnare a man to such a degree that he could not live without them—the seed of the poppy, for instance—so why not an aphrodisiac such as Kek's fungus?

There were three drawbacks to Kek's scheme. The first lay in the fact that, as far as Kek knew, the moths lived only on that particular island. Second, it took months to garner even a handful of the fungus, because so many larvae had to be culled. Kek had shown Zebengo a small leather pouch of the stuff: a pale yellow powder that resembled pounded ginger.

The third drawback was that Kek had had to pay an enormous sum just for that small amount. The ruler of the place was a shrewd man who had long used the fungus to good effect in his own realm. The fungus might be withheld from a man for any number of reasons: punishment, coercion, revenge. The ruler had driven a hard bargain with Kek, who tried to barter with silks, spices, and rare perfumes.

However, it was gold the king demanded and gold Najja Kek must procure—a great deal of it in a short time. He had promised to return within three months to buy up a portion of the existing supply and put down an advance against future deliveries.

Syrah had a hundred questions but remained silent until Zebengo finished his story. They had ridden over the rolling hills toward the sea and now sat on a high cliff that overlooked a little fishing village that belonged to the Dhions.

"Is Najja Kek certain that he can find the island again?" Syrah wanted to know.

"Yes. He charted the exact coordinates of the course of his journey back to the Western Isles."

"What of his men? They must know about the island and the fungus."

"Kek has a small group of men he trusts who have sailed with him for years," Zebengo replied. "Those less trustworthy tend to fall overboard."

Syrah stared out at the crystal waters of her island home. All her life had been spent in the warm cocoon of her little world. Disease and evil had always been out there, but they had only been the stuff of scary tales and nightmares. Now she knew they were real and no one was safe from them.

Zebengo didn't need to explain why Kek had chosen to ally himself with him rather than her cousin. A partnership with Ranulph was all well and good to conceal his smuggling activities until he had the fungus in hand, but he believed the mercenary might know where Syrah and Eben had hidden the gold.

And if Zebengo couldn't help him find it . . .

Thank God Eben was safe so long as he didn't return to the hall. But God help her.

Jibril was surprised to find only servants at the Great House when he and Orini escorted Eben and Mayenne into the hall. Lady Syrah, he was informed, was out riding with Obike Zebengo. Lord Ranulph and his guest, a wool merchant by the name of Sangor, had left early on a visit to a breeder some distance away and were not expected to return until late in the evening.

An air of celebration filled the hall as word spread that Lord Eben had returned, and Mayenne with him. Prince Jibril was looked on with considerably more favor than on his previous visit: Rather than take Lord Eben into custody he had brought him home. Clea had been just the tiniest bit disappointed that her sister had no lurid tales to tell of ravishment at the hands of lustful Gypsies. Jibril summoned Depta to a private meeting in Lord Dhion's study room, which had tongues wagging.

The unusual bustle around the hall immediately caught Syrah's attention as she and Zebengo topped the rise on their return from their ride. Soldiers were busy in the stable yard, currying their horses and flirting with the maids. Cook and a small scullion were chasing down a fat goose. Eben was . . .

Eben?

"Oh, God," Syrah gasped. "What's Eben doing here?"

"It would appear he's been apprehended," Zebengo remarked.

"He can't be. We've got to get him out of here," she cried.

"You surprise me, Lady Syrah. Aren't you happy to see your brother?"

"You don't understand," she shouted, spurring Angel into a gallop down the hill toward the Great House. Zebengo didn't understand because he didn't know she'd moved the gold. Eben didn't know, either, but Najja Kek would think he did. That made him vulnerable, and a man who ordered innocent men thrown overboard would not hesitate to use any means to worm information from her brother. When Kek discovered Eben had given him the wrong information, he would kill him.

That she herself was equally vulnerable did not cross her mind at that moment. Right now her chief care was to protect Eben, and that meant keeping him out of Kek's clutches.

Worried as she was, Syrah laughed as Eben charged toward her, grabbed her about the waist, and lifted her high into the air with a joyous whoop. His strength surprised her, and when he set her down on her feet she realized he was taller than she was. Had he grown so much in just the few weeks since she had last seen him at the inn? There was something else that was different about him: a look in his eyes and a certain set to his jaw that she couldn't quite define.

"So you went and got yourself caught after all," she teased, smiling up at him. "You don't look the worse for it, not nearly as bad I did after I got finished rolling around in the dirt with that wretched Captain Ankuli."

Grinning, Eben glanced over at Zebengo, who was in the process of unsaddling his gray gelding. "I see you've forgiven our perfidious mercenary."

"I wouldn't say 'forgive' exactly. Let's say we've come to an uneasy truce. But tell me everything. Is Mayenne with you?"

They laughed and gabbed as they made their way to the hall. When Mayenne spotted Syrah she hurled herself into her arms, sobbing and laughing all the while. An air of celebration pervaded the hall and for the moment Syrah could almost forget her worries, happy to be with the people she loved. Yet behind her smiles and lighthearted words lurked the dark shadow of Najja Kek.

"The prince was ever so kind to us, my lady," Mayenne was burbling. "He didn't tie us up. Well, I got tied up but it was only because the blob man didn't believe me when I was trying to tell him about the dromedary, and one minute there was a dock and the next minute there wasn't a dock. . . ."

As Syrah tried to follow Mayenne's disjointed tale of her encounter with the blob man, whatever that was, she caught sight of Prince Jibril across the hall deep in conversation with Zebengo. Though she now knew that Zebengo would do her no harm and the prince had returned Eben rather than arrest him and drag him before the king, she wasn't about to trust either one of them. They had conspired with the king to dangle her in front of Ranulph as though she were a worm upon a hook. They had not trusted in her

251

discretion, her intelligence, or her ability to deal with Ranulph in her own way. Now they were using the Ninth House to bring down Najja Kek as well as her cousin. Moreover, they intended to rob her of her victory over the men who had brought unhappiness, fear, and evil into her life.

Syrah gazed at the man she had loved since she was thirteen, the man she would love for the rest of her life. He had taken her innocence in more ways than one, for he had used her as men had always used women, as pawns in their games of power. She would love him, but deep in her heart she would never really forgive him.

Recalling herself to her duties as the lady of the Ninth House, Syrah made her way across the hall and curtsied before the prince. "Once again you do us honor, my lord. Thank you for bringing my brother back to us."

"There really was no choice, Lady Syrah," he said with a grin. "If I had to ride all the way back to the capital with him, he would have talked of nothing but dromedaries and worms. I understand he has added frogs and cannibals to his repertoire. It was too much to contemplate, so I brought him home instead."

"Very wise, my lord. Your gain is our loss, however, since it now falls to us to have to listen to him."

"Your cousin is away from the hall yet again, I am told."

"We expect him home this evening. Will you be staying with us again, sir?"

"I won't impose on your hospitality. We're camped nearby."

Syrah wondered if they would swoop down on Najja Kek when he returned to the hall. Then it occurred to her that Kek would not be so foolish as to walk into the hall with Ranulph, not when he learned the prince's troops were in the area. He might even return to the safety of his ship, but he would be back.

"I hope you will dine with us," Syrah said.

Jibril lifted her hand to his lips. "Thank you, Lady Syrah. I should be honored."

"Well," Syrah murmured as sparks whirred up her arm and whisked along nerves from the top of her head to the tips of her toes, "I should, um, go see to the arrangements."

She could tell by the devilish look in Jibril's eyes that he knew exactly how he had affected her. It irritated her that she was so transparent. Still, if he had slung her over his shoulder and carried her off to the nearest bed, she wasn't sure she would let out so much as a squeak of indignation.

Drawing herself up with all the dignity she could muster, she started toward the doorway that led to the kitchens. Suddenly, she turned around and told him at least part of what was in her heart. "Thank you, my lord, for bringing my brother safely back to me. I will never forget it."

Najja Kek had taken one look at the soldiers camped beside the road two miles from the Great House and slipped off into the darkness. Ranulph Gyp was not sorry to see him go. He would be back, of course.

Ranulph's first reaction after hearing the conversation between Kek and Zebengo had been such rage that he thought he would go mad. He had ridden to the village to the cottage of Fat Thuma, the whore who, for a few extra coins, willingly participated in his more savage pleasures. Lust and anger had ever been conjoined in his nature, the gratification of the former enabling him to master the latter. So skillful had Thuma been in her ministrations that Gyp returned to the Great House with a clear mind and the certainty that he would outwit Kek and become the sole purveyor of an aphrodisiac that would make him rich beyond his wildest dreams. Combined with his ultimate victory over the Ninth House, he, Ranulph Gyp, would achieve a stature to rival that of the king himself.

Even the sight of Eben Dhion sitting at the high table in the company of Prince Jibril could not disturb Ranulph's affable countenance as he strode across the hall and bowed low to the prince. "Welcome, my lord, welcome. Had I known of your arrival in the area I would have cut short my visit to Master Cobhan's farm and returned at once. I apologize for not being here to receive you."

Jibril sat back in the carved high-back chair and swirled the dark wine in his cup. "Please don't apologize, Lord Ranulph. I understand you were looking at new breeding stock today. I'm glad my visit didn't interfere with such important business."

"Indeed, sir," Ranulph said, signaling a servant to bring a chair for him, "these rams were exceptional. Despite my new duties here I could not resist the opportunity to bid on them. Eben, my boy! It's good to see you home. Syrah and I have been worried about you."

Eben settled back in his father's chair. "It's good to be home, Ranulph. I see you've kept my hall in good order while I was gone."

For a moment Ranulph sat in stunned silence, then reminded himself that Eben Dhion was now only a minor obstacle, if even that, to the realization of his ambitions. "I take my duties to see to the interests of this House very seriously, Eben."

Jibril suppressed a smile; Eben had handled that very well.

"I took Lord Eben into custody a few days ago. Since the king had already pardoned Lady Syrah I saw no reason to drag him back to Suriana."

Ranulph smiled. "Truly magnanimous, sir. With his return we can finally put all these misunderstandings behind us."

"I was told a merchant rode out with you today," Jibril said.

"Yes, Master Sangor. He trades in wool; we've done business together for years."

"He didn't return with you?" Jibril inquired idly as he selected a sugared date from a platter before him.

"No. He decided to visit a distant relative who lives not far from the capital. I expect him back in a few days. I would be honored to introduce you to him. He's a most interesting man."

"I'm afraid I'll have to delay that pleasure," the prince replied. "Unless I should happen to meet him on the road; I leave for the capital myself in the morning."

Tension at the high table eased as Ranulph turned his attention to his food. Syrah excused herself to speak to the musicians in the gallery. When the lower tables had been moved against the walls, they struck up a lively tune and a number of couples took up positions for a dance. Syrah declined Ranulph's request to partner her on the pretext that she was weary from her long ride that afternoon.

Satisfied that the company was well occupied with the entertainment, she went in search of Eben. She found him flirting with the pretty daughter of one of the tenant farmers. With a charming smile that left the girl blushing hotly, he followed his sister from the hall. They climbed the wide worn stone steps to the old battlement walls and leaned against the waist-high parapet looking out over the orchards.

"I want to know everything," Syrah said. "Start at the beginning, where you went after the inn, how you met up with Mayenne, how you were captured. How in the world did you contrive to meet me on the road and where did you get that awful cassock? It was all I could do to keep from laughing. Did you get the note I left in the tunnel—"

"Stop, stop," Eben said, laughing. "If you keep asking questions it will take all night to get through it."

For the next hour they told each other everything that had happened since the moment Syrah was dragged off Eben's horse in the stable yard. Syrah passed over the passionate interlude with Jibril at the palace, of course, and Eben made no mention of his conversation with the prince.

"Eben," Syrah said as though the idea had just occurred to her, "I think you should go to Suriana to visit with Papa. He asked after you every day. He was already somewhat improved when I left but he hasn't seen you for a long time and I think it would raise his spirits if you were there."

"I will, in a few weeks. I just got home, Syrah."

"I realize that, but he really misses you," she pressed on. "Morgana too."

"You don't expect me to leave you alone here with Ranulph, do you? Or this Sangor fellow. I know who he is: Najja Kek. You have to be crazy to think I'd leave you with him around."

255

"Well, that's just the thing," Syrah said. "I won't be alone. Mayenne's here."

"Oh, well," Eben said dryly, "as long as Mayenne's here."

Syrah gave him a playful punch in the shoulder. "And Zebengo. You know all about him now. I understand Guardsman Orini and some of his men will be here. And there's a fearsome brute of a groom in the stables who is actually a soldier too. I'll be perfectly safe."

"I'm not leaving."

Syrah racked her brains for some other reason to get Eben away from Kek. She couldn't risk telling him she'd moved the gold. His pride would be hurt, and she doubted he would see the wisdom of her actions. Most likely he would see it as a betrayal. "You seem to have struck up a friendship with the prince. You could ride back to Suriana with him tomorrow, visit with Papa, get things straightened out with the king."

"No."

"Eben—"

"I said no. That's final, Syrah."

When they returned to the great hall, Prince Jibril politely declined another game of draughts with Ranulph and strolled over to Syrah. "I wonder, Lady Syrah, if I might have a world with you in private."

Syrah led the way to what had been her mother's retiring room, conscious of Ranulph's suspicious gaze as they left the hall. A servant hurried ahead to light a fire in the cold hearth. Another carried in wine and a bowl of salted nuts. She bobbed a curtsy and left with a little smile on her face.

"Would you care for wine?" Syrah said.

"Not at the moment."

"Shall I send for ale then?"

"No."

"You wished to speak with me, sir," she said.

"Later."

"Then—"

The prince had settled down in the big chair her father had used when her parents would sit together on cold winter nights.

"Come here, Syrah."

It was not a request.

She took a few steps, stopped a foot or so in front of him, and stared down at the carpet as though she saw something of enormous interest in the intricate design.

Jibril leaned forward and looked down. "I suppose it's a nice enough carpet," he observed gravely, "but surely not worth your undivided attention."

If Syrah hadn't been so nervous she might have laughed at the droll remark.

"Closer. You wouldn't gainsay your prince, would you?"

"I'm thinking about it," she muttered.

He grasped her wrist and pulled her forward until she stood between his outstretched legs. She could feel the heat of him, smell the scent of spicy soap and leather and male animal. And then she was in his lap and she didn't have time to give a moment's thought as to how two tongues could fit into one mouth or whether the long hard bulge beside her right hip was the buckle of his belt, or what the little pool of liquid heat bubbling low in her belly might signify.

"God, you set me on fire," he murmured against her neck. "I love your taste, your scent, the way you can feint with a bishop—"

"A knight," she gasped.

"Hmmm?"

"I feinted with a knight."

"I let you win, you know," he said with a growl.

"Not in your wildest dreams," she panted.

He shifted her in his lap. "Come, Syrah, I want you."

She stilled. "No."

"You want me. Your body tells me so."

She eased from his lap and stood up. "My body, yes."

She went to the hearth and stared into the flames. "I find it strange," she said, measuring each word, "that you have expectations of further dalliance with me. I was under the impression you and the king were eager for an alliance between Ranulph and me. That was your stated purpose in sending me home, was it not?"

257

Jibril poured wine into the silver goblet. "Yes."

"And I distinctly recall you once saying you would not wish to dishonor me, yet—"

"Syrah, you are an intelligent woman. You must know by now your presence here serves other purposes. You will not be marrying Lord Ranulph."

"You're right," she replied. "I am, after all, nothing but a pawn."

"It's not like that and you know it," he said.

She turned around and looked him straight in the eye. "Of course it is. As you say, I am an intelligent woman."

"Syrah—"

"You seek to expose my cousin and through him to capture Najja Kek. The restoration of my House is only a secondary consideration, although I imagine it will go far to assuage the king's guilt for not assisting us as was his duty in the first place." She only just managed to keep the pain and anger from her voice.

She started for the door but Jibril intercepted her. His hands gripped her shoulders.

"You know that's not so, Syrah," he said angrily. "You know too in your heart that I do you no dishonor. We—"

"I don't know any such thing!" she cried. "You seduced me on the island so I would release you and you seduced me at the palace knowing full well you were going to send me here so you could get your spies into this hall. You come here to play your games with Ranulph and Najja Kek and try to take your pleasure with me. What am I to think?"

She tried, she really did, but she couldn't hold back the tears. Jibril gathered her against him and rocked her as she wept into his tunic.

"You must trust me, Syrah. I would never willingly hurt you. When all this is over you will understand. Let me and Zebengo finish this business and then—"

Syrah pulled away and swiped the tears from her cheeks. "Then what? Shall I come to court and be your mistress until you tire of me? Will you marry me off when you take a bride?" She straightened up, in control again. "Do what you must, Jibril. I will do the same. But I will not let you break my heart."

He lifted her hand to his lips. "My lady," he said softly.

She hesitated in the doorway, waiting for him to speak again. But he did not say what she longed to hear. He did not tell her that he loved her.

Chapter Twenty-seven

The messenger galloped into camp shortly before dawn.

"An attack, Your Highness," he cried. "Captain Ankuli requests assistance immediately."

"Kek?" Jibril demanded.

"His men most certainly," the man replied. "Two coasters, possibly three. It wasn't just a landing, sir, as far as we can tell. They weren't off-loading. An outright attack on a small village about ten miles from our camp. By the time we got there one of the townsmen was dead. Two women are missing."

"That bastard," Jibril swore, kicking a camp stool across the clearing. "Majan," he shouted, "break camp. Orini, go up to the Great House and get Zebengo. Bring Eben Dhion too.

"What the hell is he up to?" he muttered as soldiers and squires sprang into action.

Noticing how exhausted the messenger was from his long ride, he ordered ale and food be brought to the man at once.

"Kek's own ship?" Jibril said.

"No sign of it, sir. But the coasters are still in the area. Captain Ankuli sent a message to the admiralty. We've a number of ships not far down the coast; it's almost as though Kek wants to engage with us."

"A diversion?" Jibril said.

"Captain Ankuli thinks so, but he doesn't know why yet."

"I do," Jibril said grimly.

A short while later the prince faced Majan, Orini, Zebengo, and Eben, who had gathered in his tent.

The prince's voice was quiet but his eyes were hard as flint. "This time he goes too far. This time we end it once and for all. Majan, you will take all the men and join Ankuli. I've sent another messenger to Admiral Arcos; we will trap the coasters between our ships and the shore. You will not find Kek's ship there. I believe it must lie here on the west coast. We may not be able to spot it if it stands far out, but I suspect it shelters somewhere at the base of the cliffs along the Dhion holdings. Orini, you will lead the search for it. Take only one or two men. Disguise yourselves and go out with the local fishermen; they know every nook and cranny of those cliffs; if it's here they'll find it. Send word to me immediately, but don't try to board.

"Kek's gone to ground not far from here," Jibril continued. "When he's sure we're gone he will go after Lady Syrah; he wants that gold. Zebengo and Eben, you will return to the Great House and carry on as before. I will keep two men with me and set up a small camp in the wooded hills nearby. I want it to appear that we have turned our attention to the crisis in the north, that we have lost interest in the affairs of the Ninth House."

Majan spoke up. "But, sir, how do you expect to take Kek if all the troops are dispatched to assist Captain Ankuli?"

"Kek cannot be taken with force of arms, commander. Guile alone will bring the bastard down."

She must never take her opponent for granted. Even the most accomplished player might, on occasion, make a mistake, but of one thing Syrah could be sure: He would never overlook one of yours.

But then, Najja Kek was unlike any opponent Syrah had ever faced across a chessboard. He might play by the rules, but only so long as it suited his purposes, and then . . . The

261

trick would be to outwit him long before he knew it, before he threw aside all pretense of fair play.

After much thought, and with fervent apologies to the shade of Great Uncle Amorgos, Syrah had come to the only conclusion possible when dealing with a player of Najja Kek's evil predisposition. She would abandon all pretense of fair play before he did.

Kek needed gold, Syrah's gold, or to be strictly accurate, King Ahriman's gold. If Kek pitched men overboard on a whiff of suspicion or the merest whim, he would not hesitate to use the foulest means to get his hands on that gold. That made Syrah all too vulnerable, and worse, those dearest to her.

It came to her in the deepest hours of the night, the perfect strategy: The game must end before Najja Kek made his first move. Syrah would already have taken the one piece she could not afford to lose.

Syrah darted into the privy and pressed against the wall behind the half-open door, grateful she had decided against bringing along a candle or lantern. The telltale smell of tallow or lamp oil would certainly have alerted the man who had just slipped into Najja Kek's unoccupied sleeping chamber to the presence of another intruder. He crept about the room, aided only by the faint light from the open window.

The intruder swore an occasional muffled oath as he systematically went through traveling satchels and chests. Bed ropes creaked. A drawer slid open. Syrah peeked through the crack of the door, trying to get a glimpse of him, but he had disappeared into the small room used for bathing and dressing. Disappointed mutterings indicated he had not found what he was looking for.

A boot dropped to the floor and a sudden "aha!" indicated he had found something of interest. Apparently, the search was not over, for several minutes passed before he moved back into the sleeping chamber. "There's got to be more," the intruder muttered. "Can't see a damned thing."

Syrah heard the sound of flint on metal. A candle flared

to life, casting the curves and ridges of the intruder's face into demonic relief. Ranulph Gyp. She should have known.

She crouched low behind the door, heart beating fast, as he moved toward the privy. Flickering light illumined the little room briefly, then moved away. "Hell and damnation!" Ranulph said. "There's got to be more. Where would the bastard hide the rest of it?"

More shuffling, more muttering, ever more inventive cursing, and then . . . "The ship! By God, it's on the ship," Ranulph exclaimed. "Kek thought he could squeeze me out. Well, no one outsmarts Ranulph Gyp." He was giggling as he tiptoed out into the dark corridor.

"Oh, I don't know about that, cousin Ranulph," Syrah said with a laugh as she emerged from the privy.

Clutching a small brown leather pouch worth its weight in gold and a tightly rolled scroll worth infinitely more, she blew out the candle her cousin had left behind.

Najja Kek, in the persona of Master Sangor, returned to the Great House two days later, accompanied by three men with mean eyes and the deeply lined leathery skin of men who have spent much of their lives at sea. He had hired them as bodyguards, he informed Syrah, when he heard of the troubles in the north. As a wealthy merchant traveling about the Dominion he was bound to attract notice. Of course, he made it a rule never to travel with gold or valuables upon his person, but one couldn't be too careful, could one? Syrah agreed one certainly could not.

Eben immediately set about making friends with their guest, appearing very much a boy in awe of a man who lived an adventurous life in far-off places. He peppered him with a thousand questions about the countries he had visited, the customs of their peoples, life at sea. He wanted to learn everything about the dromedaries native to the desert kingdoms: Did they really spit green slime when provoked? Had Master Sangor encountered cannibals in his journeys? Did they boil their victims or roast them upon spits? Eat them raw?

Syrah took on the role of the perfect hostess, observing

all the niceties, seeing to the comfort of their guest, even flirting on occasion to draw Najja Kek's notice from Eben. She grew increasingly uneasy when Kek began to seek her out in private on the pretext of consulting her on the current fashions. One question smoothly led to another. Which woolens were popular right now: cashmere, merino? Which best held the bright colors of vegetable dyes native to the island? Did she spend much time at court? Did she regret her actions in kidnapping the Crown Prince? Had she really demanded the incredible sum of one thousand gold discs?

Zebengo, too, sought out Syrah, ostensibly to worm the location of the gold from her. Jibril had instructed Zebengo not to let Syrah know he was still in the area. Better she believed Jibril gone; she might be more likely to tip her hand to Zebengo if she had some crazy scheme to take down Lord Ranulph and Najja Kek herself. Zebengo suspected she did have such a scheme in mind, but she cleverly turned aside his subtle inquiries.

Ranulph Gyp, his demeanor properly deferential, appeared reconciled to Eben's appropriation of the hall as his rightful domain. He showed Syrah every courtesy. He alluded to their betrothal as though she had already promised herself to him but made no improper advances. Each morning he descended from his chambers in better spirits than the last.

Beneath this veneer of apparent goodwill, wheels turned within wheels. Zebengo observed Kek, who studied Syrah, who kept watch over Eben, who eyed Ranulph.

Mayenne, however, went about her duties blissfully unaware of the high drama around her. She enjoyed her celebrity as a notorious outlaw, embroidering upon the tale here and there to great effect. She chattered and gossiped. She daydreamed about a certain guardsman. At night she dreamed of a fiery-eyed savage clad only in animal skins, who swooped down on her and swept her up into his thickly muscled arms and rode with her to his black tent on a windswept plain. Other times, it was an exotic potentate reclining upon silken pillows; or a lascivious pirate whose sole reason for living was to bend her to his wicked will.

When he took her to his bed—as he had every intention of doing—and failed to match the heroic proportions, inspired perversions, and Herculean stamina of Mayenne's nocturnal debauchers, poor Guardsman Orini was going to have a lot of explaining to do.

Meanwhile, Jibril had received news from Kalan that two of Kek's coasters had been boarded and a third had gone down after trying to ram its way through Arcos's blockade. Two local women had been rescued but had been badly used; the rapists had been hung on the spot. The prisoners were being taken to Suriana.

Guardsman Orini learned that Najja Kek's own ship had been rowed into an enormous cavern in the cliffs two miles to the south. Kek had spent two nights aboard and then departed with fifteen men. Another fifteen remained behind with the ship.

That news worried Jibril. He had observed only three men with Kek when he returned to the Great House. That left twelve unaccounted for; he would have to discover their whereabouts before he moved on Kek or he might find himself walking into a trap. Worse, if they had somehow insinuated themselves into the hall, Zebengo, the groom, and the three soldiers disguised as workmen would be outnumbered if it came to a fight to protect Eben and Syrah.

"We're going to have to do something soon," Zebengo said one night when he and Eben had made their way through the tunnel to meet Jibril in the cavern by the river. "Kek's losing patience and Syrah's up to something. Depta said she'd been sneaking around at night."

Jibril shook his head. "That means trouble."

"She should be locked up," Zebengo grumbled.

"I might just do that," Jibril said. "After we're married."

"You're going to marry my sister?" Eben said incredulously.

"Yes, I'm going to marry the damned woman."

Eben's laughter echoed back along the tunnel to the little door that led to the herb shed. Syrah couldn't hear what set him off, but his amusement irritated her. She crept down the steps and along the tunnel until she could hear three men clearly. One was Eben, another Zebengo. And Jibril! What was he doing here?

"Hell. I'd like to know what goes on in that woman's head," Jibril was saying. "On second thought, maybe I wouldn't."

"Why not just lock her up now?" Eben said.

"The boy's a genius, Zebengo," Jibril exclaimed. "We'll kidnap *her*. That will keep her out of trouble."

"She exercises Angel every day; you could snatch her then," Zebengo said.

"Too dangerous. We still don't know where those twelve other men are. It would be safer to take her when she's asleep."

Jibril warmed to the idea. "Obike, tell Depta to slip her a sleeping draught tomorrow night. Eben, you'll act as a lookout. Bring her through the tunnel. I'll be here with Orini. We'll take her to the camp."

"You'd better tie her up," Eben said cheerfully. "She's going to kill us."

Arrogant, domineering, overbearing wretches. Presumptuous, high-handed, sanctimonious cads. Duplicitous princes. Conniving little brothers.

Syrah paced back and forth along the graveled paths of her mother's flower garden, heedless of the whistling nightjars and the heady scent of a thousand roses on the evening breeze.

Jibril was absolutely right: He wouldn't want to know what was going on "in that woman's head" at the moment.

She was beyond furious. At him. At herself.

She'd been all kinds of fool where he was concerned from the moment he'd ridden into her father's courtyard. A fool to think she might have been his choice for a wife had fate been kinder. A fool to allow him to beguile and pleasure her on the Isle of Lost Souls, woo her in the palace garden. Make her a woman, his woman. Allow herself to love him.

How could she have forgotten that he was not just a man,

but a prince destined to rule, confident in the exercise of absolute power, schooled in intrigue, willing to use whatever means necessary to achieve his own ends? And how could she ever have forgotten that women were all too often those "means?"

She had allowed herself to become what she most detested: a pawn in the games of men. She had allowed the king, and by extension Jibril, to use her as bait to lure Ranulph and Najja Kek into a trap.

Now, while they played their game, she was going to play hers. She was going to regain control of her own destiny and find a new way to redeem the honor of her House, as was her duty and her right.

It was bad enough that Jibril had lied to her about returning to the capital, had lurked about spying and plotting, even recruited her own brother against her. But this deceit, this perfidy, this treachery! Did he think her some lackwit? Was she not to be trusted? Did he see her as no better than a child to be protected from the very sight of evildoing?

Obviously he did. But far, far worse, that he should think her incapable of outwitting cocksure fools like Najja Kek and Ranulph Gyp was downright insulting

Or perhaps he thought her all too capable of doing so, in which case his own pride might be suffering. After all, a man might recognize and admire acumen, strength, cunning, and resourcefulness in another man, even if it galled him to do so. Yet confront him with the very same qualities in a woman and he would simply ignore them, and if that were not possible, ensure that she could not employ them to his own disadvantage.

That was it, Syrah decided with a nod. He probably couldn't abide the idea that she was every bit as capable of outsmarting the blackguards as he was.

And if she had shed a few tears in her private thinking place the morning Jibril took his leave, ostensibly to return to the capital; and if she regretted not letting him make love to her one last time; and if she had wished—if only for a moment—that she did not feel so very alone, then she had

267

no one but herself to blame. The more the fool she.

The sound of men's voices coming from the direction of the orchard brought her to a sudden halt. So engrossed had she been in her meditation on the egomania of a particular Crown Prince and the insensitivity of his sex in general that her own present vulnerability, abroad and alone in the middle of the night, had quite escaped her. She moved quickly toward a dark corner where high stone walls separated the flower and herb gardens from the orchard and crouched low in the concealing shadow. As the voices moved up the hill toward the arched gateway, she heard the unmistakable accent of Najja Kek.

"We will take the boy."

"Rather take that sister of his myself, Captain. She's a right pretty piece. Wouldn't mind poking a lady, just to see if it's different. Better, you know what I mean?"

"That can come later," Kek said. "Right now it's the boy we want. It won't be hard to lure him down to see the ship. If he won't tell us where the gold is—"

"We kill him," a voice said with some relish.

"Of course not, you dolt," Najja Kek snapped. "We hold him hostage. She tells us where the gold is and we release him. Better still, we make an exchange. She'll do anything for him. We take her with us. It won't take much to make her talk once she finds herself alone at sea with forty men. We get the gold and go back to the island. Maybe I'll sell her when we're done with her. She'd fetch a good price."

Syrah could see the men now in the moonlight as they came through the arch into the garden: Kek, his three so-called bodyguards, and three or four others she hadn't seen before. She hugged the wall, hardly daring to breathe.

"What about that mercenary?" someone asked. "Thought you said he knew where the gold is."

"I'm going to give him two days to put together what he heard at the inn with what he can learn from her here. He certainly knows something about the kidnapping I don't. I'm not sure I even trust him all that much. When I told that fool Gyp we should just beat the information out of her, Zebengo warned me off."

"He said that, Captain, not to beat her?"

"Not in so many words, but the warning was there. He might be trying to double-cross me. In any event, we'll get rid of him once we have what we want."

Najja Kek stilled and signaled the others to be quiet. Syrah squeezed her eyes shut, willing herself invisible to his searching eyes. A moment later, a cat leaped from the wall just above her head and took off in furious pursuit of a small gray shadow. The men relaxed and moved off across the garden toward the stables.

"Two days," Kek was saying. "Then we take the boy."

Syrah waited a long time after their voices faded away before she crept along the wall, scuttled through the archway, and made her way across the herb garden into the kitchens. There she waited again until she was certain no one was moving about in the Great House and made her way up to her room. It wasn't until she had undressed and crawled beneath the covers that she allowed herself to feel the full measure of fear that had gripped her the moment she heard Najja Kek say he intended to kidnap Eben. And now, even if she did tell him where she had hidden the gold, he intended to take her with him. Syrah wouldn't even let herself think of what could happen to her on that ship. And being sold as a slave or a concubine . . .

This was all her fault, of course. She thought she'd been so damn clever moving the gold. It might have worked to safeguard Eben for the few days necessary while they negotiated with Zebengo if only the damned man had been what he appeared to be: a mercenary for hire. Now both she and Eben were fair game. Even Zebengo was in jeopardy if Najja Kek decided he was being double-crossed.

Setting aside her fears for the moment, Syrah scooted up against the headboard of her bed, adjusted the pillows, and settled down to review the strengths and weaknesses of her position, just as Great Uncle Amorgos had taught her.

She was playing not one game but three. The first, with Ranulph, she had already won; or rather, her cousin had achieved the dubious distinction of checkmating himself.

Syrah could almost hear Great Uncle Amorgos chuckling over that one.

Najja Kek, too, faced defeat. Of course that game was over, though he might not know it yet.

As for her game with Jibril . . . Syrah would be more than content with a draw.

Chapter Twenty-eight

The following night, Jibril wrapped himself in his blankets and settled down by the dying fire with his men. He was well pleased with the night's work.

The plan had gone without a hitch. Depta had slipped the sleeping powder into the cup of warm sweetened milk Syrah liked to drink before bedtime. An hour later, Zebengo had scooped her up in her cocoon of blankets, and with Eben lighting the way carried her out through the tunnel to the spot where Jibril waited on the riverbank. Cradling her tenderly in his arms, Jibril rode back to camp and deposited the softly snoring bundle on his own bed.

Knowing Syrah was safely out of Najja Kek's reach was an enormous relief. Knowing she slept only a few feet away was not; he finally drifted off, aching for her soft sweet body, and woke shortly before dawn in such a state of arousal that he almost wished for the efficacious waters of Lake Zando. He and the men stowed their blankets, took care of the horses, and picked through the cold contents of a large basket of food Depta had sent along.

"Lady Syrah's going to have your head when she wakes up and finds herself here, sir," Orini observed as he finished off the last greasy sausage.

"It's for her own good," Jibril said.

The guardsman shook his head. "It's my experience that there isn't a woman alive who knows what's good for her, and it only gets them all surly if you try to tell them what is. My pa always said even a chicken has the sense to come in out of the rain, but a woman'll stand there until she drowns just to be contrary."

"Let's hope Lady Syrah's feeling a little more sensible than that this morning," Jibril said as he lifted the canvas flap and stepped into the dark tent. He groped for Syrah's shoulder and gave it a little shake. "Don't be afraid, Syrah, it's Jibril."

The memory of what happened next could still raise every hair on Jibril's head years later, not to mention the heart palpitations poor Orini would suffer until his dying day.

The blanketed bundle rocketed off the cot and launched itself at Jibril, attaching itself to his tunic like a drowning cat and propelling him backward through the tent flap into the petrified torso of Guardsman Orini. The three of them went down in a snarled heap, arms flailing, fists flying, chins butting noses, knees battering buttocks, and at one point teeth gnawing earlobes. Jibril had just managed to pin a heaving body beneath him and was raising his fist for a knockout punch when he looked down to see the terrified face of Guardsman Orini gaping up at him. No sooner had the fact registered than he found himself sandwiched between Orini and a howling deranged beast hell-bent on pounding the life from him. He pulled his knees to his chest to defend the royal ballocks just before fangs sank into his neck. Orini was not so lucky as a knee found its mark. With a sickening poof, the air exploded from his lungs and he doubled over, gagging up his breakfast.

How long the melee might have gone on was anybody's guess but it ended as suddenly as it had begun when one of Jibril's squires emptied a pail of cold water on the writhing combatants with a shouted heartfelt apology to the Crown Prince for maltreating the royal person.

When the three soaking disheveled bodies finally sorted

themselves out, Jibril, Orini, and Mayenne gazed at the astounded faces gathered about them and at one another in utter bewilderment. For long moments no one moved. When comprehension dawned, Mayenne flung herself face-down in the mud before her prince babbling terrified pleas for mercy.

"What . . . the . . . hell," Jibril said, "were you doing in my bed?"

"I don't know, your p-p-princeship," Mayenne wailed. "I thought I was in m-my bed . . . No, I remember now. I was sitting on my lady's bed brushing out her hair and we were talking about ribbons and then I got all sleepy and—"

Jibril closed his eyes and held up a hand. "Stop! Don't say another word."

Mayenne burst into tears, which did nothing to improve her appearance, covered in mud as she was with her tangled hair plastered over her face. The prince didn't look much better as he clambered to his feet and held out a helping hand to Orini, whose glare at Mayenne when he finally managed to straighten up could only be described as murderous.

"I'm going to lock Syrah up and throw away the key," the prince snarled as he stormed back into his tent to change into dry clothes. "She'll eat worms and water for the rest of her evil little life. I'll hire priests to read the entire treatise on 'The Sins of Eve' day and night until her teeth rot in her mouth and her hair falls out.

"She'll rue the day she was born," he was shouting by the time he emerged, buckling on his sword belt.

He stopped at the sight of a dejected little Mayenne sitting in a large puddle.

"Get up, child," he said with a sigh. "It wasn't your fault." He reached down to help her to her feet.

"Squire, get some clean clothes for her. Orini, give her something to eat."

"I'm not touching the little hellcat," Orini said. "Sir," he added belatedly.

"Orini."

Scowling, Orini prodded Mayenne toward a fallen log

273

and fetched what little food remained in the basket.

"I'm sorry," she sniffled up at him. "I thought you were the Gypsies and you were going to ravish me. Did I hurt your . . . you know, your—"

Orini grimaced down at the worried little face. "Made of brass, girl," he said gruffly, thinking that ravishing her would prove a very pleasant pastime. Just as soon as he could walk without waddling like a duck.

"Good morning, Eben. Good morning, Zebengo," Syrah said with a sunny smile as she swept into the hall, dressed in a cheerful yellow gown trimmed with blue ribbon. "I think I'll just have fruit this morning, Clea. And some of those little muffins with raisins, if cook has any. Honey, too," she thought to add as she poured a cup of thick foamy goat's milk from a flowered ceramic pitcher.

"I thought I'd give Angel a day of rest," she said, seemingly oblivious of the incredulity on the faces of the other two. "I'll have Clim put her out in the lower pasture with the mares and the new foals."

"What are you doing here?" Eben finally managed to say.

"Where else would I be?" Syrah inquired as she helped herself to fresh berries. She glanced over at him. "What's the matter with you, Eben? You look like you've just seen a ghost."

"Nowhere," he said, stabbing at a piece of cold chicken. "And nothing's the damn matter with me."

Syrah spread honey on her muffin. "My, we are surly this morning, aren't we?"

Eben scraped back his chair and stomped out of the hall. Syrah looked over at Zebengo with a cheerful smile. "You slept well, I trust?"

The hall was almost empty now as servants began clearing the tables and people bustled off to their day's work. Zebengo moved to the chair beside Syrah that Eben had just vacated.

"Who did we carry out of here last night, Lady Syrah?" he said, keeping his voice low as a page piled platters nearby.

"Mayenne."

"That was very bad of you."

"Well, you never know what crazy idea I'm going to get in my silly woman's head," she retorted.

"It was for your own safety."

"If you three had my safety in mind," she snapped, "you might have consulted me instead of trying to cart me off like so much inconvenient baggage."

Zebengo stood up. Without ceremony he pulled back Syrah's chair, grasped her by the elbow while she still had a piece of muffin clutched in her hand, and escorted her out through the main doors of the hall. He propelled her through the stable yard and down the rutted track that led through the orchard toward the boathouse.

"Just what do you think you're doing? I'm not some child," she huffed as he marched her along.

"If you act like a child, you'll be treated like one. We're going to have a little talk."

"You have no right—"

"I have every right, Lady Syrah," he said sternly. "As His Majesty's head of internal security it is my duty to see that your cousin and Najja Kek cause no further havoc in the Dominion. Your interference seriously jeopardizes our efforts."

Syrah was feeling rather foolish by the time they reached the boathouse. She waited as Zebengo yanked open the door and dragged out a stool for her.

"If you must know, I had a perfectly good reason for doing what I did," she informed him as she settled her skirts around her.

Zebengo leaned against the railing. "I'm listening."

"The night before last, after I heard you three talking in the cave I was angry and took a walk around the gardens. I heard a group of men down in the orchard. I only just managed to hide before they came through the gate. It was Najja Kek with those three barbarians and some other men I didn't recognize. Kek was saying he didn't trust you anymore and that he was going to kidnap Eben by luring him to his ship. Is it close by?"

"Two miles down the coast," Zebengo said. "Orini found it."

"If Eben didn't tell them where the gold was, they were going to hold him hostage and then exchange him for me. I couldn't let them get hold of him, because—"

"He doesn't know where it is," Zebengo finished for her.

Syrah looked up at him, astonished. "How do you know that?"

"Eben told Jibril he thought you might have moved it."

Syrah looked down at her hands in her lap. "I thought I'd be protecting him, but now he's in more danger than ever."

"As are you."

"Yes. Najja Kek would kill Eben if he thought Eben lied to him. He really wants me, though. He's going to . . ." She looked out at the river. "He said he'd give me to his men to make me tell him where the gold is and then he's going to sell me." She stopped as tears sprang to her eyes. "I don't understand how evil men can be."

"If you'd have let us take you out of there last night—"

"That's just it, I couldn't," she cried. "If I disappear, Najja Kek's going to know something's wrong. He'll take Eben and kill you. I think he's got more men around here somewhere. Jibril probably doesn't have enough men to take them on."

Zebengo had to admit Syrah had a point. "Ankuli should be back soon with reinforcements. He and Admiral Arcos trapped Kek's whole fleet. There's only Kek's own ship left."

Syrah wanted to cry. "All I ever wanted was to protect Eben and get Ranulph out of my hall. It all seemed so simple at first. I never imagined I'd come up against someone like Najja Kek. Now all of us are in danger. You, too," she said, looking up at Zebengo. "I'm sorry."

"I'll send the groom with a message to Jibril telling him what you've told me. We will all meet tonight in the cave to decide what must be done until Ankuli arrives."

Syrah shook her head with a rueful smile. "I'm not sure

that's a very good idea. Jibril will probably kill me before Kek has a chance to."

"He might at that. When he realizes it's Mayenne bundled up in those blankets, there's going to be hell to pay."

They started up the hill toward the Great House. "May I ask you a question, Zebengo?"

"No, Lady Syrah, I did not eat my brother."

"Of course not," she scoffed. "You ate your nephew; everybody knows that. What I wanted to ask is why you're here. In the Dominion, I mean. There are all sorts of stories about you. Some say you were a prince in your own land."

"I have no memory of it, but yes, it is true. My father and older brother died in an uprising against the throne. My mother and I managed to escape with a few servants, only to be captured and sold as slaves. I never saw her again."

Syrah was too shocked to say a word.

"I was bought by the ruler of Emami. That's where I met Jibril; he was with his father on a state visit to renegotiate a treaty. Jibril and I were both the same age and I was assigned to be his companion. By the time they were to leave we were fast friends, and when my master offered the king any gift he desired, he asked for me. He brought me here to the Dominion."

"But the King would never—"

"Of course not," Zebengo said, anticipating her, "he did not bring me as a slave, although I no longer saw myself as anything else because I had so few memories of my former life. He taught me that no man is a slave in his own heart. I had been born a prince and must learn to see myself as a prince once again."

"Have you ever wished to go back, to see your home?"

Zebengo shrugged. "When I was younger, but now . . . My family is dead, or as good as. I did try to find my mother but it was as though she had disappeared from the face of the earth. She, a queen. This is the only home I have ever really known. The only family."

"Family?"

Zebengo smiled down at her. "Yes. It is not known—I do

not wish it—but the king made me his son. Jibril is my brother."

Syrah sank into a graceful curtsy. "It is an honor indeed, Your Highness, to make your acquaintance. And to think you asked only a meager one hundred and fifty gold discs when you are worth a prince's ransom every bit as much as the Crown Prince."

"You forget that we did not agree on a price for my services. Surely you do not think I would have settled for a mere one hundred and fifty when I knew you were in possession of five hundred."

"Is that so?" she said sweetly. "Perhaps we should resolve the matter; say, over a game of chess this evening?"

"If I win?"

"I will tell you where the gold is. And if I win?"

"I'll see that Jibril does not strangle you on sight."

Syrah laughed. "Then I must be sure to win."

Chapter Twenty-nine

Crown Prince Jibril and Lady Syrah Dhion studied one another across the dim expanse of the cave, much as two generals might appraise the capabilities of the enemy, calculate the parameters of the action, and divine the intention of each other. They had been standing thus ever since Eben and Zebengo had returned to the hall. Jibril intimidating, with arms folded across his chest, his stance wide; Syrah standing her ground, with hands clasped behind her back, chin high, her carriage regal.

"Give me one good reason," he said finally, "why I should not lock you up and throw away the key."

"Give me one good reason," she shot back, "why you think you should."

"I could give you ten right off the top of my head." He gazed up at the ceiling with a little frown. "Where to begin? Ah, yes, let us begin with the pride that prompts you to refuse succor and support when it is freely offered. Then there is your obstinacy. Let us not forget impetuosity, irresponsibility, and effrontery. Duplicity—"

"Never!"

"You moved the gold without Eben's knowledge."

"For his own good—"

"Which leads us to your propensity to appoint yourself guardian not only of the weak but of those who might wish to defend themselves."

"He's only fourteen—"

"He is a man, Syrah, and though he has much to learn, for the moment he stands as armiger of your House."

Syrah folded her arms across her chest. "Let us have done. You have named but seven reasons to safeguard the world from the dangers I pose."

"You have hit upon the eighth yourself. You are a danger to yourself because you will put yourself in its path. And you are mad—naive at best—if you think you can tangle with a man like Kek and emerge the winner."

Syrah held her temper, barely, as she paced about the chilly chamber. "You would admire these traits if a man wielded them in defense of his House. I find it curious that they assume the patina of character defects when a woman does so."

"These things do not lie in the province of a woman."

She pointed an accusatory finger at him. "Only because your pride will not allow it to be so."

"I misspoke then. Perhaps I should have said in a woman's nature."

"It must be in my nature," she retorted, "else I could not have done it. Am I any less a woman?"

"I have never known a woman I admire more."

Her chin went up. "With all my grievous faults?"

"With all your grievous faults. Ask me the tenth reason, Syrah."

"Go ahead," she muttered. "It can't be any more insulting than the other nine."

"If anything happened to you, I wouldn't know how to live without you."

Syrah blinked, frowned, blinked again. By the time his meaning registered he was already taking her small hands in his, pressing a kiss upon them.

"My Lady Syrah," he murmured, "my tavern wench, my captor, my turnkey. My proud, willful, impetuous, irresponsible, brash, duplicitous, dangerous, naive Lady Syrah. My—"

"Yes?" she whispered, wondering vaguely if she would ever be able to draw another breath.

"My beautiful maiden dancing in the rain."

"Rain," she echoed. How had they come to be talking about the weather? "Someone is dancing in the rain?"

Jibril smiled down at her, enjoying her confusion. "An enchanting maenad I chanced upon long ago."

"Oh."

"She looked much like you, my lady."

"Oh."

"With many of your grievous faults."

"I see," Syrah said carefully.

"Lacking one iota of common sense, she disobeyed her father and ventured out alone into the wilds where I discovered her pirouetting like some bacchante of old in the heart of a storm. As her prince, it fell to me to chastise her, of course—"

Syrah was glaring at Jibril now. "Of course."

"But she looked so pitiful—"

"Pitiful!"

Jibril nodded. "Like a sodden little bunny rabbit."

"Bunny rabbit," Syrah exploded. "Why, you—"

He silenced her with a soft kiss. "So young."

"Ummph—"

"So beautiful." He tasted her with his tongue.

"Mmmm."

"So enticing."

Syrah's arms stole around his neck.

"I knew someday I would make her my—"

So sudden was Jibril's move that Syrah nearly tumbled to the floor. "Wha—"

"Get behind me," he ordered in a whisper as he slid his sword from the scabbard.

Someone was moving surreptitiously toward them along the twisting passage that led from the river. Jibril retrieved the little lantern from the middle of the cave and handed it to Syrah. "Shield it with your skirt so I have just enough light to see. If there's trouble douse it and make your way back to the shed as quietly as you can."

"I won't leave you."

"For once, Syrah, do as you're told," he ordered. He pulled a dagger from his boot and handed it to her, then moved toward the cavern opening and pressed back against the rock.

The footsteps drew near and a voice whispered, "Your Highness?"

Jibril shook his head at Syrah, warning her not to relax her guard.

A huge shadow holding a wildly flickering candle stepped into the chamber. In an instant Jibril was behind him holding the tip of his sword to the man's back.

"Set the candle down and turn slowly so I can see your face," Jibril said.

The man did as he was told. A moment later Jibril was smiling and sheathing his sword. "Hell, Golonos, I almost skewered you like a goose on a spit."

"My lord," the groom said, "Zebengo sent me to tell you there's trouble. Kek just rode in with Ranulph Gyp looking mad as hell. At least twenty men are with him. He sent one of the servants to look for Lady Syrah; he told her to rout her out of bed if she had to."

Syrah ran toward the passage that led to the herb shed. "I have to get back."

"Stop right there," Jibril snapped. "You can't go back in there. You'll come with me to the camp where you'll be safe."

Syrah whirled around to face him. "I will not leave my people when they need me."

"You will not disobey me in this, Syrah. You face the greatest danger of all. You know what he plans for you."

"Jibril," she said quietly, "you once told me that wisdom lies in asking for help when you cannot possibly carry the full load. Allow me the wisdom to do so now. I cannot carry the full load but I can carry my part. I trust you to protect me and every soul in my hall. In return I ask you to trust me. I have something that will keep Kek in check until you can deploy your men."

For long moments Jibril said nothing, then nodded at her and turned to the groom. "Get a message to Zebengo that Ankuli and thirty men arrived two hours ago. We will secure the area around the Great House. I will send another group to board Kek's ship. Station a man here so that Zebengo or Lady Syrah can apprise us of the situation in the hall."

"Yes, sir."

Syrah didn't move as Jibril walked over and lifted her chin. "Before you go, Syrah, let us finish our kiss."

Her brows snapped together. "Really, Jibril, this is not the time—"

"I believe I was telling you what I planned to do about that bunny rabbit," he said as he cupped her face in his big hands.

He muffled an irritated "hmmph" as his lips settled softly on hers.

"I decided," he murmured, "to make her . . . my . . . queen."

"Oh."

He tweaked the tip of her nose, turned her around, and gave her a little push toward the passageway.

Chapter Thirty

Eben looked around at the appalled faces of Kek's men. He lowered his voice. "God help the man who tries," he said darkly.

"Never heard such nonsense in my life," one man snorted as he cast his dice onto the scarred tabletop.

"You willin' to have a go at her then?" another taunted.

The man lifted his chin. "Not sayin' I would, not sayin' I wouldn't. All I know is people is different from bugs. Women can't go 'round bitin' off the heads of the men pokin' 'em. Bugs can do it 'cause the females are bigger."

Eben nodded his agreement. "You're absolutely right. That's what's so horrible about it all. They don't have to." He chewed at his lower lip, looking worried. "Maybe I shouldn't be talking about this. If my sister ever found out . . ."

"Aw, go on," one of the men urged. "We won't tell no one." Seven men leaned forward in anticipation.

Eben looked around the hall to make sure no one was eavesdropping. "While you're poking her, the woman licks your neck and gives you a love bite. Except it's not a love bite. It's more like a vampire bite. She injects a poison that paralyzes you. Then you're stuck in there right up to the hilt and you can't move. She can take her pleasure as often as she wants—I hear they're insatiable—and then afterward she gets to feeling hungry from all that exercise, so she makes an incision and—"

"And?" breathed the seven men as one.

Eben shuddered. "I can't say it. My father—"

"Wait a minute," the doubter said suspiciously. "If the women in your family are like these bugs, how come your pa didn't get his brains sucked out?"

"He was one of the lucky ones."

"Lucky?"

"We never know which of our women are like that and which aren't. You can't tell just by looking at them. I guess it must skip generations. My great-grandmother went through five husbands and heaven only knows how many of their soldiers. My grandmother and mother were normal, but we were due for another odd one soon. That's why I pity any man who tries to poke my sister. He'd be taking an awfully big chance."

"No poke in the world's worth takin' a chance like that," someone said. A chorus of agreement swept around the table.

"I still say it's nonsense," the first man maintained, not sounding quite so sure of himself this time.

"You said the same thing about the fungus, but that turned out to be true."

The man jerked his head toward Eben. "Keep yer mouth shut."

Eben leaned forward, boyish curiosity on his face. "Fungus? What does it do?"

A tall pockmarked sailor at the end of the table emptied his mug and wiped his mouth on his sleeve. "Makes a man big as a bull. If I hadn't seen it with my own eyes . . . Thank God I don't need no fungus to do the job for me."

"Me neither."

"Poor bastards, gotta buy their damn ballocks."

"I got all a woman can handle as it is."

"I sure as hell don't."

"Course, not every man's hung like us."

"Ain't that the truth."

The first thing Syrah noticed as she walked into the hall was a group of men gawking at her with expressions of vulgar curiosity, wary suspicion, and outright dread. Eben sat among them grinning like a crocodile after a particularly tasty meal. She didn't want to think about what preposterous tale, undoubtedly lurid, he had concocted with her as the protagonist.

Apart from the fact that there were more people in the hall than usual at this time of night, nothing seemed amiss. Zebengo lounged in the chair he had by now appropriated as his own, drinking ale and discussing horses with two of Kek's men. Ranulph's guards were occupied with games of chance and draughts; several had passed out on benches. Her father's three favorite hounds lay sprawled near the hearth, emitting an occasional snort or growl as they chased after dream rabbits.

Syrah noted, however, that Najja Kek and Ranulph were nowhere to be seen. One of Kek's men seemed to be standing guard at the bottom of the staircase; another slouched against the wall beside the door that led to the kitchens; a third straddled a bench near the tall brass-embossed mahogany doors that led to the courtyard.

All told, the number of armed men in the hall totaled twenty-three: twelve of them Kek's and eleven Ranulph's. Three others, ostensibly tenant farmers, belonged to the king's guard; Syrah had no doubt they carried knives somewhere on their persons.

The only truly unusual thing was that there was not one woman to be seen. Syrah was surprised the men hadn't noticed yet. Pitchers and mugs hadn't been refilled, and if a willing female had caught a soldier's eye earlier in the evening, now would be the time for her to signal that her work was almost finished and she was ready for a bit of sport.

The protection of the women had been Syrah's first order of business. Depta had been dispatched to round up all women and children who might have business in the Great House at this time of night. She assigned Clea to herd the younger women and the children out through the kitchen garden to the safety of the servants' quarters, which stood at some distance from the main house.

Next, Syrah had sent a page to the village and outlying farms, calling all men to meet at the dairy to await further instructions. Stable boys saddled the fastest horses. Cook piled platters high with tempting spiced wafers, honeyed dates, and gingered nuts. The housekeeper swept through the sleeping chambers, gathering coverlets, quilts, and blankets.

Throughout Syrah's whirlwind preparations, Mayenne remained steadfastly by her side. It would never occur to her to take offense that her mistress had drugged her and allowed her to be carried away into the night. However, when Syrah ordered her to leave with the other younger women, Mayenne displayed a mulish streak that surprised even her and plopped herself down in the middle of the floor and refused to budge. So it was not to be wondered at that when Syrah entered the great hall Mayenne hovered around her like a mother hen with a recalcitrant chick.

Syrah nodded to a maid who had poked her head through the kitchen door, giving the signal for serving women to bring out the sweets. They passed among the men, smiling and flirting and urging them to eat their fill, even going so far as to cuddle in their laps and feed them from their own hands. Only Zebengo, Eben, and the tenant farmers were not served. Syrah, too, made her way around the hall very much in the way of the lady of the manor, offering sweets and seeing to the enjoyment of her guests before she settled down beside Zebengo and took up a piece of embroidery.

"I understood Najja Kek wished to speak with me," she said as she bit off a thread, "but he isn't here. What's going on?"

Kek's men had moved away, and for the moment she and Zebengo were alone.

"He went directly to his chamber," Zebengo said, keeping his voice low. "Took Gyp with him. Found him nosing around the ship."

"Jibril and Ankuli are surrounding the hall," Syrah said. They have about forty men. I don't know what he plans, but we've got to keep this lot occupied. I sent a page to the river end of the tunnel to tell him how many men are in here and I've sent most of the women and children away."

Zebengo beckoned one of the serving maids. "Those wafers look good."

"They are, but if you eat any you're going to have a heart attack later on."

"Poison?"

"Trust me, you don't want any."

A commotion on the far side of the hall drew everyone's attention. A white-faced Ranulph Gyp stumbled down the last step of the stairs that led from the gallery, prodded along by a wicked-looking dagger in the hand of Najja Kek. Kek's men were on their feet in an instant with swords and daggers drawn. They crowded Gyp's soldiers back against the wall.

Zebengo got to his feet with deceptive nonchalance and positioned himself halfway between Syrah and the stairs. She set her embroidery aside and stood to face Kek.

"You will explain yourself, sir. Is this any way to repay the hospitality of this hall? Release my cousin at once."

"Your cousin," Kek said, all pretence at civility gone, "is a thief. And if he doesn't tell me where he's hidden the rest of it, I'll cut his heart out." He shoved Ranulph to the floor and planted a boot on his chest.

"I don't have any more," Ranulph almost sobbed. "I swear it. I went to your ship because I thought you'd have a stash hidden there."

"There were two pouches, Gyp. You took one from my boot. Where's the other?"

"Please, this is most unseemly," Syrah said. "It is obvious my cousin doesn't have what you're looking for."

"Perhaps, Lady Syrah," Kek said softly as he moved toward her, "you do?"

Syrah stood her ground. "I have no idea what you're talking about. Please, calm yourself. Let us sit down and try to reason out the true culprit."

Beyond Kek's shoulder Syrah caught a flicker of movement in the kitchen doorway. No one else noticed; all eyes were turned on her and Kek.

Hand resting lightly on the silver hilt of the dagger at his waist, Zebengo moved between Kek and Syrah.

"Or perhaps our mercenary friend here is playing me false," Kek said, his black eyes narrowing. Two of his men moved to flank Zebengo.

Praying desperately that Jibril and his men would be making an appearance sooner rather than later, Syrah launched her plan.

"I insist that you tell me what article you are missing. I will have the hall scoured from top to bottom to retrieve it."

"I think you know what's missing, Lady Syrah," Kek snarled. "The fungus."

She grimaced in distaste. "Fungus? What in the world is so important about such a distasteful thing? Is it valuable?"

Kek smiled. "Men would kill for it."

"Really," Syrah said with a shudder, "I can scarcely credit it. Is it some rare spice?"

"Enough, Lady Syrah. I tire of this game of yours. No doubt you are in league with Zebengo here and you know very well that the fungus is worth more than gold. Once a man has experienced its special properties, he will do anything to obtain it."

He sneered down at Ranulph. "So you tried it, did you?"

Ranulph nodded, frightened and miserable.

"And you became more of a man than you'd ever dreamed possible? You'll no doubt be wanting more of it now?" Kek inquired, toying with him now.

Ranulph blinked up at him.

"You obviously don't know what's really special about it."

Ranulph shook his head.

"You will never again be able to perform without it."

An anguished squawk escaped Ranulph Gyp's bloodless

lips as his eyes rolled back in his head and he fainted dead away.

Kek laughed as he nudged Ranulph with the toe of his boot and turned his attention back to Syrah. "I know you took the second pouch. Tell me where it is or I will kill Zebengo."

"I have no love for the man." Syrah shrugged, but she made a show of trying to come to some difficult decision. "All right, yes, I took it. I hid it in the herb shed. Mayenne, please have Cook fetch the brown leather pouch on the top shelf by the powdered ginger."

She sat down, smoothed the skirts of her brown tunic, and folded her hands primly in her lap. Mayenne returned, followed by a very agitated cook.

"I'm ever so sorry, my lady," Cook said, wringing her hands. "One of the girls must have emptied that pouch into the powdered ginger jar, thinking it was a new supply. She swears it looked just like ginger. I'm afraid it's all gone now. I used it tonight in the sweetmeats we just served here in the hall. I'm ever so sorry, my lady. If I'd have known . . ."

Her voice trailed off into an appalled silence as the significance of the woman's words penetrated each male skull, rattled about in each male brain, and triggered a response that would have made Armageddon look like a pleasant morning's exercise in the lists.

Frenzied bodies crashed into one another as men tried to claw their way toward the exits, trampling fallen comrades and cursing God and all His saints. A few managed to keep their wits about them and crawled beneath the tables where they groaned and gagged and tried to empty their stomachs by sticking their fingers down their throats.

"Aieeeee," a voice screamed above the fray like a berserker in full battle mode. Eben seemed to drop out of nowhere directly onto Kek's head. At the same time, Zebengo whirled on the two guards. He knocked one out with a single punch but went down bleeding from the shoulder from the dagger of the other.

Blankets, quilts, and coverlets floated down from the gallery and settled over Gyp's and Kek's men, blinding them and preventing them from wielding their weapons. Jibril's soldiers seemed to materialize out of thin air, blocking exits and sorting through the tangle of bodies for Kek's henchmen.

Jibril had wasted no time in searching out Syrah, Eben, and Zebengo. Sword drawn, he elbowed through the standing and leaped over the prone, his eyes fixed on Kek with deadly intent.

Eben's airborne assault had stunned Kek only momentarily. After a brief struggle, he managed to pull a knife from his boot, giving him the advantage over the unarmed boy. He hauled Eben up against his chest, wrapped an arm around his neck, and laid the edge of the blade across his throat.

Jibril came to an abrupt halt.

"Drop your sword or I'll slit his throat," Kek ordered.

Jibril let his sword clatter to the floor, his body tensed for attack.

Without taking his eyes from Jibril, Kek addressed Syrah. "One or the other of you is going to tell me where that gold is."

"My brother doesn't know!"

"Yes, I do," Eben croaked.

"He doesn't," Syrah cried, "I swear it. I moved the gold. I didn't trust him. I'm the only one who knows where it is."

Kek tightened his grip on Eben and eyed her speculatively. "You know, I believe you. You're just clever enough to do that. So you'll come with me. I'd prefer that actually."

"Let him go," Jibril said with a thread of steel in his voice, moving slowly toward them. "You won't get away this time, Kek. The hall is surrounded. Admiral Arcos has seized your coasters and by now my men will have boarded your ship."

Kek laughed. "I haven't survived all these years without having learned a trick or two. Arcos took three coasters, I believe. Where is the fourth, hmmm? No, I'm going to walk out of here with sweet Lady Syrah. She's going to take me to the gold. And then we're going back to the island and

I'm going to become the richest, most powerful man in the world. Who knows? Perhaps Lady Syrah will come to enjoy my company."

"I don't think so," Syrah said calmly.

All eyes turned to Syrah, who still stood by the hearth.

She reached beneath her tunic and pulled out a parchment scroll. "I believe this belongs to you, Kek."

"Just what is it that you think you have there, Lady Syrah?"

"I think—no, in fact I know—that this map contains the coordinates that you need to find your island again."

Kek studied her for a moment. "Surely you don't imagine I would be so foolish as to keep but one copy."

Syrah shrugged. "I hardly know you well enough, sir, to say one way or the other." She held the parchment out toward the fire. "If that should be the case, however, and I . . . Well, let's just say the gold would avail you little."

"Gold is gold."

"Are you saying that this is the only copy of your map and you would be willing to settle for me and the gold?"

"I might be," Kek conceded. "You are an extremely clever woman, Lady Syrah. I think we could work well together. Suppose I release your brother, you take me to the gold, and we use the map to return to the island together. You will be rich beyond your wildest dreams."

Taking advantage of Kek's preoccupation with Syrah, Jibril had been moving toward him little by little. Zebengo, too, had inched along the floor to within reach of Kek's ankle.

Syrah appeared to consider the suggestion. "Very well. Bring my brother here to me. I will give you the map and you may take me as your hostage."

Sensing victory within his reach, Kek walked Eben toward the hearth, released him with a shove, and reached for Syrah.

Jibril lunged.

Kek seized Syrah by her long hair and swung her around, thinking to use her as a shield against Jibril. However, the momentum flung her against the wall, where her head met stone with a solid *thwack*. Still clutching the map, she slid down the wall and squinted at the scene that seemed to unfold before her eyes in dreamlike slow motion: Jibril charging Kek, Zebengo flinging out his arm to trip him, Eben grabbing at his knees, and Mayenne launching herself onto his back like an enraged tigress.

Somehow Kek kept hold of his knife and slashed Jibril across the cheek.

"Kek!" Syrah screamed as she thrust one end of the parchment into the fire and held it out like a burning torch.

"No!" Kek shouted.

For the fraction of a second the flaming map held his horrified attention, Kek's knife wavered. Jibril knocked it from his hands and slammed his knee into his groin. The pirate rolled into a ball, gagging out imprecations in impotent fury.

Syrah never saw the downfall of the most notorious pirate the southern ocean had ever seen.

She had sunk into black oblivion.

Chapter Thirty-one

"Tempting, isn't it?" said a voice.

Syrah stopped pacing around the little table upon which rested a small brown leather pouch and a parchment scroll. "Who are you? Where are you?"

"I am your Voice, and I am always with you."

Syrah shook her head. "You are not my Voice."

"There are many voices, Syrah. Did you think you had but one?"

"I have only heard the one. Why haven't you spoken before?"

Soft laughter rippled around her. "It has never been necessary. You have known only the harmless temptations of a child. You are a woman now, and you have learned of the need for power, the love of power. One might say, the power of power."

Syrah grimaced. "I certainly have."

"And what has it taught you?"

"It is a game, a tool, a toy of men."

Evidently the Voice approved. "Very good, Syrah. But what of women? They use the power of beauty, the body, the children they bear to men."

"And their wits, wisdom, and common sense," Syrah retorted.

"I stand corrected," said the Voice, not sounding chastened in the least. "I expect you believe a woman uses her power only for the good. What of the objects on the table before you? They offer you power that men—and women—can only dream of.

"Consider, Syrah," the Voice continued seductively. "They can be used for good; a man feels more a man, and his woman rejoices in the greater pleasure he bestows on her when he takes her to his bed."

Syrah did not like the drift of this preternatural conversation. "You are wrong, Voice. This innocent-looking powder enslaves a man; this chart that leads to its source assures that no man will ever be free again."

If the Voice had been attached to a body, it would have shrugged. "It is his choice to use it or not."

By now Syrah had taken a serious dislike to this Voice. "You are wrong again. I do not like to say it of my sex, but women will seek out those men who possess the, er, attributes this substance offers, just as they seek out men who possess wealth and power."

The Voice laughed a nasty laugh. "We're back to power."

"I tire of this conversation, Voice. Go away."

"As you will, my lady," it replied smoothly. "But remember, I will always be with you."

Syrah settled into the chair beside the table, leaned her chin on her hands, and contemplated the pouch and parchment.

"I'm afraid you're right, Voice," she sighed.

Jibril sat on the edge of the bed holding Syrah's hand. More than once Depta had tried to scold him from the room but he wouldn't leave Syrah's side. Mayenne, too, refused to budge and had stationed herself at the foot of the bed like a sentinel with her feet nailed to the floor.

Syrah had been mumbling for some minutes, almost as though she were having a conversation with someone.

"Syrah, it's time to wake up now. Please, love."

"I told you to go away," she said angrily.

"It's Jibril, Syrah, and I will never leave you."

"That's what I'm afraid of . . ." Her eyes popped open. "Jibril? Oh, it's you."

Jibril smoothed back her beautiful hair from her forehead. "You have a nasty bump there. Do you remember what happened?"

Syrah reached up to touch his swollen cheek. "You're hurt. I remember him slashing at you, but everything after that is a blur. Thank you for bringing him down."

"No, Syrah, truly it was you who brought the bastard down."

"I did? How?"

"It's simple, my love. You played a better game of chess."

Epilogue

King Ahriman flopped into bed with a heartfelt sigh of relief. Had his own wedding taken so much out of him? He didn't think so. Of course, he'd hidden out in his fishing lodge for a full month until it was time to show up at the cathedral, so the question really didn't pertain.

Alya snuggled up against him. "Still awake, my love?" she murmured and promptly went back to sleep.

Never in his life had the king had to settle so many inane, embarrassing, and downright acrimonious disputes, or soothe the ruffled feathers of so many offended parties in so short a time.

The royal seamstresses had threatened to walk out of the palace when they discovered Lady Syrah intended to wear a wedding gown embroidered with the colors of the Ninth House instead of the ivory silk and cream lace creation they had envisioned. Thank God Syrah had the sense to come up with a clever compromise: She would wear the silk and lace gown if the seamstresses would set aside their own design for the veil and fifty-foot train, and create one of golden mesh threads intertwined with green vines and tiny yellow suns and azure stars for flowers, the colors of her House.

Poor Master Sprum, who had charge not only of the King's Rolls but of the archives that detailed the time-honored texts of coronation, royal marriage, and christening, had taken to his bed when informed the Crown Prince wished to include some nonsense about keys in his marriage vows. Master Sprum rose from his bed only when the king sent a message to say that Jibril had agreed to excise the offending words from his vows. The king thought it wiser, however, to withhold from the little keeper the fact that keys would, nonetheless, play an important role in the ceremony.

Cooks from the Ninth House actually came to blows with cooks in the royal kitchens over who would prepare the delicacies to be placed before their beloved mistress at the wedding banquet. Ladies of the court had been horrified that Lady Syrah would allow a mere maid to carry her train. Traditionalists complained bitterly to the king when informed that both Lord Dhion and Lord Eben would walk Lady Syrah down the aisle, not to mention the inclusion of a lowly guardsman, a steward, and a deaf mute among the prince's groomsmen. Even the intimidating Zebengo came in for criticism, albeit discreet, when he refused to remove his gold ear stud when he stood up beside the prince at the altar.

One serious issue had arisen: the fate of Lord Ranulph Gyp. The king had spent hours closeted with his Minister for Matters of Justice, but it was Syrah who had brought a sensible, compassionate solution to his dilemma. No one had been more surprised than Ranulph himself when Syrah pleaded his case before the king.

"I would heal the rift between the Ninth House and the Twenty-seventh, Your Majesty. I do not ask you to absolve my cousin of his crimes, but I ask that you spare his life. My brother, Eben, would welcome the good counsel of Ranulph's younger brother, Lord Pin, an honest and wise young man, until he can take the high seat. Allow Ranulph to go into exile with some means to assist him in the world in whatever way he chooses to live."

King Ahriman chuckled as he swung his legs over the

edge of the bed. The last they had heard of Lord Ranulph Gyp, he was outfitting a ship. Apparently, there was some island he desperately needed to find.

The king padded through his dressing room to the comfortable little privy where a beeswax candle cast a dim glow. Hiking up his sleeping gown, he reflected that Alya had been right: He'd had far too much to drink.

Something caught his eye as he prepared to relieve himself. Something shiny.

"I'm never going to move again," Jibril murmured against his wife's neck. "Someday in about fifty years they'll suspect something's wrong and come looking for us. All they'll find is white bones and this"—he kissed a small gold key that hung on a delicate gold chain about his wife's elegant throat—"and do you know what they'll say?"

"They'll say," Syrah said, wriggling contentedly beneath her husband's warm strong body, "that it served them right for breaking tradition."

She laughed, remembering the archbishop's perplexed face when, after the final blessing, Jibril and Syrah had remained at the altar and Zebengo had stepped forward bearing a purple velvet cushion. Syrah had placed the long silver chain bearing a silver key about Jibril's neck, and he had placed a similar one, only gold, around hers.

"Syrah, I've been meaning to ask about the fungus—"

"I thought you'd get around to it eventually."

"Just what exactly happened to the rest of it? It really was powdered ginger in the sweetmeats, so the fungus must be around somewhere."

Syrah smiled a little smile. "I suppose it must."

"Hmmm. And the map. Could someone, say, a beautiful princess, have made a copy?"

"Anything's possible."

Jibril scowled down at her. "I'm going to have to be a perfect husband, aren't I?"

She giggled and pulled his mouth against hers. "You certainly are."

Much later, Jibril raised his head, frowning at a strange

sound that intruded on the silence of the sleeping palace. Great peals of laughter boomed down the marble corridors of the royal apartments, swirled up and down carpeted staircases, bounced from one tapestry-covered wall to the other, drifted under heavy mahogany doors. Soon another voice joined in, this one more delicate, its silver tones merging with the deeper ones.

Dozing guards leaped to their feet, scanning for danger; servants appeared pulling on uniforms over sleeping garments; guests peered out apprehensively into hallways. Cats howled. Dogs bayed.

"Can't a man enjoy his wedding night?" Jibril said with a growl as he prepared to go in search of the cause of the disturbance.

Syrah reached up and pulled him back down to her. "Stay, my love. All's well."

"Why do I get the feeling you have something to do with this?"

"I might," she conceded with a grin.

"Syrah."

"I believe His Majesty has just recovered his gold."

The laughter of a king and his queen echoed down the corridors to unite with that of a crown prince and his princess.

And somewhere, you may be sure, Great Uncle Amorgos was laughing too.

ACROSS A STARLIT SEA

REBECCA BRANDEWYNE

They were betrothed before she was born. She has no say in her future, no voice with which to protest the agreement made by her father that irrevocably binds her to Jarrett Chandler, a man whose hot blood and swift temper can make him as savage as their native Cornish moors . . . a man determined to claim what he's been promised. Unwilling to be a helpless pawn, Laura fights him in every way she knows. But even she has to admit that the tingling which courses through her body as Jarrett takes her in his iron embrace is not fueled solely by fear. Yet to succumb to the tortuous longings means she may have to forfeit the security of innocence and delve into desires that threaten to drown her in a sea of passion.

___52440-6 $5.99 US/$7.99 CAN

Swan Road
Rebecca Brandewyne

The lady Rhowenna feels her approaching destiny as surely as she feels the brisk sea wind caressing her face. She is no stranger to the "second sight," a trait prized amongst the people of her native Wales. And the sight is telling her of invaders from the north lands. Rhowenna should be afraid, but instead she feels a heightened anticipation, an awareness that tells her an answer to her prayers is sailing toward her. An answer to her dreams. a way to escape her dreaded betrothal to a cruel English prince.

___52420-1 $5.99 US/$6.99 CAN

THE SEA WIFE

HOLLY COOK

When Myles Dampier saves her from drowning, Sabina Grey imagines him to be a selkie: a legendary seducer from the deep who means doom to foolish maidens. He is no myth, however, but a flesh-and-blood Englishman, one she falls in love with and marries on the high seas.

Yet once in London, Myles becomes a virtual stranger. He returned from exile in Australia to avenge himself on those who had stolen his youth. But he will not destroy her spirit and her heart with his obsession. This time, *she* will rescue *him*. She will show him that punishing the sins of the past isn't worth sacrificing the love in his future.

What She Wants
LYNSAY SANDS

Earl Hugh Dulonget of Hillcrest is a formidable knight who has gotten himself into a bind. His uncle's will has a codicil: He must marry. And Hugh has just insulted his would-be bride by calling her a peasant! How can he win back her hand?

Everyone has advice. Some men-at-arms think that Hugh can win the fair Willa's love by buying her baubles. His castle priest proffers *De Secretis Mulierum*, a book on the secrets of women. But Hugh has ideas of his own. He will overcome every hindrance—and all his friends' help—to show Willa that he has not only what she needs, but what she wants. And that the two of them are meant for a lifetime of happiness.

Lynsay Sands

Bliss

If King Henry receives one more letter from either of two feuding nobles, he'll go mad. Lady Tiernay is a beauty, but whoever marries the nag will truly get a mixed blessing. And Lord Holden—can all the rumors regarding his cold heart be lies? The man certainly has sobered since the death of his first wife. If he were smart, Henry would force the two to wed, make them fatigue each other with their schemes and complaints. Yes, it is only fitting for them to share the bed they'd made—'til death do them part! Perhaps they will even find each other suitable; perhaps Lord Holden will find in his bride the sweet breath of new life. Heaven alone knows what will happen when the two foes are the last things between themselves and the passion they've never known they wanted.

___4909-0 $5.99 US/$6.99 CAN

LYNSAY SANDS
LADY PIRATE

Circumstances have changed; they're worse. Valoree has been named heir to Ainsley Castle. And the will distinctly states that in order to inherit, she must be married to a nobleman . . . and pregnant. Upon learning that, the virgin captain is ready to return to the seas, but her crew puts the issue to a vote—and for those rascally cusses she will do anything. Reluctantly, she agrees. If they can find a way—Henry and One-Eye and Skully—to put on her a sweet face that will fool the ton, she will handle the rest. Even with a drunken prostitute as an "aunt" and her merry cutthroat crew as "servants." But to herself she swears one thing: She can only marry a man who fires her blood, a man who is not afraid of a lady pirate.

___4816-7 $5.50 US/$6.50 CAN

Dorchester Publishing Co., Inc.
P.O. Box 6640
Wayne, PA 19087-8640

Please add $2.50 for shipping and handling for the first book and $.75 for each book thereafter. NY, NYC, and PA residents, please add appropriate sales tax. No cash, stamps, or C.O.D.s. All orders shipped within 6 weeks via postal service book rate. Canadian orders require $2.00 extra postage and must be paid in U.S. dollars through a U.S. banking facility.

Name_____
Address_____
City_____ State_____ Zip_____
I have enclosed $_____in payment for the checked book(s).
Payment <u>must</u> accompany all orders.☐Please send a free catalog.
CHECK OUT OUR WEBSITE! www.dorchesterpub.com

LYNSAY SANDS
The Reluctant Reformer

Everyone knows of Lady X. The masked courtesan is reputedly a noblewoman fallen on hard times. What Lord James does not know is that she is Lady Margaret Wentworth—the feisty sister of his best friend, who has forced James into an oath of protection. But when James tracks the girl to a house of ill repute, the only explanation is that Maggie is London's most enigmatic wanton.

Snatching her away will be a ticklish business, and after that James will have to ignore her violent protests that she was never the infamous X. He will have to reform the hoyden, while keeping his hands off the luscious goods that the rest of the ton has reputedly sampled. And, with Maggie, hardest of all will be keeping himself from falling in love.

____4974-0 $5.99 US/$7.99 CAN

Whispers
in the
Stars
PATRICIA WADDELL

The only female sovereign in the galaxy, Lady Zara is descended from women who can telepathically sense people's emotions. But her gift feels more like a curse as she faces the raw strength of her betrothed—a stranger sent to uncover her secrets, to breach her defenses both as a monarch and a bride.

As Commander of the Galactic Guard, Logan has sacked many a stronghold, and the defiant ruler of Nubria will be merely one more conquest. As he schools his new spouse in the ways of passion, though, Logan longs to trust the whispers in the stars that speak of a warrior and a priestess joined by the love that links their very souls.

THE LADY AND THE LION
CYNTHIA KIRK

Blaming herself for her husband's death, archaeologist Charlotte Fairchild has given up her greatest love: Egypt. Then Dylan Pierce strides into her life. Reputed to be the infamous "Lion," he is said to plunder ancient tombs and a woman's virtue with the same disregard. But with a kiss as searing as the Sahara and as dangerous as a scorpion, he ignites a passion that rivals anything she's felt before.

Welshman Dylan Pierce disdains European women and their well-bred sensibilities. But there is nothing cold or uptight about Charlotte Fairchild. She is as hot as the Egyptian sun and as fiery as its sands. Dazzling and mysterious, she embodies everything he loves about Africa. And loving the English lady will prove to be as wild and scorching as a desert whirlwind.

Ann Lawrence

Lord Of The Mist

As he kneels in the darkened chapel by his wife's lifeless body, he knows the babe she has birthed cannot be his. Then the scent of spring—blossoms, wet leaves, damp earth—precedes an alluring woman into the chapel. As she honors his dead wife with garlands, she seems to bring him fresh hope, just as she nourishes the little girl his wife has left behind.

Even though this woman is not his, can it be wrong to reach out for life, for love? He cannot deny his longing for her lush kiss, cannot ignore her urge to turn away from yesterday's sorrows and embrace tomorrow's sweetness.

___52443-0 $5.99 US/$6.99 CAN

Sacrament
SUSAN SQUIRES

It begins with an illicit kiss stolen under a hot Mediterranean sun. It makes the blood sing in her veins, burn in her body in ways she has never felt before. It is a pulsing need to be something else . . . something she doesn't yet understand. It is embodied by Davinoff. The dark lord is the epitome of beauty, of strength. He is feared by the ton, and even by fleeing to Bath, Sarah cannot escape him. His eyes hold a sadness she can hardly fathom. They pierce her so deeply that she feels penetrated to her very core. What they offer is frightening . . . and tantalizing. All Sarah knows is that the sacrament of his love will either be the death of her body or the salvation of her soul. And she can no more deny it than she can herself.

___52472-4 $5.99 US/$7.99 CAN

Dorchester Publishing Co., Inc.
P.O. Box 6640
Wayne, PA 19087-8640

Please add $2.50 for shipping and handling for the first book and $0.75 for each additional book. NY and PA residents, add appropriate sales tax. No cash, stamps, or C.O.D.s. All Canadian orders require $5.00 for shipping and handling and must be paid in U.S. dollars. Prices and availability subject to change. **Payment must accompany all orders.**

Name _____

Address_____

City_____ State_____ Zip _____

E-mail_____

I have enclosed $_____ in payment for the checked book(s).
  ❑Please send me a free catalog.
      CHECK OUT OUR WEBSITE at www.dorchesterpub.com!

The
Very Virile Viking
Sandra Hill

Magnus Ericsson is a simple man. He loves the smell of fresh-turned dirt after springtime plowing. He loves the heft of a good sword in his fighting arm. But, Holy Thor, what he does not relish is the bothersome brood of children he's been saddled with. Or the mysterious happenstance that strands him and his longship full of maddening offspring in a strange new land—the kingdom of *Holly Wood*. Here is a place where the blazing sun seems to bake his already befuddled brain, where the folks think he is an act-whore (whatever that is), and the woman of his dreams fails to accept that he is her soul mate . . . a man of exceptional talents, not to mention a very virile Viking.

Spellbound
KATHLEEN NANCE

As the Minstrel of Kaf, Zayne keeps the land of the djinn in harmony. Yet lately, he needs a woman to restore balance to his life, a woman with whom he can blend his voice and his body. And according to his destiny, this soul mate can only be found in the strange land of Earth.

Madeline knows to expect a guest while house-sitting, but she didn't expect the man would be so sexy, so potent, so fascinated by the doorbell. With one soul-stirring kiss, she sees colorful sparks dancing on the air. But Madeline wants to make sure her handsome djinni won't pull a disappearing act before she can become utterly spellbound.